THE RISING

ALSO BY KATHERINE GENET

The Wilde Grove Series

The Gathering

The Belonging

The Rising

The Singing

Wilde Grove Series 2

Follow The Wind

The Otherworld

Golden Heart

Wilde Grove Prayer Books

Prayers Of The Wildwood

Prayers Of The Beacons

Wilde Grove Bonus Stories

Becoming Morghan

The Threading

Non-Fiction

Ground & Centre

The Dreamer's Way

The Rising

KATHERINE GENET

Wych Elm Books

Wych Elm Books

Otago, NZ

www.wychelmbooks.com

contact@wychelmbooks.com

ISBN: 978-0-473-56302-8

For Catrin & Bear Fellow.

1

I AM RAVENNA, AND MORGHAN COMES TO ME, STEPPING HER spirit from her body to travel through the mists of time back to the stone circle when age was only beginning to pit the stones with wear.

I greet her from the tree line, from the sidelines, for what is playing out is a story neither of us were there for in the flesh of our current incarnations.

A woman screams, high and anguished in the rushing breath of the day and I want to cover my face with my hands so that I do not have to see. I will not, however, for we are here to look and to watch.

None of us can turn our faces away anymore. We must see the truth, be able to trace the scars.

And so the past replays itself in front of us.

More screams, shrill in the thinness of dawn. A bright, blank, and innocent dawn, the sky bluing above us even as blood spills upon the ground. The young women of the

Grove run, some with dresses already torn, their faces pale with fear, eyes wide like the doe startled in the forest.

Men chase after them, scooping them up with a thick arm around the waist, to carry them off, or to lean over them, the better to pierce their flesh with the cold iron of their knives.

Morghan's hands whiten around her staff, as, I imagine, do my own. These are our kin, our sisters, and although the life we lived at this time was played out elsewhere, we knew these women then, and we recognise them now.

The scent of smoke reaches us where we stand in our spirit bodies, unseen but not unfeeling. There is a hot breeze upon my face, and I know that flame leaps and roars down the hillside as the Grove's dwellings are set alight.

By the tallest of the stones, a young woman, the spirals of our Grove etched blue in woad upon her cheeks, is thrust to the ground, and a soldier fumbles with himself above her. I allow myself a prayer for her, a wish to take this suffering from her.

Morghan reaches for me and her fingers are cool against my own. We pray together, to the Goddess, in sorrow at what has come to pass.

Men – soldiers in their short tunics and bright armour – have overrun our Grove, and now Grandmother Oak suffers a blade as sharp as those that bite into our Grove mates' flesh. I hear her scream as her sap spills, as she is toppled, our beloved mother whose songs have woven in and out of our own for a hundred or more years.

And then the fire is come closer, the trees of our Grove turned to tinder, and Morghan and I must turn to look through the smoke to see the rest.

The maiden, raped upon the sacred ground of our circle is dragged away. She is our only survivor, the only one of our own to live through the destruction.

There is a boat, and a strange land far away where our Grove maiden is taken. A land where she does not speak the language, where she is kept prisoner, unable to steer her own fate, unable to walk outside and away.

Her belly grows round, and a daughter is born nine months into her new exile. The baby is small, and luminous as a pearl. I hear her mother whisper the old prayers and songs as she nurses the child at her breast. She does not forget. She will not forget. Her heart and life belong still to the Grove.

Her child is almost grown to a young woman when they leave their imprisonment, heads down under the light of a wan and distant moon as they run.

They know where they are going. They have been long in planning this.

The land of the Grove still bears the scars when our Grove mate returns. But she remembers. The songs live on in her heart, on her daughter's lips. Their magic burns inside them, and another oak is planted beside the stones, and blessings breathed over her.

So that what was begun might continue.

So that what was harmed might be healed.

So that the truth might be carried down the years, generation to generation.

She sang the wheel in its turning, as I did in my time, so that Morghan may still in hers.

So that you may in yours.

The wheel turns.

The ancient path leads us onward.

2

CHARLIE HAD HER EYES OPEN, WATCHING THE DIM FIGURE walk along the path towards them. Except, whoever it was, she thought, was not walking – they were slinking. There was something shifty in the woman's movements, something furtive, that reminded Charlie of the dark rustlings of an animal restless and on the prowl.

It was a woman though; she was sure of that.

Charlie glanced over at Morghan, but Morghan was still...wherever Morghan had gone. Eyes closed, hands loose and relaxed around her staff. Every part of her looked relaxed, but she still wasn't there.

Someone else was, though, and Charlie narrowed her eyes, watching the woman creep her way up the path to spy on them. Was it Minnie, she wondered? Then decided not. Minnie didn't skulk around following them anymore, or not usually.

The woman on the path stepped momentarily out of the

shadows, saw Charlie staring at her, gasped, then turned and hurried back down the hill.

Charlie barked out a cough in disbelief, leaning forward on her own staff to peer between the leaves to watch the black figure scuttling down the hill.

'Don't break a leg,' she whispered, watching the woman hurtle down the path that was thick with ropey tree roots easily able to trip you up.

'Who's going to break a leg?' Morghan asked, blinking, coming back to her body.

'You wouldn't believe it,' Charlie told her, shaking her head.

Morghan breathed in the crisp air. Imbolc had just been and gone, spent quietly for the Grove, each on their own rather than in ritual, due to the lockdown. They'd had much to contemplate, sinking into the season's first stirring, the new pregnancy of the world, giving thought to what they wanted to birth with the turning of the wheel, both individually, as a Grove, and as part of their village community.

She lowered her gaze to the path between the trees that would lead down to the village if followed for long enough. Almost she sniffed the air, but she wasn't looking to catch a scent of tree or bud. Morghan closed her eyes and looked for the energy of the fleeing person.

'Huh,' she said, then sighed. 'Has she been making a habit of this? Following us?'

Charlie glanced at Morghan. 'You can see her?'

'Sense her. As you can too, I'm sure.'

Charlie looked back down the path. Mariah Reefton was out of sight now. 'I don't know,' she said. 'This is the first time I've spotted her.' Charlie closed her eyes and reached out with her senses, relaxing into them, sending her spirit wider, searching.

And she found Mariah. The cloud left behind by her, already shredding and dissipating in the early spring air.

Charlie wrinkled her nose. 'She's like a cloud of rancid smoke.'

'She's an unhappy soul,' Morghan said. 'She nurses her resentments even though they twist her and make her miserable. They have become what she's comfortable with, because of their familiarity.' Morghan rolled her head on her neck, stretching the muscles there. Was it a coincidence that Mariah should show up while she was travelling, seeing the vision that had been shown her? Morghan decided not. Things were moving, she thought.

An image of a millstone grew in her mind and she frowned at it, seeing the two giant stones turning against each other, heavy, ponderous, relentless. Grinding what was between them to dust.

'What do you know of mills?' she asked abruptly.

Charlie was taken by surprise. 'Mills?' she asked. 'What sort of mills?'

Morghan lifted her shoulders in a shrug. 'Flour mills, I suppose.'

'Old or new ones?'

'The ones that used stones to grind the flour.'

'Ah,' Charlie said. 'Old ones, then.' She thought for a moment. 'Almost nothing,' she said. 'Only that the wheat was ground to flour between two heavy and round stones.' She blinked. 'That's it. That's as much as I know.'

Morghan nodded.

'Okay,' Charlie said after another minute. 'Why are you asking about that?'

Morghan turned in the stone circle where they stood and walked slowly over to Grandmother Oak, feeling the old tree's sturdy vitality, the dreaming self that was readying to wake, to bud with the new spring. For now, her branches were still bare, but soon, Morghan knew, in a few weeks, the old tree would become tinged in a bright green cloud of new clothing. She reached and touched the stout trunk with reverence and apology.

'Grandmother,' Morghan said, her voice low. 'Grandmother, I'm sorry.'

She lifted her eyes and looked over at Charlie.

'Once upon a time,' she explained, 'Grandmother Oak felt the bite of an axe and was felled and burnt while the women of this Grove and all the others were chased down, captured, raped, slaughtered.' Morghan looked up at the sky, smelling smoke from a fire that was centuries old.

Charlie looked at her.

'Only one woman from this Grove survived, and they took her across the ocean, kept her captive until she escaped, came back here to this isle, and picked up her work where she'd left off.'

Morghan looked back at the old oak tree. 'She replanted Grandmother here, and along with her, tended and grew the Grove back to life.'

'This is true?' Charlie asked. 'This is what you just saw?'

Morghan looked around the stone circle, at the trees that crowded forward, their roots toeing the clearing. The grass between the stones was kept short by the dancing steps of the Grove members, and in the shadowed light between the trees, yellow celandine flowers swayed silently as though hearing the echoes of Maxen's faerie flute.

But she could also see the Grove razed to the ground. The forest blackened and laid low from fire, the dirt scorched, a wide swath of destruction.

There was no outward trace of the damage now, on this sunny early spring morning, almost two thousand years later. The scar of it was carried deep in the soul of the land.

And in the souls of those who had been there.

'This is what I was shown,' Morghan said.

Charlie gazed around, imagining the trees being torn down, the Grove burnt around them. She shivered despite the sunlight on her. Suddenly its warmth and light seemed wan, barely there at all. She cleared her throat.

'When was this?'

Morghan closed her eyes again. She had thought she was done with that terrible time. And yet, here it was once more, coming back to haunt her. When she answered, her mouth was dry.

'Around 60 AD.'

Charlie turned and looked at her. 'That is remarkably specific,' she said.

'Yes.' Morghan walked over to the nearest standing stone and touched a hand to its pitted surface.

'Wait,' Charlie said, shaking her head. 'That's when the Romans invaded Anglesey.'

'And massacred the Druids, yes.'

Charlie looked around, as though she could catch a glimpse of the past looming over them.

'They also took out any of the women's woodland

Groves they happened to stumble across,' Morghan added, seeing the stone under her hand with blood spilt across it.

'It is a wonder this Grove or any has survived,' Charlie said on a long breath. Then she looked over at Morghan. 'But why were you shown this?' she asked. 'It is ancient history, surely.'

'Not so long ago, really,' Morghan said. 'Sometimes I wonder if there really is anything such as ancient history. The land remembers everything.' She touched her heart. 'We remember everything. We carry our ancestors' wounds.'

Charlie nibbled a moment at her lip. 'Were we there, then, do you think?' she asked. It was possible, after all. Sometimes Charlie felt as though she'd always lived here on this land, tended it, and loved it year upon year, lifetime upon lifetime. She'd told Martin flat out when he asked her to marry him that she would never be leaving Wellsford. She'd have kids and the rest of it, but she wouldn't leave her home. And they hadn't.

Morghan's gaze was far off. 'I wasn't,' she said flatly. 'I was nearby, dealing with...other things.'

Making the mistake of lifetimes.

She sighed. That mistake had been rectified, healed, forgiven.

Charlie watched her, watched the flicker of some deep emotion pass over Morghan's usually serene features. She'd known Morghan, at least from a distance, since she was in her teens. But it had been only the last few years that they had grown closer, that their work in the Grove had brought them together, and since Teresa's passing they were now the two oldest women in the Grove – and wasn't that the oddest thing to think on?

'Okay,' she said, pulling herself together and speaking with a briskness she hoped would wipe the sudden shadows from Morghan's eyes. 'So, you were shown a terrible part of our history here – the slaughter of the Grove, so long ago.' She paused for a moment, the hairs on her arms standing up at the thought of the young women who had been hounded to their deaths.

Charlie found her voice again. 'Why were you shown that, though?' she asked. 'And why now?'

The image of the millstone rose in Morghan's mind again and she listened to it turn, to its creaking, grinding turning.

Her eyes found Charlie's. 'There are stirrings in the village,' she said. 'We've felt them, both of us, I'm sure. We contribute to them, with our plans for the village, the things we've been doing to make the community healthier, stronger. Not everyone is so pleased with us taking such an active role.'

Charlie nodded. 'Mariah Reefton,' she said bluntly. 'That woman is against everything we try to do, even those things that will directly benefit her.' She looked down at her hands, nails short and skin rough from farm work. 'Maybe even especially those, if we are behind it.'

Morghan inclined her head in agreement. She thought of the young woman she'd once been, hanged in this very county in the 1600's for witchcraft. Remembered Mariah's link to that lifetime, her familial link to the one who had instigated the hanging. And she sighed. Things always came back around until they were dealt with.

'Before Erin arrived in Wellsford,' Morghan said, choosing her words carefully, 'I was reaching out to a past lifetime that was bothering me.' Her grey eyes flicked towards the sky, then back at the ground. Earth, sky, sea, she thought, anchoring herself in the landscape around her.

'Blythe Wilde, as she was.' Morghan's lips lifted in a slight smile, then flattened. 'Hanged for witchcraft – brought to the gallows by the testimony of the woman who is now our own Mariah Reefton.'

'This is recorded history?' Charlie burst out, appalled.

'Oh yes,' Morghan replied. 'Although not, of course, my knowledge of Mariah being set against the Grove then as she is now.'

Charlie nodded her head slowly. 'I think I've heard the stories, now that you mention it. About the hanging.' She walked a few steps to one of the stones and leaned a hip against it, grateful for its solidity, the serenity that she could feel inside the stone. 'But that was Mariah?' Charlie shook her head, touching her fingers to the rock. Without waiting for a reply, she answered her own question. 'Of course it was – it explains just about everything about her – her almost pathological hatred for you, and the rest of us. But you in particular.'

'History is a convoluted thing,' Morghan said, gazing down at her golden hand, seeing the way it gleamed and wondering still, months after she had been given it, why the Queen of the Fae had done so. She'd had no answers then, and she had none now.

'Love endures,' she said, moving to the centre of the circle and lifting her arms to the sky. She stretched her fingers toward the sun, digging her roots down deep into the coolness of the earth. By sky and root, she reminded herself. By sky and root we dedicated our lives.

She lowered her arms and turned to look at Charlie.

'Love endures,' Morghan repeated.

'But so does hate.

'And pain.'

3

TODAY, WINSOME WAS GOING SOLO. IT MADE HER STOMACH churn, and she looked longingly towards the kitchen and the teapot sitting on the big, scrubbed table.

Another cup of tea to settle her nerves. One of Stephan's blends. She'd pretty much become addicted to his passionflower tea. It always made her feel just a bit calmer.

And she could certainly do with a dose of serenity right now.

Winsome shook her head, wiped her palms on the thick black fabric of her cassock, and took a deep breath.

'Come on, you ninny,' she told herself, then bared her teeth in a wince. She was supposed to be watching the language she used with herself. A glance at the dog standing by the door waiting for her, and she swallowed. Huffed out a breath. 'Okay,' she said. 'You're not a ninny.' She grimaced again. 'I mean, I'm not a ninny.' Another puffing breath. 'I'm understandably nervous. This is my first time doing the work alone.'

The dog lowered his head and looked at Winsome from under wheaten, wiry eyebrows.

'You're right,' Winsome apologised hastily. 'Not alone. Of course not.' She closed her eyes and took a deep breath, feeling the spirit dog's silent gaze upon her.

'Okay,' she said. 'All right, Mr. Guardian of the Mysteries, let's go do the deed, shall we?'

She'd brought the dog back with her apparently, after helping poor Minnie Abbott back in December. It was February now, the snowdrops were out, and the dog had followed her back into the real world.

The waking world, she hastily corrected.

It was actually quite nice having the company. Once she'd gotten over the quiver of nerves at having a dog almost no one else could see trailing around after her most of the hours of the day.

It gave her someone to read her sermons to before she had to get up and deliver them. Not that they were very long, these days. With the lockdown, she could still hold services, but felt terribly obliged to keep them short – and as sweet as possible.

She was still prevaricating, standing in the hallway, her hand on her little bag of equipment. Why was she nervous? She'd done this, more or less, with Morghan more than once now, and good grief, she was even taking a course online for it.

Soul midwifery.

She liked that name for it, and the course was very good. She'd been surprised how closely it backed up what Morghan had been teaching her. It didn't go quite as deep, but then, Morghan didn't give her a certificate and official qualifications at the end of things, either.

And Winsome preferred the term soul midwife to what Morghan called it with her characteristic bluntness – death worker. Winsome shivered. That gave it an extra level of spooky she liked to do without.

She picked up the bag before she could dither any further and walked to the front door. The dog disappeared and she unlatched the door of the vicarage, stepping out into a morning that was cold and crisp and somehow clean. It was still early in the season, but Winsome could feel spring's breath over the village already. She glanced at the ancient yew tree in the neighbouring churchyard, like she always did now, and took in its fine head of greenery. It stood proudly in her churchyard, with its needle-like leaves, as though it owned the place.

This was Wellsford, Winsome thought. Wellsford and Wilde Grove. The tree probably did own the place.

The thought made her smile, and she nodded a sort of greeting to the tree. Later, she decided, she might wander over to it and ask if it needed anything.

She shook her head quickly – what was she doing thinking like that? Honestly, Morghan was rubbing off a little too well on her. But still, Winsome's gaze lingered on the wide-spreading green tree, as though it might impart a little of its strength to her. Yew trees were, after all, a symbol of immortality. She'd looked that up, just like she'd looked up the attributes of spirit dogs, and it seemed just right. Once, it had been custom to carry yew branches on Palm Sunday. Perhaps she ought to reinstate that custom?

'Or not,' Winsome said, and turned her face away from

the tree. She decided to walk to the care home and not take her car. The home was only down the street, and Winsome was becoming embarrassed by her old petrol-guzzling car. The next one she bought, she promised herself, would be electric.

Or maybe the lockdown would go on forever, and she'd never need to drive anywhere again.

Putting on all the PPE gear flustered Winsome, and she had to spend an extra minute calming herself again, taking deep breaths, holding them, counting to four.

In, one, two, three, four.

Hold, one, two, three, four.

Out – slowly – one, two, three, four.

The dog stood and watched. So far, he'd proved to be the strong, silent type.

Mary let her in, nodding her head. 'Thanks for coming, Vicar,' she said.

'Of course,' Winsome replied around the lump in her throat. 'Of course,' she repeated, not knowing what else to say.

'He lapsed into silence some time ago,' Mary told her, leading the way to Bernie Roberts' room. 'I think he hasn't long left.'

Winsome nodded. 'I'll make him comfortable,' she said. 'Be with him as he passes.'

Erin stood white-faced outside Bernie's room. Even behind the face mask, Winsome could see she was distressed. She wanted to reach out, touch Erin on the arm.

She didn't, of course. Winsome smiled instead, knowing it was barely visible, but her eyes still crinkled, didn't they?

That was now how you could tell if someone smiled, not by looking at the lips.

'He's going to be fine, Erin,' she said. 'He's been ill for some time. This is the natural progression.' She didn't know why humans were so fragile, why their bodies wore out so soon, but maybe that was okay. It wasn't the end, after all, except of one adventure.

Erin shook her head. There were tears in her eyes. 'I've grown fond of him, that's all,' she said.

'Then he will go on his way knowing he was loved,' Winsome said. 'And that will be of great comfort to him.'

Erin nodded, looked down at the floor for a moment, then straightened, as though taking a deep breath of her own. 'May I help?'

Stephan had told Erin about helping to sing Teresa on her way, and hadn't she done that herself for Kria at Midwinter?

Winsome didn't know how to answer. She hadn't been expecting this – someone in there with her, watching what she did. Or didn't do, as the case may be.

But it was Erin, and she was attached to the old man. How could Winsome say no?

Morghan's voice spoke in her ear. *You have the authority in this work and must agree or decline according to what you need.* Morghan. Winsome wished she were here too.

Her mouth was dry when she spoke. 'Perhaps you could warm a bowl of water for me,' she said.

Erin nodded immediately and hurried away to the kitchen. Winsome put her hand on the door and closed her eyes for a moment.

'God be with me,' she said. 'God guide my hand and my heart.'

Then she pushed the door open, stepped through into the next phase of her life, and closed it behind herself.

Of course, at the bedside of the dying was a natural place for a clergyperson to be – but Winsome had come prepared to do more than just pray over the dying Mr. Roberts.

She was prepared to ease him, as gently as possible, from one life onwards to the next.

Soul midwifery. She liked the term even more.

'Hello, Mr. Roberts,' she said softly, going to his bedside and putting her bag down on the chair beside it. She touched him gently on the forehead, smoothed his silver hair back, and wished she didn't have to be wearing gloves.

But at least he wasn't on his own. She was there with him.

'I've come to help you on the next part of your journey,' she said, her voice calm, loving. 'We'll make the crossing as easy as slipping from one place to another.' She glanced around the room, but it was empty yet, apart from Dog, who sat on the floor at the end of the bed, his toffee-coloured eyes fixed on Winsome. She would have found the gaze unnerving in any other animal, but the dog was like no other she'd met. His stare was lively with knowing.

'First,' Winsome said, turning back to the man in the bed, whose breathing was shallow, dry and rattling. 'We're going to make a nice safe space for you.'

The course she was taking had prepared her to do this part too, using scent and sound to clear any stagnancy and disturbance from the room, and to this, Winsome added the ways Morghan had been teaching her.

This was the first time doing it on her own, though.

Another deep breath, and Winsome closed her eyes, the better to concentrate. She let loose her spirit, feeling her energy spread unbounded, relaxed, her senses turning calm and sure. She made a bubble of energy with her mind and her will, spreading it to the corners of the room so that it became a warm, smooth cocoon, a safe place for Bernie Robert's transformation.

Winsome raised her hands as though to touch the shimmering energy, then let them drop, satisfied. The room itself was clear now, a bright, warm, safe space. She hoped she could hold it there because that, she'd learnt, was the trick. She had somehow, to hold it with the back of her mind – or at least, that's what it felt like – while she went about the rest of her business. She paused for a moment, examining the sensation. The back of her mind, the back of her head, her neck and shoulders.

Life had become very weird, she decided.

The door opened, and Erin slipped through. 'I brought the water,' she said, speaking softly. She closed the door behind her and sighed, trying to let the tension fall from her shoulders as Winsome took the bowl from her.

Erin looked at Bernie. Sometime in the last six weeks, he'd become frail, his body taking up less and less space in the bed, barely making a bump there under the covers.

She had become fond of him. And Burdock adored him.

Burdock was in the sitting room being comforted by the other residents right now.

Erin let out a long low breath through pursed lips,

making herself relax, stepping clumsily, but stepping none-theless, into that state she was coming to think of as *far and wide*. That relaxed, spread-out state where she was inside and outside of herself at the same time. Where she felt like she could see far. And narrow.

Morghan said there was more to come after she'd mastered this *far and wide*, and whenever Erin thought about that, she shivered in anticipation. And anxiety. What if she ended up somewhere like the glen again?

The room felt sort of shimmery around her and she closed her eyes, soaking up the sensation, then glanced over at Winsome.

'You did this?' she asked. 'It wasn't like this before, although I've tried to keep it clean and clear.' She meant energetically, of course. After helping Stephan and Krista to clear the psychic gunk from Rosalie Busby's house, she wasn't keen on letting any of that stagnant dark energy accumulate anywhere anymore.

Especially here, she'd realised, at the care home. It quickly became stuffy in the corners, dirty with old memo-ries and regrets.

Winsome smiled and nodded slightly. Of course Erin would be able to see, or sense, what she'd done, the soft cocoon she'd knitted together around the space.

'Will you help me wash him?' she asked. She'd tipped a handful of herbs into the water to steep. Morghan had given them to her. Elder leaves, for transformation and birth.

Erin came over and accepted the soft muslin cloth, dipping it into the warm water and whispering a prayer over it.

'Let our friend be blessed and softened by you, water

and elder,' she said. 'Let him be washed of fear and regrets, ready for the next world.' Erin thought briefly of Kria.

She smoothed the warm cloth over his brow.

Winsome let her tend him. They knew each other after all, had become friends. It was right for Erin to care for him at this hour.

And besides, Winsome had to concentrate on holding the space. It wasn't as easy without Morghan there. Morghan did it seemingly effortlessly.

But then, Morghan had long years of practice under her belt.

Winsome forced herself to stop fretting over doing it, and just do it instead. She relaxed, and the protective cocoon steadied. She held space for the dying man with her calm mind, her strong back, her soft heart. She held him safely in it.

And she began to sing. Slowly at first, haltingly, her cheeks flaming momentarily with embarrassment. The song was wordless, a humming that reminded Winsome of the fresh early spring breeze that had pushed and tugged at her hair on her way through the streets of Wellsford. It reminded her of the deep well in the lawn at Morghan's Hawthorn House.

Erin dipped her cloth back in the warm water, and wiped it gently over Bernie's neck, his wrists. She drew it down his fingers, knowing she was clearing away his hurts, his worries. She hummed as she worked, her voice twining in and out with Winsome's.

Winsome came nearer and sat, taking Bernie's hand as Erin put the cloth away and dried him with a soft towel.

'That's it,' Winsome said, her voice full of a sudden,

sweet tenderness. 'You're doing so well, Bernie. Letting go of it all. Leaving the mistakes and the hurt behind. Taking the love with you. Forgiving yourself for everything you've left undone, every hurt given and received.'

The words were those she'd learnt from Morghan, and they resonated within her heart. She spoke them, knowing them to be true.

'You've no need to carry your burdens anymore. Leave them here, leave them behind you.' Winsome licked her lips, carried on. 'It's time now to put on your shining brow, to become again what you and all of us truly are.'

Bernie drew in a rattling breath, his hand cool and dry in the palms of Winsome's own. Winsome turned, sensing movement on the other side of the bed. Movement that wasn't Erin, who stood at the foot, humming softly.

Bernie's kin had come for him. His family. A smiling woman stepped forward, leaning over the bed, her face beaming. Behind her, a strong young man stood, eyes sparkling.

Winsome thought there were more behind these two, but they faded away into the shining light surrounding them. She drew a deep breath and watched as the woman reached for the dying man in the bed.

And she put a hand to her chest, felt the thumping of her heart as Bernie Roberts sat up, leaving his body behind in the bed like a husk, to go with his family. He stood beside the bed, strength returned, glowing, and turned a moment, glancing at Winsome with a smile before staring at Erin. His expression clouded and he turned to Winsome, aware that she could see him in his spirit form, that she would be able to hear his words as though he spoke out loud.

'Take care of the girl, if you can,' he said. 'I've not had the heart to tell her my suspicions.'

Winsome's brow knotted. 'Your suspicions?'

Bernie nodded, his spirit glowing gently, luminous around the edges. 'About her mother's death. It not being an accident. I probably should have told her.' He turned and gazed at Erin, who did not see him, then a moment later, he was with his family, being ushered onwards into the light and through into the next world.

Winsome closed her eyes, feeling her dog come to lean against her. She was troubled by Bernie's words, knowing exactly what to make of them, and what was coming next for Erin.

The girl had a great trial ahead of her.

She wanted to think more upon it, but this was not the time. Closing her eyes, she sang Bernie Roberts over to the rest of his life. She sang the crossing like a prayer, like a sigh and a wish, a blessing.

'Our Father, who art in heaven,' she said, her voice low and lilting.

'Our mother, whose body is the land.

'Hallowed be thy name, blessed it be thy flesh.

'Thy kingdom come, thy will be done, on earth as it is in heaven.

'Give us this day our daily bread and forgive us our trespasses as we forgive those who trespass against us.

'Your bounty is also our own. We are in service to your needs.

'Lead us not into temptation but deliver us from evil.

'For compassion lives in our hearts and kindness moves our hands.

'For thine is the kingdom, the power and the glory, for ever and ever.

'For we are eternal and connected and we grow in the spirit of love.

'Amen,' she sang, drawing the word out.

'So it is, so it has always been, and so shall it remain, world beyond time, world without end.'

4

STEPHAN WAS WAITING FOR ERIN AND BURDOCK OUTSIDE THE care home, and grinned when he saw them. Then his face fell.

'Erin,' he said. 'What's wrong?'

Burdock pressed his cold nose into Stephan's hand, leaned his weight into the cupped palm.

Erin screwed her eyes up for a moment then sniffed. 'Sorry,' she said. 'Bernie Roberts died today.'

Stephan had been expecting the news, but it was still a blow. He put his hand to his heart and bowed his head for a moment. When he looked up, his eyes were damp.

'Happy travels, Mr. Roberts,' he said, then sighed. 'He was a real good guy.'

Erin nodded, and stepped onto the footpath, making sure to keep the requisite distance between them. It was hard, because she wanted nothing more than to walk into the circle of Stephan's strong, comforting arms, and bury her face in his shoulder.

Instead, she just let herself look silently at him, his blue eyes like pools she could swim and soothe herself in.

'Were you with him?' Stephan asked, scratching Burdock's ears and reluctant to turn and start their walk. He wanted to reach for her, but that was against the rules. They weren't part of the same household, so there was no touching. Stephan had thought that perhaps Ambrose and Morghan would relax the rules a little for some of them, but they hadn't. If anything, they'd been extremely clear that all the lockdown rules would apply to each and every one of them. He sighed again.

He understood, of course. It made sense, when Ambrose and Morghan also made clear the ways in which they would be supporting and caring for their community. And their community wasn't Wilde Grove – or not just Wilde Grove. It was the whole village.

Erin nodded. Blew out another breath and tugged her scarf tighter around her neck. 'Yeah,' she said. 'I was there. Winsome came and sung him over.' She held Stephan's gaze. 'I helped,' she said. 'And that helped.'

Stephan nodded. He wished he'd been able to be there as well. But even when he was delivering the boxes of vegetables, he didn't go inside the care home now. No more watching Alfred Hitchcock movies. No more card games, either. That at least, was helping his wallet. Mrs. Sharp played a real mean hand.

'I'm glad,' he said. 'It was good when I was there to sing Teresa over.'

Erin drew in a breath, nodded. 'He knew my mother,' she said. 'He was like a link to my past. I'm sad that's gone. I'm going to miss him.' She dropped her gaze at last and turned to walk. Burdock trotted ahead down the footpath, keen for the walk home and the bowl of biscuits that would be at the end of it.

'It's still weird,' Erin said, 'being the one around here who knows the least about myself.'

Stephan fell into step beside her, an arm's distance away. 'How are your mum and dad?' he asked.

Erin's shoulders tightened. She shook her head. 'Nothing's changed there,' she said. 'They're still furious with me.'

'Yeah, well, they wanted you at home with them for the lockdown. I can understand that, I suppose.'

'I'm not going anywhere near them, the way they're being about me living here,' Erin said, her chin jutting out stubbornly. 'Especially now that I'm working in a care home – they think that's well beneath me.'

'I WISH YOU COULD COME IN,' ERIN SAID WHEN THEY REACHED Ash Cottage.

Stephan looked at her flushed cheeks and autumn eyes. 'Me too,' he said, his heart suddenly in his throat.

Erin nodded. Swallowed. Smiled slightly. 'Touch me,' she said.

Stephan's eyebrows shot up and he giggled. 'You have to do it too,' he said.

Erin nodded again, eyes glowing in the early evening light.

It only took a moment – they were getting good at it. Practice did that, they'd discovered.

The energy rush made Erin sway slightly where she stood on the path in front of the cottage. She breathed deeply and slowly and let her own spirit sweep and soar around her. It reached for Stephan, drawn to him with the knowledge of lifetimes.

For some reason, Stephan thought, the energy between them was blue when they did this. Blue and green and serpent-like as it twisted and twined around them, almost its own thing. He didn't understand it properly, or at all, really, but it made his head swim, and his heart pound, and every nerve in his body thrum with life and excitement.

Erin closed her eyes and reached out a hand to steady herself on the little covered entranceway to Ash Cottage. The feeling between them was electric. It tingled in every nerve, seeped in through every pore. She thought, if they kept at it, kept getting better and better at reaching for each other like this, the touch of their spirits together would bring her to orgasm. What was it going to be like to actually make love to Stephan? She shivered.

Burdock barked and leapt up at her, planting his great feet on her shoulders and licking her face.

'Burdock!' It broke the spell and Erin laughed, shoving the huge dog away and grinning over him at Stephan.

'He likes the energy between us too,' she said.

'I'm not surprised,' Stephan replied. 'It's...' He couldn't think of the words. Just shook his head.

'Yeah,' Erin agreed. 'It's that all right.' She gave a big sigh, but she felt good, flushed and alive, almost enormously happy. Well-being always flooded through her after they did their little trick. 'Will I see you tomorrow?' she asked.

Stephan nodded immediately, leaning over to give Burdock a good rub. His voice was scratchy when he answered, and his knees felt a little weak, but that was okay. That was good, actually. It was all pretty damned good, considering.

'I'll walk you to work,' he answered.

But Erin shook her head. 'I'm not working tomorrow.' She chewed at her lip a moment. 'We can meet for a walk sometime later, though?'

Stephan ticked through his job list for the next day. 'The new glasshouse is arriving next week, so I'll be preparing the ground for that in the morning, and I've another batch of teas and tonics to mix up.' He had to do that in the flat he shared with Krista now, instead of the potting shed here at Ash Cottage, much to his regret, and he shook his head. 'Then, I'm working with Ambrose for a couple hours after lunch.' He shrugged and wrinkled his nose. 'Early evening?' Stephan looked up at the sky. 'It's supposed to be fine tomorrow as well.'

Ash Cottage wrapped itself around Erin as she closed the door behind her and Burdock and set her bag down on the table so she could shrug out of her jacket and unwind the scarf from her neck. Burdock was already standing over his bowl, his eyes fixed on her.

'You're a great, greedy beastie, you know that, don't you?' Erin said, hanging her things up and heading for the big tin in which she kept Burdock's food. She doled out his evening allowance and stood back with a smile on her face as he set to crunching the biscuits.

She'd found a stash of them – his dog biscuits – under his bed by the fire the other day. He'd been sneaking some away to hide since the morning she'd got in such a bad mood and forgotten to feed him.

That made her think of Bernie Roberts again, and Erin went over to put the kettle on with a weight in her heart. She poked the embers to life in the cooker and listened for a moment to the bright rustle of the flames.

So much had happened since she'd opened that letter from Block and Ward, Solicitors. Now, she was living here, Ash Cottage officially hers. Now, she was walking the Ancient Path. And she'd got the whole thing with Kria and the valley sorted. She still dreamed of the place, but Kria was never there, only the glen as she'd left it, filled with trees, their branches reaching out to each other, fringed limbs touching. And the loch, deep and dark, a huge, shadowed form rising from it. A dragon – and it should have scared her, but it never did. It was simply there in the dream, the moon shining on its scales, like magic made real.

She took her cup of tea and wandered past Burdock in his favourite chair where he was watching the sun seep slowly from the day out the window, and she went into the little room off the sitting room. There, on Teresa's old desk lay her sketchbooks and pencils, but she didn't pick them up. Instead, she set her cup down and went over to the table she'd set under the far window and touched her fingertips lightly to the edge of it, drawing in a deep breath and holding it for a long beat before releasing it slowly and closing her eyes.

'Go in peace, my friend,' she said, thinking of Bernie Roberts. 'Your company meant a great deal to me, your stories of my mother, my grandmother, and her mother too.' He'd told her some corkers and she smiled through her tears at the memory of them. Bernie Roberts had been a natural storyteller, and the family she'd never met had come alive to her through his telling.

Erin opened her eyes and gazed down at the altar she'd made, working with the guidance of Teresa's books, the ones that weren't about plants, that was. And her own intuition and inclination, Erin had used those too, with the result being something of a chaotic spread of things.

Except to her, it wasn't chaotic at all. She touched her fingers to the small bowl of water that reflected the dying light of the sun coming in through the window to Erin's left.

It was in a shallow pottery bowl, glazed with a rich swirl of blue and green. Erin had chosen it because it reminded her of the well in the garden of Hawthorn House, the one she'd tumbled so unceremoniously down the first time she'd gone there.

Down and down the dark shaft of water she'd gone, and then, suddenly, out into a wide nothingness, twisting around to look back up at the underside of the earth.

The womb of the world, she'd thought.

Another breath and an effort to quiet her mind, and Erin moved her fingers to touch the raven feather she'd placed on the table. It was long and fine, a strong feather gifted to her by the raven that even now haunted the grounds of Ash Cottage. She smiled at it and then frowned slightly as she looked at the feather next to it – this one was from a seagull, and she could not look at it without thinking of both blood and flight. She turned her mind from the memory of blood and took wing instead, remembering the exhilaration of flying out over the ocean, the wind in her feathers, the spray cold and salty against her.

It made her sigh with a joy that had quietened but not gone away since the experience. She resolved to go out and see if she could repeat the performance as soon as she could.

Erin continued her way around the wheel of her altar. Water, Air. Then Earth, and she lightly stroked the leaves of the ivy plant that spilled from its pot and curled around the circle. How could she not have a living plant on her altar? Soil, and tree of sorts, and the honouring of her grandmother Teresa.

Then there was fire, and Erin nipped a sharp tooth at her lip, narrowing her eyes at the tiny cast iron cauldron in which there were fragments of herbs waiting for a spark of fire to set them alight.

She was too tired to try plucking the spark of fire from between her palms. She hadn't succeeded to do it at all yet, and tonight was not going to be the night. She knew that. She'd come over here for a different reason.

In the centre of the wheel on her altar, Erin had placed a tiny handful of crystals that gleamed like the diamonds the Goddess had given her, but it was not these her eyes sought now. She looked instead at the photos she'd propped up behind it all. Teresa looked back at her, face creased in a moment of wry amusement. Teresa's mother smiled from the next one, and next to that, a picture of her mother Rebecca, given to her by Charlie. It showed a young woman with long dyed blonde hair and a face giving the camera a hard look. She was sitting on a concrete step somewhere, elbows on her knees, a glass in her hand.

It wasn't a flattering photo, but the only ones Teresa had upstairs in the box at the back of the wardrobe showed her daughter as a child. Somewhere in Becca's early teens, Teresa had stopped taking photos of her. Or she'd gotten rid of the ones she had taken, because there weren't any now.

Erin narrowed her eyes. There were photographs of other people though, and she had the sudden, niggling idea that one of those other people might be Bernie Roberts. Turning on her heel, Erin dashed up the stairs, found the shoe box and dumped the loose photos on the bed to sift through them.

She'd been right. Holding the picture showing a grinning – and much younger – Bernie Roberts, in his police uniform, no less, standing next to Teresa, who had also cracked a smile for the occasion, whatever it was, Erin ran lightly down the stairs again, flung Burdock a passing grin, and went back into the little snug.

She put the photograph on the altar and sighed in satisfaction and a little sadness.

'You belong here for a while,' she told the beaming man in the photo. 'To honour your life and your passing.' Erin reached for a box of matches and lit a tealight candle.

She would let it burn, with its bright dancing flame.

For her friend, to light him on his way.

5

ERIN WOKE WITH BERNIE ON HER MIND. AND HER MOTHER.
She felt unsettled, as though she'd dreamed something, and
it niggled and prickled at her.

She lay still in the bed that had been her grandmother's,
the covers tucked up tight around her. She could hear
Burdock snoring on his bed by the fireplace and screwed
her eyes shut, trying to draw the dream back to herself. It
teased at the edges of her consciousness, but like it was a
slippery fish, and she couldn't grasp it.

It had been about something dark. Darkness behind a
door. And stairs, maybe? And the dragon there too, even
though it belonged in Kria's loch.

Erin opened her eyes to stare at the ceiling. The dragon
notwithstanding, she knew what she'd been dreaming
about, and no surprise there, was it? She'd come to learn
about her mother and grandmother even more from Bernie
than she had from Charlie.

When she asked Charlie about her mother, she always

felt as though Charlie was hesitating over her answers, never being quite straight-forward.

But Bernie had liked their little tea breaks. More and more he'd been happy to ramble on down memory lane, his mouth twisting wistfully whenever he spoke of Teresa.

They hadn't touched again on the way Becca had died, though. Bernie had just shaken his head and changed the subject whenever she'd brought it up. And she'd let him because who wanted to dwell on such a stupid accident?

Erin sat up in bed, her raised knees making a tent of the blankets. She hugged her arms around them and looked down at the sleeping dog and the low orange embers in the fireplace.

Who did want to dwell on such a stupid accident?

But, she realised, she thought she'd just dreamed of it.

For the first time, she let her thoughts turn consciously towards the boyfriend. Becca's boyfriend. The one who had called the ambulance while her mother lay at the bottom of the stairs, her head staved in.

Burdock heard the sharp intake of breath and raised his head, yawned widely, and saw his person awake and sitting up. He sat up as well, yawning again.

'Who was the boyfriend, Burdock?' Erin asked, then shivered. 'I think I'm glad I don't know him, Burdock. Something about the whole thing is just weird. A bit off.'

Burdock came over to the side of the bed and plonked his head on the covers. Erin scratched behind his ears, in the exact place he liked best. Her fingers were gentle, but the scritches were thorough and he sighed with pleasure.

'Why am I even thinking about them, Burdock?' Erin asked.

Burdock didn't know. He thought about his stomach. Was it breakfast time?

'I mean,' Erin continued. 'It's not as though Becca even wanted me.' The thought pricked at her heart like a needle.

But still. She was dreaming about it – she was sure she was.

ERIN LEFT BURDOCK DROOLING OVER HIS BREAKFAST AND slipped out through the utility room and into the garden. Her breath fogged in the cold air in front of her as she stepped between Teresa's garden beds, heading for the well.

She did this every morning now, particularly since the winter solstice. Now, even if she was late getting out of bed, she came down here before putting the kettle on for tea, before breakfast, before everything except relieving herself, letting Burdock out, and then feeding him.

The rising morning blued the sky, and she lifted the lid to the well, breathing deeply of the cold tang that rose from the water and made her shiver. She wet a finger and anointed her forehead with the clear spring water.

'Bless me, holy water, with your clarity,' she murmured, wishing it to be so.

The well in front of her was a dark, deep, watery tunnel that made her feel slightly dizzy every time she looked into its depths. She forced herself to anyway, then after a moment, closed her eyes, feeling for the water instead. It was there, right beside her, a cool, dim presence, full of secrets, rising from deep in the earth, from some hidden land.

Erin lifted her head slightly, feeling the chill of the

morning on her skin. The air was crackling sharp this morning, and she breathed it into her lungs, imagining it flooding forth into her bloodstream, carrying oxygen and the wild joy of spring around her body, out into her fingers, down into her toes.

She stepped from the raised well and stood on the path in the centre of Teresa's garden – her garden. She held her hands cradled in front of her belly for a moment, then swept her arms out and up around in a circle, standing up to stretch them to the sky, breathing in the dawning day, letting it out slowly as she lowered her arms down in front of her. She moved her arms back out to the side, embracing the air, then drew her hands forward towards her chest, breathing in again, breathing the world into her lungs. Then she exhaled, offering her breath back to the world with an outward gesture.

Air, she thought. Breath of life.

She reached upwards again, this time towards the sun, feeling for its fire with her fingertips, seeing them sparkling with diamond flames.

Fire, she thought. Spark of life.

She let her arms float down, drawing them through the air as though it was water. She floated in the well for a moment, the water stirring through her fingers as she shimmied in the waves she made.

Water, she thought. Womb of life.

And she lifted her feet, back on land again, the ground solid and fertile under her padding feet. She lifted onto her toes, sank onto her heels, then spread her arms over her head and around and down, feeling them as branches bursting with buds as her toes dug roots into the secret soil.

Earth, she thought. Root of life.

She reached back to the sky, then down to the earth, then drew her tingling hands to her chest, to her heart.

Above, she thought. Below. All around. I am part of the wheel.

And all around her, the great wheel turned, the universe spun, and she was there in it, where she was supposed to be. One, small, great, precious piece of it.

She felt it there, the vastness of space, the prickling of dimensions.

She felt it there, the land and sea beyond her garden, the sweep of its hills, the crags of its mountains, the tug and pull of its tides.

She felt it there, the trees of Wilde Grove, their roots dug deep and dreaming into the earth, their sturdy trunks rising to bridge the sky.

She felt it there, the walls of her garden, the paths leading inwards to where she stood.

She felt it all and held it. This was the song. This was Kria's song, the one the girl had forgotten to sing.

This was the song of the wheel, of the world.

And Erin was learning it.

6

THERE WAS A TAPPING AT THE FRONT DOOR AND ERIN LOOKED up from her drawing, surprised. Burdock sat up too, hearing the brass knocker in the shape of his own face. He looked at Erin, then untangled his legs from his bed by the fire and trotted to the door to sniff out who was there.

He recognised the scent at once and turned his head to look at Erin. 'Woof,' he said, telling her their visitor was a friend.

It wasn't Stephan though, who was his best friend ever, but that didn't matter. He'd see Stephan later. He saw Stephan every day.

Erin propped her lap desk against the bookcase and went to the door holding a bunch of pencils and frowning. She wasn't expecting anyone. This was her drawing time, an hour or two to devote to her art.

'Morghan!' Erin blinked at the sight of Morghan standing there in her little entranceway. 'I wasn't expecting you!'

Morghan shook her head. 'I'm sorry for my intrusion during your own time,' she said. 'But we have both been so busy and I would like us to talk together.'

Erin's eyes widened and her heart started up a harsh thumping against her ribs. 'Why?' she asked. 'Is something wrong?'

Morghan shook her head, her eyes steady and clear. 'No,' she said, although she frowned slightly. 'May we walk in your garden a few minutes?'

Erin nodded dumbly, looked down at her fistful of pencils, at Burdock thrusting himself out the door to demand a pat. 'Of course,' she said. 'Um...'

'I'll go around the side and meet you,' Morghan said, then smiled down at the dog. 'Burdock can remind me of the way.'

She turned with the dog before any reply came, and Erin stared after her for a moment before closing the door and standing behind it, frowning. What could Morghan possibly want? There had been faint strain lines around her eyes too, hadn't there? Did she have bad news?

Erin went straight to the door into the utility room from the kitchen and thrust her feet into her grandmother's old wellington boots. When she stepped outside, the late morning air was as still as spun glass. It crackled in her throat when she took a gulping breath.

'Is it my parents?' she asked. 'Has something happened to them?' It didn't make sense that Morghan would know something about her parents back home when she didn't herself, but the questions burst forth anyway.

She still gripped the pencils in her fist.

Morghan shook her head. 'I'm sure your parents are fine,' she replied. 'Have you heard from them lately?'

Erin shook her head, then scowled, remembering she was still angry with them. 'No,' she told Morghan. 'They're still being unreasonable about everything.'

'I'm sure it doesn't feel unreasonable to them,' Morghan said evenly, stepping away down the garden's central path. 'They've never experienced anything like Wilde Grove, remember.'

But the comment had Erin shaking her head. 'Just because you don't know something doesn't mean you oughtn't be open-minded enough to learn about it.'

'Perhaps,' Morghan agreed. 'But people are rarely simple or even reasonable, and we have to remember that every person has an inner life of which we generally know nothing.' She stopped in front of the well and looked at it, then lifted her face to the sky, seeing still in the edges of her vision, the roof of the world torn and ragged with lightning.

'I don't know,' Erin said. 'I think Krista's right – that there's a lot of illness in people's heads these days. It's as though our software has been corrupted, or something.'

Morghan nodded. 'The illness is caused by losing our connection to spirit,' she said. 'We have become divided people, not knowing the most important part of ourselves.' She blinked and turned to smile at Erin. 'But that does not mean we should not treat those suffering like this with compassion and as much understanding as we can muster.'

'Even while they're hurting us?'

'Ah,' Morghan said on a long sigh. 'There's where it gets difficult, doesn't it?'

'There's where we need boundaries, you mean.' Erin scuffed her toe in the gravel of the path.

'Yes. Those too.'

'That's the problem, isn't it?' Erin asked, suddenly passionate, squeezing the pencils in her hand. 'I mean – how do you walk this line, or whatever? Have compassion for someone's ignorance when they're basically trying to bulldoze you with it?'

The smile that appeared on Morghan's face was wide and unfeigned. 'Being bulldozed is not an option,' she said. 'But it doesn't preclude trying to understand another's situation. Or our own, if it's our ignorance that's at issue. It might even make things easier.'

'Or more exasperating,' Erin muttered. 'I don't know,' she repeated. 'I don't know any of this. The world's sick. How do we fix that?'

Morghan knew the question – she'd asked it of herself often enough. 'We fix ourselves,' she said. 'And we take care of our communities.'

Erin stared at the ground and said nothing. Just shook her head slightly.

Eventually, she looked up and gazed at Morghan. 'Fixing yourself is hard,' she said, thinking of Kria, her own doubts and struggles.

'Yes. It takes constant effort. Every day.'

'Is it worth it?' Erin wondered.

'You are truly asking that?'

Erin thought of her parents. They lived every day comfortably, oblivious to most of what went on in the world. Caring only about material things, never giving their souls a thought. Didn't that seem easier?

Morghan watched Erin thinking, seeing the slight frown between her brows. She kept herself still, wondering if Erin would find her way towards an answer for her own question.

'Yeah,' Erin sighed, lifting her head, and looking around her garden, turning a moment to gaze back at the solid stones of Ash Cottage. Burdock was nosing around by the back door, tracking some sort of interesting scent. She looked over the top of the walls at the trees of Wilde Grove and felt her heart lift.

'Yeah,' she said again. 'It's worth it. It's important.'

'Good,' Morghan said. 'I'm glad you know that.' She turned away and looked over the garden again. Teresa had designed it very particularly. It was time to use that.

'It's not an easy job,' Morgan said, reaching out gently to touch the lid of the well, tracing the design with a fingertip, 'being Lady of the Grove.'

'But you love it, surely?' Erin interrupted, somehow shocked. She'd never expected Morghan would say such a thing.

'I do,' Morghan said. 'But like most important things, it is not easy. Responsibility and duty seldom are easy, I think, and this job comes with plenty of both.' She paused a moment. 'I'm telling you this because I hope that you're going to be taking my place one day, and you need to know it.'

Morghan had never said this quite so bluntly, and Erin's mind filled with the white noise of shock. She sucked in a deep breath and the cold air pierced her lungs, brought her mind back to her.

'I have been learning it since the moment I got here,' she

said, and a little bitterness crept into her voice. 'Being trapped with Kria was hard.'

'You cannot begrudge her the mistakes she made,' Morghan said. 'She got lost.'

Erin nodded, not knowing at all where this conversation was going.

Morghan smiled. 'But you retrieved her, and the initiation was complete.' She hesitated. 'Or begun truly.'

Erin glanced sharply at her. 'What do you mean? Begun? I'm not going back there – she's not there anymore.'

Morghan didn't reply straight away. She had not been looking forward to this conversation. She felt she had been keeping things from Erin – and she had. She'd been keeping Wayne Moffat from her. Had she been right to, or were things unfolding as they were supposed to? If she'd told Erin straight away, the young woman would have had time to brood upon it and become fixed in her opinion – something Erin was prone to doing as it was. If meeting Wayne would be a shock, it could force her mind to stay open.

For a moment, when Morghan looked up over the walls of Teresa's garden, the trees of Wilde Grove were alight with fire, the flames shooting silently towards the sky, leaping from one tree to the next, intent on burning the Grove to the ground. Echoes of the past destruction.

The past never truly went away.

'What is it?' Erin asked, seeing the lines around Morghan's eyes deepen. 'What are you seeing?' She looked in the same direction over the wall, but there was nothing but the twiggy limbs of the Grove's trees and clouds bunching like white candyfloss on the far horizon.

Morghan looked at Erin. She was so young, she thought, then gazed away back at the trees. The fire was gone. Too young? she wondered. Was Erin too young?

Did it matter?

She turned back to the woman who would one day – hopefully – take her place in Hawthorne House and Wilde Grove.

'There are things I need you to begin learning,' she said.

Erin looked steadily at her, but her heart was thumping in her chest.

'The first of them,' Morghan continued, 'is the way of walking between the worlds. Of stepping into the Wildwood, of finding your way around the Otherworld. She touched a hand to her chest. 'This is one of our duties – to be an axis point around which the Waking and the Wildwood spin. So that we may walk in each, know the truth of each, and navigate between them for the good of our community and our world.'

Erin's mouth was dry. She tried to think of something to say, but she didn't have the slightest idea of how to respond.

'I do not think you will find this difficult to learn,' Morghan said with a soft smile. 'You already have experience of travelling back to other lives – this will not be too terribly different in its method.'

'Method?' Erin frowned. 'I don't know that there was much method there. Mostly I went in my dreams, and occasionally, I sort of...followed a thread.' She grimaced at how difficult that was to explain.

But Morghan was nodding. 'Your experience of altered states of consciousness will ease the learning,' she said, then looked around the garden and waved a hand at it. 'Teresa

designed this garden very specifically, and I think we will
use it as an aid to walking between the worlds.'

That made Erin gaze around at the plant beds in the
walled garden in astonishment. 'How will a garden help?'
she asked. 'Even this one?'

'There are many wells in the Otherworld,' Morghan
said, looking down at the well in Teresa's – now Erin's –
garden. She put her hand flat on the lid and felt the water
underneath, felt the way it went down deep into the secret
places of the earth.

'There are?' Erin looked at her own well. 'Is that one of
the reasons why there are so many here too? I mean, you
have one, and Charlie has one.' She shook her head slightly.
'There are probably others I don't know about.'

Morghan nodded. 'We try to echo as many things as
seem applicable. It helps us move from one world to
another, and to remember that there is more than one reality.' She smiled slightly. 'Wells, caves, pools of water – all
things you find a lot of in the Otherworld.' A pause. 'But the
well is special, at least in my own experience. They are
tended in sacred temples in the Upper World, and it is my
belief that they run from one world to another, to another,
the lifeblood of them all, perhaps.' She frowned over the
mystery. 'They are the wheel well, the axis around which
the worlds spin.'

Erin listened, trying to follow.

'But as that may be,' Morghan said. 'I want you to use
this garden as your fixed point in all the worlds.'

'What?'

For a moment, Morghan grinned. 'When we begin to
travel to the Otherworld, it is best at first, if we establish a

place on the border that is ours, a liminal space we can go to where we are safe and at ease, where we may rest and just be, and where we can see that which needs tending in our own psyche.'

'You have a place like this?'

Morghan inclined her head. 'I do.' Her eyes took on a faraway gaze. 'This is also a place where we may stand there at the same time as here.'

'I don't understand,' Erin said, shaking her head.

'I know. It is hard to explain these things, unfortunately, which is why we mostly push ourselves into experiencing them.' Morghan tapped her fingers on the well lid. 'But I will try, at least for this part. Because we must begin somewhere.'

'Uh huh. That would be good.'

Morghan laughed. 'Be patient with me, Erin. I was taught this myself many years ago, and this is the first time I've tried to pass the lesson on.'

Erin was immediately contrite. 'Sorry,' she said. 'I'm listening. There's just so much, isn't there – to learn, I mean?'

Now Morghan shook her head. 'Not so many things, really,' she said. 'They're just all rather large things.'

That made Erin more nervous. She rubbed her palms against the wool of her dress and waited. Burdock came over and sat beside her, ears cocked as though ready to listen and learn as well. She reached out and rested a hand on his warm neck.

'All right, then,' Morghan said. 'Most of the time when we travel in the Wildwood, and in the Otherworld, our spirit has left our body to do so, and we are not conscious of where we are in this world. Our consciousness is in the Otherworld, do you understand?'

Erin nodded. Then shivered. 'Like when I was with Kria, I couldn't see or feel myself here at all.'

'Yes, that's so. Which is why it is good to also have a fixed point, where you can stand there and here at the same time.' Morghan frowned again. How had Selena taught her this? It had been so long ago. 'Because we must hold the worlds in us,' she continued. 'If we are to do the work we must, we need to be able to hold both places within us, to be aware of the truth and reality of the worlds, that they exist within us at the same time.'

'Okay,' Erin answered slowly. 'So how do we do that? And how do we find this place?' She narrowed her eyes. 'How did you find yours?'

But Morghan shook her head. That didn't matter right now. 'You,' she said, 'are going to use this garden to do it. You will explore this garden and develop a counterpart garden inside you.' She paused and drew breath. 'Initially, this will be done through your imagination.'

'My imagination?'

'Yes.' Morghan smiled. 'The imagination is a gateway drug, believe me. It leads straight to magic.'

Erin burst out laughing and Burdock turned to look at her, his jaw dropping in a doggy grin of his own.

'All right then,' Erin said. 'A real garden and an imaginary garden.'

Morghan nodded. 'Explore this one so that you are familiar with it, with the way it is laid out. Draw it – that would work well for you. Make plans of it, detailed drawings until you know every inch of it. Then, come out here, and after your regular morning devotions, go inward, and bring the garden inside you.' She blinked, looking around the perfectly laid beds, several bare, waiting for spring to come properly so that they might be replanted. A garden was good, she thought. A garden must be cared for. It would work.

It would help Erin with what was coming. The second thing she needed to learn.

'Like, imagine it?' Erin asked, checking.

'Yes. Model it on this one, because this one is very special. And when you have it inside yourself, walk around it in your mind, your imagination, and check what needs tending, what needs planting, what needs clearing and weeding. And take care of it.'

Erin narrowed her eyes. 'I'm no gardener,' she said. 'You want me to imagine gardening?'

'We are all gardeners,' Morghan corrected. 'We all must tend the gardens of our spirits.'

'What will it achieve, though? I thought this was about learning to travel to the Otherworld.'

'It is. But we also want you to be as steady and stable and safe as possible, and this is a good way to do it. To begin the travelling.'

'By imaginary gardening?'

'By imaginary gardening,' Morghan agreed. 'You see, you will find that certain beds relate to different areas of your life and spirit, and when you tend to them, you will be seeking healing and steadiness.' She raised her eyebrows in an arch look. 'This is magic, remember. What is within is also without.'

Erin nodded. 'Garden magic.'

Morghan reached out and touched Erin lightly in the centre of her chest with a finger. 'Soul magic,' she corrected.

Then Morghan turned and looked around Teresa's garden without waiting for a response from Erin. 'Once you have tended your garden, and built it in the spirit world, it will be time to open the gate and venture forth.' She turned back to Erin. 'We all need an entry point to the Otherworld, you see. So we may as well have one that also serves us.'

'Is your like, safe place, a garden?'

Morghan decided to answer. 'No,' she said. 'But I did not have the luxury of Teresa's garden when I was learning this.'

Erin shook her head. 'I'm not sure I understand yet,' she said.

'Then explore Teresa's garden, and unravel the mystery of it while you do what I have said.' Morghan smiled. 'It will come to you.'

Erin looked back at her, doubt and confusion clear on her face. Morghan contemplated her for a long moment and decided to leave the other thing she'd come to talk about for another day.

If she told Erin about Wayne Moffat now, Erin would probably not try the exercise she'd just been told.

And that was important.

To step in and out of the world of spirit was the job of the Lady of the Grove.

Perhaps it was everyone's really.

7

'We know what's back there, you know.'

Winsome startled at the voice and almost tripped over her own feet. She felt her face go red and made herself, through sheer stubbornness, not put her hands to her flaming cheeks.

'I'm not sure what you're talking about,' she squeaked, then winced.

Mariah Reefton curled her lips in contempt. 'It's that pagan temple you've been visiting,' she said.

Now, Winsome's voice wasn't a squeak any longer. It was just gone. She stared at the old woman in dismay. And at Julia Thorpe standing next to her on the church's shaggy lawn, the low spring sunshine simpering at them from the blueness.

'You've been cavorting with the devil,' Julia said, and there were twin spots of colour in her cheeks too, although Winsome didn't think they were from embarrassment. She thought they might be there from indignation.

And jubilant, righteous indignation, at that.

If Winsome hadn't been taken by surprise, and suddenly worried for her own skin – she wasn't foolish enough to think this wasn't leading somewhere she didn't want to go – she might have sighed, shaken her head, and tried to laugh it off.

Instead, her smile was a wretched grimace and she had to clear her throat twice before she could speak.

'Erm,' she said.

Inside her head, she screeched at herself. Erm! That was it! That was all she could manage?

'We've caught you red-handed, this time,' Mariah said, nodding her head like a chicken at its feed, bobbing up and down, her eyes small and beady in their wrinkled folds.

Now, Winsome's voice made an appearance, fuelled by sudden outrage. 'Caught me red-handed? This time? Caught me at what?' She shook her head, wondering whether to simply push past the pair, dismissing them.

But dismissing them could be as dangerous as letting them accuse her of not being the Christian vicar she was supposed to be.

And honestly, hadn't they been skirting around this issue for a while now? Since, in fact, Winsome thought, looking at Julia, whose eyes were almost glassy with excitement, since Julia had come across her stumbling from the church that morning as though drunk.

The morning she had seen off the souls of Reverend Robinson and his parishioners to rest in Christ's love.

'Caught you at using that damned pagan temple for worship, that's what,' Mariah crowed.

'Because I am coming back from a walk in that direction?'

The problem with this, Winsome thought desperately, was that they were right. She was coming back from the small temple.

She had been praying there.

And if she told them that she hadn't been, then she was a liar. And if she told them that it wasn't a pagan temple, but instead a sort of summer house, then she was still a liar.

'Because you've been praying there.' Julia spat out the words from behind her mask. 'We know you have – and that's not the least of it either, is it? You've been doing a lot more than praying to whatever heathen gods you've met in these cursed woods.'

Winsome stared at the pair of women, feeling the blood leach from her face. Underneath her, clad in jeans and boots rather than the cassock, her legs wobbled and threatened to let her down. Literally. Just dump her into the grass in a shocked, limp heap.

She cleared her throat. Looked wordlessly from Mariah to Julia. Blinked. Opened her mouth.

'Look at you,' Mariah said, gleeful contempt bubbling to the surface and making her almost shiver with pleasure. 'You can't even think of a way to answer us, can you?'

'No,' Winsome said, shaking her head. 'I can't, as a matter of fact.' She rallied herself, pushing her shoulders back. Whatever these two thought of her, she was doing good work. She was helping people. Her faith, if anything, was stronger than ever.

It was just that her world was also bigger.

'I think you need to be very clear about what you are accusing me of,' she continued. 'You are two of the more... superstitious, shall we say, members of the parish, and as such, I'm not entirely convinced you're seeing things clearly.'

Mariah tipped back her face and laughed, her long yellow teeth showing. Julia glanced at her, then started laughing as well.

Winsome locked her knees and managed to stay upright.

The laughter finally died away, and Mariah looked at her with eyes lit with a foul sort of joy. She licked her lips and hooked her clawed hands onto her hips. 'Oh, Vicar,' she said. 'We know exactly what we're accusing you of, and when we've spoken to the Dean, so will he.'

'Look,' Winsome said desperately, shaking her head, knowing that now the Dean had been mentioned, things were serious. 'There's no need to bring the Dean into any of this. I am discharging my duties perfectly well. I am supporting the community to the best of my ability, and we are all doing as well as we can in these trying times.'

But Julia was shaking her head. 'Discharging your duties? Is that what it's called these days, when you go cavorting around with the enemy?'

Winsome narrowed her eyes. 'Excuse me?' she said, her temper rising. 'Cavorting with the enemy? Is that what you said?' She shook her head. 'What is this – the Inquisition all over again? We have no enemies, especially not here in Wellsford.'

Mariah and Julia did not look persuaded, however. Julia rubbed her knuckles compulsively against the hem of her puffer jacket, making slippery little synthetic noises that threatened to unravel Winsome.

'The Inquisition,' Mariah said slowly, feeling a great calm and certitude sweep over her so that the cold was no longer nipping at her joints. She nodded and said the words again. 'The Inquisition.'

Winsome stared at her.

Julia rubbed her knuckles against her jacket.

A dog barked in the distance.

Winsome tried to move her head, to look for her dog. Her spirit dog. But her neck would not turn, as though some more mechanical part of her had seized up. Perhaps it knew something she didn't. That it would be foolish to turn and search for a spirit dog when you were being accused – for all intents and purposes – of being a witch.

'I think I told you when you first got friendly with that Wilde woman,' Mariah continued, 'that we'd once had one of them put to death.'

If there had been a tree next to her, Winsome would have put out a hand to steady herself against it. It felt as though there were almost no blood in her head. She wanted to hang it between her legs and take a few deep breaths.

'Of course,' Mariah said conversationally, 'there was no burning of witches in England, back then.'

'Nor now,' Winsome managed to squeak.

But Mariah ignored the interjection. She was feeling strange inside her skin, almost...happy. As though she'd just suffered a great vindication. Where was the sensation coming from? It was almost a memory, she decided, yet as fresh and new as though it was born moments ago. She shook her head a little. What had she been saying?

Ah. Yes. 'We had to be content with hanging.' She touched her neck and stretched her lips into a wide, loose smile.

'We can't possibly be having this conversation,' Winsome said.

But Mariah didn't hear her. She'd cocked her head to one side, as though listening, perhaps to the jeering, boisterous cheers of a crowd. The crack and swing of a rope.

Perhaps.

She breathed in, blinked her eyes, focused again on Winsome. The vicar. A weak woman. Seduced by the devil, by the ways of the foul Grove that had been the nemesis of the good God-fearing folks of this town for all of memory.

Mariah knew this. Hadn't she been on the look-out? Hadn't she kept perch near her window each and every day, so that she could see the comings and goings from the vicarage?

She glanced at her niece. Hadn't Julia told her about coming across Winsome Clark that morning, the woman stumbling out of the church in her cassock and surplice, with slippers on her feet, and not a Sunday, and drunk as a skunk, reeking of the communion wine?

And hadn't she heard through her carefully tended grapevine, that Winsome had been seen with those young people from the Grove, and at Rosalie Busby's house? And that Morghan Wilde herself had been there too? Her informants said as well, that it had been Winsome, outside on the footpath, bold as brass, who had telephoned for Morghan to come.

It irked Mariah that she didn't know precisely the reason why there had been these events at Rosalie's house. Rosalie was a good churchgoer, but she wasn't in Mariah's small, tight circle of cronies.

Which was exactly why she'd had that word with her after service last Sunday.

And the last piece of the puzzle had fallen into place. Mariah leered. Or was that the last nail in the coffin?

'I had an interesting chat with Rosalie Busby after service on Sunday, Vicar,' Mariah said, following the threads through her mind.

Winsome said nothing. She waited for what was coming next, whatever it would be.

'I wanted to know as what had happened at her house, the week before Christmas.' Mariah nodded sagely, and Julia grinned at her.

'As it turned out, however, I was given a much juicier bone to chew upon for consideration,' Mariah continued. She smacked her lips together as though the bone hadn't been metaphorical but instead, she could still taste it, that perhaps the juices were still running down her chin. 'It was that granddaughter of hers who let the cat out of the bag.'

Minnie, Winsome thought, and remembered the look on Minnie's face when she'd seen her dancing around the stone circle at the Winter Solstice.

Winsome's stomach sank. She really needed to sit down.

She should have known better. Better than to have left her house and gone traipsing into the woods with everyone that low dark dawn. Better than to have taken a place in a pagan celebration of the returning sun.

Her mouth tasted bitter, of sudden bile.

It would have been different, if she'd organised some sort of celebration in the village that brought both faiths together, honouring each. But she hadn't done that, had she? No.

She'd gone off and joined the Grove's ritual. As though she was one of them.

As though she'd belonged there.

'Striking child, that one,' Mariah said, wrinkling her nose. 'Dyed her hair black, for some ungodly reason.'

'Minnie is not an ungodly child,' Winsome said.

Mariah waved a hand dismissively. 'I was giving Rosalie her due, for dragging the child along to services.' She fastened her small, currant eyes on Winsome and grinned suddenly. 'Until the child herself told me the reason she was willing to attend our church.'

Winsome thought she might throw up. Right there where she stood. All over her own feet.

'Well, it turns out, doesn't it Julia?' Mariah threw a glance at her niece and Julia nodded enthusiastically.

'Yes,' she echoed. 'It turns out completely.'

Winsome shook her head. She wasn't going to throw up, but she was suddenly very tired.

'It turns out that you're the attraction at the church on a Sunday,' Mariah said, crowing the words as though they were some sort of victory.

'That's very generous of her,' Winsome said. 'I do try to make things youth-friendly.'

But Mariah wasn't finished yet. 'Oh,' she said. 'That's not quite all, is it, Winsome? The reason you're such a hit with this girl? What would that be, then, do you think?'

Winsome just looked at her.

'Because according to her...'

'Minnie,' Julia interrupted, unable to stop herself.

'Minnie,' said Mariah. 'Yes. According to Minnie, you're the first vicar she's met who also participates – quite willingly and enthusiastically – in local pagan rituals. Did you greet the dawn with Wilde Grove on midwinter's, Winsome?'

Winsome closed her eyes.

'I'm sorry, Winsome,' Julia said. 'Could you speak up?'

Snapping her eyes open, Winsome looked steadily at her Churchwarden.

'Yes,' she said. 'I did.'

8

'Winsome?' Ambrose hurried down the steps from his front door, taking in Winsome's wild halo of hair and pale face in alarm. 'Winsome, what is it?'

He had his arms out as though to reach for her, and it was an effort to make himself stop short on the path, keeping the requisite distance. He shook his head. 'You look...'

'A fright?' Winsome answered, shaking her head, wondering what on earth had possessed her to come up here to Blackthorn House, to Ambrose of all people.

Maybe Mariah and Julia were right – maybe she was no longer fit to be vicar. The thought stuck in her craw and she touched her fingers to her throat.

'Distressed,' Ambrose said, then looked helplessly back to his house. It was cold out here and warm in there and Winsome certainly looked as though she could do with a sit down, but he couldn't take her inside with him.

Those were the rules. He held up a finger. 'Wait just one

moment,' he said. 'Don't go away. I'll be right back.' He looked at her again. She was shaking, and he didn't trust her to bolt away through the woods like some shy, frightened deer. 'Promise me,' he asked. 'That you won't go anywhere?'

Winsome shook her head, then planted her gaze on her feet. God, she thought. What am I doing here? Why is this happening to me?

Everything was going wrong.

Ambrose turned back to the house, dashing inside and snatching up his coat, which he shrugged himself into, and his cloak, which he carried back outside and held out to Winsome.

'Wrap this around yourself,' he said. 'It's cold out here, and you look like you've had a shock.' He peered at her as she took the cloak from him and held it in her hands, as though she didn't know what it was or what to do with it.

'Are you all right, Winsome?' he asked, his voice quiet.

She looked up at him, his cloak still in her arms. The wool was thick, and it smelled of him. Of wood fires and magic, of drumming and dancing.

Winsome burst into tears.

'Oh no,' she moaned through them, seeing Ambrose step towards her, and holding her hand up to stop him. 'I'm sorry, oh Jesus, I'm so sorry.'

Ambrose wasn't sure whether she was apologising to him, or Jesus. Either way, she was in pain, and that hurt him as well. He wanted to step over to her. He fought with himself, to stop from going to her, taking the cloak from her arms, and wrapping it tenderly around her to warm her, and then putting his arms around her too, and just holding her. Holding her against his chest.

'Tell me,' he said instead, in agony. 'Tell me, Winsome, what's happened?'

But she shook her head. Not because she didn't want to speak, but because the words were buried under the enormity of it all. She moaned instead.

'Winsome, darling,' Ambrose said.

She stared at him, shocked to silence, the tears wet on her cheeks. Her throat worked as she tried to swallow. 'What did you say?'

'Winsome,' Ambrose repeated. 'Darling. Tell me what's wrong.' There was something heavy and solid that seemed to slide from his heart. Darling. He'd called her darling. It had just come tripping off his tongue as though it belonged there. As though she were his darling, as though his heart and tongue loved her, even before his head knew for certain.

She continued to stare at him, eyes wide now, the tears forgotten. Slowly, she shook her head. 'Everything,' she said, then cleared her throat and tried again, glancing down at the cloak in her hands. 'Everything has gone wrong.'

'Wrong?'

Winsome shook her head and rolled her eyes, a feat which left her a little dizzy. 'First, I saw ghosts.' The ends of her hair flew about her shoulders as she whipped her head from side to side. 'The dead, just standing around on my lawn as though they'd been beamed down by some flying saucer and didn't quite know what to do with themselves.'

Ambrose frowned. 'You saw a flying saucer?'

'No,' she said. 'But I might as well have, when you have your predecessor dead on your lawn, scratching his backside with one hand and holding his Bible with the other.'

Oh God, she thought. She was having a nervous break-down. This was it. She'd spilt her Wheaties. Lost her marbles. Lost the cucumber from all her sandwiches. The cheese had slid from the cracker.

Suddenly, she was mortified that she'd come here – come here of all places! To Ambrose! So that she could do what? Show him what a complete mess she was?

But Ambrose had one eyebrow raised in that quizzical way she loved. 'You saw the dead Robertson scratching his backside?'

Winsome stared at him for a moment, and then her lips twitched. A giggle escaped. A little bit high-pitched and hysterical, but it was a giggle, nonetheless.

Ambrose's lips quirked.

Winsome covered her face for a moment with the cloak, then let her hands fall and gaped at Ambrose, laughing, tears squeezing again from her eyes. She laughed and laughed.

'Oh my sides,' she wheezed. 'Stop me from laughing, please. It hurts.' She bent over, holding her middle, trying to stop.

'Come and sit down,' Ambrose said, walking past her to a bench under the trees. It was a spot he liked to sit in during the evening, as the trees gathered the night around them, drawing it down and close like it was a grand, silken cloak. 'Winsome?'

She nodded weakly and followed him, planting herself gratefully on the bench seat and looking up at him.

'I'm sorry,' she said. 'I should go, really. I'm a complete mess. I should never have come here.'

'But you did,' Ambrose said, standing gazing down at

her. 'And I want you to stay. I want you to tell me what has happened because I know something has.'

Winsome leaned her elbows on her legs and shivered. 'Oh boy, has it ever,' she conceded.

Backing away another step, and wishing he could sit down beside her, Ambrose nodded. 'Pull the cloak around you,' he said. 'I'm going to make us a cup of hot, sweet tea.' He looked at her. 'You'll wait for me, won't you?'

Winsome didn't know. She shook her head. 'I should go,' she said. 'That's what I should do. I should go back down to the vicarage. I shouldn't be here.'

'Please don't,' Ambrose said. 'You've obviously had a shock. Won't you at least tell me what has happened?'

Winsome nodded wearily. She supposed the man deserved that at least, after she'd landed on his doorstep, hysterical, crying and laughing like a madwoman.

HEADING BACK DOWN THE HILL AN HOUR LATER, WINSOME tried to sort out what she was feeling. But her emotions were all over the place, messy and contradictory.

On the one hand, she felt elated. She tried to stamp down this one, tried not think about how Ambrose had called her darling, how it had just slipped off his tongue as though he'd been poised to call her that for a long time now and it had simply, finally happened.

He'd been the complete gentleman after that, of course, although, Winsome reflected, tripping clumsily over a tree root and automatically apologising to the tree, it may have been a different story had Ambrose been able to sit beside her on the bench.

Social distancing, she thought with a sigh. Maybe in this case, it had been a good thing.

The vicar and the...what was Ambrose? What had Morghan called him once?

The vicar and the alchemist.

She flattened her lips together. Somehow, that didn't have any sort of ring to it. The vicar and the alchemist. The couple who couldn't.

Not, she reflected, that she would necessarily be a vicar for long. Or not here, anyway. Once Julia Thorpe called the Dean, all bets were off. She'd be shipped away from Wellsford, forced to leave the vicarage and her parishioners with her head down and her tail between her legs.

The thought of tails made Winsome look up and glance about the shadows of the woods. The afternoon was dimming, clouds sweeping in from the sea to douse the weak sunlight, but she could still see the dog.

Her dog. Her spirit dog, her kin, her – who knew what it was, really.

But it was there, and she couldn't deny it. She could see spirits of the dead, and she could see the spirit of the dog she'd called to her side while working with Morghan.

That made her groan.

The worst of it, she decided, reaching the edge of the woods and slipping quietly, head down, to her kitchen door, was that Julia and the dreadful Mariah were correct.

She shouldn't be the vicar anymore. She was consorting with pagans.

She had participated in the winter solstice ritual.

Winsome stopped with her hand on the door, the key in the lock. Yes, she thought. She had gone traipsing through the snow up to the stone circle in the woods, and she had danced this way and that in a circle, a lantern in her hand to light the way for the rising sun.

And it had been beautiful.

It had been so beautiful. She dropped her hand from the key and turned, leaning against the door and looking at the sky, at the church, at the trees.

It had been a full mind and body experience, that ritual in the ancient stone circle.

And yes, they had called spirits to them, but the spirits had actually come. She had heard the faery man playing his flute. She had seen the wavering figures of Otherworld beings.

Winsome blinked.

She had seen the large, beautiful eye of the whale during the call to the spirits of the west. She had swum with it for a moment, feeling its age, its ancient wisdom.

The church, she thought, had forgotten how to do ritual. It was all words, rote and trite. The prayers – they were something, but did her parishioners really feel them? In their body? Did they feel them in their body, in their spirit, in their soul?

Which led Winsome back to another thing Julia had had something to say about. Winsome's 'stress exercises'. Winsome shivered against the door to the vicarage kitchen. They were wrong, Julia had said. Winsome had learnt them from the Wilde Grove lot. They weren't wholesome.

Winsome grimaced. She'd lost her temper, just a little, when Julia had said that. Had said obviously Julia herself hadn't tried them, because they certainly hadn't done anything for her level of stress.

And then they'd just all stared at each other for a long, silent moment.

It wasn't good, whichever way Winsome looked at it. She turned, finally, and unlocked the door, pushing it open and stepping into the kitchen she'd gotten so used to. She closed the door carefully behind her.

There was the big oak table she sat at with a pot of tea every morning. This was the table where she'd sat across from Morghan that very first time. That very first meeting. She frowned slightly, trying to remember.

Had Morghan ever told her what she'd been doing in the church that day? Morghan had never been back to the church, for reasons that were pretty obvious, really. Mariah would have had a fit of apoplexy and made a terrible scene about it, and well, why did Morghan need the church when she had so deep a practice of her own?

Winsome sat down at the table and laid her head on it, the grain large at eye-level. She sighed. What was she going to do?

The telephone rang, interrupting her thoughts and she sat up, staring towards her study with a sudden, sharp dread. Swallowing, her throat clicking dryly, she got up, her body now heavy and cumbersome, with knees that didn't want to bend, feet that didn't want to carry her weight.

She walked as though through syrup to her study and stared at the old green telephone on her desk.

9

AFTER A LONG MOMENT OF LETTING IT RING, WINSOME snatched up the handset and pressed it against her ear.

'Hello?' she said, then cleared her throat and tried again. 'Hello?' she asked. 'This is Reverend Winsome Clark; how may I help you?'

At first, Winsome didn't think there was anyone on the other end of the line. Perhaps, perhaps – and her heart leapt at the thought – it was just a crank call, or a wrong number, and this was her reprieve.

Her heart sank. Even if it were any of those things, it would still only be a reprieve. The phone call she was afraid of would come no matter what.

'Winsome.'

The voice was low, serious, and Winsome recognised it straight away.

'Dean,' she said. 'Dean Morton, how can I help you?'

Again the pause, and when Dean Morton finally spoke,

he was as grave and serious as Winsome had been afraid he would be.

'Winsome,' he said, and she could hear the sigh in his voice, a sigh that gave her a tiny, sneaking measure of hope. The Dean liked her; she was sure of it. And although she didn't consider that they really practised the same sort of Christianity, on the whole, she guessed that that was probably what a great deal of non-stop administration did to one. Or at least, she knew, she could certainly give him the benefit of the doubt.

'Winsome, I expect you know this already, but I've had a troubling conversation with your Churchwarden.' There was the rustling of papers on his desk as Winsome stood in her study clutching the phone with a hand white with tension.

She made herself ease it away from her ear, but she couldn't stop herself from holding her breath.

'Julia Thorpe,' Dean Morton said. 'She called me with some concerns that I'm afraid I feel compelled to address.' There was a long pause. 'Winsome? Are you there?'

'Yes, Dean, I'm here.'

'Good,' Dean Morton said. 'I thought for a moment there I'd lost you.'

The handset was slick against her palm and Winsome cleared her throat again. 'No,' she said. 'I'm still here, Dean.' She gathered up her last shreds of courage and spoke as brightly as possible.

'Have you ever met Julia Thorpe?' Winsome asked.

'No,' the Dean said. 'I've only spoken to her on the telephone, although she was a great blessing when Reverend Robinson passed away. But I believe,' he said, 'that you yourself have been having some trouble with her?'

Winsome closed her eyes, shutting out the shade of the dog that stood in the doorway of her study, its wheaten fur soft enough to want to touch.

'Julia Thorpe means well,' Winsome said. 'And I'm sure she was very helpful during the transition period between Reverend Robinson's duty here and my own.' Her voice was even enough, Winsome thought, but her legs shook, and she planted a palm on her desk to steady herself, eyes still closed. What had she been saying?

'I have not however, always found her the easiest person to get along with.' The wood of her desk was cold under her hand. She squinted an eyelid open, and the dog stared at her. She wanted to shoo it away, but she was afraid of losing her balance. And she was afraid that it would not move.

There was silence at the other end of the line.

'Winsome,' Dean Morton said on a sigh. 'I fear I have done you no favours with your first solo posting,' he said. 'Wellsford is not the easiest parish at any time. It never has been. It has had a long history of conflict with, shall we say, a certain element that lives in the parish.'

'Wilde Grove,' Winsome said flatly.

'Yes. Wilde Grove.'

'I have found,' Winsome said, 'that each and every member of Wilde Grove is an upright, honest, and sincere person. Wellsford would not be thriving as much as it is, if not for their tireless work on behalf of the entire community.'

On her desk Winsome's hand made a fist. She squeezed her eyes together even tighter.

'Yes,' Dean Morton said. 'I have the same understanding. I did after all read, like most of the rest of the county, if not the country, the interview of...' More rustling of papers. The Dean cleared his throat. 'Ah, yes, here it is.'

Winsome heard the sound of a newspaper being raised. She waited, opening her eyes as she did so. Her spirit dog stared unblinkingly back at her. She wanted to ask what he wanted, why he was there, but she knew he was there because she herself had called him to her. Had called him to her while with Morghan Wilde, leader of Wilde Grove, Lady of the Grove, Lady of the Forest, Lady of Death, while travelling to the Otherworld for the healing of a lost and hurting soul.

That was why the dog was there.

The Dean was talking and Winsome blinked, struggling to make herself listen over the confused static in her head.

'Impressive work they've been doing,' Dean Morton said. 'And most of it while in lockdown.'

'Actually,' Winsome said, 'most of it during the first and second lockdowns. And even busier during this one. I have to say that it is through their efforts that Wellsford is as fit and healthy and prospering as it is. I wish that I could take some credit for it, but my efforts have been puny in comparison.' She stumbled to a halt and listened to the Dean clearing his throat.

'Let's see,' he said. 'They've opened up their own care home for your elderly, and have instigated their own community outreach programs, so to speak. They distribute food parcels regularly to every household in the entire village in need of them. Their plans are extensive – a new state-of-the-art glasshouse for a community garden. Even a doctor – they're planning to bring a doctor to the village. Your village, Winsome. How many people live in Wellsford?'

Winsome, realising after a moment's silence at this was not a rhetorical question scrambled for the answer. 'There are around about 360, Dean,' she said.

'Yes. Indeed. An exceedingly small village for all this.'

Winsome, unsure completely about the direction of this conversation, kept her mouth shut, staring at the dog again. He really did look like Erin's Burdock. Same size, same shaggy fur, same, dare she say it, slightly goofy face. He pricked up his ears and cocked his head at her as though hearing her thought. Winsome wondered suddenly what having a dog as your spirit animal, or kin as Morgan called it, meant. Guardian of the mysteries was what Morgan had said, but what mysteries? And why did she need a guardian – or why did the mysteries need guarding?

'And what have you been doing for the community in Wellsford, Winsome?'

Winsome was jolted back to her conversation on the phone. She winced and thought rapidly.

'Oh, erm, well, in these times it's almost as much as one can do to keep services going and to provide the spiritual care that our parishioners require,' Winsome said.

'I hear that you have established, according to Julia, some rather odd suggestions for coping with stress?'

'A small series of stress-easing exercises,' Winsome said. 'And I will not apologise for those either, no matter what my Churchwarden has to say about her opinion of them. They have been a hit, Dean, and you know why? Because this has been an extremely frightening and stressful time for all of us. And if I have found a way to help people relax and cope with the pressure then that surely is a grand thing.'

'And these are available how?' There was a slight scratching sound and Winsome frowned still holding the phone tightly against her ear. Finally she realised it was the Dean rubbing a hand against the stubble on his chin.

'Oh, erm, I made a video,' Winsome said, her face flushing at the memory of her fumbling effort to record something resembling anything useful and professional on her phone. She stifled a sigh. And who had she gone to help her navigate the means of uploading it and distributing it to those of her parishioners with Wi-Fi and computer access?

Krista. Krista, member in good standing of Wilde Grove, proprietor of Haven for Books which had, by any standards, and overly large occult section. Although, Winsome had to admit, inside that section was a good selection of Christian literature – heavily curated towards Celtic Christianity and the works of those such as John O'Donohue, Winsome's favourite writer. She'd been delighted when she'd first seen his books on the shop's shelves.

But the Dean had asked her a question.

'I, erm, also produced something of a brochure, I suppose you could say,' Winsome said. 'For those who don't have computer access.' She wound down into silence and held her breath.

The Dean was also quiet for a long moment and Winsome winced as she heard the clicking of his computer mouse. The Dean, of course, would have access to the Wellsford parish website, such as it was. She grimaced again.

Wellsford also wouldn't have had a parish website if not for Krista. Winsome cleared her throat and waited.

'I see,' the Dean said after several minutes perusing the site. 'You've done an awfully good job with the website, Winsome – it's easy to navigate, and nice and simple.' Some more clicking, and another long moment's silence while he read from his computer screen.

'This blog of yours is quite wonderful,' he said. 'Some very thoughtful posts, and they're positive, but not gushing.'

Finally, Winsome sat down, unlocking her knees, and sinking onto her office chair. She rested her elbows on the desk and pushed the fingers of one hand into her hair.

'Thank you, Dean,' she said, her voice faint. 'I rather enjoy writing for it, actually. And I find, now that we must keep our sermons a little shorter, that being able to use this format to reach people is complementary.' She nipped a tooth at her lower lip. 'I'm posting my sermons, after the Sunday service, and then writing again during the week, either to expand upon the sermon, or to, well, write whatever's on my mind, really.'

'And these exercises...'

Winsome could hear the frown in his voice.

'A little on the new-age side of things, perhaps, but in all, some very healthy suggestions, I think. I don't know what Ms. Thorpe's objection was.'

Winsome sat up, hope sparking through her.

'But,' the Dean said on a sigh, 'this doesn't mitigate her other allegations, I'm afraid.'

The spirit dog stalked over to Winsome and sat down beside her, his gaze fixed on the telephone receiver in her hand. Winsome wanted to push him away, but she knew –

from experimenting – that her hand would go right through the animal. Apparently, her new companion only felt solid when she was walking with him in the Otherworld.

'You're going to have to come in, Winsome,' Dean Morton said.

'Come in?' Winsome squeaked, startled. The dog turned his caramel-coloured eyes to her.

'Yes. To my office. We need to talk in person, I think. Figure out what to do about this mess.' He sighed.

'Really,' he said. 'I am growing a little tired of the village of Wellsford.'

10

Krista looked at her watch. It was only four in the afternoon. 'You look beat,' she said.

Stephan dropped his jacket onto the table and collapsed into a chair. 'That would be because I am,' he said.

'You look like you haven't shaved in a week.'

'I've quit shaving. I'm growing a beard for the duration of the lockdown.'

Krista raised an eyebrow. 'Really?'

'No idea,' Stephan answered. 'But now that I've thought of it, it isn't a bad idea. Who has time to shave anymore anyway?'

'Yeah, I know what you mean, Krista answered, looking around for her keys. They were there somewhere. She picked up Stephan's jacket, tossed it at him and snatched up her keys. 'Even without the shop open, I'm just as busy. Maybe even more.'

Stephan, draped over the table, his head on his arms,

turned and looked at her through one eye. 'We're doing good work though, right?'

She stopped on her way out the door and smiled back at him. 'Stephan,' she said seriously. 'There isn't anywhere I'd rather be than here through all this. Wellsford is going to end up better off, and it's in large part thanks to you. So, there you go. Have something to eat. A growing boy like you needs fuel to run on.' She narrowed her eyes at him. 'Did you sleep at all last night? You look like a raccoon over that scruff you're calling a beard.' His blue eyes were rimmed in red.

Stephan sat up and stretched his arms over his head, groaning. 'Not much. Erin and I were talking on the phone.'

'Hmm. Things are progressing between you two. Despite having to keep six feet apart.'

Krista had said it as a statement, but Stephan answered anyway. 'Yep,' he agreed amiably. 'Progressing nicely, as it happens.' He rubbed at the sore muscles in his neck. 'And there are ways around the distance if you know how.' His lips stretched in a grin.

That made Krista shake her head, looking at him. 'I take it you're not just talking about phone calls?' She held up the hand with the keys in it. 'No, wait. I don't think I want to know.'

Stephan laughed. 'Let's just say that energy between compatible souls can be a mighty powerful force.'

Krista shook her head gently. 'Lucky boy,' she said, and sighed.

'Yeah. I am,' Stephan agreed, then changed the subject before he asked for the hundredth time why Krista didn't do anything about how she felt about Clarice. 'Where are you off to, then?'

'My daily walk and talk with Minnie,' Krista answered, pocketing her keys and shrugging into her coat.

'How's Minnie getting along?'

'Good. Real good, actually. She's a bright kid, and she's healing.' Krista stopped with one arm in the coat and one out. 'I wish something could be done for her mom though. Natasha has stopped thinking she has the virus, but she's going out of her mind there, I'm sure, in that little place all day.'

Stephan scratched his head. 'You know Simon and Lucy are leasing the Green Man, right – the pub next to The Copper Kettle? Maybe she can see if they'll need someone to help out.'

'They're reopening the pub? I'd forgotten.'

Stephan shrugged. 'Someone has to, right? It's been closed for ages.' He stretched again, his neck cracking. 'It'll be amazing to be able to pop in there for a pint again. And music – they're bound to have live music, right? Maybe they'll let us have a few low-key jam sessions, or something.'

Krista nodded. 'You know,' she said wonderingly, 'Wellsford is truly getting to be a fantastic place.'

'Yeah,' Stephan agreed. 'It's like, blossoming.' He waved a hand goodbye as Krista slipped out for her walk, then sank his head down onto the table again. Really, he thought, he could sleep for a week.

But soon, his new glasshouse would be delivered, and the thought made him smile happily. A glasshouse to grow food for the community year-round. Even better than they were managing now.

There was only one thing he wasn't sure about, right now, and that was what to do with the healing training he was going through with Old Bear Fellow.

But, he decided for the millionth time, he'd just wait and see how that unfolded.

'Follow the path,' he reminded himself out loud. 'One step at a time.' He looked at the clock. Time to get some late lunch, then meet Erin and walk her back to Ash Cottage.

The smile that spread over his face was beatific.

'Why did Teresa design her garden the way she did?' Erin asked, wishing she could reach out and tuck her hand into Stephan's. She put it in her pocket instead and watched Burdock duck in and out of the trees at the side of the road as they walked home.

This was her favourite time of the day now. Late afternoon, still cold and damp to make her tuck her chin down into her scarf as they walked down the narrow, invariably empty lane that wound its way through the woods to Ash Cottage. The clouds had come clustering in around the hills as though seeking the novelty of land over sky.

Burdock, nose swinging this way and that as his tail did the same, exploring the undergrowth.

A glimpse of the red fur of a fox in the dimness between the craggy trees.

And Stephan, stepping along beside her, muffled inside his jacket and hat, skin so winter-pale it was translucent, and eyes so blue, blue as the sky when the clouds cleared.

It was half an hour of peace and wonder and joy. Her skin tingled inside her clothes, feeling half a size too small as though she would burst out of it. The air in her lungs was cold and thin, and so fresh that it felt as though she could live on breathing alone.

'It's all aligned to the elements,' Stephan answered.

'What?' Erin asked. She'd forgotten her question.

Stephan glanced at her. 'The garden – you know the well has the directions on it, right? And everything radiates out from that? Well, all the plants in each direction are chosen because they align with each particular element and direction. And the well is like, the axis point. The centre of it all.' His brows knotted together a moment. 'Haven't I told you this before?'

'Probably,' Erin admitted. 'But a lot's gone on over the last few months, so I just thought I'd ask again.'

'Why?'

'Morghan has given me a sort of...task...I guess.'

'To do with the garden?'

'Yeah. She wants me to learn to step between the worlds, and to get really comfortable doing it.'

Stephan nodded. 'That makes sense. That's what she does, right? That's kind of like, her job.'

Erin nodded.

'And yours, one day.'

'That's just weird,' Erin said, her sudden breath out a rush of foggy air in the chill. 'I don't know that I'm ready to think about that, yet. I mean, I don't even really know what it means.'

But Stephan had thought about it. Daydreamed about it, really. Because it was Erin's future, and that hopefully meant it was his. So, of course, he'd daydreamed about it.

'Well, you'll have to live in Hawthorne House, I expect,' he said.

Erin blinked. 'Why would I have to do that? I have Ash Cottage.'

Stephan shook his head. 'Every Lady of the Grove lives there in Hawthorne House. That's the way it's done. It like, comes with the job.'

'I don't know,' Erin said. 'I mean – Morghan's not that old, right? When does she stop being head of the Grove, and I take over?' Saying the words made her shiver. She was so far from ready for that, she couldn't even imagine it. 'I can't imagine Morghan moving into Wellsford Care Home, you know?'

Stephen agreed. He couldn't visualise that, either.

'What happened to the Lady before Morghan?' Erin asked. 'What was her name?' She frowned, realising there was a lot of history that she didn't know yet.

'That was Selena, Morghan's aunt,' Stephan said.

Erin nodded. 'Yeah. What happened to her? Did she die, or something?'

'Nope,' Stephan said, swinging happily along beside Erin. They couldn't hold hands, or anything, but simply being near her was intoxicating. In the best way.

'No?'

Stephan drew himself properly back to the conversation. 'Nah,' he said. 'She left, that's all.'

'Left?' Erin was confused. 'What do you mean, left? How can the Lady of the Grove just leave?' A frisson of unease had Erin suddenly hugging herself.

'Well, she didn't like, just leave – she trained Morghan

first, obviously. And left Morghan in charge, so it was all right.'

Erin stopped walking and stared at Stephan. 'But she left – I didn't know that could happen.'

'I guess they agreed between themselves,' Stephan said, looking across at Erin and frowning. 'Selena went travelling – following the wind, she called it. This was according to Teresa, anyway.' He shrugged. 'She's in Australia or somewhere now, I think.' His voice trailed off and he looked nervously over at Erin who stared at him, eyes wide and wild. 'What's the matter?' he asked.

Erin shook her head slowly. 'I didn't know you could just leave. Like train up the next one and then go.' The realisation terrified her, and she rubbed at the sudden goosebumps on her arms. 'What if that's what Morghan decides to do?'

Stephan shook his head. 'I can't imagine Morghan ever leaving the Grove, can you?'

'But her aunt did.'

'Yeah.' Stephan shrugged. 'But Morghan's different. She's like, totally dedicated.' Inspiration struck. 'And if she'd ever been going to leave, she would have done it when Grainne wanted to go off adventuring, you know?'

Erin shook her head again. 'I don't know. I don't know anything at all, remember? I've only been here a few months.'

'Right.'

Erin lifted her brows.

'Right,' Stephan repeated. 'Well – you gotta realise I was only a kid when this happened, okay? I only know what everyone knows.'

'Which is still more than I do,' Erin repeated. She scuffed her boots on the surface of the lane and sighed.

'Yeah,' Stephan said. 'Well, Grainne – she was Morghan's wife – she was like this restless soul, and happiest when she was out on the ocean, sailing. So about five or six years ago, she cooked up this big sailing trip, right, after years of living here with Morghan, and Morghan wouldn't go with her. She said she had to stay here, and the trip was going to be like, six months or a year, or something. All around the world, anyway.'

'What happened?'

Stephan looked glumly at the ground. 'Grainne never came back – she drowned.'

'Wow,' Erin breathed. 'That's awful.' She shook her head. That was a big thing to happen. How on earth had Morghan gotten through it?

'As for Selena,' Stephan continued, breathing in the soft scent of the trees next to the road. 'She left – I don't know when, really – maybe like, ten years before that? obviously she and Morghan had worked it out between them.'

Erin shook her head, trying to do the maths. If Selena had left fifteen years ago, then Morghan had been only thirty-five when she'd taken over the Grove.

There were thirteen years until Erin was that age. How much would she be able to learn in that time?

Not nearly enough, she thought, and hoped Morghan had no intention of going anywhere.

11

THE NEXT MORNING, AMBROSE TUCKED HIS HEAD DOWN AND
shrugged his collar up higher around his neck. The rain had
come in again during the night and it was cold hard pellets
that threatened to turn to sleet. He thought it suited his
mood, tired and melancholy, tramping along in the woods
achieving not much at all. Winsome danced around at the
edge of his mind but he didn't know what to do about it.
What was there to do about her? – this is what he'd known
from the beginning, when he'd realised how he felt about
her. She was untouchable, the local vicar, for crying out
loud. They were each on a different side of the fence.

Except that Winsome had been hopping over that fence
more and more often, and now look where that had got her.
She'd been in such a state of the day before and Ambrose
hadn't known what to do for her, had only ached to take her
in his arms and comfort her, but even that was out of the
question.

'Ambrose,' Morghan said. 'I didn't know you were up

and out already.' He'd been staying at Hawthorn House since the lockdown. It was easier for them that way.

Ambrose sighed, shaking the rain from his coat and shrugging it from his shoulders as he stepped into the dim hallway of Hawthorn house. 'Went for a walk,' he said. 'Trying to clear my head for the day.'

Morghan looked at him in the dimness of the hallway, then touched him briefly on the arm. 'Something to drink?' she asked.

Ambrose nodded gravely and followed Morghan into the sitting room where a fire burned brightly, the red flames dancing in the hearth. He moved automatically towards it and stood holding his hands out to the heat, his back to Morgan.

Morghan stood in the doorway for a moment her hand on the door, regarding him with steady eyes. 'I'll get some tea,' she murmured.

When she returned, Ambrose had moved to the window to stare out over the garden towards the trees behind which his own house lay tucked as though it had grown there at the same time that the trees had dug their roots deep into the soil.

Morghan put the tea tray down and poured them each a cup. She carried one to Ambrose and handed it to him. He took it silently.

'What is it?' she asked. 'There's something on your mind.'

The cup of tea in his hand, Ambrose continued to stare out the window. A blackbird pushed its beak between blades of grass on the lawn, searching for its breakfast. And the rain fell in silver sheets over the trees and lawn. He lifted the cup to his lips and sipped automatically at the tea, not tasting it at all.

'I've had word, by the way,' he said. 'That Wayne Moffat is ready to take up his residence in the home.' Now there was a second bird with the blackbird on the lawn, this one with feathers of a plain wooden brown. A female, then. The blackbird's lady.

Morghan looked at Ambrose. That's sooner than I expected,' she said.

'The ambulance is bringing him tomorrow afternoon.' Ambrose's voice was flat, inflectionless. But he turned at last and regarded Morghan with eyes that were clear and direct. 'I trust you have everything ready for him?' Ambrose raised his eyebrows with the question.

Morghan nodded. 'Yes, she said simply. Now was her turn to gaze out the window.

Even amid his own preoccupations, Ambrose noticed. 'But?' he asked.

Morgan sighed. 'But,' she sighed. 'But I have not yet told Erin.'

'Was that intentional?'.

'Not entirely, I confess, Morghan replied. 'I meant to tell her, but I had other important things that she had to take notice of, and if I had told her both she would have favoured the news of Wayne over the other task that she must begin to work on.'

Now they both stared out the window. The blackbird and his lady searched for worms.

'Moffat's arrival is important,' Ambrose said. 'This will have consequences.'

'Everything has consequences,' Morghan replied. 'We

must remember however,' she said, 'that this was not put into motion by us, but by those who know greater and wider and deeper than we do. We follow the path of the soul.'

Silence stretched out between them again for a long minute. 'Mind it though,' Ambrose said. 'Mind that you aren't using that as an excuse not to do an unpleasant task.'

Morghan pushed away from the window and went over to the chair by the fire. She sat down and crossed her legs, put her cup on the table next to her, and regarded her friend silently for a moment.

'Why don't you tell me what is really bothering you?' she said.

Ambrose turned and there was agony on his face. In his hands the cup trembled just a little. 'It's Winsome,' he said at last.

'Winsome?' Morghan asked, surprised. Whatever she'd expected, it hadn't been this. 'What about Winsome?'

'She came to me yesterday in a terrible state, when I was at home,' Ambrose answered, remembering the heaving sobs and the tears streaking down Winsome's lovely cheeks. He lifted his hand and drew it through his hair, the way he always did when he was agitated.

Morghan looked across the room at him. 'Winsome came to you?'

'Yes,' Ambrose said. 'She came to me. Is that relevant?'

Morghan lifted her shoulders in a slight shrug and decided to wait for him to elaborate.

'Julia Thorpe, her Churchwarden, and Mariah Reefton, who is Julia's aunt, are laying a complaint with the Dean,' Ambrose said. 'About Winsome – her coming to our solstice ritual.'

Morghan sat forward in her chair, her hands gripping its arms. 'I knew things were being stirred,' she said. 'Things are shifting.' She shook her head. 'The wheel turns, and what has been passed comes around again.'

Ambrose narrowed his eyes at her. 'This is something you have had a vision of?'

Morghan nodded and sat back in the chair again. 'It is going to affect all of us, I fear,' she said. 'And now that you have told me this, I can see that I am right to think so.' She paused for a moment tapping a finger. 'Only a while ago, at the circle with Charlie,' Morgan said. 'I travelled and Ravenna, the Ancient One, showed me things.'

'You did not tell me this?'

'I have been busy,' Morghan sighed. 'And you have been even busier.'

Ambrose inclined his head. It was true. Taking care of the village was becoming a full-time job. So many new things they were instigating in the name of community and resilience. He had been working tirelessly alongside Stephan and Charlie's husband Martin, and Krista, to make it so.

'What did she show you?' he asked.

'She showed me an event from the Grove's past,' Morghan said. 'She showed me a time when the Grove was overrun by Roman soldiers who raped and slaughtered the women of the Grove and stole one away with them, sending her back over the sea to their own land where she had a child and lived with there for many years, always yearning for home, for the Grove.'

Morghan fell silent and for a moment they listened to the rain spitting against the windows.

Ambrose frowned down at his hands holding the cup and shook his head. 'I didn't know specifically of this,' he said. 'It is another piece of our history here.' He blinked over at Morghan. 'An important one.'

Morghan picked up her cup of tea and looked into its amber depths, sighing. 'Yes, an important one,' she agreed. 'And it makes sense to be shown it now. It is to be expected that the world's disturbance will also echo here in our lives, to some extent.' She looked over at Ambrose frowning by the window. 'But more than that, we have long had an unresolved issue here between Wellsford and the Grove.'

Ambrose nodded his agreement. He walked across the room to the fire and gazed at the leaping, hissing flames.

'Mariah Reefton,' he said.

'You and I have known for a long time that she carries the burden of her past, and its intertwining with my own.' Morghan laid her head back on the chair and stared at the ceiling. 'Do you think,' she mused, 'that there will ever come a time when peace and harmony and balance has been restored to this world?'

The question made Ambrose snort. 'Yes,' he said. 'There is no choice but for that outcome.' He swung around on his heels and walked back to the window. When Ambrose was agitated, he liked to move. Perhaps, after his tea, he would stalk the woods for another hour or two. 'But I do not fancy the chances of it happening in this lifetime, Morghan,' he said. 'Despite that we must strive toward it at any cost.'

'Yes,' Morghan agreed. She thought of Erin, of Winsome. 'At any cost.' A pause. 'What does Winsome intend to do?'

But Ambrose shook his head. 'I don't know,' he confessed. 'What can she do?'

'And someone, you say, saw her join us for the winter solstice ritual?'

'Minnie told either Mariah, or Julia. I'm not sure which, and nor do I know why she did it.'

Morghan thought she likely did. 'Minnie is quite entranced by the thought of a vicar who dances in a pagan circle. She probably thought she was defending Winsome.' Morghan sighed. 'The girl is only young still.'

Ambrose reached out and pressed a palm to the glass. It was cold under his touch, and condensation gathered around the outline of his hand. He pulled it back, set down his tea and rolled his shoulders.

'I need to walk,' he said. 'You will take care of Erin, regarding Mr. Moffat?'

Morghan nodded. 'Yes,' she said, watching Ambrose with sympathy in her eyes. She knew full well of his feelings for Winsome, no matter how he had tried to hide them. She'd watched them grow as they'd all worked together over the last four months.

This would be agony for him.

IT WOULD ALSO BE AGONY FOR WINSOME, MORGHAN thought, stepping like a wraith from the woods behind the vicarage and striding through the rain to the kitchen door where yellow light spilled outwards, beckoning her.

'Morghan!' Winsome stared at her for a moment, flustered, then opened the door wider before remembering that she couldn't invite Morghan inside.

'Are you busy?' Morghan asked. She glanced around the kitchen. The doorways to the rest of the vicarage were dark. 'No visitors? I thought we might take a walk together.'

Winsome glanced back into her kitchen, then leaned out to peer down the side of the vicarage towards the street.

'Is Mariah Reefton able to see this door?' Morghan asked bluntly. 'She can see us here?'

Winsome grimaced. 'I don't know what she can see, but I can tell you, she knows an awful lot.'

A heavenly aroma wafted out from the kitchen. Morghan sniffed appreciatively.

'Ambrose told me,' she said. 'But if you are busy, we can speak another time.'

The colour rose in Winsome's cheek. 'I was upset,' she said. 'I don't know why I went to him.'

Morghan edged closer to the door, out of the worst of the rain and smiled. 'Ambrose has an aura of strength and competency about him that draws us all to him in crisis,' she said. Then she shrugged. 'He made you feel safe, and you're in love with him.'

Winsome yelped, then stared at Morghan. Suddenly, she couldn't think of a single thing to say.

With a smile, Morghan nodded towards the kitchen. 'Does that marvellous smell belong to something in the oven, or may you spare half an hour to tell me about what has happened?'

Winsome shook her head. 'It's not in the oven.' She glanced back at the table where two cakes and a batch of scones sat cooling. 'Stress baking,' she grimaced, and looked down at her floury apron. 'I never thought I'd sink to it.' Winsome shook her head. 'At least, though, you've come just in time to save me from the next step in the process – stress eating.' She reached for the apron tie. 'Give me five minutes and I'll meet you on the path, shall I?'

There was no need to say which path. Certainly, it wasn't the footpath on the street. Morghan nodded and sank back into the greenery behind the house.

Winsome stood at the door for a moment longer, looking blankly out into the dimness of the afternoon. The rain had come with the dawn and found her as she'd scurried across the lawn to go pray. Not at the small temple in the woods this time, but at St. Bridget's, as was proper for her position. She'd unlocked the heavy door and slipped into the silent shadows, walking slowly up the centre aisle to kneel before the altar.

The prayers had come easily, but she'd soon stopped whispering them. They all sounded...different now. Wild, somehow. Deeper and wider, she'd thought. But...wild. After a few minutes, she'd turned around and sat on the step under the altar, staring out at her church.

There, in those front rows, had sat Alfred Robinson's flock, waiting for her to help them find their way, to listen to their last, whispered, prayers, the messages they were carrying for their families. They'd sat there, looking to her, shining.

Tears had wet her eyes.

After that, there'd been no going back to the way things had been, before she'd come to Wellsford. Before she'd learnt to see and love the spirits of the dead, to help them. Hadn't she helped old Bernie Roberts just the other day? She'd sniffed, sitting on the step in the cold church and wiped her eyes with the sleeve of her jumper.

She couldn't imagine not doing such work anymore.

And Minnie – hadn't Winsome done what was necessary there too? A parishioner had called her for help, and she'd helped.

Wasn't that the job, really, when it came down to it? Stewardship? Leading the flock of God's lambs?

Winsome had winced then. She didn't like the vision of people as sheep. It wasn't a flattering one. She pressed her hands to her sides. What she wanted, most of all, she supposed, was to help the people of her community to lead their best lives, and when they were done, and tired, to die their best deaths, prepared for what came next.

THE RAIN HUNG IN HER HAIR LIKE DROPS OF GREY PEARLS, AND Winsome shook them loose. She had her long coat on, and stout boots. 'Morghan?' she called, keeping her voice low, unable to help the thought that Mariah would appear from between the trees instead of Morghan.

'You brought that delicious smell with you,' Morghan said, coming down the path towards her.

Winsome looked down at the quickly-buttered scones wrapped in a tea towel that she held. 'I know,' she said ruefully. 'Turns out, stress eating is the requisite next step to stress baking.' She sighed. 'But at least you can help me eat them.'

'I would be delighted to stress eat with you,' Morghan said, ushering Winsome onto the path.

'That sounded like you have things niggling away at you too.' Winsome tucked the cloth parcel of food under her elbow and concentrated on where she was walking. It was dark in the woods, even with the trees bare of leaves. It was just a dark sort of day all around.

'Although, my things are gnawing, rather than niggling, come to that,' she added.

Morghan was silent a moment before replying. Around her, the woods of Wilde Grove rose dreaming from the deep soil, soaking in the rain, and letting the cold breeze press against their bark like an old friend. Her golden hand glimmered in the low light, and all around them, she could see the sparkle of rain as though it were falling diamonds. The threads of the web gleamed.

Despite niggles, despite gnawings, life was lush. The world remained beautiful.

If only, Morghan thought, everyone could see it like this. Perhaps, she decided, this was the human race's next evolutionary step. Awakening to this true vision of the world.

'Do you know what else a spirit dog is adept at?' she asked Winsome walking beside her as they made their way further from the village and into the ancient boundaries of Wilde Grove.

Winsome turned to look at Morghan, a startled frown on her face. Whatever she'd expected Morghan to say, it hadn't been this.

'Erm,' she said, and turned her eyes to look for her dog. He walked behind her and as she settled her gaze upon him, he lifted his head and grinned at her, quickening his pace to walk at her side. He'd never looked so solid in this world. Winsome swallowed around the lump in her throat and looked over at Morghan's other side.

Her wolf was there, padding along beside her, head low, great black ruff thick around his neck.

Winsome swallowed and straightened. 'Tell me,' she said.

Morghan smiled. 'Cù comes to walk with us often when we are in a position of having to defend and protect that which is sacred to us. That which we value, whether it be a way of life, a vocation, a world view.'

'Cù?'

'It's Gaelic,' Morghan said, and smiled. 'For dog.'

Cù. Winsome liked it. She could call him that, perhaps. It was better than no name – a dog, she thought, should be named, whether flesh or spirit. 'Oh goodness,' she said out loud.

Morghan glanced at her. 'What is it?'

But Winsome shook her head and stopped walking. She held her hands up hopelessly. 'I don't know how to manage this,' she said.

Morghan waited, quiet.

Winsome shook her head again. She looked down at the dog. Cù, she'd just decided to call him, as though he were real. 'That's the problem,' she said. 'He is real – and I can't go back to not seeing him.' She blinked. 'Or any of the other things I've seen since...since...'

'Since you came to Wellsford,' Morghan finished for her.

Winsome sucked in a great lungful of cold, damp air and blew it out in a rush. 'I don't know how I thought this was going to go, really – or even if I thought of it at all.' She tipped her head back to the sky, looking at it through the pattern of tree branches. Underneath their protection, the rain was gentler. Or perhaps it had eased as they walked.

She lowered her head. Looked at her dog. Cù. She

would call him Cù, she decided almost mutinously, her fists clenching, the scones getting crushed under her arm.

'It's come to it,' she said. 'That I will have to act to protect all the things and my way of life that is precious – sacred – to me.' Winsome lifted her gaze to meet Morghan's. 'Are you telling me the truth? About the dog, and what he means?'

Morghan wasn't offended by the question. She simply nodded. 'Yes,' she said. 'That's how it works, in the flow of the world. That which you need is given to you.'

'Knock and you shall be answered. Ask and you shall receive,' Winsome murmured.

'Yes. Although not always in the way we foresee or would necessarily want.'

But Winsome shook her head again. 'Why is it,' she asked, 'that I am being put in this position?'

Morghan laughed. 'I don't think any of us get through life without asking that question at least once.'

'I know,' Winsome said, turning to walk again. It felt obscurely better to be moving. As though by moving, she could outpace the reality of what was happening.

What was going to happen.

'I have an appointment to see the Dean in a bit over a week's time,' she said. 'At his office, nonetheless. Which shows you how seriously he is viewing my...offences.'

'And what has he been told your offences are, exactly?' Morghan asked.

They'd come to a halt again, this time because they'd reached the clearing where the stone circle was. Morghan gazed out at the crooked ring of stones, seeing them again as they'd been in her vision, strong and tall, and sprayed with blood. She blinked, then closed her eyes. When she opened them, the blood was gone.

'Drunkenness, for starters,' Winsome said.

Morghan turned and gaped at her. 'I beg your pardon?'

Winsome shook her head and laughed. 'You should see your face!'

'Drunkenness. You said drunkenness,' Morghan replied, eyes just as wide.

'Yes. Because Julia is convinced that I was drunk when she saw me that morning after I'd helped Reverend Robinson and the others.'

'And you cannot, of course, tell her what you were really doing.'

'No. I cannot. I cannot tell her that I can see and help the spirits of the dead.'

'And the living,' Morghan added.

'Isn't it ironic,' Winsome mused. 'That my official job as a clergyperson is to see to the souls of my parishioners, and yet, if it were known that I do that in such a comprehensive way, shall we say – I would be removed from my position?'

'Would you, do you think?'

Winsome looked at Morghan. 'What? What do you mean?'

'If you were to tell the Dean, when you see him, that you can see and communicate with spirits, what would happen?' Morghan asked.

'He would think I had lost my marbles,' Winsome answered.

'But he believes in the soul, surely?'

'As may be,' Winsome replied. 'Although I might have my doubts about that. But he would not be open to me seeing and speaking to ghosts. That's too...well, let's just say, that's the realm of the spiritualists and occultists.'

Morghan laughed. 'And the pagans, don't forget. Or at least, our variety of them.'

'Goodness,' Winsome said, shaking her head, looking down at the spirit dog who stood at her side. 'My life is such a mess.' She wished she could stroke Cù. 'What do you do when things feel out of control like this?' She glanced over at Morghan who was gazing at the stones. 'Or do things never feel out of control for you?'

Another laugh from Morghan, this one more rueful. 'Indeed,' she said, 'you know that sometimes they do.'

'So what do you do then?' Winsome persisted.

Morghan shifted on her feet, turning towards Winsome, her face smooth, smiling.

'Winsome,' she asked. 'Would you like to find out for yourself?'

12

WINSOME HAD THE DISTINCT FEELING THAT SHE OUGHTN'T TO have agreed to this.

'I should be back at the vicarage,' she said. 'I should be baking another five loaves of bread, and minding my own business, and thinking about what to say when I see the Dean next Friday.' She blinked in the dim light of the fire and looked over the flames at Morghan. 'You know that, don't you? I shouldn't be here doing this.'

'You may leave, of course, if you wish,' Morghan answered. 'I will even walk you back down the hill and see you to your door. And if it is better for you, I will also not come knocking at it again.'

The thought horrified Winsome. She shook her head quickly. 'No,' she said. 'That can't be the answer, surely?'

Morghan reached into the bag she'd had slung over her shoulder and brought out a handful of herbs. 'I admit,' she said, 'that I for one, would suffer from the lack of your friendship.'

Winsome gazed at her over the fire. 'You would?' she asked.

'Yes.' Morghan's answer was simple, certain.

Winsome looked into the flames for a moment, watched Morghan sprinkle some herbs upon it, her lips moving in what, a prayer? An invocation? The flames leapt up, burning brighter for a moment.

'What was that you put on the fire?' Winsome asked. The scones in their tea towel were on the dirt floor of the cave beside her. Shadows leapt and danced over the walls and ceiling of the cave, their movements jerky, fantastical. She tried not to notice them.

She wasn't entirely sure all of them were reflections from the fire.

When Morghan had led her to the cave and told her they would go into it, Winsome had shaken her head.

'Nope. That's a nope. Uh uh,' she'd said. 'And why, anyway?'

Morghan's reply had been gentle but unwavering. 'It is easier to feel close to the world when we are inside the womb of the Goddess.' She lifted a hand and gestured at the cave. 'In a cave,' she said. 'Or in a circle of trees...'

'Or in the comfort of your sitting room,' Winsome said, aware that she was grumbling.

Morghan laughed. 'It is possible,' she said. 'And some of us have the knack to walk wherever we are, but in general terms, a particular spot in nature, or of our own conscious design and effort, evokes the necessary state of mind and body better.'

Winsome had looked over at Morghan. 'It's all very complicated, isn't it?' she asked, then turned to look back at the cave. 'No wonder Christianity caught on in the end. It's very civilised, just sitting inside a church each week, letting the priest do most of the work.'

Morghan was silent, and after a minute, Winsome had let her lead her into the darkness of the cave.

Sitting in a church once or twice a week might have been simpler, but by God, Winsome thought, she had never marvelled so much at the world, never felt so close to her own spiritual nature, never helped so many in truly meaningful ways, since Morghan had begun showing her a different way.

The Ancient Path.

She gasped, turned it into a deep breath, and closed her eyes, seeking stillness.

'What am I supposed to be doing here?' she asked, her eyes still shut, feeling a little woozy, as though the oxygen in the cave had thinned to a small trickle into her lungs. Winsome took a deep breath, but there was plenty of air.

Perhaps the dizziness was from the herbs. She felt something warm come and press against her thigh. Her hand touched fur. It was the dog.

'Cù,' she said softly, under her breath.

'When Minnie was in your healing clearing,' Winsome said suddenly, 'she had an angel come to be with her.'

Morghan sat on the other side of the fire, eyes closed to narrow slits, breathing deeply. 'Our kin, our spirit guides come in many forms,' she said. 'I don't know what brings us one rather than the other.'

'There's so much not to know,' Winsome whispered.

'From this vantage point, yes,' Morghan answered. She could feel the worlds spinning about her, the space and form of them opening so that all she needed to do was to tip over, to slip lightly down in the direction she wanted to go.

But she held herself steady, sitting beside the small fire, her wolf at her side, and listened to answer Winsome's questions.

'I have a dog,' Winsome said, her voice faraway, drifting on the smoke from the fire.

'Yes,' Morghan agreed.

'Are there...' she hesitated. 'Others?' she asked. 'Others who...walk...with me?'

'Yes,' Morghan said. 'Always there are.'

Winsome shook her head slightly. Now it felt like the air was thick inside the cave, dense with oxygen. She felt the weight of Cù's paw on her thigh, of the heat of him against her. How could a spirit animal have weight? Heat? She swallowed.

Because she wasn't quite in the real world anymore, she thought.

'Who?' she asked. 'Who are they?'

Almost, Winsome wanted to clap a hand to her mouth, to take the question back, ask something else, something smaller. Something inconsequential.

'I don't know,' Morghan said, holding herself still. 'You would have to go seek them.'

Winsome shook her head a little. 'I think I'm afraid to do that.'

This time Morghan didn't answer.

She didn't need to. Winsome licked her lips, shook her head. 'If I were to do that,' she said, talking to herself as much as to Morghan, 'then there would be no going back, would there?' She blinked. 'Unless it were an angel as well, my...erm, guide.'

'They come as they are,' Morghan said after a pause. 'Or as they wish – I do not know which.' She looked down into the glowing heart of the fire and thought about Erin's Kria and her ability to conjure fire from the spark of the worlds. 'And there is more than one, Winsome,' she said. 'They share the task of your guidance between them, according to need.'

'Whose need?'

'Yours.'

Winsome touched the dog beside her. 'I feel odd,' she said, then breathed in deeply, raggedly. 'Is it the smoke from the herbs you put on the fire?'

'No,' Morghan answered. 'They were simply an offering to the spirits of this space, bringing them greeting and honour.'

'Then why am I feeling like I'm about to keel over?'

'You are open to shifting now,' Morghan said. All around her the cave was open with different places to go. One step to this side or that, and she would be somewhere else.

Winsome's throat was dry. 'Shifting?' she whispered. 'Would you come with me?'

Morghan thought before replying. 'No,' she said. 'But if you need me, you've only to call.'

The answer made Winsome flick her eyes open. 'No?' Her breath was fast in her chest and her eyes stung suddenly from the smoke, and the shadows had moved forward to dance in the space between fire and wall.

She shut her eyes again, swayed slightly.

'We have different paths today,' Morghan said, feeling

the need to let go now, to tumble down into one of the worlds waiting for her. She held herself still. 'Sometimes, the only way to go is on your own and yet not alone.'

'On your own but not alone?' Winsome repeated. She thought for a moment that didn't make sense, but before she could say so, she found that it did. Somehow. She touched the fur of the dog again. 'Cù,' she said.

'He will go with you,' Morghan agreed. 'And if you've need of me, I will come.'

'How will you find me?' There was only the dirt of the cave floor under Winsome now. She could no longer feel the walls of the cave around her.

'I am the Lady of the Forest,' Morghan said, the words coming as from a great distance away now. 'If you are amongst trees, I shall find you.'

She couldn't hold on any longer. The urge – need – to let go and tumble was too strong. And so, Winsome let herself go, her hand on the dog's back to take him with her.

She blinked, lifting a hand to her face, feeling sudden yellow sunlight on her. With effort, Winsome made herself stand straighter, opening her eyes to look around. A panic swept over her when she could not see Morghan with her, but she tucked her gaze down, looked at the dog, who turned his head to grin up at her, tongue lolling to the side.

'Cù,' she said. 'Where are we?'

But the dog did not answer. He turned his head again and looked with interest to something in the distance. Winsome made herself follow his gaze.

They stood on a sloping hillside, all long green grass waving in a breeze under a wide blue sky. She lifted a hand to her forehead, shaded her eyes, and squinted up into the sky. A flock of birds, plump-bodied and long-necked flew past in formation, intent on getting where they were going. Winsome frowned up at them, trying to see what sort of birds they were.

But something was approaching them from the forest below where Winsome stood with her canine companion. For a moment, remembering what Morghan had said about being able to find her, as long as she was near trees, Winsome was relieved to see the forest, but then all thought fell away from her mind as she saw the horse come closer.

It was a white horse, tall and silky-maned, tossing its head as it climbed sure-footed up the slope towards her. Winsome watched in astonishment. It seemed to her as though it shone and gleamed in the sun.

Surreptitiously, Winsome lowered her hand to her thigh and pinched herself. Hard.

She rubbed the sore spot.

Not dreaming then, she thought. Or not dreaming the way she was used to dreaming.

Suddenly, she wished Morghan was with her. She was used to going to these places with Morghan. Tagging along behind her, mouth open in amazement, and always safe in the knowledge that she wasn't on her own, wasn't in charge, didn't have to find her own way.

Now, though, there was no Morghan. There was a dog, and a horse, and her.

And overhead, in the far distance, crossing the horizon, a flock of birds.

The horse reached her, stopping in front of her and Winsome felt its hot, snorting breath on her skin. It looked at her with bright, warm eyes.

'Erm, hello?' Winsome said, surprised she was able to find her voice.

Cù grinned at her again.

The horse too, seemed to find the greeting amusing.

It shook its head, the long white mane catching in the breeze and making Winsome shiver to see it. She wondered if she was supposed to get on the horse's back. She'd never ridden a horse.

Surely though, in this strange, Otherworldly place, she'd be able to do such a thing?

She felt as though she might.

But the horse turned and began picking its way back down the hillside, its hooves lifting delicately over the grass. It didn't look back at her, and simply seemed to assume that she would follow it.

The dog followed it, as though it was a matter of course to do so.

Winsome took a breath of air that tasted like grass and sky and walked down the slope after the dog and horse. Her heart tripped wildly in her chest and she placed a hand upon her breast, willing it to calm.

'Everything is all right,' she whispered to herself. 'You've done this before, remember.'

Or a variation of it. Although not alone, not without Morghan.

What had Morghan said, though?

Sometimes the only way to go is on your own but not alone.

Winsome swallowed and felt her tongue thick and dry in her mouth. Well, she thought. She was on her own.

She looked ahead at the dog and the horse. The horse's white coat was bright and clean in the sunlight.

Well, she thought again. She supposed she wasn't alone.

The shade of the trees was sudden and cool and Winsome found herself blinking, getting used to the dimness. Wherever she was, however, it wasn't the tail end of winter. There was no sign of frost or snow upon the ground, and the trees stretched luxuriously leaf-laden limbs overhead, glorying in the sunshine.

Neither of her animal guides hesitated before stepping into the forest, and nor did they glance back to make sure she followed. Winsome frowned at this, irritated for a moment that they would take her trundling along after them for granted.

And then she wondered at her own thought. What else was she to do here but go where they led her? If she were to believe one part of this – and she did believe that Cù was something like a guardian spirit – then oughtn't she accept the rest as it appeared?

It was a leap of faith, she told herself. And God knew, she'd made plenty leaps of faith in the past on less evidence than this. Why was she worrying now?

They picked their way through the forest in silence, Winsome staring all around her with eyes she thought were probably as round as the proverbial saucers. For a moment, she thought about calling for Morghan, to see if she really could do so, if Morghan really could hear her somehow and find her; and, well, so she could ask what Morghan thought was going on.

But Winsome didn't do it. It wouldn't be fair, she knew. Morghan had said they had different paths to travel that day, and she wouldn't have said that for no reason. It had been kind to even tell Winsome that she would come if it was necessary.

So Winsome followed the horse and turned her mind to wondering about it instead. Was this horse another of her guides, since it was obviously guiding her?

Or was it sort of like...the normal greeting party? A sort of *let me lead you to your...*

Tree. The horse had pulled up short at an enormous tree. It was so big and old that one of the branches sweeping out low across the ground from it was the thickness of Winsome's own waist. Or almost, she thought. More like a trunk than just a branch, anyway. The horse had had to duck down her head to get under the canopy of the tree's branches, and now they stood within a delightful green and brown tent, with the huge circumference of the tree's actual trunk rising solidly and marvellously in the middle of it all.

Winsome felt a strong desire to go up to the old tree and lean against it, as though they knew each other, as though the tree – a horse chestnut, she saw – was something she'd always been able to count on.

Not something, she corrected herself. Someone.

13

MORGHAN WAS RIGHT. WINSOME KNEW THEN WITHOUT A shred of doubt.

Morghan was right when she maintained that everything had spirit. That trees dreamed and sang and lived in ways no one seemed to give much thought to anymore.

Stepping up to the venerable old tree, Winsome pressed her palms against its bark and leaned her forehead against it, as though to hear it whisper some of those dreams and songs to her. How, she wondered, had she not known this about trees?

Or horses? She glanced over at the horse, who stood regarding her with bright, intelligent eyes.

Or dogs? Winsome smiled down at Cù, beamed suddenly at him.

'I'm amazed by you all,' she said out loud to the tree, horse, dog. To the whole world.

The horse pawed at the ground as though in answer and shook her mane. Her great nostrils flared. Winsome took a stumbling, dazed step back from the tree and grinned at the horse. 'Okay,' she said. 'What am I supposed to be doing then?' She looked up at the tree, at its spreading branches. Was she supposed to climb all the way up there?

Surely not. It had been thirty years at least since she'd last scrambled up a tree.

Winsome glanced around rather wildly. Where was a guide when you needed one? Maybe she'd need to call Morghan after all.

Cù stepped forward and then, somehow, he was gone.

Winsome blinked at the space where the dog had been, feeling her head suddenly swimming. Honestly, one moment he'd been there, and then the next, not even the flash of a tip of a tail. It was as though he'd fallen into a hole in the earth.

Then Winsome dropped to her knees and peered down into a burrow under the roots of the tree. It was large enough for Cù to have disappeared into it, she decided. And there was nowhere else for him to have gone like that, there one moment, vanished the next.

When she swallowed, there was the taste of dirt in her throat and she cleared it, looking at the horse, eyebrows raised.

'In there?' she asked, her throat scratchy with soil. The horse lifted her head up and down. Nodding.

Winsome peered into the darkness under the tangle of tree roots.

In there.

'Where does it go, though?' she asked. Her teachers in school had always told her off for asking so many questions, she suddenly remembered, and closed her mouth. Then shook her head at herself and opened it again. 'Am I just supposed to go along and find out?'

The horse regarded her with a steady gaze.

'I, erm, guess so, then,' Winsome decided. She wished Cù would come back for her. He could be anywhere by now since she'd dithered so long.

'Okay then,' Winsome said and took a breath, looking down the hole again. 'Wish me luck.'

The sound of her voice made her pause, biting her lip. She looked over at the horse and nodded her head to it. 'Erm,' she said. 'I mean to say – thank you for leading me here.'

Winsome touched the tree above her gently with her fingers. Almost, she thought, she could feel the thrum of its sap inside the trunk like blood. Or perhaps the faint vibration was its song. Either way, she chastened herself, how could she have gone on without saying something to it? She cleared her throat again, reminding herself of all that she'd learned so far from Morghan, who, she was sure, walked these worlds, had likely been right here at some stage, crouched in front of this very horse chestnut tree that felt so much like a beloved grandmother.

'Thank you,' she said, her voice hesitant but sincere as she groped for the words. 'Thank you for being here, for being you, for being so special.' She scrunched up her face. That hadn't been what she'd wanted to say – but what did she want to say? She didn't know what she was doing.

After a moment, she simply nodded. It would have to suffice. Her gratitude had been real, and wouldn't that count for something? Even if she didn't have the right words?

Yet, she thought. Even if she didn't have the right words yet.

The thought frightened her. What was she doing? Again, she peered into the darkness down the hole.

The problem, she decided, was that once you knew the world to be bigger than you'd previously realised, than anyone had ever told you, then you couldn't unknow it. Once you learnt you had the gifts or the know-how to see things and go places you hadn't previously even considered to exist, you couldn't unlearn that.

It wasn't how things worked. Or at least, Winsome decided, gathering up her courage, it wasn't how she wanted it to work. She supposed she could run home like a frightened rabbit and stick her head in the ground. She frowned, knowing she was mixing her metaphors, or something, but it didn't matter.

She knew things now. She knew that trees lived and breathed and dreamed. Not necessarily in the same ways as herself – but they did it all the same.

She knew that there were places a person could go. Worlds beyond the one that existed outside the front door. Maybe these worlds were inside herself, deep into her own psyche, or maybe they were actual, literal places; it didn't matter.

What mattered was that she knew about them.

And she couldn't unknow it.

Which only left one more question. Should she go down the hold head-first or feet-first?

Winsome opted for feet-first, discovering that it was only a scramble for a moment, a small drop, and then she was in a tunnel in which she could stand. Cù was waiting for her, and his tail gave a gratifying wag when he saw her.

'Nothing to it,' Winsome said, brushing the dirt off her dress. Frowning at the feeling of the fabric under her hands, she looked down at the clothes she wore and realised in the dim light that they weren't what she had been wearing before slipping sideways back in the cave with Morghan.

'I've fallen down the rabbit hole, all right,' she muttered. She wore something like she'd seen Erin wearing. A woollen dress, plain, old-fashioned. And leaf green in the light.

Which was coming from where? Cù turned and trotted down the tunnel, ducked around a large rock and was lost to sight again.

'Wait for me,' Winsome called, and hurried after the spirit dog. 'Wait for me,' she whispered.

And the dog was waiting for her, his head turned back to the short tunnel, ears cocked in expectation. Winsome thought he might have looked relieved when she finally popped out of the tunnel and caught up with him.

'I'm coming,' she told him.

And as if he'd been waiting for her to say just such a thing, he took off at a trot again, and Winsome scrambled after him.

They were in a forest still, although Winsome wasn't exactly sure it was the same forest she'd been in just minutes before with the horse and the chestnut tree. They looked similar, perhaps, but even so – she had a niggling idea that they were now in a different place.

'I need a map,' she said, and felt her cheeks heat with the thought that came tumbling after that one. Ambrose would have a map. Or would help her draw a map. Or would know where she had been.

Whatever. Ambrose would know.

Ambrose. He had called her darling. He had looked at her with such...longing.

Her face heated even more.

'Stop going so quickly,' she called to the dog. 'I can't keep up.'

Cù turned his head and flung her a dubious glance she had no trouble reading.

'Okay,' she mumbled. The colour in her cheeks wasn't from exertion. But what was she supposed to do about Ambrose?

What was she supposed to do about any of this?

Abruptly, Winsome and Cù were on the edge of a clearing and Winsome pulled herself up short. There were people there, in the broad, leafy clearing deep in these strange woods. A man and a woman of such strange features and looks that Winsome just wanted to sink to her knees and cry.

I don't know where I am anymore, she thought and clutched handfuls of her skirt in clenching fists.

The woman, her skin dark and swirled with strange designs that did not look tattooed on, but part of her, turned and regarded Winsome with eyes the colour of winter oceans. A white sow pushed its nose from behind the woman's dress and regarded Winsome and Cù, its nostrils quivering.

The man next to her had antlers on his head. Or growing from his head. Winsome wasn't sure which. There was no colour in her cheeks now; she felt faint, her legs unsteady.

These people, she thought. They're not human. They're not from earth, even. She didn't know who they were, and she didn't know what they were, but they looked and smelt of an ancient wildness that threatened to bring Winsome to her knees.

Just as she was afraid her legs really would buckle beneath her and drop her in an undignified huddle upon the ground where she'd probably squirm and wriggle in the dirt like some sort of small snuffling and frightened animal, the woman smiled at her and spoke.

'Ah, you are in time for a story,' she said.

Winsome glanced around. Was this woman talking to her?

There was no one else there, apart from Cù, of course. Winsome put her hand to her chest.

'Me?' she squeaked.

'Of course, you,' the woman replied. 'Why else would you be here?' Her voice sounded like the wind, like the rain, like the shifting and settling of stone.

'I don't know why I'm here,' Winsome said, barely able to believe she was saying anything at all. 'I followed my dog.'

All eyes lowered to gaze at Cù, who took the examination as if nothing else were to be expected.

'An impressive hound,' the antlered man said, speaking for the first time. His voice too, seemed older than the trees around them, as old as the sky above them, the oldest thing, perhaps, that Winsome thought she'd ever heard.

Overwhelmed, she grew light-headed, dizzy. 'I think I

need to sit down,' she said, her hands going out to grasp at the air for balance.

'Of course,' the woman said, and gestured at a fallen tree trunk. 'Be comfortable and I shall tell the story.'

Winsome blinked at her, blinked at the log, then stumbled towards it and almost fell upon it, turning to sit, astonished, unsteady.

Perhaps she was dreaming. Perhaps she had fallen asleep by the fire there in the cave with Morghan. It was not beyond the realm of belief. She'd barely slept the night before for tossing and turning over the news that she had to go see the Dean, offer some explanation for her inexplicable behaviour. And when she hadn't been thinking about that, and Mariah Reefton and Julia, and trying not to be mad at Minnie for saying what she had, Winsome admitted that she'd been thinking of Ambrose.

Darling, he'd called her. My darling.

So maybe she was dreaming. Vividly.

A hawk had settled silently upon the woman's arm, and she stroked the soft feathers as she told her story. The hawk looked at Winsome with yellow, unblinking eyes.

'Once,' the wild woman said, 'of a dark night with the moon the only bright thing in the sky, a woman stumbled through the forest, blinded by her tears, caught in her despair, her mind filled with problems she did not know how to give up.'

Winsome winced, then tried to hide her grimace. She knew what it was like to have a mind filled with problems and not know how to stop going over and over them. Still, she thought, risking a glance around the forest surrounding them, she didn't think anyone could pay her enough to go stumbling through this lot, even with the moon out fully bright.

She shivered slightly and tried not to look at the two strange people standing in the clearing. Were they even people? What were they doing there? Had they been waiting for her?

That surely, was impossible. But on the other hand, Winsome thought, why would they just be standing in a random clearing in the woods?

She sighed and reached out tentative fingers to touch Cù where he sat on the ground beside her. His fur was warm, and she was comforted.

The woman spoke again, and still her voice was the sound of waves coming home to shore. 'As the woman stumbled and tripped her way through the forest, the wind chased after her, having an inkling where she was going, and it plucked at her clothes and caught at her hair, trying to stop her.

'But the woman put her hands to her ears, so that she could not hear the wind's urgent voice, for she did not believe it could speak to her. She believed the wind was merely an irritant, pushing her about, picking at her.'

Winsome looked at the woman standing in the clearing, her strange gaze fastened on Winsome so that Winsome thought she might faint under it. Inside her head, she could hear the nickering, huffing voice of the wind, and the woman from the story, the way she stumbled and panted as she stumbled through the forest. Winsome drew her gaze away and looked at the trees, between them, imagining herself thrusting her way between them, seeking...what?

Quiet from the incessant problems. She shook her head

in a minute gesture. All she wanted was to tend her village, and her own spirit. Why was that so difficult?

Why did those who knew next to nothing about it, want so badly to stop her doing either? She closed her eyes.

The woman's voice washed over her, and now it was the wind, each word the puckering and sweeping of a breeze, a wind that had been around the world a hundred million times, had tasted of everything, had poked into every little corner, had spied every secret.

'And the woman came at last to her destination, a cliff from which to throw herself, from which to seek the oblivion she so desperately wanted, and so she did, hurling her body off the edge and into the coldness of the night, seeking the blackness and relief that would surely be hers at the bottom.

'But the wind, it caught up her soul and cradled her to itself, whispering that what she thought she sought was not to be found, that instead, she would never die.'

Winsome waited for the woman to say more, but she did not, looking at Winsome instead with a slight smile curving her lips.

Cù got up and stretched, as though this were all ordinary, and everything was as it should be. He looked at Winsome, then walked across the clearing the way they'd come and stepped back into the trees and along the faint path that had brought them there.

Winsome gazed after him in consternation, then stood up and looked at the two others in the clearing. Both stared back at her without saying a word. She cleared her throat.

'Erm, thank you for the story,' she said. It was clearly over, and Cù was clearly ready to continue this strange and odd journey. She sank down in an awkward little curtsy, surprising herself, then hurried from the clearing, head down, hands clenched.

A curtsy! She'd curtsied to them like she was some weirdo. How did Morghan find her way around these places? How did she know what to do?

And who the heck had those two been?

And what the heck did that odd little story mean? Winsome shook her head. That even death didn't save you from your problems?

Well, she thought with sarcasm dripping in her inner voice.

Wasn't that just fabulous?

14

ERIN LOOKED OUT THE KITCHEN WINDOW AT THE RAIN THAT fell about the cottage like mist, a long slow fog of drops too small to see except as a whole. She glanced back at the inside of the cottage, all cosy and dancing with shadows from the fireplace in the sitting room where Burdock was spread out on his bed, long legs overhanging.

It wasn't really the day to go outside and do anything, and she'd been working all morning. She was tired. Working at the Care Home wasn't exactly taxing, but it did mean getting up and walking into the village – she still didn't have a car – then walking home again, and it was cold out.

She was a great deal fitter than she'd used to be though, with all the exercise she got on the walk there and back, head down, hands tucked under her arms for warmth.

What she wanted to do was to go sit in her favourite chair by the fire, legs tucked up under her, a steaming cup of coffee on the table beside her, and she just wanted to sit there, ignoring the pile of Ambrose's books which she was only part way through. She just wanted to sit there and think about Stephan.

About how it felt late at night when they were both in their beds talking on the phone, feeling as though they were right next to each other. They were learning some very odd, very special tricks. Erin shuddered slightly, remembering how she had felt Stephan's energy right there with her, almost a real, three-dimensional thing. And how she could reach for him with her own spirit, and they could be together even though their bodies were miles apart.

It made the lockdown and enforced separation easier, that was for sure.

The thought brought a smile to herself, and she put down the cup she held and wiped her hands. She would begin Morghan's exercises, whether it was drizzling out there in the garden or not. The thought sent a frizzle of excitement through her, undercut with a tiny thread of fear. Did she want to be the next Lady of the Grove? Did she want Morghan's job? And would Morghan leave when she was trained, the way that Selena had?

It was all a bit crazy. She didn't even know exactly what Morghan's job was, except that...well, no, not really she didn't.

Erin pondered the question, going into the utility room to put on boots and cloak. Morghan oversaw and led all the rituals, of course, although organising them was a team effort and everyone had something of a part to play in them.

Morghan kept the truth alive too, Erin supposed.

The truth. What was the truth?

Erin stepped outside and sheltered for a moment under

the eaves overhanging the back door while she gazed around the walled garden.

The raven – the one she'd come almost to think of as hers – perched atop the roof of the well, its grey back glistening with rain.

The truth, she knew, had learnt, and was still learning, was that the world was a bigger place than she'd known. The truth was that one could reach out and touch things in spirit. The truth was that everything had spirit.

Like this garden, she supposed. If a house could have its own spirit, then so too, surely, could a garden? Erin toyed with the idea, a frown marring her forehead, as she looked out at the winter beds, so carefully arranged in a radiating pattern from the well in the centre.

How did you talk to the spirit of a house or a garden, though? How did you hear it if it spoke back?

So many questions, Erin thought. Always so many questions.

And she'd dreamed of her mother again the night before. She knew that was what the dream of the door and the darkness was about. This wasn't a door like in her other dreams, with the letters slipped underneath them. Erin shook her head.

No. This was a real door, and the blackness behind it was also real. It made her want to back away, the sight of that black hole behind the door. The blackness in which lurked the dragon from the loch. What did that mean?

Erin shook her head. Why had her mother fallen down the basement stairs? And her newest question - why hadn't she turned the light on before stepping across the threshold?

Erin huffed out a breath. These were the questions that wouldn't leave her alone and it wasn't much fun. If it weren't for Stephan, she thought, she'd be brooding on them practically all the time. Especially now that the dream was coming back to her night after night.

It was better than dreaming of the loch, but only just.

Another breath, that steamed in the damp air. Erin corralled her thoughts and tried to focus.

The garden. An imaginary garden that would become a real garden, although not in this world.

'Should be easy,' she said out loud. The raven looked at her, fluffed out its wings then tucked them back sleek against its side, dark eyes shining.

'Okay,' Erin told the bird. 'Seriously. A fixed point in both worlds, that was what Morghan said, right?'

The bird didn't answer, but its gaze never wavered.

'Yes,' Erin said, agreeing for it. 'That's what she said. *A place in which to stand both here and there.*' A frisson of excitement coursed through her, making her smile. She could do this, she thought.

She really could.

Stand between the worlds. Walk between them, one foot in each. The knowledge of how was there; she was sure of it. There deep inside her like something vestigial, something long unused but just waiting.

She wrapped her arms around herself and grinned, then stepped out into the garden, walking down the main path to the well, where there was space in front of it for her to stand, greet the elements whose symbols adorned the well.

She'd begin there, she thought.

The rain misted her hair, and she pulled the hood of the

cloak over her head, then realised she would get wet anyway, as soon as she started moving.

Well. There was nothing for it. And there was a toasty fire in the range inside to warm up beside afterwards.

Erin turned herself towards the east, where the sun rose in the morning, lighting the air with its golden breath. She bent her head for a moment, then swept her arms down and back up, around in a circle, stretching her fingers to the sky, feeling the rain upon her skin, tipping her face back, the damp breath of the day upon her cheeks. She breathed in, filling her lungs with air, then let it out slowly as she lowered her arms. She spread her hands out to the side, embracing the air, then drew them forward towards her chest in a gathering gesture, breathing in again, breathing the world into her lungs, and then she let her breath go, offering it back to the world with an outward gesture.

'Air,' she said. 'Spirits of Air, I greet and honour you. Breath of my life. Hold this space with me.'

A pause, held, letting herself feel, be, part of the air. Part of everything.

Erin reached upwards again, then, turning her body towards the south, aligned by the directions on her garden's well, she reached for the sun, feeling for its heat and light even through the rain. She thought of Kria, bringing forth the spark of life, of fire, in cupped hands and her fingers sparkled with diamond flames.

'Fire,' she said. 'Spirits of Fire, I greet and honour you. Spark of my life. Hold this space with me.'

Erin let her arms float down, turning to face the west, imagining the sea out there past the edge of the land, spreading out towards the horizon, and her arms floated for a moment as though in water. Her fingers shimmered in the waves she made.

'Water,' she said. 'Spirits of Water, I greet and honour you. Womb of my life. Hold this space with me.'

Turning for the final time, Erin lifted her feet, feeling the earth underneath her, feeling its strong, solid ground spread out from her. She breathed deeply of its secret musky scent and lifted onto her toes, sank onto her heels, then spread her arms over her head and around and down, and they were branches pregnant with buds as her toes dug her roots down deep into the ground.

'Earth,' she said. 'Spirits of Earth, I greet and honour you. Root of my life. Hold this space with me.'

She was almost there, and reached back to the sky, then bent down to spread her fingers towards the earth.

'As above, as below,' she said, bringing her tingling hands back to her chest and pressing her palms to her heart. 'As outwards, so inwards. We are the wheel.'

And it was true; she felt it in every vibrating atom of her body. Was this not already holding the worlds in you – or standing in both this world and the Otherworld? It felt like it. Wasn't this what Morghan meant when she talked about standing with the spirit flexed, senses so much wider than how everyone went about most of the day?

So, Erin wondered, where was the difference? Why the garden?

She held the thought and pondered it for a moment, then found herself sinking back inside her head again to do so. It was so hard to hold herself like this. Inside and outside her skin. Not in her head, but in her heart.

Erin took some slow, deep breaths, holding them and

exhaling slowly to the count of four, as she'd been taught. She let herself sink down out of her head again, focusing her consciousness outwards from her heart, letting her eyes and ears just be instruments of her heart, not her mind.

She could feel her feet, her knees, her stomach that gurgled just a little. Her heart, wide open and strong, her neck, slender, protected. Her lips, nose, eyes, the top of her head. It was funny, to be so aware of her body at the same time as she felt so free of it. It was an odd trick.

So, Erin decided, closing her eyes, letting her spirit stream beyond her skin. A garden. A garden inside her that echoed the garden in which she stood.

Her visualisation was as much a knowing as a seeing, she thought, casting her eyes around behind their lids, not feeling the rain upon her cloak and cheeks anymore as she stood in the centre of the walled garden her grandmother had built. It was the same for her when she was drawing, when the difference between knowing there ought to be a tree with leaves like *that* and seeing them were only milliseconds apart.

Behind her, she could feel the well, but with a faint sensation of surprise, she realised the one in her imaginary garden was different. Her brow puckered for a moment, then smoothed and she smiled unconsciously, turning in her mind to gaze upon the garden that unfurled in the space inside her. Vines grew up about the ancient stones of her well, vines with great, green leaves and white, waxy flowers shaped like trumpets. They twined up and around, the flowers wagging slightly in a breeze and Erin lifted her face as though she could smell their fragrance on the wind. And perhaps she could. It was sweet, like the echoes of an old, half-remembered lullaby.

Her eyes still closed, Erin stepped over in her inner vision to her imagined well, placing a hand on the stones around its watery eye. The stone was dry and slightly warm, and she leaned over to look down into its depths, for there was no lid to this well, just the water, reflecting the waving heads of the flowers, the green leaves like elephant ears. Where did it go, this well?

Erin remembered the well in the garden of Hawthorn House. She remembered how she had fallen into it, tumbling down the shaft until she floated on her back looking up through the great darkness to the underside of the world, feeling all around her the great pregnancy of being.

She wondered where she would find herself if she were to topple down this well.

But that, perhaps, if she were brave enough, if she dared, would be for another day. For now, she lifted her closed eyes and looked around at the rest of the garden.

To begin with, it was blurred in front of her, as though not quite formed, uncertain of what shape to take, what configuration. But Erin reminded herself to model it on the real garden, and she brought it into as much focus as she could.

How different it was! Startled, she felt her body gasp out loud, and almost lost her concentration. She breathed deeply again, stilling herself into the vision of the garden until it stopped wavering in front of her and settled back into her mind's space again.

It was not so early in spring in this garden that the earth

lay in the beds without stirring, the plants still too young under the soil to push their ways towards the strengthening sun.

In this garden, the plants crowded forth and Erin stood before them, open-mouthed in shock at their unruly chaos.

It was true – her imagined garden was beautiful, a kaleidoscope of colour and shape – but there was something wrong with it. Erin pressed a finger to her lips and tried to pinpoint why it made her feel unsettled, uncomfortable.

Life grew in her garden, green and vibrant, with complete abandon wherever she looked. There might be places where it did not, she supposed, but the beds immediately beyond the well blocked her view. She couldn't see to the wall at all unless – and so she did so – she stepped onto the path and peeped beneath the wild tangle, squinting and peering.

There was the wall, so at least it was still there, although she could not see its bricks and stones, only the great mass of thistle growing in front of it.

What did this mean, Erin wondered, gazing around as the vision of the garden grew and steadied in front of her as though she had no part in the making of it. What did it mean that this imagined garden of hers was so wild and overgrown?

She didn't know, and backed up a step, her heel scuffing against something and causing her to cry out in alarm, looking down at the path, where a thick root snaked across from one bed to another. She'd almost tripped on it, fallen over on her backside in the garden she'd conjured.

Confused, unsettled, Erin drew herself up, found she was rubbing at her arms, and let her hands drop to her sides. This garden had come so easily to her imagination, but it wasn't at all as she'd expected it would be.

What had she expected? Erin thought about it for a moment. She'd expected that she would walk, in her mind, from bed to bed, choosing what would grow there. Roses in this bed, pink ones, frilly and delicate, one of Stephan's tea roses, old-fashioned and lovely. Lavender in that one, soaking up the sun and dreaming of sunsets and drowsy buzzing bees. Tender and new shoots of pansies in the next, unfurling and growing until their pretty faces would turn towards the sun, smiling.

Not this jungle, this riot of plants, overgrown and untended.

She hadn't been expecting this.

Was this the way it was supposed to be? And how was that? How could you imagine something, and yet not control what you imagined?

Erin shook out her hands, drawing in deep breaths, turning from the garden in her mind and towards the garden she knew within the stone walls of Ash Cottage. She sought the cold wetness of rain upon her cheeks and shivered, coming back to her body.

Coming back to the real garden.

Where everything was tidy and in its place, awaiting the fullness of spring.

15

AT FIRST, ALL MORGHAN COULD SEE WAS SKY.

Thick clouds raged and roiled across the arching bowl of the sky, dark veins through them where thunder lurked, and when the lightning struck, they were lit from within, their great shadowed bulk hissing and steaming, the sky streaked with black and gold.

She thought she was on the cliff-top again and reached for her face with her hands, pressing her palms to her cheeks, pulling the skin down as she stared up at the sky, feeling the deep vibrating hum of burnt ozone, the sharp crack of thunder that wrenched open the sky in every direction.

But then she sank down to her knees and realised she wasn't on the cliff-top at all, but inside a building, the storm raging now outside, hard nails of rain pounding upon the roof tiles, drowning out every other sound.

Her knees were pressed against something hard, and Morghan groped out a hand, touched wood, and heaved herself off her knees and into a sitting position, blinking, looking around, trying to place where she was.

And then realising.

St. Bridget's. She was in the church, and it stank of unwashed bodies and spluttering candles. The pew grew slick under her hand and Morghan closed her eyes, her heart sinking. Hadn't she known though, that this was one of the possibilities? That she could end up back here, considering the state of things between Wellsford and Wilde Grove?

Yes. She'd known. On the face of it, Wellsford and Wilde Grove had been working hand in hand more so than ever before in their long, fractious history. Working together for the good of the community, making sure everyone could get through in difficult times, working to implement Morghan's and Ambrose's vision for a safe, sustainable community. The natural extension of their work.

For what was the individual without their community?

Two steps to the work, Morghan knew. The strengthening of the soul on each individual level. The outward manifestation of that in the caring for those around them. It was impossible to work to alleviate the suffering of your own soul without realising that the person next to you suffered just the same.

Her fingers tightened on the wood of the pew. How tiring sometimes this world was. How much could so easily be avoided, how much of that suffering lifted.

She coughed, her throat working, and she flung her hand from wood to flesh, touching the skin of her throat.

Which of course, was not the skin of her own throat. It was younger, firmer, and the hands with which she touched it were longer fingered, and the panic that bloomed suddenly in her mind was not her own either.

She could not stop coughing. There was something in her throat, caught there, as though she had swallowed a breath of this heavy dust and it had turned to a hard knot, a twist of something that lodged there and would not be removed.

She could not draw breath and now there was almost no space for Morghan's own thoughts as they subsided under those of the woman whose body she was in. She could not breathe! Her hand fisted and she thumped at her chest. Her fingers flexed and clawed at her throat and she knew that she would be leaving great scratch marks there, as though the devil had got her.

Blythe rose in her seat, although it was not time to stand, and stood bowed over the bench in front of her, her throat working, working, trying to expel that great knot stuck down deep in it. She coughed, hacking, and knew her eyes bulged, knew that the priest had stopped his preaching to stare at her, that everyone was turned to stare at her, horror on their faces.

But still she could not stop clawing at herself, trying to draw breath, her chest heaving with the effort to suck the dirty, smoky air into her lungs, and she staggered, one hand out grasping, reaching for help as she coughed and hacked and tried to howl and breathe.

The priest backed away, his eyes locked on hers, his hand going automatically to make the sign of the cross, warding her away. She stumbled from the bench, tripping on her skirts, and she looked wildly around the tiny church, at the faces of the people she'd known since birth, all of them shying away from her, some of the small children crying now, burying their faces in their mother's arms.

Morghan felt Blythe's skittering, panicking terror, and her legs locked, holding her barely upright in the smoky interior of the church as she worked frantically to clear her airways, her hand fisted, pounding upon her own chest, while her eyes bulged, staring at those looking horrified back at her from their pews.

No one reached to help her. The priest backed further away, shaking his head, mouth moving in words Morghan couldn't hear. She turned her face from him and lurched into movement, staggering for the door.

If she was going to die, Morghan heard her long-ago self think, then it wasn't going to happen in the church.

She made for the trees, rain immediately soaking her, one hand outstretched, groping in the air until it touched a sturdy trunk.

And like that, the obstruction in her throat loosened, and Blythe took a great whistling breath, then leaned forward and threw up, splattering the hem of her gown and the roots of the tree with her vomit.

She stood swaying for a moment, the back of her hand against her lips, eyes closed, other hand grateful for the steady support of the tree. After a moment, she shifted to lean her forehead against the trunk, the bark rough against her skin, but that was all right. She could feel the tree's young, vibrant energy inside the wood and sap of its body, and it shared it with her, letting it spill over into her body, until the faintness grew less, then passed.

Blythe Wilde, with Morghan looking also through her eyes, stood slowly, pushing herself upright.

'Bless you for sharing your strength,' she whispered to the tree, then turned slowly to look back across the lawn to the church.

Morghan felt the rising swirl of bitterness in the young woman's mind. Her mind. It captured her and she stared at the crowd from the church through a dark haze of anger.

'I nearly died,' she shouted suddenly at them. 'Choking on my own breath, and none of you lifted a hand in aid!' Blythe swung her head slowly from side to side, watching them with a snarl on her lips. 'What sort of neighbourly love is that, then? Do you not listen to your priest, then?'

She smacked her lips shut, realising the mistake she'd just made, hoping none of those with eyes narrowed to stare at her heard it. She dropped her hand from the tree, and turned, back stiff under the gaze of her neighbours, and stepped forward onto the path that would lead her through the woods back to Hawthorn House.

Her dress stunk of vomit and her throat was raw, chest sore from heaving breaths that wouldn't come. Her hair too, had come undone and hung down from her cap, draped over her shoulders in long dark wet ropes.

'Witch,' someone hissed from behind her. Louder than they'd ever yet dared.

Blythe swung slowly back around and looked at the crowd of those she'd known all her life.

'Who said that?' she asked, but her voice cracked and broke halfway through the question, her throat hurting too much to bear speaking.

There was rustling movement in the congregation, and the small children hid their faces in their mother's skirts again.

'Twas the work of the devil, making you choke like that, in God's house.'

Inside Blythe's chest, it seemed like her heart stopped for several beats. They'd never spoken like this before. Not out loud. Not on church ground.

Not before Agnes Reefton's babe had sickened and died, despite Blythe's remedies.

She shook her head. 'You'd best be careful with your accusations,' she said, putting greater bravado into her voice than she felt.

'Nay,' another said over the hammering of the rain. ''Tis you best be taking care.'

Blythe had no wish to leave them with the last word, but she could only shake her head, aware of the muck down the skirt of her dress, and her disarray.

There was nothing she could think of to say anyway, and she turned again, stepping forward into the quiet embrace of the woods, feeling her mind become wild and dark with foreboding.

This would lead nowhere good, she thought. Nowhere good at all.

MORGHAN CAME BACK TO HERSELF, TOOK A DEEP BREATH AND coughed on a mouthful of smoke from the small fire. She pressed a hand to her chest, suddenly frantic as she tried drawing in a breath of air. For a moment she was Blythe again, struggling to breathe in the church, all eyes on her, hostile and afraid.

She coughed, tried to catch her breath, and then there was someone thumping her gently on her back.

'There,' Winsome said. 'It's all right, take it easy now. It's just smoke. Take a breath nice and slow.'

Morghan bent over her lap, stilling herself, letting herself breathe, concentrating on the simple rush of air in and out of her lungs. They hurt. Her whole chest hurt. She touched her throat. It too felt raw and shredded. When she opened her eyes, she half-expected to see her clothes streaked with vomit.

'Thank you,' she whispered, and her voice was strained, hoarse.

'No problem,' Winsome said, sitting back and looking at her friend. 'Just a splutter.' Although for a moment there, she'd seen real panic in Morghan's flailing.

Morghan nodded, closing her eyes again.

'Are you all right?' Winsome asked. 'You haven't, you know, seen something like last time?'

Last time. That terrible vision of the lost souls, the creeping darkness over the earth. Morghan shook her head, swallowed, tried out her voice again.

'No,' she said. 'Nothing like that.'

Winsome was almost bursting to know what Morghan had seen. She was also full fit to bust of what she'd experienced, where she had been.

'I think we need to eat these scones,' she said.

Something to eat would be good, Morghan knew. Bring her back properly. She'd gone hard and fast, when it had come to it. Thrust sideways right into the life she'd lived so long ago.

But her throat was sore. 'I think I'd need some honeyed tea to go with it,' she answered. She'd never be able to swallow down a scone, no matter how fresh and buttery it might be.

Winsome nodded. She was a bit parched too. 'Your place?' she asked, hoping that Morghan would agree. 'Mine's well, not really the place to be seen together right now. And there's nowhere but the church to sit out of this wind and drizzle.'

She didn't want to imagine what sorts of bother Morghan stepping into the church for a socially distanced chat with the vicar would get her into. As soon as the words were out of her mouth, Winsome regretted them. It was wrong, she thought. Just so wrong on so many levels. 'I'm sorry,' she said. 'It's all just crap, isn't it?'

Morghan felt again, for a fleeting moment, the growing suspicion of the villagers for Blythe and the life she lived.

'It's all right,' Morghan said, and her throat felt red and sore. 'This is an old story.'

For a moment Winsome looked at her, frowning. 'An old story?' she asked. 'I don't understand.'

Morghan paused before answering. 'Tea,' she said at last. 'You are able to make visits, correct? Come for tea, and then I've a story for you.'

A story. Winsome rocked back on her heels. Everyone had a story for her, it seemed these days. She licked her lips and tasted the dust of the cave. She hadn't wanted to slip in through the narrow entrance to this cave, to feel the heavy weight of the hillside above her, but her fear had ground to dust quickly and easily.

As though there'd been nothing to fear in the first place. She thought of the story the wild woman had told her in her own travelling to the Otherworld. Where the wind had caught the woman's soul even as her body had tumbled to the bottom of the cliff. What had it meant?

But Morghan was leaning forward to put the fire out, and Winsome tucked away her questions for the moment, picking up the parcel of scones, cold now, and waiting for Morghan before scooting out of the cave.

The wind greeted her, blustering in her face, and tugging at her shaggy hair. She pushed it away, wondering whether she ought to, or if it was trying to tell her something.

Of course it wasn't trying to tell her something, Winsome scolded herself. This was the real world. The wind didn't speak. It didn't carry messages across the hills and valleys.

Did it?

She shot a secret look at Morghan, but Morghan was brushing down her clothes, a tight frown between her eyes. Winsome decided she'd ask about the wind later when they were sitting down with some tea.

She shook her head. Fancy, she thought. Making plans to ask someone if the wind could talk to you.

But it had in her dream, or her travelling, or whatever it had been. Her vision.

It had spoken to her then and promised her she would never die.

Whatever that meant.

16

MORGHAN OPENED THE DOOR OF HAWTHORNE HOUSE, grateful to get in out of the wind and cold, thinking of her seat by the fire and something soothing for her throat. She turned to look at Winsome.

'Go through to the sitting room,' she said. 'I'll get us some tea, and a plate for those.' She nodded at the scones in Winsome's hand, still wrapped in their cheerful tea towel.

Winsome handed them over and watched Morghan disappear down the hallway towards the kitchen. She looked around for a moment, taking in – like she always did – the pleasing proportions of Hawthorne House. And then, she thought – like she always did – that she shouldn't be there.

She hung her coat on the stand and sighed, then pushed open the door to the sitting room. She'd warm herself in front of the fire, and then talk it all over with Morghan.

'Winsome?'

She looked up, startled, then flushed a deep scarlet. 'Ambrose,' she said. 'What are you doing here?'

He looked at her, not speaking, his eyes as green as the ocean in the dim room. He pushed back the flop of fair hair.

'I moved into Hawthorn House for the lockdown,' he said.

'Of course you did,' Winsome said. 'I'm sorry – what a question to ask you, what you're doing here. You have every right to be here.' She was rambling but couldn't seem to stop herself. Her mouth was a runaway train. 'You've more right to be here than myself, that's for certain.'

'Winsome,' Ambrose interrupted her, his voice gentle. 'It's okay.' He frowned slightly. 'Isn't it?' He cleared his throat but made no move from where he stood by the fire. 'Are you all right?'

Winsome bit down on her bottom lip, suddenly afraid that she was going to burst into great sobbing wet tears. Again. She sucked in a deep breath, let it out with effort. 'Yes,' she answered. 'Well, at the moment at any rate.'

Ambrose nodded, and an awkward silence fell between them.

'Are you...?' Winsome asked.

'Are you...?' Ambrose asked.

They were silent again.

'You go first,' Winsome said. 'What were you going to say?'

'Oh.' Ambrose didn't remember. 'Oh,' he repeated. 'I was just going to ask if you were here to see Morghan, but that's a silly question, isn't it?'

Winsome shook her head. 'I came here with Morghan.' She looked down at her hands. They had dirt from the cave in the lines on the palms. She ought to wash them. 'We, erm, went to the cave,' she said.

Ambrose's eyebrows shot up. 'The cave?' he asked.

'Morghan took me there,' Winsome said, and rubbed her palms against her thighs, looking at Ambrose. He needed a haircut. She wished she knew how to cut hair. She buried her hands under her arms.

Ambrose was still surprised. 'For what purpose?' he asked.

'Oh,' Winsome answered. 'Erm, I asked her what she did when she needed guidance.'

Ambrose's eyebrows raised even higher, disappearing under his sandy hair. 'And she took you to the cave?'

Winsome nodded.

'What, ah, happened then?'

'Well,' Winsome said with a sudden sigh. 'It's very dusty and dirty in there.'

Ambrose barked an astonished, startled laugh. 'Yes,' he said. 'I suppose it is,' He shook his head. 'I'm sorry,' he said. 'I had no right to ask what happened. Most of what each of us goes through in that cave is personal, and a story to tell only if one wants to.'

Winsome shifted on her feet. 'It's not that I don't want to tell what happened,' she said, then trailed off before starting up again. 'It's just that...'

'You'd prefer not to tell me.'

She shook her head. 'No, no that's not it at all.' Winsome hesitated. 'Or not all of it, at least.' She quit trying to explain herself, tongue-tied.

And then, suddenly, in a rush, she said, 'it's just that being in the same room with you makes me feel flustered.'

They stared at each other.

Winsome looked down at her feet. 'After,' she said. 'After, you know, the other day.'

Morghan pushed the door open carrying the tray of tea things. Mrs. Palmer had heated the scones for a few minutes and put out some jam and cream. They looked marvellous, but Morghan mostly wanted the tea.

Her throat hurt.

'Winsome,' she said, her voice rasping. 'I've got the tea.' She rounded the door and all but bumped into Winsome who stood a few steps into the room.

'Sorry,' Winsome yelped, moving out of the way and edging across the room.

Morghan stood with the tray in her hands and looked from Winsome to Ambrose and back again.

'I see,' she said after a moment.

And she did see – the energy was there in the room like a great swirl of colour, looping from one of them to the other.

'Something has happened between the two of you.' There was no point saying otherwise. It was obvious. Morghan set the tray on the table and stood for a moment with her hands on her hips, reading the energy.

It was strong, but fraught. As, she supposed, it would be.

Winsome and Ambrose stared back at her, their expressions twin looks of discomfort.

But after a minute, Morghan's face blossomed into a delighted smile. 'I can't help it,' she said. 'I think you would make a wonderful couple.'

Winsome's mouth fell open, and finally she sat down, letting herself sink into the deep cushions of the chair. 'It's impossible though!' she said without thinking. 'I mean, with me being the vicar and all.'

There was silence in the room except for the usual chatter of flames in the fireplace.

'Although, I'll likely not be vicar here for much longer,' Winsome said, staring red-faced at Ambrose.

Ambrose said nothing. He couldn't ask Winsome to give up her calling, just as he could never give up his.

He cleared his throat instead. 'I think, ladies, that I will give you the room to continue your visit with each other undisturbed. I've work to do.' He picked up the book he'd been reading, nodded to Winsome. 'Excuse me,' he said, and walked to the door, pulling it closed behind him.

Winsome groaned. 'Now I've gone and upset him,' she said.

'I shouldn't think so,' Morghan replied, then coughed. Her throat bothered her still, part of the experience with her past self she'd brought back with her. She waited for the fit to pass then shook her head. 'Ambrose won't want to make anything harder for you.'

But Winsome lowered her head into her hands. 'This is ridiculous,' she said. 'Nothing like this should go on these days. There shouldn't be this sort of division.' For a moment she perked up. The Dean couldn't stop her seeing whomever she liked, no matter their religious persuasion. Wasn't that so?

But it wasn't just a matter of a romantic attachment, was it? It was the whole long list of other things she'd been doing.

Been caught doing.

Raising her head again, Winsome looked at Morghan. 'You're pale,' she said suddenly. 'Sit down. What's wrong?'

Morghan, surprisingly, did as she was told, grateful to rest a moment. She touched her throat. 'Hurts,' she said.

'And your voice is all raw and hoarse. Was it the coughing fit in the cave? It was only a little smoke, though.' Winsome got up and hurried over to the tea tray to pour a cup of tea for Morghan. She added a generous dollop of honey and took the cup over. 'Here,' she said. 'Drink this. Do you want something to eat as well?'

'No, thank you,' Morghan said, wincing. She took a sip and the warm sweet liquid helped. 'That's better.' She sighed. 'Winsome,' she said. 'I barely know where to start.'

Winsome picked up her own tea and a scone with a lovely helping of cream on top of it. She couldn't help herself. Stress eating. It came after the stress baking no matter what. Her hips could attest to it.

'Where to start?' she repeated.

Morghan nodded, then, in a hoarse whisper, told Winsome about what she'd experienced while in the cave. While back in the body of Blythe Wilde, priestess of Wilde Grove all those many years ago.

When she'd finished, Winsome sat still for a moment, her plate forgotten on her lap. 'Wait,' she said, holding up a finger. 'Two things.'

Morghan nodded. Waited.

'First thing – is this what you were doing the time I met you? In the church that day? For some reason I feel like it has something to do with this.'

'Yes,' Morghan said. 'That was my first serious attempt

to contact her. I thought it would be easiest to reach her from a common spot, so to speak.'

'The church?'

'Yes. It was a stressful place for her, so her energy would be easier for me to track there. It's the same building that she would have worshipped in when she was alive.' Morghan hesitated a moment. 'Or she would have attended services there, at least.'

'Because she wouldn't have worshipped there, would she? Just as you don't.'

Morghan inclined her head in agreement. 'That is true,' she said. 'As Lady of the Grove, she would have lived much as I do, although of course, in greater secrecy.'

'And they called her a witch,' Winsome said, thinking sadly upon it. She looked over at her friend, a woman many would still call a witch.

'Members of the village would eventually lay a complaint of witchcraft against her with the local magistrate,' Morghan said. 'There are records of it. She was sent to the gallows for it.'

Winsome raised her hands to her face, smoothed them over her hair. She shook her head.

'What was the second thing?' Morghan asked.

'Agnes,' Winsome answered. 'You said Agnes Reefton.' She swallowed, felt ill suddenly to her stomach as though this was recent, not ancient, history.

'Yes,' Morghan said and now it was her turn to sigh. 'And yes, Agnes is ancestor to Mariah.' She blinked. 'If not an aspect of the same soul.'

Winsome stared at her, trying to fathom it all. If she bought into this belief system, and she could feel it inside her that she did, that it felt like the truth, that it made sense of so much, then there were...implications. Weren't there?

'So, things are what?' she asked. 'Playing out over again?'

Morghan sipped at her tea, then nodded. 'You could say that, I suppose. The trouble is, you see, that ancestral wounds need to be healed, or they simply play out again over and over.'

'The sins of the fathers,' Winsome said.

'And this is one ancestral wound that we've never dealt with,' Morghan said ruefully. 'I imagine after Blythe met her fate that Wilde Grove was simply occupied with the issue of survival, and protection, and until now, it's not seemed urgent.'

'Why now, then?' Winsome asked.

'The wheel turns,' Morghan said. 'Things must always come back around.' She sighed. 'And the whole world is in turmoil now as we approach a great time of change again. Another Time of Turning is upon us, and what we shall end by turning to is still up in the air.' She looked down at her golden hand and shook her head.

'And of course,' she added. 'Wilde Grove has never been so open before. For centuries, the Grove has been a secret thing, its practices hidden.' Morghan shook her head. 'Now, society has changed, and I am able to be who I am without hiding it. We are able to work for the good of the village without being shunned.' She blinked. 'The increasing secularisation of society has done that for us, anyway.'

'But there are still some who don't like it,' Winsome finished for her. 'Who want you back in the shadows, who think you're doing evil.' She paused, remembering her very first conversation with Mariah Reefton. 'We put one to death once,' she said. 'But it didn't kill the serpent – that's what she said. That's what Mariah Reefton said, right to my face, as though it was a good thing, putting someone, anyone to death.' The horror of it coursed like cold liquid through her blood all over again and Winsome shook her head. 'I know it's uncharitable of me, but I cannot, no matter what, bring myself to like Mariah Reefton.'

'She is an unpleasant woman,' Morghan agreed. 'An unpleasantness she has had a long time to cultivate. And justify.' Morghan leaned forward slightly. 'Because justify it she must, otherwise how to live with it?'

'With what?'

'With condemning another to death.'

Winsome nodded slowly. 'But she would have believed it then, wouldn't she? Agnes Reefton? Their world view was different back then. Witches and spirits existed – I mean, they exist now, obviously – but back then, it was a world full of spirits that people lived in, not like now. Now we're all about materialism, and it's a miracle if anyone can see anything deeper than that in our world, but then, it wasn't the same. Agnes's belief in witches would have had the same reality as her belief that milk came from cows.'

Winsome shook her head, shrugged. 'So, in a way, she was only acting in accordance with the world she believed in.' She frowned. 'Or am I missing something and tying myself in knots?'

'No,' Morghan said. 'You are right. Agnes's worldview would have made the accusation against Blythe normal. Acceptable to many, even. But what motivated her accusation, really? Did she really believe that Blythe had killed her child? That Blythe cavorted with devils? That Blythe's proficiency with herbs and healing was fine when it worked, but an evil thing when it didn't?' Morghan took a deep breath and barked a half-laugh. 'Listen to me,' she said. 'I'm letting my closeness to Blythe colour my emotions.' She set down her tea and sighed. 'It is a difficult thing even for me not to carry around the resentments and hurts of other lifetimes, even when I know that's where they're from. Imagine then, how hard it must be for Mariah not to succumb to them as her own feelings.'

'I doubt she's made much effort, Morghan,' Winsome said. 'You're being awfully kind about it.'

'I'm doing my best, yes,' Morghan said. She looked toward the fire, not really seeing it, but staring past the flames backwards in time to Blythe Wilde's time on earth.

'Blythe died young,' she said. 'Before she'd grown fully into her training – which takes maturity, as well as learning. And her death was a shock to her. It was full of pain and suffering and she died full of that pain, mad with it.' Morghan paused, searching for the right words, searching for the truth.

Winsome waited, fascinated. Honestly, she thought. She'd never had such an immensely interesting time of things until she'd come to Wellsford. Difficult, trying, even frightening at times, but so deeply, incredibly interesting. She couldn't regret it. No matter what was to happen, she didn't know if she could ever bring herself to regret all the experiences, all the things she'd learnt.

'It would be hard not to die resentful in those circumstances,' Winsome said softly.

Morghan nodded. 'That's it,' she said. 'And that's the task ahead.'

'The task ahead?'

'To heal Blythe, for she is still caught in this terrible death, and to heal Mariah too, for she suffers the echoes of Agnes's cruelty and fear. Her whole family line has.' Morghan looked over at Winsome. 'But,' she said. 'The good news is, that if we manage this, we heal a whole village.'

Winsome stared back. 'We?' she asked.

Morghan nodded and smiled. 'I hope so.'

17

WINSOME WALKED BACK THROUGH THE WOODS TO THE vicarage barely watching where she was going. Everything she'd seen that day swirled around in her head, everything Morghan had said.

Everything Ambrose had said, every expression on his face.

She sighed and shook herself a little. 'Get yourself together, Winsome,' she said. 'Your brain's turning to porridge.' It felt thick and glutinous inside her head.

The wind rose, splattering her with thick droplets of rain, even through the spiky canopy of branches. It pushed and shoved at her, buffeting at her clothes, tearing at them, then swooping away to whoop with glee in the trees.

Winsome stopped walking and stared around at the forest. She'd passed the crossroads where the boundaries between Wellsford and Wilde Grove began and ended. She could feel them now – just the slightest tension, as though her ears were about to pop, then back to normal. Or she imagined it. That, she considered, was just as likely. It was easy to imagine things once you knew about them.

Just like she was imagining now that the wind might be speaking to her.

Trying to speak with her.

Because of her wee jaunt to the Otherworld. Morghan's Wildwood. Or some part of it anyway.

'What?' she asked out loud. 'What do you want?' She turned her face towards the wind and listened to its cold breath on her skin.

She'd told Morghan, eventually, when the conversation had wound around to it, about her visit to the Otherworld. She'd sat there on the chair, the fire crackling away merrily, all nice and normal, and said how a pure white horse had met her on a hillside and led her away into the forest and told her to climb down a tunnel under the roots of a great horse chestnut tree. The biggest, oldest chestnut she'd ever seen.

And Morghan had nodded along, as though this were all the most normal thing in the world.

A secret glee had snuck into Winsome's voice as she'd told her story. She'd wanted almost to hug herself in sudden happiness – that it had happened to her, that she had had this experience. That she had been brave enough to explore the world that was so much bigger than she'd ever once imagined.

Explore it with her dog and the horse to lead her, that was. She'd never want to venture there on her own. She'd be lost in a matter of seconds and who knew then where one might end up?

She'd asked Morghan who the two people were, in the clearing. Who was the woman who had told her the story?

Morghan, bending forward and pursing her lips, had shaken her head. 'The sow makes me think it could have been Cerridwen,' she said. 'And there are several horned gods. Cernunnos? Herne?'

The names had seemed ancient on Morghan's lips, and even now, standing on the path, her face to the wind, Winsome shivered. Cerridwen. Cernunnos. Who were these people? How could she have interacted so easily with them? Weren't they gods?

'Or,' Morghan had also said. 'Perhaps they were just spirits of the Wildwood.'

Not gods. That explanation was easier for Winsome. And they'd certainly had that ancient, wild look about them. She remembered the swirling patterns on their cheeks, their deep eyes that seemed to look so far and wide, and their voices. She shivered and tugged her coat tighter around herself.

Their voices had sounded like oceans, rivers, mountains, winds.

Wind. 'Are you speaking to me?' Winsome asked again, feeling vaguely idiotic, but unable to help herself, to stop herself from talking to it. In the story – hadn't it harried the girl, plucking at her, wanting to communicate?

But how did a wind communicate?

Winsome tucked her chin down and closed her eyes, letting the cold breeze press the rain in wet smatterings against her cheeks. Her thoughts drifted to the ending of the story she'd been told.

Where the wind had caught the soul of the woman and told her she would never die.

What did that mean?

Winsome believed in everlasting life, obviously. Her brows knotted over her closed eyes. How much had she thought about it, though? Really truly deeply thought about it? Beyond the resurrection of Christ, beyond the dinner at the right hand of Jesus, beyond all the dogma of the church?

She discovered she was trembling where she stood on the narrow dirt path between the trees. She felt as though she were on the verge of tipping over. Off a...

Off a cliff.

'Oh God,' she moaned. 'I don't know what I'm doing.'

And she didn't. Winsome didn't have the slightest idea. Everything was different. Everything had been different since she'd come to Wellsford only five months ago. It seemed a lifetime ago.

Everything was changed. She was changed.

The only problem was – she didn't know what she was changed into.

That was enough. Winsome turned her back and hurried down the path, almost running, her hair catching on her wet cheeks, her eyes blinking rain from her lashes. Or tears.

THERE WAS SOMEONE LOITERING OUTSIDE HER KITCHEN DOOR and Winsome groaned deep in her chest. Why was she never come across when she was composed, dignified? She reached up to smooth her hair and felt a leaf stuck in it. She pulled it out and went to drop it, then stopped and frowned at it, even as she kept walking reluctantly towards her own door and whoever it was awaiting her there.

They would have seen her emerging from the woods.

The leaf was bright green, and she recognised it. The five leaflets, arranged almost in a fan. How had she been walking around with this tangled in her hair and not known? For how long?

'Where'd you get that? The trees aren't in leaf yet.'

Winsome stared a moment longer at the leaf, then stuck it in her coat pocket.

'What can I do for you, Minnie?' she asked.

The girl's eyes were red-rimmed under the black mascara and liner. As though she'd been staring open-eyed into the wind. Or crying.

Winsome imagined she might look much the same, for all that. Minus the heavy eye makeup.

But wild-eyed all the same.

Minnie bit at her lip, worrying at it as she stared at the vicar. 'I'd never have said it, what I did, if I'd known it would cause you trouble,' she blurted.

'It's just,' Minnie continued, shaking her head so that her hair, with long blonde roots and black ends, slapped wet with rain against her jacket, 'it's just that I hate that woman, and she was slagging off at you and I couldn't bear it – she was saying the worst things to my Gran.' Minnie blinked and scowled. 'I couldn't let her get away with it, not when you'd helped me like you did.'

When Minnie looked back over at Winsome, her eyes shone with admiration. 'I mean like, I've never met a vicar like you. They should all be like you. You're the only reason

I let Gran drag me along to services; well, that and the fact that, you know, it makes Gran happy.'

The words tumbled from Minnie's lips and then she snapped her mouth shut and gave a miserable shrug. 'So, you see, I'm sorry, I guess is what I came here to tell you. I wouldn't have done it if I'd thought...' Another shrug. 'Well, I suppose if I'd thought, I guess, you know?'

Winsome let out a long breath of air. 'It's all right, Minnie,' she said. 'I know you weren't meaning any harm.'

'I wasn't,' Minnie said. 'I was defending you! That bitch Julia Thorpe – she thinks she's better than everyone, and she doesn't hold a candle to you and Morghan.'

'Please don't call Julia names, Minnie,' Winsome said.

Minnie shook her head and looked as though she wanted to argue the point. 'Sorry,' she mumbled, then raised her eyes in anguish to Winsome's. 'Are you really going to lose your job?' she asked.

Even though Winsome had been thinking the same thing herself, hearing it asked so boldly, put as such a black and white question, shocked her and she rocked back on her heels. When she opened her mouth to answer, she had to swallow first, her mouth suddenly dry.

'I don't know,' she said, then sighed, her shoulders sagging. 'Probably.'

Minnie shook her head fiercely. 'You oughtn't. You're an amazing vicar. No one else could have got me to come along to church. It's dead boring usually.' She blinked, then narrowed her eyes. 'And I still believe the church ought to, you know, apologise.'

Winsome was lost. 'Apologise for what?'

'Putting all those witches to death, that's what.'

The world was spinning. It was starting slowly, but Winsome could feel it moving under her feet. A slow tilting, just slight, and then a dizzying slow-motion spinning. Why were witches being mentioned again? She knew Minnie had a thing about the witch hunts, but all the same...

She looked up, lifting her face to the grey sky, imagining the web of energy that Morghan saw, imagining how it criss-crossed and wove in and out, each strand leading some-where, so many of them intersecting.

She couldn't leave Wellsford, she thought suddenly, vehemently. She could not leave Wellsford.

Not now.

Not yet.

'Anyway,' Minnie said. 'I wanted to come and say sorry, and I'll speak to whoever as well, if you need me to.'

'Whoever?' Winsome asked, dragging herself away from the insistent feeling – premonition – that things were... well...intersecting. Coming to a head. A crisis.

She wasn't the only one having a spiritual crisis, she realised with a jolt.

One was coming to the village as well.

'I don't know,' Minnie said, speaking on, oblivious to the frantic flurry of Winsome's thoughts. 'Your boss, I guess. I'll tell anyone you like, anyone I have to, that you're the most fantastic vicar. And that it ought to be perfectly okay if you get on well with the, you know, pagans.'

'I went to one of their rituals,' Winsome said faintly.

'Yeah, and what's wrong with that?'

'I participated in it,' Winsome said, knowing she shouldn't even be answering. Minnie wasn't going to under-stand the gravity of what she'd done. Minnie thought

Winsome was a better vicar for having one foot in both religions.

Winsome closed her eyes. Was that what she had? One foot in both?

Her mouth was dry again. She needed a cup of tea.

Or a big glass of wine.

She had more than a foot in each. She was bloody well playing hopscotch between them.

'I need to get inside, Minnie,' she said. 'Thank you for your apology.'

Minnie ducked her head. 'Yeah. I'd not have said anything if I knew they were going to be such pillocks about it.'

Winsome decided to accept that one without scolding the girl about her language. Or correcting her. They weren't being pillocks. For once, Winsome thought, Julia Thorpe and Mariah Reefton were actually in the right.

'And don't forget, I'll tell anyone you like that you do a really good job,' Minnie was saying. 'Ask just about anyone at church – you're real popular.' She wrinkled her nose. 'Except with that old bat and her cronies, but it's just them. Everyone else loves you.'

'Thank you, Minnie,' Winsome said. 'That means something to me.'

'Yeah, you bet. If you're made to leave, half the village is not going to be happy about it.' Minnie stared at Winsome, her eyes wide and owlish. 'More than half, likely.' She nodded. 'Anyway, I'll see you. And don't forget. I'll tell anyone you like.'

Winsome collapsed against the kitchen door, watching

Minnie walk away around the vicarage and appear a minute later down the street.

The girl needs a woolly hat, she thought, then let her own head fall back against the glass.

It had been lovely of Minnie to come apologise and offer to speak on her behalf to *whoever* but Winsome didn't think that would help any.

There was one thing though that she suspected Minnie might be right about, now that it had been said.

If she, Winsome, had to leave her position of vicar of Wellsford, there would be quite a few who wouldn't be happy.

Because what Julia and Mariah might not fully realise, was that there wouldn't be another vicar after her, to take her place.

The church would simply be shut up, the vicarage empty. A service once a month, that's what Wellsford would be lucky to get.

Led by someone who didn't live in Wellsford.

Who didn't have a relationship to the place or its people.

18

'You've got that look again,' Stephan said, thrusting his hands in his pockets and straightening his arms against the chill. The sun was a faint watery tint on the horizon and the air, even though the rain had stopped during the night, felt wet and heavy in his lungs.

'What look's that?' Erin asked, whistling for Burdock, and pulling the door closed behind them. She narrowed her eyes at Stephan in mock suspicion.

Stephan laughed, pulled his hands from his pockets, and held them palm up towards her. 'Hey,' he said, laughing. 'Don't zap the messenger boy.'

Erin's eyebrows rose. 'Zap you?' she said and shivered suddenly, all the hairs standing up on her body. 'That sounds like fun. That sounds like what we do already, when, you know...'

Stephan did know. When they wound themselves energetically around each other. He could feel her right now, the vibrancy of her, and her aura seemed sweet to him, as though dripping with honey.

Erin laughed and snapped her fingers at him. 'Come back, gorgeous,' she said. 'We don't have time for that sort of carry on.' But she vibrated a little anyway, inside her coat, and grinned at him.

'Right.' Stephan blinked, looked at her. 'It's gone now, though, that look of yours.'

She widened her eyes. 'What look was it? And this better be good, Stephan Reed. We've not been seeing each other long enough for you to know all my looks.'

Stephan sent her one of his own. He knew all her looks. He knew the way she smelt, the way she tasted, the way she felt against him, and they hadn't even touched yet. Not properly. Not since the bloody lockdown.

Still, as it turned out, there was more than one way to get to know a person. To be close to someone you loved, especially, he thought, if you'd loved them over and over and over the way he surely must have with Erin.

'Ah,' he drew himself back to the present. 'Right. You looked preoccupied. You had your preoccupied look on.'

'I have one of those?'

'It's pretty much the one I see most,' Stephan told her.

'Yeah,' Erin conceded. 'Well, it's been like that, hasn't it? Since I came here to Ash Cottage.'

'True enough,' Stephan said and Burdock, wearing his smart plaid jacket to keep himself warm, bounded up to Stephan, licked his hand in belated greeting, then went galloping back down the road.

Burdock loved the walk to work in the mornings. Everything fresh from the night when he wasn't allowed outside.

All the new trails, all the overnight comings and goings of small animals to sniff out. Every morning was pretty much the best morning ever.

And he liked going to work too, with Erin. The old humans were kind with their hands. They gave most excellent scritches.

And they always told him how handsome he looked in his coat.

Erin had bought him boots to wear when it was really cold, but he'd drawn the line at those. He couldn't figure out how to walk in them. They made him feel clumsy and slow. When Erin wasn't looking, he'd taken one of them and hidden it.

'So,' Stephan said, drawing in a big damp breath and turning his feet back towards the village, Erin falling in beside him. 'What's on your mind?' They hadn't managed to talk the night before, in their separate beds, on the phone to each other.

Erin tucked her chin down into her scarf and her hands into her pockets. She would be so glad when this physical distancing thing wasn't in place anymore and she could reach out and link her hand with Stephan's.

'You do the travelling thing, right?' she asked. 'I mean, you know – journeying to the Otherworld. Walking between the worlds. Whatever you want to call it.'

Stephan nodded. 'Yeah, but only recently. With Ambrose, when he started taking me to the cave. And then it began happening spontaneously. You know this. Why are you asking?'

Truthfully, there hadn't been so much time to dedicate to that side of things since the Grove had stepped up their work in the village since the lockdown. But he and Ambrose still went up into the hills once a week, and he still crossed over into the Otherworld, and met Bear Fellow there while Ambrose beat upon his drum.

Not that he'd figured out where it was all leading yet. Mostly, Bear Fellow was showing him how, well, how to heal people, Stephan guessed. Turned out there were lots of herbs in the Wildwood too, and Bear Fellow was pretty much systematically showing him how to use them, and when and what for. It was fascinating, if Stephan were honest, and boy did he have plans for a proper herb garden. No pesticides, or anything. Had to be organic, had to be exactly right. He hadn't found the place for it yet.

Part of him wanted to ask whether he could use the garden at Ash Cottage for it. Since it was already set up so well – Bear Fellow had been showing him how each plant embodied the spirits of the directions – and the Ash Cottage garden was already organised like that. It was kind of the obvious place, and Stephan was fairly sure that while Erin loved the garden, she didn't have any plans to be, well, hands-on with it.

'Morghan told me to start gardening,' Erin said.

'What?' Stephan stopped walking, turned to look at her. 'What?' he repeated.

Erin shrugged. 'Well, not real gardening.' She shook her head. 'Everything we do is so hard to explain, it drives me nuts.'

'Okay,' Stephan said, walking beside her again. 'Morghan wants to you start gardening, but not real gardening. Are you talking about the exercise she wants you to do?

You started telling me about that the other day, remember, and then we went off on a bit of a tangent.'

Erin laughed. 'Yeah, I remember. You freaked me out saying I'd have to live at Hawthorn House one day, and then scared the crap out of me by saying that it could be sooner than later, if Morghan does what Selena did.'

'Which Morghan will never do,' Stephan said. 'Morghan belongs here. She wouldn't even leave when Grainne did, and she was practically married to Grainne.'

Erin nodded, hoping that Stephan was right, and wishing she knew more about it all. But she was getting side-tracked again.

'Right. So,' she said. 'It's like this.' She blew out a breath between her lips. 'Okay, so I think it's like this, anyway.'

Stephan's full attention was on her.

'So, Morghan said,' Erin continued, 'that the job – like, the main job – of the Lady of the Grove, which I will one day be...' She had to stop after that bit. It just sounded so...huge.

'She really said that?' Stephan asked. 'Wow. It must have been weird, you know, hearing it put just baldly like that. Just out there plain as day.'

'You're telling me,' Erin said. 'I'm going to be the least qualified Lady of the Grove in the history of it, which as we all know, as Ambrose keeps telling us, goes back thousands of years.' She shook her head. 'That's a lot of Ladies of the Grove.'

Great. She was going to psyche herself out before she'd barely begun. She shook her head, and somewhere off in the trees she thought she heard Macha laugh.

'I wonder if Macha was ever Lady of the Grove?' she said out loud.

'Probably,' Stephan answered, not hearing anything but Erin's question and the clamour of birds in the woods lining the lane. 'Don't you think? So it won't be your first time, if that's any help.'

'Hmm.' Erin thought about it. 'I guess that helps. Kind of.'

'Anyway.' Stephan turned the conversation back to the garden. 'What are you supposed to plant in the garden? You never did get to telling me what the gardening task Morghan set you was.'

Erin shook her head. 'No, I don't need to do any real gardening, not like actually planting things, which is good really, because I've enough to learn to do without adding gardening to it. Real gardening, I mean.'

'It's going to be time to replant the empty beds in a couple weeks,' Stephan said.

'Have at it, babe,' Erin answered. 'You know that Ash Cottage's garden is really yours. You can do whatever you like to it. In fact, I wish you would, because then I can sit there and draw you while you work.' She flung him a sudden, sly smile, then just grinned widely. 'Seriously though. It's yours, you know that.'

Stephan hadn't really known that until right that moment, and his heart sang. 'Thanks,' he said. 'That's awesome. I'll start making plans.'

He already knew what they'd be.

'So, tell me,' he said. There was so much going on for them both that it was easy to get distracted. But he sensed this was important, especially if Morghan was getting Erin to do it. So he wanted to hear.

'Yeah. Where was I?' Erin thought about it for a moment, watching Burdock, nose down, zig zagging across the road in front of them. There was no traffic. There never was, not at this time of the day. Besides, hardly anyone went anywhere now.

'So, the main job of the Lady of the Grove is to walk between the worlds. To have, like a foot in each, right?'

'Right. Yeah. Sounds good.'

Erin nodded. Talking to Stephan always made things easier to understand. Having to say it out loud, hear her own thoughts, get it all straight. Or as straight as was possible, she thought.

'So, to make this job easier, Morghan says I need to have, like, a base in both worlds. A safe place, you know?' Erin frowned. 'Somewhere I can stand in both at the same time.' She blinked. 'Consciously.'

Stephan's eyebrows rose. 'At the same time?' he asked. 'Consciously?' he scratched his beard. He'd been joking when he'd told Krista he was growing it, but he'd not shaved since, and it was going through an itchy phase. 'I mean, when I go over to the Otherworld, I don't know what I'm doing in this one. Just standing there like a gormless nutter, usually. Or sitting in the cave, preferably, tucked out of sight of everyone.' He shook his head. 'I mean, I'm one place or the other, you know?'

Erin nodded. 'Yeah, well, that's the difference, I think. Morghan wants me to learn to be both places, however that works.'

'How does she say it works?'

Erin lifted her hands in a hopeless gesture. 'I've not the faintest idea. But, Morghan says to start with this gardening exercise.'

They would be in the village soon. It was taking ages to explain.

'What I'm to do,' she said, 'is to use your –' She flashed Stephan a brilliant smile. 'Your garden, because it's been designed so particularly, I guess with the directions and everything, and the well at the centre, and use it as a sort of fixed point.'

Stephan nodded.

'Right?' Erin continued. 'And to imagine another garden, same layout and everything, but an imaginary garden, and sort of stand in them both.'

'An imaginary garden?'

'Yeah.' Erin spread her hands out, waving one over the top of the other. Like one is superimposed on the other, I think. And eventually, this imaginary garden, I don't know how, becomes like a place in the Otherworld?'

'So,' Stephan said slowly, 'you kind of design a space there for yourself, to go to and from, I suppose, and because it's your particular place, a sort of still, secret place, you can be there at the same time as you're here.' He gave a low whistle. 'That's pretty brilliant when you think about it.'

Erin was glad he thought so. She wanted it to make sense to him, since she felt like she could only really grasp at the edges of its meaning, yet. 'You think so?'

'I do, yeah,' Stephan said, nodding enthusiastically. 'Have you tried it yet?' He stopped walking and turned to Erin. 'Wait,' he said, eyes wide and blue in the greyness of the morning.

'What?'

Burdock came up and sat down in front of him, ears perked as though to ask the same as Erin had. What?

But Stephan was shaking his head slowly from side to side. 'Wait,' he said. 'What if, well, what if that's why Teresa designed it that way? So it could be used like that?' He laughed. 'Like, I don't know, what's the word? Prototype?' He shook his head. 'That's not it, but something like that, anyway.'

Erin was still nowhere near asking the question she'd wanted to, that had started all this, but she was caught up by the notion as well. 'When did she design it?' she asked. 'Did she ever say why it was in that particular layout?'

Stephan pursed his lips, thinking, and rubbed at his new beard again. 'She was getting it underway when I started working for her,' he said. 'She got me to fill all the beds, actually. They were new then, and she said I had the better back for it.' He shrugged, then grinned. 'I was only sixteen and it was my first time lugging and chucking dirt around, so I don't know that she was right about that, but I got plenty fit in short order, I can tell you.'

Erin nodded, trying not to think about the muscles lurking in Stephan's slim frame. She looked away, swallowing. 'Did she tell you why she'd laid it out like that, though?'

'Only that she'd always wanted to, I think. And that it made sense to her to do it in honour of the directions.' Stephan turned and squinted back towards Ash Cottage, although it was long out of sight. 'And she said it made sense because it's the worlds in microcosm.' He frowned. 'Do you think that's it, then?'

The world in microcosm. No wonder Morghan wanted

her to use it, Erin thought, and sighed. 'Yeah,' she said. 'I think that's really it. And you know what everyone's like here about wells.' She rolled her eyes briefly. 'Which are another thing I still haven't figured out.'

Stephan grinned. 'Well, you've got to save something for later, don't you?' He looked at his watch. 'Wow,' he said. 'I've got to get a move on. I've got help coming this morning to dig the foundations for the new glasshouses.' A shadow crossed his face.

'Your father?' Erin said, and her voice was low, gentle. She knew Stephan had barely spoken to his father since he'd left home.

Stephan nodded. 'Yep. Dad's going to be there. I'm going to be giving him orders.' He winced. 'Directions,' he corrected. 'Though they'll sound to him like orders, I'm sure.' He lifted a hand and gnawed at the knuckle there before realising what he was doing and forcing his hand to drop. He'd kicked that habit years ago.

'It'll be okay,' Erin said. 'Just talk to him like he's anyone else.' She gave Stephan a smile. 'Be your normal, lovely self. Don't let him make you feel any other way. This is your project, and you should be really proud of it.'

'I am really proud of it,' Stephan said. 'I can't believe that Ambrose and Morghan have let me do it in the first place. But they have, like they knew I could.' He huffed a breath. 'And it's not like, cheap, either. They're really investing in it.'

'They're investing in you, because they know you're going to make a real difference to this village,' Erin said. 'So don't you let him get to you, and don't let him get away with anything either, you hear?' She looked at him until he met her gaze. 'Promise me?'

'I love you, Erin,' Stephan said.

The words, still new to her ears, made her grin. 'I love you too. Now go feed the village, Stephan of Bear.'

He smiled back at her, blue eyes alight. 'I wish I could kiss you, Erin of the Grove.'

'You do,' Erin answered. 'You already do.'

19

THERE WAS A PATIENT TRANSPORT SERVICES VAN OUTSIDE THE Care Home, and Erin put a restraining hand on Burdock's collar as the driver slid open the door and helped a man down onto the pavement and into the wheelchair Mary had waiting.

'Erin,' Mary said. 'You're just in time. Get your coat off and your gear on, and you can prepare Mr. Moffat's room for him.'

'I thought we weren't expecting Mr. Moffat until the day after tomorrow?' Erin looked down at the thin man in the chair. He'd turned his head to stare at her at the mention of her name, and something in his gaze made her still. She grew quiet inside, and something seemed to open up inside her, something dark, a doorway to a dark place. She blinked, licked her lips.

'Well, as you can see, that's been changed.'

Mary's words made Erin jerk her head up, breaking

whatever it was that she'd just experienced. The sudden...something.

'Erin?' Mary narrowed her eyes at the girl. Ambrose had said she didn't know anything yet.

But the girl looked as though she'd seen a ghost.

Mary shook her head slightly, not knowing exactly what she thought about this whole thing. Somehow, it seemed underhanded, and almost cruel, bringing this man to be cared for here, by the very girl whose mother he'd...well... contributed to the death of.

But, Mary decided, on the other hand, it did make sense, depending which sort of view you took. Mary wasn't part of the Grove. She preferred a solitary practice, but she was perfectly familiar with shadow work, and this seemed to her an – extreme, admittedly – extension of it.

She only hoped Erin would be up to the task.

But then, wasn't it just the way of the world to force you in the deep end, to sink or swim? Life was one trial after another, in a lot of ways, and they either strengthened you, or well, you buckled under them.

Mary decided she wouldn't let Erin buckle. Not if she could help it.

And besides, she thought, wheeling the silent Wayne Moffat through the door the ambulance man was holding open, if you could get through this one with grace and strength, then you really would make a fine leader of the Grove.

And that was not a job for pussies.

'Mr. Moffat,' she said, leaning forward slightly over the wheelchair. 'Your room's not ready yet, so how would you feel if we went to the dining room and got you a nice cup of tea? You've had a bit of a journey, I'm sure.'

Wayne Moffat nodded. 'Thanks,' he said, his voice as gravelly as only a heavy smoker's could be. 'That'd be welcome.' He paused a moment. 'Was that Erin?' he asked. 'Erin Lovelace?'

'Erin Faith,' Mary corrected. 'Her grandmother's name was Lovelace.'

For a moment, there was only the vague squeaking of the wheelchair over the carpet and Mary manoeuvred them towards the dining room.

'And her mother's,' Wayne said. 'It was her mother's name too.'

'I'M NOT SURE I UNDERSTAND,' ERIN SAID, SPREADING THE clean sheet out over the bed for the new man. 'Why's he coming here instead of Banwell? He's not a local, is he? I don't recall anyone saying he is.'

Mary pressed her lips together, at a loss as to how much she was to tell the girl. Ambrose had explained the situation, but it didn't appear that anyone had told Erin about it at all. She knew nothing. Surely, that wasn't right?

Mary wondered whether she ought to skirt around the edges of the matter. But it would come to light sooner or later, would it not? Sooner, most likely.

And wasn't that the whole point of it?

She took a breath. 'He's not local,' she agreed. 'But he does have a connection to the village, and when a place was offered to him here because of it, he accepted.' She tucked in a corner of the sheet, helping without even thinking about it.

'What's the connection?' Erin asked, then frowned, reaching for the second sheet. 'And who offered him a place? It doesn't sound like it was you?'

The girl asked too many questions. She should have been told already. Mary had understood that she would be ready. Why wasn't that the case? It couldn't remain a secret.

'Morghan offered him the place,' she said, unable to help the sigh that came with the words.

'Morghan?'

'Yes,' Mary said. 'It's my understanding that she helped him when he was at the Banwell Home for some respite care, and when she learned who he was, she offered him a place here for when he needed it. He has no family, I believe. Or they're in Australia, or something, and he's estranged from them.' Was she saying too much? Too little?

Really, the situation she was being put in was unacceptable.

'Oh,' Erin said. 'I guess that makes sense. What's his link to Wellsford, then?'

Mary bent down to smooth the sheet, and tucked it in. 'Right,' she said. 'When you've done that, will you help Mr. Moffat into the bed and make sure he's comfortable?'

'Of course,' Erin said. 'But you've not answered my question.'

And Mary didn't want to, either. 'You can ask Morghan herself if you're wanting any more information. I'm sure it's not my place to say anything further.' She nodded, emphatically, and spun on her heel, striding from the room, and muttering at herself in her head.

She'd handled that one poorly.

But honestly. Why hadn't they prepared the girl?

Erin stared out the door after Mary, wide-eyed and astonished. What had she said wrong, she wondered? She'd only asked the obvious questions.

Maybe Mary had known the man once. Or something. Erin frowned. But Mary wasn't from Wellsford. Mary was from somewhere in Scotland, wasn't she? Nowhere near here.

She picked up the pillow and plumped it before looking around for the pillowcase and stuffing it inside without thinking about it.

Something was going on, but she didn't know what. Erin's brow wrinkled as she shook her head. And what had been that weird feeling that had come over her when she'd looked at Wayne Moffat?

Or rather, when he'd looked at her.

She'd felt like she was falling.

She stuck the pillow on the bed, turned the covers down and stood up, drawing in a deep breath. It was time to bring the man himself in. The man of the hour. The mystery man.

The man with some sort of connection to Wellsford.

That could be anything, she told herself, smoothing her hands down over her uniform before drawing out another pair of gloves and popping them on. Her palms were sweating, and the gloves stuck to her. She wrestled with them for a moment, then drew in a deep breath, shook her head, and made for the dining room.

'Mr. Moffat,' she said, making sure her voice was cheery. 'Oh, I see Burdock has introduced himself. I hope he hasn't been making a great nuisance of himself. He does like to hoover any and all crumbs that come his way.'

Wayne turned his head and looked at the young thing walking towards him. With a sudden clamping certainty, he knew he oughtn't be here. Didn't want to be here.

And look at the girl, he thought. There was no way she was going to want to pay him the time of day when she knew who he was. What he'd done. Wayne ducked his head down and stared at the carpet. The dog had wriggled under the table and stared up at him hopefully. Damned big beast it was too. He missed his dog. But Bullet had passed away years ago and now it was just himself left. His sad old carcass still walking around like it had life in it.

He shook his head. 'I want to go home,' he said, the cup still in his hand. 'I've decided,' he said. 'I don't want to stay here.'

Erin rounded the chair and sat down at the table, looking curiously at the man from behind her smile. 'It's all arranged, Mr. Moffat,' she said. 'I've just made up your bed, the pillows are all plumped for you, and you'll be comfortable, I promise.' She blinked and went on quickly, pushing aside the vision of emptiness that yawned in the background of her mind. 'There aren't many here right now,' she said. 'Only Mrs. Sharp, and Mrs. Ruston. We could do with some more company.'

But Wayne was shaking his head. 'No,' he said. 'I've changed my mind. I don't want to be here.'

Erin stared at him without answering. Her fine brows inched downwards. 'What is it?' she asked, and there was that door again, and blackness behind it.

But this man couldn't have anything to do with her dreams, could he? Why would he?

Who was he, anyway?

'Who are you, Mr. Moffat?' she asked, barely knowing the question was on her lips, her head tilted softly to the side. Burdock came scrambling out from under the table and sat beside her, watching her with cautious eyes. She wasn't going to go wandering off again, was she? She hadn't done that for ages, no dreams that smelt of cold water. It had been good.

Wayne flung his head about, looking around the room, but there was no one else. Just this girl who looked too much like her grandmother. Not like her mum, except maybe a bit around her eyes.

And it was her eyes that were bothering him. There was something in the way she was looking at him.

'They haven't told you, have they?' he rasped.

Erin felt the blood drain from her face. So, there was something going on here. She wanted to stand up, suddenly, walk out of the room. She should do it; she should just get up and walk out of the room; every nerve in her body told her to. But the muscles weren't getting the message. They stayed put, kept her sitting there, staring at the man.

'Told me what?' she asked, and it might have been her imagination, but the words sounded as though they came from her mouth in slow motion. She shook her head, and that movement was slow as well. 'Nobody has told me anything,' she said. Then again, 'told me what?'

Wayne licked his lips, his tongue still wet with tea. He sniffed, put the cup down. 'I'm tired,' he said. He was too, he wasn't lying about it, but this had all been a bad idea. He'd let that woman, that Morghan woman talk him into this. Her and the vicar, both. They'd said it would be a good idea. He could make amends, they said, like this was just another twelve-step programme.

Well, it wasn't that. It was a two-step programme. Tell this chit of a girl the truth and let her hate him. No making amends. And she would hate him, he could see that. It wasn't like they'd said to him.

Wayne stared down at the table, forehead creased, confused. He deserved to be hated. Hadn't he been doing a good job of hating himself all these years – why not let her have a go as well. He glanced sideways at her and she was still staring at him, white-faced and wide-eyed like he'd already told her. It confused him more.

'Who I am,' he said at last, picking up the thread of their conversation. 'I knew your mum.'

There. It was said now. He couldn't take it back. It was like he was on a train and it was heading for the station no matter what, and taking him along with it, because if he jumped off, he'd still have to get to the station somehow, wouldn't he?

He didn't really know what he meant, by thinking all this. But it was too late, he'd told her now. Maybe he did want to cling to the slight chance that she'd forgive him. Maybe he did, at that.

And if she didn't – well, it was only what he deserved, wasn't it?

'You knew my mum?' Erin asked. 'You knew Rebecca?'

'Becca, yeah.' Wayne sniffed. 'I was her boyfriend.' He scratched a spot on his face with a dirty nail. 'When she died, right?'

White shock filled Erin's head like noise. She slapped a palm down on the table as though to steady herself and Burdock thrust his nose onto her lap, whining under his breath.

And behind the shock loomed a door and behind the door grew the darkness and now Erin knew what the darkness was.

It was the darkness of the basement where her mother lay at the bottom of the stairs, her head staved in from the fall.

She shook her head, wordlessly. Just shook it back and forth, one side to the other.

'No,' she said at last. 'No, you can't be him.'

But the last of Wayne's strength had drained from him with the confession. It had been a long morning, dragging himself from bed early to be ready to meet the fella from the patient travel service. His bag packed, not that he had much of anything. It was all much of nothing, really. Just a few bits and pieces. Clothes, mostly, a pair of pyjamas. Nothing else. He'd not managed to keep much of anything else.

He opened his mouth, but no words came out, and he slumped over in his chair. He still wanted to leave, but there was nowhere else for him to go. He'd never go back to his room at the boarding house again. They'd be stripping his dirty old sheets right now and chucking them out. They wouldn't let him back.

He was here to stay. Till the end, whatever that brought.

There was a bumping outside the room and Mrs. Sharpe came hobbling her way slowly into the dining room.

'Is there a fresh pot on, Erin?' she asked, then peered

over at the table. 'Goodness, is this our new inmate? He looks a bit done in, dear.'

Erin jumped up from her chair, knocking it backwards. 'Yes, um, of course. This is Mr. Moffat, Mrs. Sharpe, and I'm about to take him to his room.' She swallowed, sucked in a breath, blew it out. Autopilot, she thought. Just do this bit on autopilot.

Pretend everything is all right, she thought.

But it wasn't and she couldn't.

Another deep breath, Mrs. Sharpe frowning at her, and Erin straightened, tried to pull herself together. For a fleeting moment, she saw herself standing in her imaginary garden, and it almost helped, until she realised that it ran too wild and overgrown to offer her any strength.

'Okay,' she said. 'Mr. Moffat, I'm going to take you to your room now, get you comfortable.' She blinked, her voice coming to her own ears as though from far away. 'You can have a rest; I'm sure you need it after your busy morning.'

It was true. The man was sinking sideways over the armrests of the chair even as she spoke. He was done in. She tried to remember what Mary had told her he was dying from. Hadn't it been cirrhosis of the liver? An alcoholic, then.

That didn't help much. Had he been drinking with her mother the night she'd died? She'd thought a while back that it would be good to meet this man, that he'd be able to fill in bits of her history – but it wasn't like that, after all. All she could think was that he'd been there when Becca had died. He was part of all that and whatever he had to say, it wouldn't be good. Wouldn't be anything she wanted to know.

'Erin, love?' Mrs. Sharpe asked, stopped in the middle of the room staring at her. 'Are you all right? You've gone all pasty.'

Erin nodded quickly. 'I'm fine, thank you Mrs. Sharpe.'

Tilda Sharpe nodded dubiously. If the girl said so, but she didn't really believe her. 'You don't need me to fetch Mary?'

'No,' Erin said, stalking around to the back of Wayne Moffat's wheelchair on legs made of wood. She grasped the chair with hands that were slick in their gloves. 'Okay then, Mr. Moffat,' she made herself say, her ears still ringing with shock so that she could barely hear herself speak. 'Just a minute more and you can have that rest.'

Wayne grunted. 'I don't have anywhere else to go,' he said, the words slurred with fatigue. He worked his mouth, stirring his tongue. 'I didn't mean to,' he said.

Mean to what? Erin pushed the wheelchair carefully past Mrs. Sharpe and through the doorway. Wayne Moffat was going into Bernie's old room, and wasn't that just a joke, she thought, alarmed to feel hot tears at the corners of her eyes. She wiped them away with her wrist.

Didn't mean to what? She shook her head. Why was this man here?

Wayne Moffat's duffel bag waited on the end of the bed, and Erin unzipped it, rooting through it and pulling out the pair of pyjamas.

'One more minute, Mr. Moffat,' she said, 'and we'll get these pyjamas on you, then you can rest until lunchtime. You'll get a nice lunch here.' She was babbling, but she didn't care.

'We grow all the vegetables right here in the village,' she

said, thinking of Stephan. It was good, thinking of Stephan. It calmed her hands a bit so that they didn't shake so badly as she helped Wayne Moffat – her mother's boyfriend! – unzip his jacket and get his pyjama shirt on.

'And the meat is local too,' she said, blowing short breaths through pursed lips to keep herself calm. 'All ethically butchered.' Her head swam and she blinked rapidly, bending down to help get the man's shoes off.

'Wellsford is a wonderful place,' she said.

'How did you come back here?'

It was the first time Wayne had spoken since they'd left the table. He sat on the side of the bed and scrabbled at his belt. 'I can do this bit,' he said.

Erin nodded, and turned away, moving the chair to the door. She wiped cold sweat from her forehead.

'My grandmother,' she said. She was hot. It was too warm in here. She needed to step outside for a minute. 'I inherited her cottage after she died.'

'And you stayed?'

There was a hint of incredulity to his voice that had her spinning around to face him. He was drawing his pyjama bottoms over his bony rump.

'Why wouldn't I?' she asked, and closed her eyes for a moment, before stepping forward to help him swing his legs into the bed and drawing the covers up.

He stared at her, his head on the pillow.

She didn't think he was going to say anything else, but then he did.

'Found you a good family though, we did. Rich they were, and all.' He licked his lips. 'Better than here.'

It took a moment for Erin to find her voice. 'You were with Rebecca when she gave me up?'

'Adopted you out, that's right,' Wayne said. The bed was comfortable. It was a relief to be lying down. He looked at the girl. 'She gave you the best start she could. It was better than you staying with us.'

'Why?'

The question was out of Erin's mouth before she could stop herself.

Wayne Moffat laughed, a deep, grating sound like cement in a mixer, then closed his eyes.

'You were better off, love,' he said. 'Better off away from us.'

He lifted a limp hand from the covers, flapped it at her, then dropped it to the blanket and closed his eyes, sleep drawing him down into darkness.

20

ERIN STARED AT HER PHONE, THEN SHOVED IT BACK INTO HER pocket with a sigh. Just when she needed to see him, she thought, Stephan couldn't get away.

He was busy with the glasshouse. She pulled the door of the care home shut behind her and stood on the footpath, staring blindly out at the village. Burdock gazed up at her, wondering why they weren't doing something about lunch?

It was only a half day at work for Erin, but she wasn't ready to go home. Not that there was anywhere else to go. Everything was still shut. Except for the church, she thought, her gaze drifting that way. Winsome didn't lock the church during the day; it was open for anyone to step in, slide into a pew, ask god for help.

Except she wasn't Christian, was she? So that was out. What was she supposed to do instead? Who was she supposed to ask?

The conflict inside her was making her stomach hurt. On the one hand, she wanted to go storming up to see

Morghan, ask her what the hell she was thinking springing this on her.

On the other hand, she just wanted to sit down on the kerb and cry like a child.

'Erin?'

It was Krista, and Erin gave her a wobbly smile.

'Are you okay?' Krista asked, peering down into Erin's face. 'You're a bit pale.'

Erin laughed, but there was no humour in it. 'I don't know,' she said.

Krista nodded. 'Do you want to walk?'

There wasn't anything else to do. Erin nodded dumbly and fell into step beside Krista.

'What's happened?' Krista asked, when it became obvious that Erin wasn't going to say anything. 'Good grief, nothing's happened between you and Stephan, has it?'

Erin shook her head. 'No. Nothing like that.' She lapsed into silence again.

They kept walking. Erin frowned.

'You know,' she said, 'Part of me, I've just realised, has always wondered about the way my mother died.'

Krista's eyebrows shot up. Whatever she'd been expecting, it hadn't been this. 'What about it?' she asked.

Erin dug her fingernails into the fleshy palms of her hands.

Burdock walked beside her, head down, unsettled by her mood.

'Tell me,' Erin said. 'When you get up in the night – or anytime it's dark, really – to go to the loo, do you turn the light on before you go into the room, or afterwards?'

'Isn't that how your mother died? Something about opening the wrong door?'

Erin nodded. 'She was going to the loo, apparently, and she wasn't really familiar with the house, and she opened the wrong door.' She paused a moment and shook her head. 'Instead of the bathroom door, she opened the door to the basement, and stepped in and fell down the stairs.'

Krista was silent. They walked another few steps before she answered.

'I always turn the light on before even going in the room.'

'Yeah,' Erin said. 'Me too.' She rolled her head from side to side, her shoulders tense. 'Every single time, unless I'm not going to turn the light on at all, and that would only be because the moon was out, and I could see anyway.'

Krista shrugged deeper into her coat, suddenly shivering. 'It's odd,' she said. 'She was still alive though, wasn't she?'

'Yeah. She died later, at the hospital when they were operating on her.'

The more Krista thought about it, the weirder it was. 'So an ambulance was called?' she asked.

'I guess so,' Erin replied.

'What about police? Wouldn't they come out too, in a situation like that?'

'I don't know.' Erin frowned. 'Is there any way to find out?' She shook her head suddenly, hair flying. 'Bernie knew. Oh my god, he knew, and that's what he wouldn't tell me.'

'Bernie?'

'Bernie Roberts – he was at the care home until just a little while ago when he passed away,' Erin said. 'I really liked him. He knew my mum, and my grandmother, and he was a policeman, see? It was him who had to tell Teresa when my mother died. So he would have known all about it.'

'I guess it was officially an accident, then,' Krista said.

'Yeah, I suppose so. Only I think Bernie thought there was something odd about it too – he always stopped talking about it after a certain point, as though he didn't want to upset me, with you know, speculating, or something. I always wondered why, but he'd never say.'

'Was anyone else with her when she died? With your mum, I mean?' Krista looked down at the road. She'd have to get back to the shop in a minute, she had things on the go there. But at least there was colour back in Erin's cheeks now.

Erin nodded slowly. 'Oh yeah,' she said. 'There definitely was.' She lifted her head, saw that she was almost to the road up to Ash Cottage and pulled a smile onto her face. 'Thanks, Krista, I'd better get home and on with stuff.' She gazed out at the trees for a moment, thought about the path through them up to Hawthorn House. 'Thanks for answering my question though.'

'Okay,' Krista said. 'Are you going to be all right?'

Erin nodded. 'I'll see you later.'

As much as she really liked Krista, Erin was glad to be on her own. She needed to think.

It had been such a shock, meeting Wayne Moffat like

that. She wrinkled her nose in distaste. He'd obviously wasted his life, to end up how he was.

Maybe that was good, she thought. Maybe he deserved that.

Because maybe her mother's death hadn't been an accident at all. Maybe she'd been murdered – wasn't it usually murder when someone fell down the stairs and hit their head? Did the police even check that she'd hit her head on the stairs, and not been bashed by someone?

By Wayne Moffat?

And hadn't Wayne himself said that Erin had been better off without them? Without her mother and him?

She stopped walking abruptly and stood in the middle of the lane, arms straight, hands in fists. She wanted to scream.

Everything – everything about this was wrong!

And why was Wayne Moffat at the care home? Where she worked? Where she was going to have to help him eat and drink and go to the toilet, for crying out loud? It was obscene. She'd gone to ask Mary that very question, only Mary hadn't been there, and Pauline, the nurse, didn't know anything.

Even if he hadn't killed Rebecca, he'd been there when she'd sold little baby Erin to the highest bidder.

Instead of giving her to her grandmother. So she could have grown up in Wellsford and Wilde Grove like she was supposed to have.

He and her mother, laughing as they counted their cash, thinking about how much booze they could buy. Because booze was better than a daughter.

Then having the temerity to tell her to her face that

she'd been better off without them. Well, he was right there; they were losers.

It was like a sticky web, all the thoughts circling around her. Catching her in their threads, tying her up and the more that she struggled against all the thoughts going round and round in her head, the tighter they bound her.

Burdock stared at her. Why were they standing in the middle of the lane? 'Woof,' he said, wanting to go home. It was going to rain again. He could smell it on the air. There'd be a nice warm fire at home. They should go there. Be warm and happy. He could sit on his cushion by the fire, and she could sit in the chair she liked and play with the sticks and the paper. Make the squiggles.

He pushed his nose at her, relieved when she turned and walked down the road with him again.

'Sorry, Burdock,' Erin said, shoving her hands back deep into her pockets and shaking her head. She strode down the lane, dog at her side, head tucked down, an ugly scowl like a gash across her forehead.

Every now and then, she shook her head and wanted to scream.

THE RAVEN WAS THERE, BY THE FRONT DOOR WHEN SHE GOT home, but she ignored him, fumbling with her key, scraping it across the lock before fitting it in and twisting it. She shoved the door open, let herself and the dog in, then flung it closed, dropping her bag on the table to stand in the middle of the kitchen looking around.

Still shaking her head.

What was she going to do?

Well, she knew what she wasn't going to do. She wasn't going back to the bloody care home, for starters. She wasn't going to help that man get dressed, or make cups of tea for him, or listen to him bleat about how they'd done her a favour giving her away to some nice rich family that wasn't her own.

She wasn't going to do any of those things. The care home didn't need her. Mr. Wayne bloody Moffat could go to hell.

Erin pressed her lips together. Stared at Burdock staring at her, his tail down, a worried look on his face.

And Morghan Wilde. What about her? Erin's fingers were white with tension, curled into a fist, the nails biting into her palms.

What right did Morghan have arranging things like this? Like some master manipulator of other people's lives? What did she think she was playing at? Erin wasn't some little chess piece to be moved about on some mighty board of Morghan's design.

Erin pushed her hands through her hair, grabbed twin handfuls and tugged.

'That's it,' she said out loud. 'That's it. I've had enough.' She shook her head, hands still knotted in her hair. 'I'm not doing this anymore.'

She dropped her arms, looked over at her bag, thinking about getting out her car keys and just getting out of there. Driving.

Maybe even going back home. Her parents might have adopted her, but at least they wanted her, didn't they?

She laughed. What a joke. She didn't have her car keys.

'Because I had my car taken away from me, like I was

being a naughty little girl,' she said, spitting out the words.

Burdock turned and slunk away to sit on his cushion by the cold fire.

Erin stalked into the kitchen and picked up the kettle, slammed it under the tap and twisted water into it.

'I'm trapped here,' she said, disbelief colouring her voice through with bitterness. 'Just trapped.' She shrugged, turned the tap off and dropped the kettle onto the cooker. Picked up the poker, opened the woodbox and dug it around in the embers.

'Trapped,' she repeated. 'No way to leave.' Not unless she rang her parents.

She dumped some wood into the box, listened to it hiss and spit. 'Imagine how that would go,' she said, knowing she was talking to the empty room and not caring.

'Finally come to your senses!' She mimicked her mother's voice.

Yeah. Well, maybe that was better than staying somewhere where you had to change the trousers of the man who helped your birth mother sell you off, and then who, from any direction you cared to look, probably killed her after that sordid little job was done.

Erin slammed the woodbox door shut, then went like a whirlwind across the tiny kitchen to pick up a mug. She held it for a moment, staring down at herself and realising she was still in her uniform.

'Argh!' she yelled, and she dropped the mug back on the kitchen bench and made for the stairs, pulling off her coat and scratching at the uniform under it.

She dropped the blouse at the top of the stairs, shimmied out of the trousers as she stumbled down the short hallway to the spare room and left them in the doorway. A moment later, not noticing she was shivering from the sudden cold, Erin wrenched open the wardrobe door and pulled out her suitcase to fling it on the bed.

Her mind a red blur of anger, she ripped open the zip and pulled out an armful of her old clothes, letting them drop onto the spare bed before pawing through them. She pounced on a pair of jeans, still stiff and new despite being bought months ago, and dragged them on. Buttoned them up. Rifled through the clothes for something to wear up top, found a Burberry jumper and shoved her arms into it, tugging it on.

Standing up, Erin turned and pushed all the clothes back into the suitcase, then closed the lid.

She spied a pair of her old boots and leapt upon them, pulling them on.

There. She was dressed. Like her old self again. Before she'd come to Ash Cottage.

Before she'd even known Wellsford was a place.

Well before she'd known anything about Wilde Grove.

She sucked in a breath and caught sight of herself in the wardrobe mirror, stopped to stare.

It was like looking at someone she no longer recognised. How long had it been since she'd worn a simple pair of jeans?

Wow, Erin thought. She'd really been sucked in. Wandering around like a fool in linen and woollen dresses like it was the Middle Ages again and she was some sort of fairy princess. Didn't matter if they were comfortable and warm. She'd been sucked in all right.

Caught, hook line and sinker.

21

BLYTHE LEFT THE HOUSE UNDER COVER OF THE SHADOWED
dawn. Tomas had told her not to go, to do her work here in
the house, where it was safest, but she couldn't bear that.
How could she raise her hands to the trees, to the sky, when
she was under a low roof in a house that stank of guttering
fires and whatever Cecily was making in the kitchen?

She couldn't take it seriously, despite the looks she'd
seen in the eyes of those who had stood there on the church
lawn and bid her take care and the dark premonition she'd
felt at the sight of them. What would they do to her?

Blythe shook her head. They would do nothing. They
wouldn't dare. The Wilde's weren't overly powerful in the
district – it didn't pay to draw too much attention, that
wasn't their way – but they had one of the bigger houses
and more land than many, even if much of it was wooded.
Tomas kept a tight fist on the finances, so that most didn't
know all their security, but even so.

Tomas was careful to work their land himself. He acted

not as a lord, but as a tiller of his own fields. A farmer, prosperous for certain, but a farmer, nonetheless. Without sons to work beside him, he had to employ help but that just brought them pity for her childlessness, nothing more, and men were always glad of extra work.

The first birds woke with the rising sun and opened their throats. Blythe ducked under the trees and gave a whistle, low and clear. She stood waiting, then, when she heard the answering call, she straightened and carried on to the stream that wound its way deep in the woods, between the roots of the oldest trees.

No one came here to these woods. They had a reputation of being shadowed. Unwelcoming. Perhaps spirits wandered between the trees, half-seen forms. The villagers of Wellsford muttered of the faerie, lurking there to steal the unwary away.

All of which meant that Blythe could walk between the trees unaccosted. Particularly at this hour when the day was neither begun nor the night done. She paused on the path and closed her eyes, reaching with her fingers to feel the charm she'd spun in the air, to keep strangers away from Wilde Grove land.

It was still intact, and she reached out with her spirit to strengthen it, using her will and her own energy to make it shine, setting into it the vision of all being repelled who came this way, suddenly uncomfortable, itchy to get back to their own homes, out of these woods.

Blythe turned and took a different path, satisfied that her wards held strong. A silent stirring of the air had her looking upwards and she smiled, holding out her arm.

The owl landed upon her outstretched sleeve, tucking her wings to its side, and smoothing her tawny feathers.

'Have you had a good night's hunt?' Blythe asked the bird quietly, stroking her feathers. The owl blinked at her then swivelled its head to look along the path.

Blythe brought the tawny owl to her lips and dropped a kiss upon the feathers of her head. 'Away with you to your bed,' she said, and smiled when the bird launched herself from her arm and was gone in seconds on her silent wings.

The stream could be heard before it was seen and Blythe took a deep breath of the cool dawn air, calming her mind. She reached out and touched the mossy side of an oak, smiling at its serious wood and sap conversation.

'Leah?' she said, arriving at stream's edge.

'I'm here,' the girl replied, stepping out from between the trees.

'Good,' Blythe said, nodding at the sixteen-year-old. 'We've much to discuss, but first – shall we greet the day?'

Leah glanced around her, a frown upon her features.

'What is it?' Blythe asked. 'The wards were strong where I passed them. Were they not along your pathway?'

'They seemed untouched,' Leah said. 'But I've heard talk, after what happened at the church on Sunday.'

Blythe shook her head. 'That,' she said. 'It was a farce, all of it. I choked, and no one came to my aid.' She closed her eyes for a moment, not wanting to admit that the event had unsettled her. 'Still,' she said. 'We'd best hurry things along, I think.'

That word came into her ears again. Hissed at her. *Witch.*

Leah stared at her, face pale. Blythe didn't like the look of her. 'Is it something to take seriously, do you believe?'

'You know how it is in the village,' Leah said. 'Word takes flight like it has wings. From one mouth to the next.' She shook her head. 'And since Agnes's baby.'

'I tried to help that baby like I've done so before with others,' Blythe said, furious at the turn of matters. 'Like I did my very own.' She peered with the first glimmers of the rising sun through the trees and examined Leah. 'Aye,' she said, straightening. 'You think there is cause to be concerned.'

It was a statement, not a question, but Leah answered anyway.

'I think you can't be too careful at the moment.' Her light brown eyes moved around the streambank. 'You will be followed, I think. If not this day, then soon. We ought not to come out here for this purpose.'

'I will not hide my face from the Goddess,' Blythe hissed, suddenly furious with a mixture of fear and desperation. 'I will not turn from the trees and the sky and the ground beneath my feet.'

Leah shrank back, but she said nothing.

Blythe took a deep breath and looked out over the stream where the sun was touching it in isolated spots that turned the burbling water to diamonds.

'How am I supposed to continue to teach you if we cannot come out here to do what is necessary?' she asked, her jaw locked.

'I should move in,' Leah said, her voice barely more than a whisper over the noise of the stream. 'We should bring that forward. My mother will miss me, but not so much that she won't be glad of one mouth less to feed, and a share of my wages.'

Blythe nodded, then held up a hand for the girl to be silent. She tipped her head back and listened, closing her eyes, the better to hear with her ears and her spirit.

Birds.

Her owl tucking herself into her nest, great eyes closing against the rising sun.

A vole in the undergrowth.

Something larger, the footsteps of a deer.

For a moment, the shade of something else, someone. But it was just a glimmer, a shimmer, and Blythe looked upon it for a moment, then dismissed it as one of the faerie. The boundaries between the worlds were thin here.

It was part of her job to keep it that way.

But there was no person. No human. No one from Wells-ford ducking their head under the branches, sneaking where they ought not.

Not today, at least.

She nodded again, then spoke to Leah. 'Let us greet the day then. The sun strengthens, and we will shortly be easily seen.' A sigh, unsettled. 'Should someone desire to look.'

Leah nodded, slipping off her shoes. She took a deep breath and held it, let it out slowly, but she couldn't relax. It was three days since Sunday, and the rumours were flying. A fleeting presentiment settled a moment upon her, and she shivered under it rather than from the chill of the stream water about her ankles.

Things would not go well.

And another thought on top of that one.

Had she learnt enough?

Not nearly enough, she knew, as she closed her eyes and set the world to spinning around her.

MORGHAN STOOD, THE WATER OF THE STREAM AROUND HER ankles, the skirts of her tunic hiked up in her belt, free of the water flow. She took a breath of air that tasted of water, of memory, and forced her eyes open, forced herself back to her own time.

Here was the truth: she travelled so easily now. As though unlatched from any particular life, any particular time. She'd become so adept at stepping from one world to another that...

That what?

She shook her head, her long hair draped over her shoulders. That wasn't it. She'd always been adept at walking between the worlds. Stepping from here to there. From the woods of Wilde Grove into the Wildwood of the Otherworld.

This was different, this slipping and sliding. This was more than before.

Morghan lifted her hands and the sun, puny in the sky as it was, caught her golden hand in the light. This was what had been done to her, that day in the realm of the Fae Queen, in that small stone temple, a knife across her wrist, a new hand. One that shone in the light.

'Follow the pincushion,' she murmured, and a slight smile twisted her lips at the memory of Ambrose's story. What had the words been?

'I will give you a pin cushion to guide you. This you

must throw in front of you and follow whithersoever it goes.'

It made as much sense as anything, she supposed, and looked again at the golden hand glowing from her right arm. It felt no different, and she knew it looked no different for those looking with ordinary sight, but in her eyes, it glowed and gleamed, even as she flexed fingers that felt flesh and blood.

Her mind loose and flexible, she let it muse and wander. Ravenna had shown her the past destruction of the Grove. Morghan flicked her gaze up at the trees, seeing them as they had been that dreadful day, their limbs burning in a great conflagration. She heard, for a brief moment, the echoes of their screams.

And now there was Blythe Wilde, once Lady of the Grove – for too short a time.

Morghan looked down at her feet, bare beneath the clear, eddying water, conscious that she stood in almost the exact place that the other woman had done, four hundred years ago in the past.

Where she herself had stood, all those centuries ago, when she was Blythe.

Difficult times, she thought. Difficult times were upon Wellsford. The balance, always delicate, was disrupted.

Blythe Wilde, Morghan thought once more. The Lady of the Grove who had not made it past her death.

Morghan tipped her head forward and took a breath, knowing what was to come over the next few days or weeks. Knowing how much the coming would cost her.

Still. Was that not her purpose? To keep the way? To

maintain the balance? To be unafraid of death, even of pain?

She straightened again.

'Blessed stream through sacred land,' she murmured into the cool air. 'You have tumbled down through these woods and these hills for hundreds of years. You have heard the prayers of my ancestors and my sisters and brothers. You have born witness to conversations and kept secrets. I honour your long memory and your song.'

She raised her face to the sky, and inhaled deeply, thinking of Blythe, who once stood on this very spot, and what must come next, for them both. Morghan let go of the breath she held and stepped a foot into the Otherworld, seeking that place there that was hers, that was home to her, that soothed her.

So, she stood in water there too, her feet on the stony shore of a lake, trees crowding around the beachline to dip their rooted toes into the clear water. She looked down at her feet under the water, and turned, stepped dripping into the loosely wooded clearing behind her. This was her place. Her place where she could breathe and be, from which she could step back and forth, which she could conjure with the merest thought, and walk through any part of her day both there and in the physical world.

The air was scented not with the woods that grew around Wilde Grove, with their oaks and birch, but with the clean astringent freshness of pine. Morghan walked up the short slope from the lake with its tiny island out from the shore and stepped into the coolness of the trees.

She hadn't come here often the last few years, and she stopped on the soft and familiar ground to look around. All was just the same, just as she'd left it, just as it always was. Something stirred in the trees, a movement in their shadows and Morghan's breath caught.

'Amara?' she said, her voice barely a whisper.

Movement again, and a golden mountain lion padded out of the trees and over to her. Morghan dropped to her knees and reached for the cat, and then the cat's head was on her shoulder, heavy and warm, and the big cat was twisting around, almost sitting in her lap.

'Amara,' Morghan repeated, and there was that catch again in her throat, even as her heart pounded. 'How I've missed you.'

The cat climbed from her and stared instead at her with her eyes of flecked amber.

Morghan bowed her head. 'I know,' she said. 'I will come more often.'

She didn't know how it worked; indeed, Morghan often reflected upon how little she knew about how much of it worked, but here, in this place, she could still find Amara, the cat that had walked lifetimes with Grainne.

Grainne herself was not to be found in this light-dappled clearing where the breeze smelt of conifer trees and far-off snow. Morghan had used to bring her here some-times, when the nights were too hard and too long for her, when all the hurt Grainne had been through as a child had threatened to catch her up and overwhelm her. Morghan had brought her here too, shards of her retrieved, to heal, to sleep, curled up in nests lined with soft feathers, to rest and grow strong again.

But she'd not come here so often herself since Grainne had embarked on her long voyage from this life to the next.

Loss, even with the knowledge it was neither total nor permanent, was still difficult, and here Morghan felt her heart ache all the stronger for the one she'd loved through so many lifetimes.

She stood up, brushing needles and mulch from her clothes, and nodded. It would be good to come here again, to draw strength for what she knew she would soon be going through.

And likely, she'd need somewhere to bring Blythe, when it was time.

The cat gazed at her, then yawned and turned, wandering off amongst the trees, flicking her long tail, and Morghan drew breath, braced herself, and stepped back into Wilde Grove again.

In the water of the stream, Morghan knelt down, feeling the cold shock of water around her knees, soaking her almost to her thighs. She dipped her hands in the stream, scooped up a palmful of water and let it run down over her face.

'I hold myself in bond to you, water, earth, sky,' she said. 'I walk in balance between you, world to world to world.'

Bowing her head, Morghan listened a moment, hearing whispered voices from the past in the song of the stream, hearing one word repeated over and over.

Witch, the stream hissed. *Witch.*

Morghan took a deep breath, held it, let it out. 'By sky and root, through all worlds,' she said, paying attention to the familiar words so that she was sure of them, not saying them merely by rote.

'From each birth to each death, my life dedicated, my service offered.'

22

Erin came clattering down the stairs and stopped dead at the bottom to stare at the raven. It perched on the back of one of the kitchen chairs and stared unblinkingly at Erin.

'How did you get in?' Erin asked slowly, taking her gaze reluctantly from the bird to scan the room quickly. None of the windows were open, were they? Of course not, she was only just home, and they would have been closed when she left. She swivelled back to look at the bird.

'What do you want?'

The bird sat and looked at her.

Over on his cushion, Burdock whimpered. He didn't mind so much when the birds stayed outside in the trees like birds were supposed to. But he wasn't so happy when they came inside and sat around looking at his stuff in his home. There was a biscuit still in his bowl, left over from breakfast, and Burdock thought about it warily – the bird wasn't going to steal it, was it? He didn't trust it one bit, no matter that it smelt of wind and trees and magic.

'This is absurd,' Erin whispered, still standing at the bottom of the stairs, still eying the bird. 'You can't keep me a prisoner here.'

The raven lifted his wings and spread them wide for a moment, beating them against the still air of the kitchen before tucking them back against his sides, the feathers smoothing.

'You can't.'

Burdock whimpered and Erin glanced over at him. He sat on his cushion looking nervous and miserable.

'It's all right, Burdock,' Erin said, making an effort to sound convincing for the dog.

But that was something she hadn't thought about, wasn't it? What to do with Burdock if she really did plan to go running off and leaving all this behind. Her mother certainly wouldn't welcome him, if she was thinking of going back there.

'What am I thinking?' she asked, speaking to herself. She shook her head. 'I can't leave.'

There was Burdock.

There was Stephan.

There were all the things she loved about Ash Cottage, Wellsford.

Wilde Grove.

There was everything she'd been working for. Kria – if she left now, what would that all have been for?

The bird stared at her and she peered back at him. How had he gotten in the house?

Erin edged around the table and the chair with the bird on it, making for the front door. She opened it and held it open.

'There you go,' she said. 'Outside.'

Burdock got up from his bed and slunk reluctantly out the door, head down, tail tucked between his legs.

'Burdock,' Erin called. 'Not you,' she said. 'I meant the bird.'

Burdock looked back at her, confused. She'd said *outside*, hadn't she? He was a good dog. He knew that word.

Erin shook her head. 'Come back here, boy,' she said.

Burdock turned around, crept back into the house and sat back down on his cushion. He thumped his tail against the floor, twice, hopefully.

Erin closed the door. 'Okay,' she said. 'I'm sorry. I lost my temper.' She wasn't entirely sure who she was talking to. Maybe herself. She rubbed her knuckles on her jeans. Glanced down at herself and felt suddenly ridiculous. She looked so.... normal.

And she wasn't warm either. She should get the fire going.

Make a proper cup of tea. Soothing lavender. Sit down and be sensible.

Erin shook her head. She wasn't ready to be entirely sensible. The injustice of it all still burned inside her.

'I'm not going back to the care home,' she said.

The raven stared at her.

Burdock whined softly.

'I'm not,' she said. 'That's just going too far.' She blinked. 'And I'm sorry, but Morghan has some questions she needs to answer.' Erin shook her head. 'What the hell did she think she was doing? I mean, that's taking things way too far.'

The atmosphere in the room thickened suddenly, and

the hairs on the back of Erin's neck stood up. She tipped her head to the right, looking over her shoulder, knowing who to expect to see.

Or feel, rather.

'Macha,' she said.

The air in the room shimmered with Macha's energy. 'You walk the Ancient Path,' Macha said. 'You passed your first initiation, and now you run from the next?'

Erin shook her head. 'It's not like that this time – this isn't fair.'

But Macha was gone, as though nothing Erin said would be important. As though she couldn't possibly be right about this.

But she was. This was going too far.

The bird stared at her.

'Nope,' Erin said to it. 'I'm not doing this. I'll stay, and I'll learn all the stuff. I'll do the garden thing, and all the rest. But I'm not doing this.' She narrowed her eyes at the bird and folded her arms. 'That man helped my mother get rid of me – to the wrong people. The last thing I'm going to do is take care of him now.'

Her phone rang, cawing out the sound of a raven's cry from inside her bag on the table. Erin rolled her eyes at the noise – Stephan had set up the ringtone, thinking it was funny. It had been funny, until the real bird had somehow found its way in through closed windows and was sitting watching her.

She edged around the bird and snatched up her bag, dug out her phone.

'Stephan,' she said. 'I thought you were busy?'

'I am,' he told her on the other end of the line. 'Listen, I need your help – I'm supposed to make the grocery run, you know? Deliver the boxes around the place? But I'm stuck here with the construction for the glasshouse.' His voice dipped as though things weren't going well. 'Can you give me a hand and do the run instead? Craig was supposed to do it, but his dad's gotten sick, so the whole household is isolating.'

Erin frowned. 'Isn't there still someone else who can do it?' She shook her head. 'I'm only just home and I've had a rough morning.'

She heard Stephan scratching at his beard. She hadn't decided yet whether she liked it or not. It made him look like a bit of a pirate, and that didn't necessary have to be a bad thing.

The bird on the chair back raised himself up as though about to launch into the room. Erin flinched and backed up a few steps, but he only stood there looking at her. She turned her back. The bird's gaze was unnerving.

'Well, I could try finding someone else,' Stephan was saying. 'But that would need a fair bit of ringing around, and I really don't have time, you know?' There was a pause. 'It would just be brilliant if you could step up and do it.'

Erin chewed on her lip. She really didn't want to go out and drive around dragging box after box of groceries onto people's steps. It really had been a hard morning.

'Fine,' she said. 'Can you come pick me up?'

Another pause, longer this time. 'Well, not really,' Stephan said, and his voice lowered. 'Look, my dad is being a real prat, and I'm having a hell of a time getting anything done because of it. I don't have time to go haring off to do anything at the moment. You'll be all right though, won't you? It's only a twenty-minute walk. The van's at the back of the grocer's and it'll probably be loaded up by the time you get there. The list of addresses will be on the seat.' Stephan blew out a breath. 'You'll be being a real lifesaver, Erin, I promise.'

Erin opened her mouth to ask why the deliveries couldn't be put off until the next day, but she closed it on the question and sighed instead.

'Okay,' she agreed. 'I'll be there in a little while, okay?' She put a smile in her voice. 'Just for you.'

'Well, for the village, really,' Stephan said. 'But thanks. I have to go now, I'll call you later, okay? Though I reckon by the time I'm done today, I'll be taking a shower and crashing. I'm beat already.'

Erin pressed end on her phone and shoved it back in her bag. 'You want to go for another walk, Burdock?' she asked, ignoring the bird who had settled back down in a fluff of black and grey feathers.

Burdock looked up at her from his cushion. Another walk? He was always up for a walk. He got up, wagging his tail experimentally, and went to the door.

THE VAN WAS WHERE IT WAS SUPPOSED TO BE, AND THE address list was on the driver's seat. The keys were in the ignition. Erin looked at it all, then over at Burdock.

'Front or back, do you reckon?' she asked.

Burdock looked hopefully at the vehicle.

'Yeah, let's see if there's room in the back,' Erin decided. 'You are a big dog, Burdock.'

Burdock swooshed his tail. He was a good dog.

'Good grief,' Erin said, sliding the van's side door open. 'How many boxes are there?'

Blue Harvey stepped out of the back of his shop. 'Thirty-two of them,' he said. 'You doing the delivery this week?'

Erin nodded. 'Yeah. I was hoping Burdock could fit in the back.'

'Shove the boxes towards the back a bit and there'll be room for him to stand – he can look between the seats and out the front window. Should be tall enough to see, and all.'

'Yeah,' Erin replied. 'That will work.' She stepped back a bit so he could get in there and do that, but the grocer made no move. He just stretched and yawned.

'Better get back to it,' he said. 'You'd think in a lockdown you'd be less busy, right?' He shook his head ponderously. 'Not so. Not here in Wellsford, that's for sure.' With a brief wave, he disappeared back into his shop.

Erin stared after him for a moment, then looked at Burdock who gazed hopefully back at her. 'Okay then,' she said. 'I guess I'll do it, right?'

'Woof,' Burdock agreed.

She clambered into the back of the van and hauled the boxes about until there was standing room for Burdock. The boxes were heavy with potatoes and jars of pasta and rice. Not plastic bags, but actual jars. It weighed the boxes down even more. Although some of them, she noticed, had rice packed in pretty, home-sewn cloth sacks. But even they were heavy.

'There!' she said at last, backing out and grinning at Burdock. 'In you get, then.'

Burdock did not need telling twice.

Erin swung herself into the driver's seat and got the van going. It was strange to be driving again, she thought, adjusting the rear vision mirror so she could see. She picked up the list and checked the first address, then put the van in gear and pulled out onto the road.

23

IT WAS BARELY LIGHT WHEN ERIN CAME TRIPPING DOWNSTAIRS
a few days later with Burdock at her heels. She blinked in
the half-light and rubbed sleep from her eyes and decided
she was looking forward to summer and light mornings and
bright days. This spring was still wintery, and winter had
been going on forever, it seemed, since so much had
happened in the space of it.

She threw open the front door and Burdock bounded
out, heading for his favourite stops. He paused for a
moment at the figure on the path, then scooted on his way.

Erin, however, froze with her hand on the door,
squinting into the half-light.

'Morghan?' she said at last, and shock at seeing her
standing there, motionless, made her tremble.

'Erin,' the quiet voice answered. 'May I meet you in the
garden?'

'How long have you been standing there?' Erin

demanded, her temper flaring from the fright of seeing Morghan motionless on the pathway, staff in hand.

But of course Morghan was going to turn up. It had been three days and Erin hadn't gone to the care home.

Morghan didn't answer and Erin stared at her. She wouldn't have been standing out there for long, right? Why would she?

'All right,' Erin said at last. 'I'll meet you out the back.' She withdrew into the house and snatched her cloak off its peg, pulling it around her shoulders over her dressing gown – still the one that Teresa had used to wear.

Burdock came into the walled garden with Morghan and now he rumbled over to Erin, wondering why they were doing everything different this morning. She was supposed to be out here, but he ought to be back inside having his breakfast. Breakfast was an especially important meal.

Erin looked down at his shaggy head and gave it a pat. 'Breakfast in a minute, okay?' she whispered, then lifted her gaze to Morghan.

Morghan looked faraway, as though only half her mind was on the matter she had come to speak to Erin of.

That, for some reason, irked Erin. She knew Morghan was here to tell her to get back to work – why else would she be – but the look on her face said she was totally thinking of something else. Something not to do with what she'd done to Erin at all.

'I'm not going back,' Erin said, crossing her arms under the cloak and staring out over the garden before looking again at Morghan.

'You have a responsibility to turn up for your job,' Morghan said. 'Tell me why you are not.'

Erin's eyes widened. 'What? You can't figure that out?'

Morghan's gaze gentled a little. 'I would like to hear from your perspective,' she said.

'I would have thought my perspective would be obvious.'

'No,' Morghan said. 'It isn't, actually. You are here to walk upon the Ancient Path, to deepen into who you truly are, and to carry forward the legacy of this Grove, walking in truth and compassion as best you may do, and yet you are not engaging in your own soul's challenge.'

Erin gaped at her, open-mouthed, her ears suddenly ringing. 'My own soul's challenge? You're calling this my soul's challenge – to what, care and tend to the man who helped my mother get rid of me to strangers, and then maybe chucked her down some basement stairs?' She shook her head violently. 'You organised this. You manipulated me into it – I had nothing to do with it.' Erin stared at Morghan for a moment. 'Where's your compassion for me?' she asked, the words harsh from her mouth. 'Tell me that? Tell me why you don't give a fig about how I feel in this?'

There was a whisper of Ravenna in Morghan's mind, and she sighed. 'You are as undisciplined as Macha once was,' she said.

'Don't give me that Macha bollocks!' Erin screeched into the morning air. Burdock shifted, looked from woman to woman, and whined. 'I'm not Macha, I'm me. This isn't, like, 2000 BC or whatever. This is now – the twenty-first century and...and...' Mortified, Erin felt hot tears in her eyes.

'Erin,' Morghan replied softly. 'What did you learn from Kria?'

Erin blinked at her, caught off guard at the change of subject. 'What?'

'Kria,' Morghan repeated patiently. 'What did you learn from her?'

'Ah,' Erin swallowed, flailing around for an answer to the unexpected question. 'Um.'

Morghan waited, turning her mind from what was happening in the woods behind her. From the events replaying themselves there. She would go back there, to Blythe, when she was done here.

Erin decided to go back to the real subject at hand. 'Were you going to tell me about Wayne Moffat?' she asked. 'Were you going to do that, at least, and didn't get to because he arrived early?'

Morghan had half turned to look back at the woods and Erin scowled at her.

'You're not even paying attention to this conversation,' she said.

Morghan looked back at her. 'Erin,' she said. 'You are not my only concern. Other matters demand my attention.'

'Other matters like what?' Erin said, unable to help the burst of curiosity. She looked towards the woods herself but saw nothing there except trees and their long shadows.

'Such as those that one day you would be able to assist me with, if only you will care for your own challenges and learn what is necessary.' Morghan's voice was abrupt, harsh, and she shook her head. 'Erin,' she said. 'I ask you again – what did you learn from Kria?'

Erin reached a hand up and drew it through her hair, catching the fingers in its tangles. She shook her head. 'I don't know,' she said. 'That things happen that shouldn't, and that what she went through was really unfair.'

'No,' Morghan said. 'I don't think so. Tell me properly – what did you learn from singing Kria over, by completing her initiation?'

Erin felt like a chastened child, her lip pouting. She drew herself up to her full height, unable to help wondering again what sort of things Morghan was dealing with, besides her.

'I learnt that Kria shouldn't have turned her back on her training, on her knowledge of the truth,' Erin said, letting herself think about that barren glen again. She'd been glad not to go back there, to the cold steel water of the loch where a great beast lurked underneath the surface.

'What should she have done?'

Erin found herself not wanting to answer, because she could see where the conversation was heading. She wanted her anger back again, hot and righteous, so she wouldn't have to do what was being asked of her.

'She should have kept singing the wheel,' Erin said reluctantly.

'Yes,' Morghan replied simply. 'She needed to deepen her practice, to sink into it completely and have faith that it would carry her through.' She paused and thought for a moment, feeling Blythe's need at her back again. 'Do you remember the story Ambrose told us before midwinter, Erin?'

'The one about the prince with the golden hand?' Erin looked down at Morghan's right hand, which the Fey Queen had replaced with one of gold.

'Yes. In that story, the prince was given a pin cushion by Grandmother Yaga.'

Erin shook her head and drew her cloak tighter around herself. The morning was cold and the rising light ashen. 'Why was it a pin cushion of all things? It's almost absurd.'

'Because it is the simple things, the unassuming under-pinnings of things that see us through, Erin,' Morghan said. When we are faced with challenges – as we all invariably are, over and over, we must throw that pin cushion and go on the journey one step at a time, even when we know only what we are heading towards and through – a great battle, a great hurt – and not the outcome.' Morghan blinked. 'We must strive, Erin. I did not bring matters into this alignment for you. You did that – your own soul's purpose, its necessity. I only recognised it and played my part.'

'I'm still not sure I understand,' Erin said, but her voice was quiet, the fight gone out of it.

'It is your challenge to heal the hurt of your past and your mother's, and your grandmother's – and Wayne Moffat's, if you can find a way to.' Morghan closed her eyes for a moment, hearing the clamour of her own deep history. 'There are things you cannot run from, Erin. Things that will strengthen you if you face them in the depth of your practice, if you keep your practice during the hardship.'

'And if I don't?' Erin asked, shifting her feet uneasily on the path. 'If I can't bring myself to do it?'

'Then what are you here for?' Morghan questioned. 'What purpose does your life serve? The cycle only repeats, Erin, until it is dealt with.'

'I'm...I'm not sure I follow,' Erin whispered.

'We carry our wounds from life to life, Erin. We carry

our family's wounds from generation to generation until we heal them.'

'But what if we can't?'

'Then we will keep facing them until we can. You will face your pain again in another life, and your children will face it in theirs, in one form or another.'

'That's not fair!'

'No,' Morghan said. 'Perhaps not, but it is what it is, and sometimes your challenges will get the better of you, and you will not win in your striving against them, but stand up anyway, Erin. Stand up with the trees at your back, and your song on your lips, and strive anyway. Give it everything you have, because you are playing with your life, for your soul.'

Shaken, Erin stared at her. 'But...'

Morghan blinked at her. 'But what?'

Erin shook her head. 'It will hurt,' she said. 'I already went through so much, with Kria.'

'Yes,' Morghan agreed quietly. 'It hurts, and then, if we are successful in finding our way through, Erin, the sun rises, and the world is bathed in beauty.' She cocked an ear towards the forest again. 'You cannot avoid pain, Erin. Each of us suffers a share of it. But the world is large, and we are not alone. Be strengthened by your practice. Deepen into it so that you might be sustained through difficulty. Choose it at every moment you are tempted to give up.' A smile touched her lips. 'And do what must be done.'

'And if I don't?' Erin asked, unsure why she was hedging like that.

'Then your life will continue upon a different path,' Morghan answered.

'What does that mean?'

Morghan took a quiet breath, reminding herself that Erin was only young still. 'We would have to see, Erin,' she said. 'We would have to see.'

Erin frowned at the ground. That sounded ominous. They would have to see? She found, with a shudder, that she didn't much like the sound of that.

'I must go,' Morghan said, interrupting Erin's thoughts. 'I've business of my own to see to.'

'Can I help you?' Erin asked, looking over at her. 'With anything? Is there something I can do?'

Morghan couldn't help it – she smiled. 'Today, no,' she said. 'But I've high hopes for you.'

'Huh.' Erin nodded and sighed. 'All right,' she said. 'All right.'

'All right,' Morghan agreed. 'Practice standing in your gardens, Erin,' she said. 'You must learn to step back and forth between the worlds, to hold both inside you.' She turned to go back through the gate and towards the Grove.

'Wait,' Erin said. 'One more thing – I imagined my garden, just like you told me to, but it's all overgrown.' She waved a hand. 'I mean, really wild.' She shrugged. 'What do I do? I mean, about that?'

Morghan looked back at her. 'Tend it, Erin. Cut things back, prune and trim. Develop discipline.' She walked towards the gate again.

'Does it mean I need more discipline?' Erin called.

But Morghan just smiled at her and stepped through the gate and was gone.

'I guess so,' Erin muttered, looking down at Burdock.

She shook her head. 'That didn't go as expected.'

She thought she should have known that things never really did, with Morghan.

Burdock perked up his ears and looked hopefully at her.

'Discipline,' Erin sighed. 'Deepen my practice. Garden. Walk between the worlds. Heal familial wounds.'

She shook her head and walked back towards Ash Cottage, to put the kettle on, feed Burdock, and begin all over again.

'No problem,' she said. 'All in a day's work, right?'

Burdock slipped in first through the doorway. He was ready for the day, if it started with breakfast.

24

'You cannot go and do this, Blythe – surely you can see this, after the last few weeks?' Leah scurried down the path to the end of the garden with her, wanting to catch hold of her priestess's skirts to hold her physically back, but not daring. Not quite. 'Blythe, my Lady – you cannot.'

Blythe spun around on her heel, stopping to face the young girl. 'Leah, I must. Surely that may be seen. I cannot let another suffer when I've the means to relieve it.'

But Leah shook her head again. 'My Lady,' she said. 'You've no guarantee that your herbs will help, that the spirits will be able to cure the child of whatever ailment harasses her. And if you try and the girl continues to fade, and then does die, then you've no goodwill from these folks to fall back on.' She cast desperately around for an argument to convince Blythe Wilde. 'This has been a hard season,' she said. 'A hard season on top of another hard season. Crops have withered, cattle and sheep have suffered, and now a child has set to an illness no one knows. You heard what they from the village called you that day in the churchyard – they will surely blame you if the child dies.' Leah pressed her lips together, unwilling to say what would come after that.

Now it was Blythe's turn to shake her head. 'The child, Leah. I cannot ignore the suffering of a child if I've means to relieve it.'

'Means you may have, my Lady, but not the guarantee that good health will return to it. Not every soul is blessed to live long upon this earth – you've told me this yourself, your very own words. You cannot risk another child to die upon your attendance.'

'I cannot risk another child to die.'

They stared at each other, standing upon the path near the house's well. Blythe looked a moment towards the house, squaring her shoulders. She had had the same dispute with Tomas that very morning, Tomas insisting she not go to attend the child.

'It will be well,' she said through gritted teeth.

'It may not,' Leah repeated. 'You've no foreknowledge of it.' She bit down on her lip and frowned. 'Have you? Or have the spirits told you something you've not said?'

Blythe shook her head, her back rigid. 'I will not know what ails the child until I have examined her.'

'Her father is one who called you witch,' Leah said. 'You must not be foolish enough to ignore this.'

Blythe stared at her, eyes dark, and Leah knew she'd gone too far.

'My Lady,' she pleaded. 'You're all we have – all I have. You're the one who may pass through the veil. You're the one with the ability to teach me so that the Grove may carry on. You – only you.' She shook her head, increasingly desperate. 'Without you, everything is in danger.'

'Bah,' Blythe said, spitting the word. 'The Goddess will not have anything happen to me. She would not risk the loss of my knowledge, as you say.'

Tomas came striding towards them, his jaw set. 'The Goddess, Blythe, requires your cooperation. The Gods are not all-powerful. You must work with them, and Leah is right – you would be fool indeed to risk the work of us all for the life of this child.' He blinked, wanting to snatch at Blythe, drag her back to the house. He lowered his voice. 'I know you hurt, my love.'

Blythe glared at him. How dare he bring her own pain into this? The ache of her own lost child? 'I make my choice,' she said. 'I am able to help this child, and it is my obligation before the Goddess to do so.'

'And if it is not the child's time to live?'

She shook her head. 'The girl will live.' She picked up her skirts in her hand and turned back down the path. 'I will not allow another child to die.'

The child's mother looked upon Blythe standing at her door.

'Pauline,' Blythe said. 'Let me help.'

Warring emotions crossed Pauline's face. 'My husband,' she whispered. 'He said not to let you in if you came calling.'

'He is here?' Blythe asked.

Pauline shook her head silently.

'The babe is better?'

Again, Pauline shook her head. Then found her voice. 'Nay. It is worsening. I know not what to do for it.'

Blythe nodded, knowing the helplessness well. 'I would look at her, Pauline. See if there is anything my knowledge can do for her.'

Now, Pauline's eyes narrowed. 'Your knowledge?' she hissed. 'Our John says your knowledge is of the devil himself.'

'No,' Blythe said. 'You know it is only of herb lore and charms for good, nothing for ill.'

Behind them, a thin puling wail sounded. Pauline's face fell. 'It does not even chatter as is usual, according to my sister, who would know, as she has five herself. It does nothing, or if it does something, it is only to scream or wail. And Olive were such a beauty as a little one. Now I do not recognise her in this child. Surely she has been bewitched.' Pauline's face took on the cast of one who was frightened.

'Then let me look upon her,' Blythe said, even while a shadow cast over her mind, a whisper of a presentiment. She ignored it. 'It may be I can help, and I would certainly never harm.'

Pauline looked at her for a long moment, chewing upon her lips, then glanced about the lane outside the house. If any were watching, they were doing it without being seen at their windows.

She stepped back as the child cried again and held the door for Blythe to step inside.

Blythe blinked a moment, waiting for her gaze to adjust to the cottage's dimness. Smoke stung at her eyes. 'Your chimney has need of unblocking,' she said.

Pauline had her arms wrapped around her middle,

hugging herself. 'Tis not the chimney,' she said, 'but that the wood is green and smokes badly.'

Blythe nodded, unsurprised. 'I will get Tomas to bring you some dried,' she said. 'This smoke will not be good for the babe.'

'Tis not the problem, though, I'm sure,' Pauline said. 'She'll not let me touch her no more, but throws herself around, turning rigid as a board when I would hold her. As though my touch hurts her. And her father's – she is the same with him.' She paused. 'With my sister too. As though now she is weaned she will have nothing to do with any of us.'

The child sat upon a threadbare rug on the floor, a rag doll unheeded beside her. Her hair was wispy and dark, face thin, eyes two small storms.

Blythe sank down upon a bench to look at the child, making no move to touch her. Her skin looked papery, dry, and Blythe's fear for the child ratcheted up a notch. 'You've had the doctor see her?' she asked.

'Nay, for we've never been as far as Banwell,' Pauline said. 'My sister Ethel thought it likely to be worms, and gave us remedy for that, but has made no difference. The baby still ails.'

'And what think you all now?'

There was a long pause before Pauline answered, and her reply came reluctantly from her mouth. 'John and Ethel have said as how now she must be a changeling, that there is no other answer. That at some stage, the faeries must have got in and took our Olive.' Pauline lifted her skirt and pressed the fabric to her cheek, sniffing. 'What other answer is there, as this is not our Olive? It cannot be.' She cast a sudden, hopeful look at Blythe. 'In which case, you'd be able to bring our Olive back, would you not? We all know you consort with the fairies. All witches do.'

Blythe was glad of the hard bench beneath her. The word changeling rang in her ears so that she almost didn't register the rest of what the mother was saying to her.

'I'm no witch,' Blythe replied, dry-mouthed, staring at the child.

Pauline's laugh was harsh. 'Of course you are. 'Tis well known around these parts that you dabble in things most be afeard to.'

'I have skill with herbs, that is all,' Blythe said.

'You consort with spirits,' Pauline retorted. 'Up in them woods all the time, wandering around like a mad woman. We've all heard you, one time or the other, singing songs with no proper words, songs such that aren't those learnt in the church pew.'

Pauline stalked over to the child on the floor and picked her up in rough hands. The little girl screamed and thrust her body rigid, hands clenching to miniature fists.

'Take her,' Pauline said over the racket, and pushed the child at Blythe's chest. 'Take her and get my Olive back.' Now she did not just look hopefully upon Blythe, but slyly.

'Or I'll have you before the magistrate for your witch-craft – everyone in the village is about ready too, and all. There won't be any shortage of those willing to testify against you.'

Blythe ached to reach out and take the child being shoved at her, but her sinking heart told her she couldn't afford to. Leah had been right, and Tomas. She shouldn't have come.

She stood up, edging away from the furious mother. 'I shouldn't have come,' she said. 'I'm sorry; I was wrong to.'

'Aye, because we know the child cannot be cured with herbs, now, don't we?' Pauline's eyes blazed with anger and fear. 'Take the child and make your bargains with Themselves to bring my Olive back.' She thrust the little girl again at Blythe. 'We all know 'tis in your power to do so.'

Blythe shook her head again. 'That is not in my power to do. You are wrong.'

Pauline cackled and the baby's cries grew louder. 'Send your imps to do your bidding then. We've all seen you with their shadows around you. We've all seen you, Blythe Wilde, and nothing can save you now, except maybe if you bring me my Olive. That would be a good convincement for the village.' The child dangled from her hands, hanging from arm and leg, face red with screaming. 'We've tried putting this one out at night to be taken back, but its howling disturbed the village, and none could stand it.' Pauline shook the child that dangled from her hands. 'So we're giving it none but water and a scrap of bread. All know that Themselves don't like their changelings to be abused, and so will exchange them back. If the water and bread don't work, it will be on the hot coals next.'

'You are starving her?' Blythe asked, appalled. That accounted for the girl's sunken eyes and dry skin then. 'And hot coals?' She was horrified. The girl was but a tiny child. 'What mean you by hot coals?'

'All know the faeries hate the touch of iron.' For a moment, the anger and fright in Pauline's eyes were gone, and tears stood in the corners instead. 'Take her, for all that is good in the world, and bring Olive back to me. Even a faery child such as this I cannot bear being branded with hot irons.'

This time when Pauline thrust the child into Blythe's chest, she let it go, and Blythe caught her automatically, so that the girl would not fall straight to the floor.

Pauline stepped over to the door and flung it open. 'Go,' she said. 'Afore my John returns.'

Blythe opened her mouth, but Pauline wouldn't let her speak.

'Nay,' she said. 'There be no disputes to make upon this, Blythe Wilde. Take the changeling. Bring me back my Olive.'

The child's face against her breast, Blythe had nothing to do but step from the mean little house and onto the street. Pauline closed the door against her, and Blythe found herself staring at its wooden grain. She glanced down at the wispy head around which she'd cupped her hand. It was small, fitting inside her palm, and hot with dehydration.

But the child had stopped her screaming, and Blythe watched the small girl, not yet two years upon the earth, blink in the bare light of the day and reach out an arm, the tiny fingers stretched, grasping for the spirit of the great black wolf that stood at Blythe's side, visible to none.

Except Blythe.

The child threw herself to the side, both arms reaching now, hands set to grab.

Except perhaps, this child.

Blythe glanced along the street, saw with a panicked breath, the twitch of a curtain at a window. She turned her back to the eyes behind the window, and the child in her arms lurched to the other side, grasping for what she ought not to be able to see, reaching clearly for what was not supposed to be visible.

Blythe hitched Olive higher on her chest, and not knowing what else to do, hurried down the road, towards the trees, and the dubious safety of Hawthorn House.

25

WINSOME CLEARED HER THROAT, AND WATCHED HER HANDS shake as she rested them on the pulpit. Usually, she chose to stand in the middle of the aisle, perhaps on the step there, to say her sermon, but today she was not sure that her legs would not knock together at the knees for all in the church to hear. The church, for its small size, had excellent acoustics.

She needed a drink of water. Her mouth was as dry as the desert. She lifted the glass she kept there for just this situation, and sipped at the water, afraid that if she gulped, she would choke, and that would be a merry thing, wouldn't it? To choke literally as well as metaphorically in front of her congregation.

And a good-sized congregation it was as well. Attendance had, despite the virus, or perhaps even because of it, been on the rise. There were even a few families, younger couples with their children huddled together in the pews gazing at her, waiting for her to start.

Mariah Reefton was there too, of course, sitting in her regular spot, right in the front, right in the place where Winsome's gaze naturally rested when she was speaking. It was as though the woman had divined this, she thought, and placed herself there deliberately.

But that surely wasn't the case, Winsome reminded herself, and she took another sip of water. It sloshed in its glass against her lips.

Julia Thorpe sat next to her aunt, and Winsome could hardly bear the smug look upon her Churchwarden's face. She sat with her arms folded across her breasts, a smirk upon her lips as though she'd already forced Winsome from the church and her position of vicar.

Winsome shook her head slightly. What did Julia think she was going to achieve, when she had forced Winsome from the vicarage, and from the pulpit? Did she think that somehow she would be able to take her place?

After Reverend Robinson had died, and in the period of several weeks before Winsome had taken up the position – Winsome shivered slightly at her memory of arriving in Wellsford to be greeted by the sight of the dead former vicar and several of his parishioners wandering around the churchyard when they ought to have been sleeping peacefully in their graves awaiting the next world – Julia Thorpe had indeed kept things running smoothly, kept the church business ticking over. But that hadn't included services. A locum vicar had been brought in for those, and not every week.

Was Julia really happier with that arrangement, if it meant she had the church to herself most of the month? Or did she perhaps just prefer a male vicar, someone she could simper over?

The congregation grew restless, stirring in their seats, twisting this way and that, wondering why Winsome hadn't yet spoken. Julia's smile widened and Winsome looked down at her, wanting to wipe the smugness from the woman's face.

Instead, she removed her gaze from Julia and her aunt, and took a nice big breath, holding it, then letting it out. Her notes were on the lectern in front of her. All she had to do was open her mouth and start talking.

Winsome swallowed and looked out over her small and precious flock. She could see their spirits in hazy colours around each of them. She nodded.

'We're going to talk about unity today,' she began. 'And how in times of difficulty, we must look for similarities, not differences, and how we must not turn from each other, no matter who our neighbour might be.'

There was a barely concealed snort from Mariah in her front row seat, and a titter from her cronies arrayed in formation behind her, but Winsome drew another breath and carried on.

'That was a good try, I expect you think,' Mariah said afterwards, outside where Winsome was saying her goodbyes.

'Don't forget your two metres, Mariah,' Winsome said sweetly. 'We're still socially distancing, remember.'

Mariah rolled her eyes. 'What a shame you weren't

thinking about distancing when you ought to have been, isn't that right? When you went up that hill and danced with those witches for all the world like you were one of them.' She looked for a moment like she was going to spit on the ground. 'And now you have the temerity to preach unity, of all things.'

'Loving thy neighbour is a central tenet, Mariah,' Winsome reminded her.

'As may be but entering into their devil worship I think is certainly not.'

Mariah's voice was strident, and her two or three friends were near enough to hear her and snigger, nodding their heads.

'We'll see you out for that, Winsome,' Julia said, not wanting her two pence not said while all were listening. 'You can't do what you did and get away with it. You'll see.' She puffed out her chest with righteousness and crossed her arms over it, unassailable.

'Winsome did nothing!' It was Minnie, striding forward through the crowd and flinging her arms about to clear a path, her grandmother Rosalie huffing on her heels. 'You're the mad, dried up old cows who don't want anyone to experience anything but by your say-so.'

Minnie stared around at the loose knot of people, shaking her head at Mariah's lot. 'You are the ones ought to be ashamed of yourselves – you're trying to get Winsome out of here from pure spite!' She held up a finger and waggled it at the miserable old women before anyone could say a word. 'I think you ought to tell us the truth about why you're trying to get St. Bridget's shut down.' She glared defiantly at the growing crowd. Some were even drifting back from the gate where they'd been about to head home. Minnie nodded. People needed to hear this.

'Minnie,' Winsome said weakly, 'I don't think...'

'I know, Vicar,' Minnie said. 'But I do.'

Winsome wanted to hide her face. Not that everyone didn't know by now what she stood accused of.

Stood accused of. Like she was a witch, and this was the seventeenth century.

Winsome told herself not to be dramatic.

'What do you mean, shut down?' someone asked from the gathered crowd in the slanted spring light. 'Why would the church be shut down, then?'

Minnie raised her eyebrows and looked at Mariah Reefton and Julia Thorpe. 'That's right,' she said. 'Why would it be shut down?'

'Don't be stupid,' Julia snapped. 'The church won't be shut down – what will happen is we'll get a vicar who doesn't consort with the devil.'

Winsome couldn't believe her ears. 'Do you hear what you just said, Julia?' She shook her head in consternation and raised her hands to quiet the growing muttering in the crowd of her parishioners. 'Consort with the devil?'

'Yeah,' Minnie said. 'What planet do you bloody well think you're on? Or rather – what century do you think this is?'

Julia looked at Minnie with venom in her gaze. 'You can't talk, you little floozy. You oughtn't to be even darkening the door of our church – not when you're one of that lot.'

Minnie widened her eyes dramatically.

'Please everyone,' Winsome said. 'Let's be calm about this.'

'Or let's not,' Minnie said. 'I want to hear just how crazy they are.' She shook her head. 'One of that lot? Do you mean Wilde Grove?' She drew herself up to her full height, which wasn't much but just the act made her feel strong. Krista said posture was important to magic, and Minnie could see why – it made you feel powerful to stand up straight, shoulders back. 'You mean those who follow the old ways – walking with reverence upon this earth, treating every person, animal, and plant with respect?' She rolled her eyes. 'Yeah, I don't see what the problem is there.'

'Thou shalt not suffer a witch to live,' Julia said, her face mean and pinched.

'Oh please.' Minnie shook her head. 'You going to burn me at the stake? That your thing still, is it?' She glanced over at Winsome who stood white-faced and silent with shock. 'Sorry Vicar,' Minnie said. 'I mean hanged, not burnt.' She turned back to Julia. 'If you bothered to learn anything about the Grove – the people who are your neighbours, who you're supposed to be busy loving, you'd know that even if Winsome danced with us, it wasn't for sure no dancing with the bloody devil, because nothing evil goes on in the Grove, just a quiet love for the world and everyone in it, and a determination not to be overcome by this casual chaos and rot that you see everywhere.' Minnie grinned, baring her teeth. She'd done a lot of learning and reading and talking in the last few weeks and was proud of herself for it. 'By what I see when I look at you.'

'What does she mean, if the Vicar danced with them?' someone asked. One of the newer people, hugging her child to her while her husband frowned.

Winsome roused herself from the blaring of panic

between her ears. She supposed this was inevitable, but somehow, she hadn't envisioned having an impromptu meeting about her digressions on the church lawn. She opened her mouth, not knowing what she was going to say.

Minnie got in first. She was on a roll. 'The nasty old cow is talking about the fact that our Vicar was invited to the Wilde Grove midwinter ritual by Morghan Wilde,' Minnie said, enjoying what was happening – and she believed it ought to be all out in the open. People ought to know what was going on. Properly know, as well. Not just the nasty gossip spreading in whispers behind cupped hands.

There was a murmur of consternation, and Mariah Reefton rocked back on her heels, an ugly smile on her face.

But that's not all, though, is it, Vicar,' Mariah said. 'You've been praying in that heathen temple in the woods. We've seen you coming back from there, time and again.'

Winsome raised her eyebrows, her ire also finally roused. 'You saw me coming home from walking in the woods, did you, Mariah? Getting some exercise during the lockdown?'

There was a titter of laughter from the small crowd.

Mariah heard it, her slack and lined cheeks growing red. She narrowed her eyes at Winsome. 'You know full well that wasn't all you were up to. I'm no fool – I know where that path leads.' She turned her head to the crowd. 'There's a nasty little temple built back there. And we all know what those devil worshippers do in those places.' She turned back to Winsome. 'And I followed you and all, I did – saw you standing in the temple spreading your hands about, muttering words, curses, probably.'

'Mariah,' Winsome snapped, unable to quite believe

what she'd just heard. 'That's enough of your vitriol. For starters, it's some sort of half-ruined summer house, and it's quite beautiful. A nice spot along a walk, and a nice spot for contemplation.' She drew breath, all eyes upon herself. 'A nice place to lift your hands in prayer – my favourite prayer, the Our Father, as it happens.' She huffed out a breath. 'I can't believe you've been sneaking around following me.' Winsome shook her head. 'Mariah...' She bit down on her question. For a moment there, she'd been going to ask the old woman if she'd gone quite mad.

'You were drunk that day I met you coming out of the church,' Julia said, butting in, wanting things back in control again. She swung around to face everyone. 'I saw her with my own two eyes, when I came over for our usual meeting. Drunk and stumbling out of the church in all her robes, she was, and not even nine o'clock in the morning.'

Winsome closed her eyes and sighed. This whole thing was a debacle. She wanted to walk away, go and sit in her kitchen, rest her head on the table, maybe bang it a few times.

'That can't be right,' someone said. 'I've never seen our Vicar ever the worse for wear for drinking.' It was Wen Murray who had spoken up, the church groundskeeper. 'And I'm in and out of here all the time,' he continued. 'Mowing the lawn and tidying the gravestones and the like. I see our Vicar at all hours, and never once even smelt anything on her.'

'Well, she was definitely drunk that morning,' Julia pronounced, folding her arms tight across her chest.

'I bet she wasn't,' Minnie said and looked over at Winsome. 'Tell them.'

Winsome shook her head, deeply uncomfortable. She couldn't believe this conversation was even happening. 'I was not drunk,' she said, then swallowed, casting around for what to say. 'I had spent the morning deep in prayer.' She shot a pointed look at Mariah, unable to help herself. 'Inside the church – and yes, Julia, in my robes, as I am entitled to.'

'Why were you rolling around like you could barely walk, then?' Julia shot back. 'There's only one explanation for it, and that's that you'd been in the communion wine.'

Winsome couldn't conceal the horrified look on her face, and several gasps from around her indicated that others were the same way. She shook her head slowly.

'Julia,' she said. 'I'm not even going to dignify that with an answer.'

'You still went and danced with that lot with the sun rising after the shortest day,' Julia shot back, her words like a poisoned arrow.

'So what if she was invited along to the ritual?' Minnie yelled. 'I was there too, and now I'm here with my grandmother and my sister. There's no law against it! You'll really have the church closed down over that?'

Louder murmuring from the crowd now.

'What does she mean have the church closed down?' It was the woman there with her husband and child again.

Winsome held her hands up placatingly. She glanced at Minnie, wondering how the girl had figured this out. She was smart though, now that she'd settled down a bit and recovered from what had happened before Christmas, and of course, her grandmother would probably have realised this, if she'd thought about it. 'If St Bridget's loses its full-time vicar – which is me, like it or not,' she said, 'then the church will probably only have one service a month, held by a rotating district team.' She paused a moment and frowned. 'If that.'

There was a sudden silence.

It was another of her older parishioners who spoke. Mattie Robertson, who had attended St. Bridget's since she was baptised. 'One service a month, led by a stranger?' she asked. 'I don't know that I like the sound of that.'

'I'm afraid that's what would likely happen,' Winsome said, and she had everyone's attention now, although Julia shifted on her feet, scowling. 'What with everything, the Church's budget is shrinking. The district team would still be available for pastoral care, if anyone had need of a visit, but all the other things we do would likely come to an end, I'm afraid.'

'But we've only just started coming along.' It was the younger woman again, her husband nodding beside her. 'It's comforting and it's been a help, feeling like part of a community, like we're all in this together.' She blinked and when Winsome looked at her she thought she saw a sudden dampness around the woman's eyes. 'Everything has been so dreadful lately, that coming here has meant the world to us. It's given us some stability, I mean. And there's all the extra stuff – the clothes swap that turned into the charity shop – I was going to volunteer with that when the lockdown is over.' She paused. 'And the nursery group and coffee mornings? What will we do without all that?'

Her husband nodded. 'And the Men's Shed?' he asked. 'I've been looking forward to going back to that and pottering around with the other blokes. I was learning a lot.'

Mariah curled her lip. 'That was run by the Wilde Grove group,' she hissed.

'It is a joint community effort,' Winsome corrected her. 'A chance for the men of the village – whether Church goers, Grove members, or neither, to get together and share their wisdom and expertise.' She took a breath. 'Wen,' she said to the groundskeeper. 'You pop along to that too, don't you?'

'I do an' all,' he replied. 'It's been a great thing, and thank you Vicar, for organising it.'

Winsome nodded. 'That might not fall by the wayside, if we were to lose a full-time vicar here,' she said to the crowd, then looked pointedly at Mariah. 'Because the Grove shares the running of it – and put up the money for the building and the tools, I might add – but our other efforts would. The community would have to continue them on their own initiative.'

'But the Church funds some of those things, doesn't it?' Mattie Robertson asked. 'Where would we get that money from then?' She shook her head. 'I still don't understand what's going on? Why would you be leaving, Vicar? We need you here.'

'We've no need of her,' Mariah said, turning to glare at Mattie and everyone else. 'Like I said, she went and danced with those pagans.'

At least she hadn't said devil worshippers again, Winsome thought.

'Danced around under the moon – probably in the nick an' all – like the dirty pack of devil-worshiping witches they are.'

Winsome sighed.

It was another of the other younger people who spoke up this time. 'They don't worship the devil,' he said, putting his arm around his wife.

'How would you know?' Mariah crowed. 'You were there, then?'

He shook his head. Winsome plucked his name from the tip of her tongue. Michael, he was. And his wife was June. They'd moved to Wellsford to be with Michael's mother. He worked in IT – remotely, now, which had worked out for Lucy, his mother, who was very frightened by the pandemic.

'No,' Michael said. 'But nor, I'll wager, were you.'

'Bah,' Mariah spat. 'It's not me being neither here nor there that's the problem. It's that our Vicar here was.'

Everyone gazed at Winsome again.

'I was there,' she said. 'Although, since it was snowing, everyone was very well clothed, I'd like to say.' She blinked and nodded. 'You'll all be aware that the last few months has seen a lot of things happen in Wellsford for the good of us all – initiatives such as the Men's Shed, the charity shop, the community gardens, the grocery subscriptions, art and dance classes at Haven, and others as well.'

Heads nodded all round. Everyone knew.

'Almost every one of those initiatives has been able to happen because we have worked hand in hand with Wilde Grove.' Winsome sighed. 'I know it's a little unorthodox, but times have changed. If we don't come together as a community – no matter who we are and what we believe – then we will not survive these times, and I have to say that here in Wellsford, we do not wish just to survive, but to thrive. Our community is becoming more vibrant, we are caring for each other better, and I am proud of us. But it is only happening this way because we are not letting our differences come between us.'

Winsome shook her head, perfectly aware that she had hedged around the question of her being at the ritual. 'Now, I think we ought all to get home to our dinners.'

'I'll wager the Dean won't agree with you, Winsome Clark,' Mariah said, determined to have the last word.

'What's the Dean got to do with this?' It was Rosalie, and there was outrage in her voice.

'We've made a formal complaint to the Dean,' Julia said, a wide and satisfied smirk on her face. 'About the vicar's behaviour.'

'Are you trying to get the church shut down?' Rosalie asked, shaking her head in disbelief.

Julia just crossed her arms again and pressed her lips together.

'There'll be another vicar,' Mariah said. 'A god-fearing one. One not tainted by close proximity and friendship with the enemy.'

'But they're not our enemies, Mariah you old bat,' Wen said. 'They're people just like ourselves. Our Vicar's right – this isn't the Middle Ages anymore. We can get along even if we believe different things. That young Stephan, he's a miracle worker with the gardens, and always willing to lend a hand when needed. Same with the rest of them.'

'The bookshop sells abominations – tools of Satan,' Julia said.

Wen shook his head. 'They're just gewgaws, Julia, and you don't have to buy 'em.'

'She's got a good selection of Bibles and Christian books in there, if you want them,' someone else said.

Winsome followed the conversation helplessly.

'Right next to tarot cards,' Julia snarled.

'I need the cheaper groceries,' someone else said. Linda Wattle, Winsome recognised. She'd come back recently too, forced into early retirement. 'The subscription, and bulk buying them, plus the vegetables from the community gardens – I don't know that I'd be managing so well without that for the basics.'

There were nodding heads all round.

'You take the groceries too, don't you, Mariah?' Wen said. 'I've seen you – that boy Stephan, or the other one, what's his name? Craig – his dad's just gotten sick, so I hear – has delivered 'em right to your door more than a few times.'

Mariah sniffed, but said nothing.

'All right, everybody,' Winsome said. 'It really is time to bring this to a close now. I'm afraid that there has been a formal complaint laid against me to the Dean, and I don't know what will come of it at this stage. I'll be speaking to the Dean next week about it.'

'I'll come with you, Vicar,' Wen said, puffing out his chest. 'Let the Dean know we need you 'ere.'

There were murmurs of agreement all round, and Winsome looked at those nodding, not knowing whether suddenly to laugh or cry.

This was such a mess, she thought.

Why, why had she had to follow everyone to the ritual that morning?

26

'WE HAVE TO DO SOMETHING MORE,' MARIAH SAID, SETTING her back to the church and crossing the road to her own house.

Julia scurried after her. She was living with her aunt now – Mariah had insisted, on account of the lockdown. She missed her own little cottage, but on the other hand, Mariah was right. Things were easier to do if they were able to be in the same room with each other.

'Can you believe that people were actually sticking up for her?' she asked, shaking her head. 'I could hardly fathom it – how could they?'

'That's the problem, isn't it?' Mariah answered, swinging open her gate and baring her teeth at its squeal. 'Julia, you need to be oiling this gate. Its screech sets my teeth to edge.' She stalked up to the front door on hips that were stiff but still rolling and twisted her key in the lock. She resented having to lock her doors and her windows in a small village like Wellsford, but Wellsford was no ordinary village, and you did what was needed.

'We have to let everyone know the gravity of the situation,' she said, stepping inside and speaking to Julia without looking at her. 'That there is really a viper's nest in our midst.'

Julia nodded. 'I'll heat us up our lunch,' she said.

'Good idea,' Mariah answered. 'And we'll make our plans. If we're dogged and orderly about it, there won't be anyone in Wellsford who doesn't know what's what.'

'Did you really see her praying in that temple?'

Mariah set herself down at the kitchen table, still clutching her handbag. 'I most certainly did,' she said. 'My jaunts about those woods have been most instructive.' She shook her head in disgust. 'Robinson ought never to have died and put us in this position.'

Julia, who had enjoyed the few weeks between the Reverend Robinson's death and the Reverend Clark's arrival shook her head. She'd received all the telephone calls from the Dean. Well, the Dean's office, but she had been their go-to woman. 'He was friends with Ambrose if you recall,' she said.

'True,' Mariah said, forced to acknowledge the unpleasant fact. 'But he never succumbed to their wickedness. He never went and prayed to Lord knows what in that temple now, did he?'

'Maybe he did,' Julia said. 'And we just never saw him do it.' She shrugged elaborately, turning the oven on to warm their plates.

Mariah stood in the middle of her own kitchen, hands on her hips, a look of consternation on her face. She'd never considered that. Never considered that Robinson might have been just as perverted and influenced as the current one was. The realisation set to festering inside her.

'It's a – what do you call it?' she asked, lowering herself slowly to a chair and shaking her head. 'Come on, Julia, what do you call it?'

Julia wiped her hands on a tea towel. 'I don't know what you're talking about.'

Mariah shook her head. 'Come now,' she said. 'Of course you do – it's like you've been seeing on the Internet.' She laid her hands on the table and gazed at the wrinkled maps of skin on the backs of them without seeing them. 'Think about it.' Mariah Reefton looked suddenly and thoroughly pleased with herself. 'It all fits together,' she said.

Julia put a cup of tea in front of her aunt. 'What fits together?' she asked.

'Look at it,' Mariah said. 'They want to take over the village. Probably Banwell too, I'll bet my teeth on it.'

Julia grimaced. Mariah kept her teeth in a glass in the bathroom overnight. It was unpleasant to have to answer the call of nature at 3am – always 3am – to be greeted by a lipless grin every time.

'Who wants to take over?' Julia asked, still wondering why it was always 3am. Wasn't that the witching hour? She frowned. Or wasn't that the most common time for a person to die in their beds? Her eyes opened suddenly wide.

Mariah saw it. 'What?' she asked. 'What have you just come up with?'

Julia shook her head slowly. It was too fantastic for words – wasn't it? And yet, there was a symmetry to it that made her think it must be the truth.

And no one had ever accused Julia of not facing the truth, no matter how horrible it might be. Hadn't she been the one to go tell Lucky Kendricks that her old man had dropped to the ground right in the middle of the doorway to fancy Miss Jilly Deaver's little house? Dead as a doornail, he'd been, dropped like a stone, he had, and Lucky certainly hadn't lived up to her name that day, had she now? They'd gone to school together, so it was only right that Julia would be the one to march down the road to her house to tell her the news.

'Julia,' snapped Mariah. 'Are you just going to sit there with your mouth hanging open and eyes as wide as golf balls, or are you going to tell me, for heaven's sakes?'

'What?' Julia almost jumped in her seat. 'Oh. Right. Sorry, I was remembering something.'

'Relevant? Or were you just wool-gathering?'

Julia blinked and then blinked again. Her eyes felt dry. She sniffed, and just to make her aunt wait a minute longer, she picked up her cup and took a dainty sip, then reached for her handkerchief and dabbed at her lips with it.

'Relevant,' she said at last.

The thin line, which was mostly pencil, of Mariah's brows rose towards her hairline, also thin, but not drawn on, at least.

'Well,' Julia said.

'Yes?' Mariah said, pointedly.

'I've been waking up at the same time every night to visit the bathroom.'

'To spend a penny, you mean?' Mariah wasn't a prude. She prided herself on straight-thinking and straight-talking.

Julia, whose sensibilities were a little more delicate –

prissy, Mariah thought often behind her niece's back – sniffed then deigned to continue. 'Yes,' she said.

'And?' Mariah cackled out loud. 'You're not getting any younger, Julia, and not being able to get through the night without emptying the watering can is as good a sign of that as any.'

Julia pressed her lips together so tightly they disappeared. She stared at her aunt. 'Have you finished?' she asked.

Mariah's answer was to roll her eyes. Honestly, she thought, if Anne's daughter wasn't quite so useful on occasion, she could really do without her altogether. But, since she'd never married, and certainly never had children of her own, then her sister's offspring were all she was left with. And at least Julia had also never married or produced any nasty little children, so it generally worked quite well.

Except for times like now when Julia quite drove her crazy.

'Why don't you just tell me before our dinner gets burnt in the oven?' she added for good measure. 'It's going to be a busy afternoon, and I don't want to start it off with burnt pie.'

'Busy?' Julia asked. Why was it going to be busy? She had plans for the afternoon that consisted of lying on her bed with the comforter over her legs, a good cup of coffee beside her, and the third of the Mills and Boons she'd picked up at the new little charity shop.

But she wasn't about to tell Mariah that. She'd been planning to complain of a sore stomach and then close the door on the old woman, let her look after herself for the afternoon. It wasn't as though Mariah wasn't capable. The woman was as spry as they came. That's what happened, Julia thought, when you had vitriol instead of blood.

She longed a moment for her own little cottage. The first flowers would be up in the garden by now. It wasn't much of a garden, but it was cheerful. Mostly roses. She ought to go back soon and see if they were all right.

Julia loved her roses more than anything or anyone else. Secretly, she compared them to herself. They smelt lovely – which she always did, their flowers were charming – same also as herself, and if they were a bit prickly, then being a bit prickly was a good thing, she'd discovered – it saved people from taking you for a fool.

'That's right,' Mariah was saying. 'Busy. You'll not be sneaking off to read those trashy novels of yours today, my girl.' She leaned back in her chair and beamed malevolently at her niece. 'Today we begin our counterattack.'

'Our counterattack?' Julia stared dumbly at her aunt.

How did Mariah know about the novels? Julia frowned. Hadn't she hidden them in her underwear drawer?

'That's right. I've got a plan, you see,' Mariah said, and she rubbed her hands together in glee. 'People need to know the truth, don't you think?'

Why would Mariah be rooting around in her delicates? They were personal things in there. That's why she'd put the six or seven slim paperbacks in there, tucked beneath her underwear.

Mariah leaned forward over the table and snapped her fingers under Julia's face.

'Earth to Julia,' she said. 'Is anyone at home?'

Julia scowled. 'Of course I'm home,' she said. 'I'm listening to you, aren't I?'

'Are you?' Mariah asked. 'The pie's burning.'

For a moment, Julia sat in her chair unmoving, then she realised what Mariah had just said and jumped up to open the oven door. The pies steamed at her, their crusts a perfect golden brown.

'They're fine,' she said, and prodded them experimentally with a finger. Hot enough, she guessed, and if they were still cold in the middle – well, that wasn't her doing, was it?

Mariah watched Julia bent over the oven with her head practically in it. One shove, she thought merrily, and she'd be in there just like the child's fairy tale.

She refrained from leaning over to give the broad bottom a shove, just for kicks and giggles. She had more important work to do today than tormenting her dead sister's feeble excuse for a daughter.

'So,' she said instead. 'What amazing revelation did you have?' Mariah was fairly sure it wouldn't be amazing, but on occasion, Julia had said something worth the listening, and her position as Churchwarden was, it had to be admitted, and Mariah did admit it with gritted dentures when she had to, useful.

Julia brought the plates to the table then went back for the cutlery. 'What revelation?' she asked, then remembered. 'Oh, that's right.' She sniffed, gave her aunt knife and fork, and sat back down with her own.

'I was saying that I've been getting up each night, which no...' She waggled her fork at Mariah, 'isn't unusual, but it's been at exactly the same time.' Julia blinked, looked down at her pie and didn't see it. She was looking at the little alarm clock she had in the bedroom instead, on top of the dresser with her underwear drawer in it, for that matter. Not that that was relevant right now.

But still, Julia was furious that Mariah knew about the novels.

'I mean,' she said, dragging herself back to the matter at hand. 'I mean at exactly the same time – down to the minute. Always 3:33.'

Mariah stared at her, waiting for it to make sense. Sometimes, with Julia, it could take a while.

'Isn't 3am both the witching hour, and the time when most people die?' Julia asked triumphantly. She sat back, holding her knife and fork, smug.

Mariah narrowed her eyes, searching for the sense. 'You mean...?' she asked leadingly.

Julia sat forward and tucked into her pie. Suddenly, she was hungry. Not just for pie, but for revenge. She'd do whatever it took now, to get that simpering Winsome Clark out of the church, and the Wildes out of town.

'I mean,' she said, poking about in the middle of her pie, the fragrant meat and gravy oozing out of the pastry. It was hot in the middle, which was a good thing. A very good thing.

Things were going her way. And she was still alive, wasn't she? Not even been sick with the virus. God was looking after her.

'I mean,' she started again, 'that they've put some sort of curse on me, haven't they? Winsome Clark and the other lot. Morghan Wilde.' She spat the names out. 'Trying to kill me, they are.' She lifted her gaze across the table and looked at her aunt. 'They know we're going to root them out like the vermin they are and so they're using their witchcraft to try to stop me.'

She returned to her pie, nodding. It made perfect sense. Everyone knew that terrible things were being done by the elites. The people in power. And wasn't the Grove trying to take over the village now, with their deep pockets and their smug attitudes?

'The Grove is trying to take over the village now,' she said, her mouth full of steak and kidney pie. 'They've been biding their time, and now that there's this pandemic, they're making their move.' Julia nodded. She'd been keeping up with things. She didn't always just read her Mills and Boons. She could find her way around the Internet as well as anyone. She knew what was going on in the larger scheme of things. 'I wouldn't be surprised if that Morghan Wilde had a direct hand in spreading the virus.'

Mariah nodded. She wasn't entirely sure about all that, but she considered it for a moment. Where there was one nest of vipers, there was always another, wasn't that so? They couldn't be the only place cursed with a nasty lot of pagans like this. There were bound to be others, and all working together, she could be sure of it. And she knew for certain that this one had been trying to take over Wellsford for centuries. Buying up all the land – why, they must own half the county by now. And weren't they secretive about that?

Not to mention all the other perversions that went on. Mariah's lip curled. The gallivanting with the Fey. The spirits who danced in their circles with them.

She knew it. Of course she did. Her house was right across from the church, and behind the church what was there? Grove land, that's what. Acres and acres of it, and that stone circle. It was there too, not far away, as the crow flew – and didn't she often see crows flying over the trees there?

She did. She knew she did.

Mariah Reefton shivered slightly. And there had been that day. She still remembered it like it was yesterday – nothing wrong with her memory. Almost 83 now and still as sharp as the day she was born. Sharper, probably, because babies, well, they didn't really do much thinking, did they?

'You haven't touched your dinner,' Julia said.

'I'm thinking,' Mariah retorted. 'Hush.'

Julia shook her head and went back to her food. It took a while for the old woman's brain to crank around the thoughts now.

That day – Mariah usually tried not to think about it. Young, she'd been, which was always why she told herself it had happened. It was the only thing that allowed her to forgive herself for it.

She'd been beautiful when she was young, though that wasn't something to be bragging about, she knew. It was just the truth. Long dark hair down to the small of her back. A slim little waist, and a face dark-eyed and pretty. Her mother had looked at her sometimes with something in her expression that Mariah hadn't been able to quite place. It had looked a little like disquiet. Sometimes, she thought, a bit like fear.

'You mind to stay away from Them,' her mother had told her over and over. 'Only one thing on Their mind and it isn't what God meant for a woman. Lay you down as soon as look at you, one of those Fae will – and mark my words, I'm telling the truth. They're abominations, I see them in my dreams of a night, I do, come tapping on the window leering and laughing.'

Her mother's face had twisted, and she'd glared at Mariah, shaking her head. 'There was a girl come across in the woods last year by Themselves, and they laid her straight down where they were, and took turns with her, and when they were done with their evil deeds, they took a tree branch to her and used that instead.'

Mariah, whose father had walked out on the household when she was still scampering about in her naps, had listened to her mother and believed every word.

Almost every word.

Some of them, anyway, and the worst of that had been that it'd made her furiously curious. She wasn't allowed to step out with any of the local lads – her mother drove them off so that they'd go away shaking their heads cursing the thought of having that harridan for a mother-in-law.

Mariah stared down at her plate, and Julia watched her, knowing the old woman had gone off somewhere in her head again. Julia wondered if her aunt was going to eat her pie.

She'd sneaked up on them, that was what Mariah had done. Eighteen years old, she'd been then, and in a fever to know what went on in the woods, what went on at the stone circle.

It was one of their festival days. Midsummer. Which they celebrated down in the village too – May day. She'd wanted to dance the maypole, but her mother wouldn't hear of it, said it was pagan leftovers like that which invited the devil in.

And so, she'd sneaked away from the village green

where everyone was laughing and dancing, having a grand old time, and she'd tiptoed through the woods, her heart bouncing off her ribs so that she was sure she'd be found out just from the noise of it.

And they'd been dancing at the stone circle too, and Mariah had crouched in the long grass, between the trees to watch, and she'd seen them – the Others. The Fae, dancing with them.

They were beautiful. She'd never seen men so beautiful and when they laughed and sang, she thought their voices sounded like spun glass, even though that didn't make any sense.

And when one had spotted her and come to lie down in the grass with her, she didn't push him away. And she didn't get up and run for home.

Her mother knew as soon as she'd walked in the door. Mariah stank of them, she said. She could smell the Fae on her from a mile away, she'd told her before slapping her resoundingly across the cheek.

She wouldn't let Mariah out of the house then, not for a long time. Not until Mariah understood completely how the devil worked, every little in and out of his deception.

Mariah looked up, blinking, saw Julia eyeing her pie and stabbed into the pastry with her knife.

'We're going to put some posters together,' she said. 'Some, what do you call them? Flyers.' She sniffed. 'You can use the church copier to run them off.'

'That's in the vicarage,' Julia said, putting down her knife and fork. 'But I've got a printer of my own.' She smiled in satisfaction at the foresight she'd had to invest in one.

She'd gotten a good deal on it too – a year's worth of ink. Plenty of ink. She licked her lips.

'What are we going to put on the flyers?' she asked.

Mariah nodded, put a forkful of pie in her mouth, chewed for a minute.

'We'll put Winsome Clark's crimes on it. Everyone needs to know them. Itemised and in black and white.'

She swallowed, stabbed her fork at another piece of pie. 'And we'll detail exactly what Wilde Grove and that Morghan woman are trying to do to our village.' She nodded and lifted the pie to her lips.

'I've remembered the word, you see,' she said. 'That I was trying to think of before?'

Mariah leered over the table at Julia.

'Conspiracy,' she said. 'It's a conspiracy. They're trying to take over our village.'

Another nod. 'Well let 'em try,' Mariah said.

'They'll find they've got another thing coming.'

27

Erin sidled into the Care Home with a sigh heavy on her lips. She still was not sure at all that she wanted to be here, but Morghan's admonitions rang in her ears, and she'd been debating all the long walk into the village, whether she was doing the right thing or not.

She'd not fully decided. But she had determined to put her trust in Morghan and the Grove for just a little while longer.

It was just that – why, she wondered, were the right things to do always the ones that looked like being the hardest?

Wouldn't it be better if she had to do the things that she already knew she was good at? She could concentrate on her art, and just learn the magic. Why all this other stuff? That's what she'd done yesterday – just stayed at home and did some drawing. Worked on her art. Missed Stephan.

He was still messing around getting the glasshouse built. She'd hardly spoken to him the last two nights. His father, apparently, was giving him grief over every little thing they had to do. Didn't like taking orders from his pansy son, Stephan had reported.

Erin still smarted on his behalf. How dare he say such a thing to his son? She was in half a mind to march down to the gardens and tell the man what she thought of him.

She wondered what he looked like. Stephan must favour his mother. Erin hadn't met either of them. She didn't really know much about Stephan's early life at all.

But that was how it went, wasn't it, she decided, tucking her bag in the cloakroom, and fishing out several pairs of gloves to go in her pockets. Parents were problems.

If she were ever a mother, she'd be different. She wouldn't keep secrets from her kids, that was one thing. She wouldn't say stuff to belittle them, either. Stephan wasn't gay, and if he had been, then so what?

'Ah, Erin, you're back.' It was Mary, and Erin looked up at her in alarm, wondering, not for the first time how the woman managed to slink so silently about the place. It was a gift.

'Yes,' Erin said, feeling sheepish. 'Sorry about not coming in those days last week.'

Mary leaned against the door frame, arms crossed, looking at her youngest employee. 'I understand Morghan talked to you?' she asked, her voice calm and sympathetic.

Erin nodded, looking down at the mask in her hands. 'I don't understand really, why we're doing this – why I'm supposed to take care of this man – but I'm here, and I'm going to do it.'

'Well,' Mary said, standing up again, relieved to see that Erin seemed to have a grip on herself, and some perspective.

'It will give you some closure, at the least, I expect. And perhaps you'll learn things about your birth mother that you didn't know before.'

Erin nodded, biting down on her lip. 'I guess so,' she said.

'Right, well, if you could start by taking all our guests out to their breakfasts, and then changing their beds, that would be lovely.' Mary turned to go, then stopped. 'And Erin?'

Erin made herself look at Mary. 'Yes?'

'Any problems, any, you know, wobbles, do come to me before doing anything rash.'

'Rash?' Erin repeated.

'You've a bit of a knack for rash,' Mary told her.

Erin frowned. That wasn't how she would have thought of herself. Was it? 'I do?' she asked, then thought of something else. 'Mary? Can I ask you something?'

Mary raised her eyebrows and leaned back against the doorway. 'Yes,' she said. 'Have at it.' She hoped she wasn't going to get herself in too deep with that. She was conflicted over Erin. On the one hand, she didn't want anything to do with the girl, but on the other, she couldn't help but have a bit of sympathy for the situation Erin was in. She thought about qualifying her response, but it was a bit late for that.

Erin was turning the mask over in her hands, not really seeing it. 'Do you think I'm...undisciplined?' she asked.

Mary spluttered a laugh, then waved an apologetic hand at Erin. 'I'm sorry,' she said. 'I oughtn't to have laughed.'

Erin looked flatly at her. 'That's a yes, then?'

'Well,' Mary hedged, decided there was no point in

beating about the bush. 'Yes,' she said. 'You're not how as I would describe as disciplined.'

'Why not?' Erin asked.

'Well.' Mary squirmed a bit, but it was too late now. She'd invited the question, now the least she could do would be to answer it gently but truthfully and hope the hearing did the girl some good.

'You're headstrong, quick to flare into anger, and quick to feel wronged, Erin,' Mary said, lessening the harshness of her words with a soft tone. 'You're also a bit whiny.'

Erin's eyes widened. 'Whiny?' she repeated, horrified. 'I'm not whiny.'

Mary said nothing, simply gave the girl a pointed look.

'That was whiny, wasn't it?' Erin said, then heaved a giant sigh. 'I'm sorry. You're right – both of you, you and Morghan – you're right. I am undisciplined.' Her shoulders slumped. 'And whiny.'

'It's not wholly your own fault, love,' Mary said, taking pity on the kid.

'How's that?'

'You were brought up privileged, and that colours things for you.'

'Because my parents are rich, you mean?' Erin shook her head. 'I try to be aware that not everyone has had the same stuff I had.'

'It's not so much that as always having had a soft landing, so to speak, when you've needed it. It's not something everyone has the privilege of being able to rely on,' Mary elaborated. 'It's made you just a little soft and entitled, when what you need is a compassionate heart and a strong backbone. You work on that self-discipline, Erin, and you'll gain both, I've no doubt of it.' Mary hid her smile. Morghan had obviously given the girl quite the thorough talking to.

'Great,' Erin said. 'This is so hard. On the one hand I'm told I'm really talented, and on the other I'm called whiny and undisciplined.' She shook her head. 'Which is it, then?'

'It can be both,' Mary said, wondering how Erin could not have known she'd just whined right then and there.

'Even better,' Erin said, shaking her head. 'Where do I even start, then?'

'Well,' Mary said, standing up, this time for certain. 'I'd start with thinking before you speak, every single time, Erin.' She checked her watch. 'In fact, I'd begin with thinking about what you're even thinking, before you start speaking.' She sighed. 'I've got to get back to work, and you need to begin your work. Breakfast for the residents,' she said. 'And then the beds.'

Erin stared after Mary, her ears ringing with the woman's words.

'Think before you speak,' she muttered. 'Think before you even think.' She resisted rolling her eyes at that one, but only just. She sighed instead and then straightened.

Stephan had said something once, hadn't he? What had it been? Erin slipped the mask on over her mouth and nose, frowning.

She grinned behind the fabric. There. She'd remembered. He'd been telling her something Teresa had told him – about looking after his thoughts. What had it been?

Erin tapped her fingers against her thighs, trying to bring the words back. He'd said Teresa had told him his thoughts were a garden, and he had to decide what he wanted growing there.

That was it.

Erin deflated. Gardens again.

Gardens and pruning and planting. She couldn't escape it.

WAYNE WAS SITTING ON THE SIDE OF THE BED, TRYING TO GET his feet into his shoes. They were just a pair of worn trainers, but he wasn't willing – not quite yet – to give them up for a pair of old man slippers. He wasn't ready to go slouching around in knitted cardies and slippers just yet. In fact, he hoped he'd die before he reached that point.

He watched Becca's girl come into the room, thinking he was ready to die but for this one thing that he didn't want to do – he didn't believe it was possible for starters, getting this privileged little bitch to forgive him. Why was he trying anyway?

'Good morning, Mr. Moffat,' Erin said.

Wayne sniffed. 'Rather you call me Wayne,' he said. 'Mr. Moffat makes me sound like I was ever someone important.'

He looked Erin over as she raised her eyebrows at him and forced a smile for his benefit. Well-scrubbed, she was, and all that pretty red hair. Becca hadn't had red hair. He guessed that must be from the grandmother, then. He'd never met that one, though Becca had had plenty to say about her, and not a whole lot of it had been flattering. He looked around the room, feeling a pissed off amazement that he was here, doing this.

Why? What hope was there for a bloke like him anyway? He ought to go out the same way he came in – no one giving a damn.

'Would you like me to help you walk to the dining room,' Erin said. 'Or shall we take the wheels this morning?'

He looked up at her under his eyebrows. Forget about the old man cardies, he already had the old man brows. How did they get this long? How did any of this happen? He should be dead already, choked on his own vomit or something. Ugly, but quicker than this.

'Walk,' he said.

'Lovely,' Erin replied. 'Let's do it then.' She came around the side of the bed where he was sitting and offered him her arm. She was doing all right, she thought. He wouldn't be able to hear the slight bit of strain in her voice, and if she just didn't think about it, just didn't remind herself that this man knew her mother, then she could do the job. She'd just think of something else every time she was around him.

'Expect you'll be wanting to ask me things about your mum,' Wayne said, letting her help him up from the bed.

'She wasn't my mum,' Erin replied, making her mind as determinedly empty as possible. She made it very still and quiet inside her mind, then shook her head, because there was something there even so, rising from secret depths, dripping water from webbed wings. Erin blew out a breath. There were so many things rising to the surface. 'She gave birth to me, that's all, then sold me.'

'Just asked for a bit extra, is all. To cover expenses and the like. The couple were happy to give it to her.' Wayne sniffed again, remembering loitering around outside the meeting places while Becca was in there spinning her stories.

'I'll bet they were,' Erin said. They squeezed through the doorway. 'Mr. Moffat,' she said.

'Wayne.'

Erin swallowed. She was getting a headache. 'Wayne. I'm not sure that I really want to talk about my mother with you.'

'Why?' he asked. 'I'm the one what knew her best.' He blinked a couple times then spat the words out, daring fate to stick its oar in. 'I was there when she died. Don't you want to know how she died?'

'I already do,' Erin said, wishing she'd insisted on the wheelchair. That way, this odious man would be delivered to the dining room already, and she would be making beds. She'd never complain about making beds again. Ever.

'Nah,' Wayne said, swinging his head slowly around. 'I was there, remember.'

Erin didn't answer for a minute. She guided Wayne Moffat over to a table and pulled out a chair for him.

'It's a shock, you being here,' she said at last. 'I'm not ready yet, to talk about any of it.'

Wayne shrugged his shoulders, felt the plates of bone move under thin-stretched skin.

'Well,' he said. 'As may be, but I've not long to go, and I've things to tell you.'

'Why?' Erin asked, standing back and hugging herself. They were the first in the dining room, so there was no one to overhear her plaintive question.

'Why?' Wayne hunched over and stared at the table-cloth. This was a fancy place, having a tablecloth. Well beyond his means. His means only stretched to a filthy bed in a filthy boarding house where rats ran up and down the drainpipes outside at night.

Maybe, he thought, this was Becca's way of saying it was

okay. That she didn't hold it against him, what had happened. He blinked and lifted a hand to rasp over the whiskers on his chin.

'Yes,' Erin repeated. 'Why?'

He turned and looked at her. He'd forgotten her question. He forgot a lot, really. There were holes all through his mind, big enough to take a dive through, if you were unlucky.

'Why what?' he asked.

Erin drew in a breath, reminding herself to patience and compassion. Even if she had to fake them until she felt them. Even if she never ended up feeling them.

'Why do you need to tell me?' she asked.

The question took Wayne by surprise, and he answered without thinking to lie. 'Unburden myself,' he said, then looked back at the tablecloth. 'I'm on my way out, you know.'

'You mean, pass your burdens along to me,' Erin said, shaking her head.

But Wayne just shrugged.

Erin gazed at him, chewing on her lip, then nodded. 'I'll get you a cup of tea.'

'Rather coffee first thing,' he said.

'Coffee then. And some breakfast. Can you do some scrambled eggs and toast?'

Wayne nodded. He didn't have much of an appetite, but a couple bites might be okay. Then they could talk.

Erin turned in relief and hurried over to the table with the tea and coffee. She'd get him his cup, then go and make sure everyone else was okay, bring them in to breakfast. And there were the beds to make, the laundry to put on, fresh water jugs to the rooms.

If she kept busy enough, Mr. Wayne Moffat wouldn't have the chance to tell her all the things she was pretty sure she didn't want to know.

It would be easier to look after him like she was supposed to, if she didn't know.

28

THEY SAT AND STARED AT THE CHILD THAT SAT PLACID UPON Blythe's knee watching the spirit wolf.

'I'm afraid,' Leah said. 'What are we to do with it?'

''Tis not an it,' Blythe said. 'Her name is Olive.'

Cecily bustled about the kitchen, warming some gruel she'd made from goat's milk and a little oats. 'The Fae do not give their children away,' she said. 'This is no changeling.'

'I know,' Blythe said, taking the bowl gratefully from Cecily and sopping a piece of bread in it, then offering it to the little girl.

'Which means,' Leah said in a horrified whisper, 'that you cannot go to Them and find the baby her mother wants.'

'No,' Blythe said. 'This is the child Pauline gave birth to.'

'What's wrong with her, then, do you suppose?' Cecily said, coming and sitting down on a bench at the table with the other two women. She narrowed her eyes a moment. 'I seen another acted much like this one,' she said. 'It were when I was but a slip of a thing myself, but was the same, I'd swear. Couldn't stand to be petted, wouldn't talk nor look upon one.'

Leah turned to look at her. 'What happened to it?'

Cecily worked her mouth before answering. 'It were put out for the faeries.'

'And?'

Cecily shrugged. 'Did not survive. Was a cold time of the year,' she said.

Blythe held out the bread sop to the small girl and smiled when it was taken from her hand.

'She likes it,' she said, watching the child eat.

Cecily shook her head. 'I wonder if it is a kindness to feed the poor mite.'

Blythe didn't look at her. 'She would die.'

'Aye, and what are we to do with her otherwise? There can be no exchange made, we all three know this, and soon Pauline and John in the village will know also.'

'I cannot let her die,' Blythe said. 'Look upon her – she sees Wolf.'

It was true and none of them could dispute it. While the girl would not look upon any of them, she was enraptured by the spirit wolf who kept to Blythe's side, and thus for the moment, to the child's.

'Perhaps we could find her a place of safety?' Leah asked. 'Perhaps we know someone who could take her in?'

Blythe shook her head, watching the child gaze steadily at Wolf. 'We need to keep her here with us,' she said. 'She has the gift of sight.'

'But will not look a person in the eye!' Cecily retorted.

'It does not matter.'

'But what of Pauline and John?' Leah asked again, more urgently this time as she watched Blythe with the child on her lap. 'They will be expecting their baby back.'

Blythe squeezed her eyes shut. It was an impossible situation. 'I will go back and talk to them,' she said. 'Explain to them that I will keep Olive and look after her, but that she is no changeling.' She looked from Leah to Cecily, then back again. 'What else is there that I can do?'

'And of her threats against you?' Leah asked stiffly.

'I will induce her to retract them,' Blythe answered. 'I will go there on the morrow and explain things.' The child was a pleasant weight upon her knees, and although she would not bear arms around her, Olive was content to sit and eat and watch. Every now and then her gaze would drift from Wolf to search the room as if to see what other animals lurked about. A smile touched the corners of Blythe's mouth, and she imagined how the girl would react were she taken to the stream for devotions. Or to the Wildwood.

'We keep her,' Blythe said. 'Cecily, you must make up the bed for her, and I will fetch some clothes.' She thought of the clothing she had sewn for her own child. Some might fit if she adjusted the seams.

'We ought not,' Leah said, shaking her head. 'Please Blythe – I've a bad feeling on this.'

'If we return her to her parents, they will kill her surely as we sit here,' Blythe said. 'And she is special – look at her, how she gazes upon Wolf.'

Leah pressed her lips together. She could not see Blythe's wolf spirit, not without effort, and looking through different eyes. And here was this child, who saw without any training.

'Are you certain she is not a changeling?' she asked.

'The Fae do not give away their children,' Cecily said firmly. 'They rarely have them, and do not covet a human child above their own.'

'Why so many stories of it, then?' Leah demanded.

'Because not all our children are healthy,' Blythe said, letting herself cup the girl's head in a palm. 'They ail from things we cannot guess at the cause of. We wish they belonged elsewhere, so that there might be a chance we could have the child our heart cries for.' The girl's hair was soft, although in need of a wash. She reached for another piece of loaf to soak in the gruel.

'Not too much to begin with,' Cecily reminded her. 'Else will be too rich for her and end on the floor instead of in the stomach.'

Blythe nodded, and held the breadsop for the child to take.

THE CHILD – OLIVE, BLYTHE SAID TO HERSELF – HAD NOT cried out during the night, and did not now, although, when Blythe slipped from the warmth of her own bed to peer into the child's, her eyes were wide open and casting about. They slid past Blythe's face, and fastened instead on Wolf, who stood high enough to be seen over the wooden sides of the little trundle bed.

'Bide a minute,' Blythe said. 'And I'll be back for you when I'm dressed.'

The house was dim and cool, Tomas still in his bed,

snoring softly. He'd not been pleased to find Olive in Hawthorn House but had no more idea what to do with her than any of them. He did, however, make it known that he shared Leah's misgivings on the situation.

Blythe dressed quickly, used to finding her way by the dull coals of the fire and nothing more. She approached Olive with murmured assurances, and reached for her, putting her hands on the child, and leaving them there for a moment before lifting her from the blankets.

Cecily was already stirring the kitchen fire back to life, huffing and puffing as she went about the dawn's first jobs.

'How was she during the night, then?' she asked. 'Did the tight swaddling comfort her as I thought?'

Blythe was changing the child, drawing on warmer clothing against the morning's chill. 'She didn't stir, or not so as to hear,' she said. 'And now, she looks still at Wolf, and is calm.'

Cecily straightened, watched the flames leap upon the hearth for a moment, whispered a small charm to the fire, then turned to look at the child. 'What are your plans?' she asked.

'I will do my morning devotions – and I shall take the child with me for them, and then I shall go down to see her parents.' Blythe picked Olive up. 'She lets me hold her, see? When her mother touched her, she went rigid as a board. Pauline said it was the same when John or anyone would touch her.'

'She sees the spirits,' Cecily said. 'And is calmed by them.' The old woman sighed, hands on her ample hips. 'She is special, I concede it.'

'We must find a way to bring her up, Cecily,' Blythe said,

looking at the fluff of hair upon the girl's head, clean now. 'She will make a priestess, even if a silent one.'

'Do you not think she'll talk, then?'

'She has not said any word yet.' Blythe turned for the door, the child in her arms reaching down for Wolf. 'We would be glad to break our fast upon our return, Cecily.'

THEIR BREATH STEAMED UPON THE RAW MORNING AS THE SUN took its time gleaning over the hills of Wellsford. Blythe tipped her face to the sky and closed her eyes. Did she imagine it, or was there the faintest taste of salt in the air this morn?

'Salt and sea,' she whispered. 'I beg thy guidance on me.'

Olive was staring solemnly at the trees and when they stepped in amongst them, her head swivelled first this way and then that, dark eyes wide.

'You like the trees?' Blythe asked her. 'Our friends are tall and gracious, are they not?' She stepped over to an oak and took the child's hand in her own, pressed it against the tree's bark.

'There,' she said. 'Do you feel the tree singing?' She smiled. 'Seems a wordless song, a hum, but trees are like that – they sing and dream slower than we.' She looked at Olive's small face, a frown of concentration between the child's eyes. 'But they are both guardians and history-keepers,' she said. 'And we owe them much.'

She walked over to another tree, a long, lean beech this time, and again pressed Olive's hands to the trunk. 'Hear their different voices?' she asked. 'I am Lady of this Forest, and you, my littlest one, shall be a priestess of the same one day, Goddess willing.'

'My Lady,' Leah said, stumbling upon a root in the path, flustered. 'Oh,' she said. 'You have the child with you.'

'She is your sister, Leah,' Blythe said. 'She hears the songs of the trees also.'

But Leah was shaking her head, even while looking at the girl and seeing that it was true. 'My Lady,' she repeated. 'There is great stirring in the village this morning. I fear that they will be coming here to demand the child.' She blinked, her lashes pale against the dimness of the woods. 'The real child.'

Blythe turned to her. 'The real child?'

'Pauline is expecting you to bring her daughter back to her – and not the one you're holding in your arms,' Leah said. 'I spent the night there, in my mother's house, the better to have an ear to the ground.'

'And does the ground rumble?'

'It does, Lady. It rumbles so that I am worried for you.'

Blythe looked at the baby in her arms, then around at the trees. 'I will go and speak with Pauline as soon as we are done here,' she said. 'Worry not. I will speak sense to her ears.'

Leah glanced about. 'We ought not be here this morn,' she said. 'I'm afraid that the woods would have ears other than their own.'

Blythe paused at this and tipped her own head to listen and her spirit to feel. She shook her head. 'They will not dare to come in my woods at this hour,' she said. 'Let us continue with our devotions. I would have the child see who comes to be with us. I can feel Their curiosity.'

. . .

EYES WERE LEVELLED SUSPICIOUSLY UPON BLYTHE AS SOON AS she entered the village, and she stared back at them without blinking. By the time she reached the house of Pauline and John Cotter, there was a crowd following along behind her.

A restless crowd.

Pauline was in front of her house, standing next to her husband. She stared at Blythe.

'Well,' Pauline said. 'Where's my Olive, then?'

There were murmurs all around them, and the villagers moved restlessly on their feet. Blythe gazed about her, watching as none let their gaze slide away from hers as usual, but instead looked insolently at her.

Rumblings, Leah had said. And for the second time, Blythe felt a true flutter of fear in her belly. She drew herself up to full height and looked back at Pauline, standing next to her husband whose knuckles were white from being clenched to fists.

'She is at my home, Pauline, being cared for.'

'Why have you not brought her here back to me?' Pauline demanded. 'I said as how you were to do so when you got her back from the faeries.'

'Pauline,' Blythe said, focusing all her energy now on the woman and doing her best to ignore the fuming John Cotter. 'Olive was not a changeling. There is no such thing as changelings – only our own children who do not always develop bright and bonny as we might wish.'

But Pauline shook her head. 'She was fine when she was but a babe. A little slow to take her feeds, perhaps, but nothing else.' She pulled at her apron. 'Nothing like she is now. That child is not our Olive, I'm telling you. A mother knows her own baby.'

More murmurings from the crowd. It unsettled Blythe.

'Pauline is right,' John said, rousing himself to words at last. 'And you made her a promise to bring our Olive back to us – to take the child to the faeries and bring the correct one back.' His brow was thunderous. 'Are you telling me now that you've not done this?'

'I cannot do that, John,' Blythe said. 'None can do such a thing.'

John turned and spat upon the ground. 'Then that is only because you are a curse upon this village.'

There was a cheer from behind her. Feet shuffling heavier upon the dirt lane.

'It were you who put a hex upon my cattle then and sent them ailing until two of the beasts laid down and died.' John rubbed his knuckles against the stuff of his trousers, as though to shine them up.

'Aye,' a voice behind her piped up. 'And I saw you upon the road the day that my wagon threw a wheel. That were you an' all, weren't it?'

A woman pushed forward to the front of the crowd and Blythe saw with dismay that it was Agnes.

Agnes who had lost her baby when it was only weeks upon the earth. Agnes, whose eyes were bloodshot with grief even still.

'And don't forget the curse you put on my babe, so that he ailed and died still in the cradle.' She blinked hard. 'I saw the imps you sent to do him harm. Come in through the window you demanded I leave open, didn't they? Fresh air, you said – but really, you just wanted the window open for your spirits to come in and do their nasty work.' She sniffed and ran a hand under her nose. 'Jealous, you were, after your own son died. Couldn't bear for another to have the fortune God had denied to you, and so you killed my baby.'

Blythe shook her head. 'No,' she said. 'I tried to help your baby. I wanted to see him happy and healthy in your arms.'

Anges' face twisted into a look of hate. 'Them remedies you gave me – they did no good – and when you were putting your hands on his little arms and legs, and whispering things, them things were no good were they? They weren't prayers to our Lord to save his little life. They were curses, to twist his life, so that he couldn't thrive.'

'I seen yer,' another man said, shoving his way through the crowd to stare her in the face. He jostled up against her, and his breath stunk against her cheek. 'I seen yer, when you think none are watching – roaming amongst those trees of yours, touching them and praying, 'cept it ain't to no god we know, is it?' He leaned back and shook his head at her. 'What use are yer for us to tolerate in our midst if you can't even bring their Olive back to them?' He wrinkled his nose as though she were the one who smelt so badly. 'Why, I reckon then, you're no good and all harm.'

'Blythe!'

Her knees almost didn't hold her, so great was her relief at hearing Tomas's voice. But when the crowd parted to let him through, and she saw that he held the baby Olive in his arms, she shook her head violently.

'You should not have brought her here!' she hissed.

'What's this, then?' John asked, looking to the child

swaddled tightly in a blanket in Tomas's arms. 'Is this our Olive, then – our real Olive? Must be, since she screams not.'

Blythe shook her head, looking over the child at Tomas, tears springing to her eyes. He gazed back at her.

Pauline lunged for her child. 'You did get her back, then!' she crowed. 'You got her back and thought to keep her for yourself!'

Blythe pressed her hand to her mouth.

Pauline snatched the child from Tomas's arms, and tore the blanket from her, bending to inspect the girl. Olive, ripped from the comfort of the tight swaddling, went immediately rigid and screamed. Her mother froze, gazed down at the child in horror, then shoved it back at Tomas.

'You lied!' she screeched over the screams of her child. 'This isn't our Olive. Get this disgusting thing out of my sight. It's a lie, it's not my baby.'

Helpless, Tomas took the baby and held her awkwardly as she howled as though being murdered. Blythe pushed forward and picked up the dropped wrapping, plucking the baby from Tomas's arms and holding her tight against her breast.

'Hush little one,' she said, 'hush now, little one.'

But Olive kept screaming, and Blythe couldn't get the blanket tightly around her again, not while the child held herself so stiffly. She tried though; she tried to get it wrapped about her, tucked in to give comfort, but Olive fought, flinging her arms out, arching her back, and screaming, her small face turning beet red.

Blythe looked up again, over at Tomas, and he was all she could see in the crowd. Everyone else fell away for a moment, and it was just him looking at her, and she looked back at him and hoped he could see the love in her eyes, the love she held in her heart for him, and her sorrow that she'd put them in this position. He mouthed something to her, but she couldn't hear the words, could only see his mouth work, his head shake.

She shook her own, tears springing to her eyes, and then she smiled at him. A smile full of love, and apology.

Blythe looked back down at the child in her arms, and sank down to her knees, pulling Olive tighter against her and pointing. 'Look at Wolf, little one,' she said. 'Look at Wolf, he's right there.' She sniffed and spoke again. 'Look little one,' she said. 'Wolf is looking at you. Wolf is your friend, isn't he?'

Olive stopped crying. She relaxed slightly, her gaze going to the great Wolf spirit.

'See?' Blythe murmured. 'You and Wolf have made good friends, haven't you? He likes you very much, I can see. And you like him too, don't you?'

Olive reached out to touch Wolf, and Blythe nodded. 'Yes, little one. He's right there. That's the way.'

A hand grabbed Blythe by the shoulder, wrenching her to her feet. It was Tomas, and his face was in hers for a moment, furious. 'Quickly,' he hissed. 'Home. Now, before they turn to a lynch mob.'

Blythe went with him, his hand clamped around her arm, dragging her, and when they reached the safety of the woods, she saw it was no safety at all, and stared at the trees in horror.

Each of them along their way was on fire, burning silently for only her eyes to see.

Destruction was coming.

29

'Morghan?' Ambrose said. 'Are you all right? What is it?'

Morghan shook her head. 'Step outside with me – tell me whether you see it too.'

Ambrose gave her an odd look, frowning, but his curiosity was already stirred, and he stepped willingly out into the morning. Morghan's feet were bare, but he didn't think she'd had time to walk down to the stream yet.

She all but tugged him from the door and out onto the wide spread of lawn that bordered the treeline. Skirting around the well, they stopped, and Ambrose glanced at Morghan's pale, drawn face, then shook his head.

'What are we looking at?' he asked. 'I don't see anything.'

Well, not anything that wasn't what he usually saw. The morning had dawned with a clear sky that now lifted overhead, a lightening violet blue. The air held a crispness in it that had his heart leaping, and he knew that soon, the trees would let their buds burst forth and suddenly everything would be tinged with fragrant greenery.

Morghan was shaking her head, her shoulders hunched about her ears, flinching away from what she could see.

'You don't see the trees?' she asked. 'On fire?'

Ambrose looked at her face, then gazed around at the woods. 'I don't,' he said. 'Describe it to me.'

Morghan blew out a long breath in an effort to calm and ground herself, then shook her head. 'History replays itself,' she said. 'What happened once in real life is happening now - as a warning? A premonition of sorts, of danger?' She closed her eyes.

'The trees are on fire,' she said. 'The flames leap around their branches.'

Ambrose looked again at the trees but saw nothing disturbing the early peace of the morning. 'Is it just visual?' he asked. 'Or can you hear it as well?'

Morghan shook her head. 'I can only see it, thank the Goddess. Hearing it also would be too much. Far too much. I have seen it in glimpses the last weeks, but now it stays. There is an intense pressure in the air and the flames look so real I can barely lift my head to look.'

'And is it all of them?'

She made herself look, drawing in a lungful of air, unable to stop the expectation that it would taste of smoke and fire. But it was clear and fresh and sharp and that helped.

'Most,' she said. 'Not all, I think, but the ones along my way to the stream.' She lifted an arm and gestured in a wide sweep. 'It is the same as Blythe saw.' Morghan paused.

'It is the same as Ravenna showed you?' Ambrose asked.

Morghan nodded. 'It happened in real life, and now they burn again – but why, Ambrose?'

'They burned for Blythe as a premonition of what was to come, did they not? As a warning of danger?'

'I believe so, yes.' Morghan squeezed her eyes shut against the flames that danced silently upon the limbs. 'One which she was unable to act against.'

'For the sake of a child, Morghan. You mustn't be too hard on her.'

'I know.' Morghan shook her head. 'I know. And I may have done exactly the same in her position.' She pressed her lips shut on any other judgement. Then snorted a sudden laugh. 'I should say – I did exactly the same in her position.' She swallowed down another shrill giggle and opened her eyes instead. 'So, what do you think it means this time? I don't believe it is about myself. I am well.'

'The Grove – do you think it is in danger?' Ambrose posed the question out loud as much because he wanted to consider it himself as hear Morghan's opinion.

'The Grove is better established than it has been for centuries,' Morghan replied. 'Surely it cannot be that?'

Ambrose's brow furrowed. 'Perhaps,' he said. 'Perhaps it is precisely because of that.'

Morghan shook her head, still shying away from the dreadful sight of her beloved trees on fire. 'I'm not sure I understand you,' she said.

Ambrose thought upon it. 'This pandemic,' he said. 'In an effort to combat its dreadful effects, we have stepped out of the shadows, and into the full life of the village.'

'We had to,' Morghan said.

'I agree. We've done good things.' He lifted a hand and ticked them off on his fingers, still gazing around at the trees, wishing he could see what Morghan did. 'The care home, the community gardens, the co-operative grocery scheme – and now you're even planning to set up a doctor's office.'

'If we can entice any doctor out here,' Morghan said. 'That isn't guaranteed.'

Ambrose didn't allow himself to be distracted. 'What we've also done,' he said, circling back around to his original thought, 'is to make ourselves more visible. We've entered the day-to-day life of Wellsford, instead of keeping to ourselves.'

'And not everyone is best pleased about that,' Morghan said, thinking of Mariah Reefton. 'Winsome,' she said. 'We need to check on her.'

Ambrose looked suddenly startled and turned wide eyes to Morghan. 'She is in danger?' he asked, feeling the sudden urge to dive into the trees and down to the vicarage. He held himself back with the strength of will.

'Mariah knows she cannot touch us, and Winsome is vulnerable, since she bridges the gap between the Grove and the village. Mariah will wreak havoc however she can.' Morghan looked across at Ambrose and sighed with relief. 'The flames have gone,' she said.

There was not even a singed branch when she looked at them now. No blackened limbs, no scent of burnt sap or bark. Nothing. It was as if it had never been.

But there was someone on the path, stepping out from the trees towards them. It was Stephan, something fluttering in his hand.

He stopped abruptly, surprised to find them both standing outside.

'Have you been waiting for me?' he asked, briefly confused. They stood as though they'd had warning he was coming, and yet that was impossible.

Morghan shook her head. 'No,' she said. 'What is it?'

Stephan panted from the jog up the path from Wellsford. 'I found these,' he said, holding out the page. 'Plastered all over the village this morning. Thought you ought to see them.' He bared his teeth. 'They're brutal. What's going on?'

Ambrose reached out and took the paper from his hand, smoothing it open so he could look at it.

'It's a flyer,' Stephan said. 'And they've been plastered everywhere. On the lamp poles. Buildings.' He wrinkled his nose. 'I took that one from the window of Haven for Books, where it definitely shouldn't have been.'

They heard a car pull up on the gravel driveway on the other side of the house, and a moment later, a door slammed.

'Oh, you're all outside,' Lucy said, rounding the side of the house and coming up short. She spotted the piece of paper in Ambrose's hand and pursed her lips. 'I see you've already discovered what is going on,' she said.

Ambrose passed the flyer to Morghan. 'Stephan says they're everywhere.'

Lucy came closer, shaking her head. 'Whoever did it went completely overboard. They're everywhere, all right.' She held hers up, the print large and black on the page. 'This one was in the window – on the outside, of course – of

The Copper Kettle.' She was furious. 'As if we'd ever hold to this rubbish.'

'It's Mariah's doing,' Morghan said, and gave the paper back to Ambrose. 'I'm going to go see Winsome.'

Lucy nipped a tooth at her lip. 'Won't that, well, won't that make things worse – if you go see her?'

Morghan crossed her arms, realising that she was chilled, standing barefoot in the damp grass. 'I'm wary of this,' she said. 'This sudden disunity, this disharmony between ourselves and the village.'

'It's not everyone,' Stephan said. 'Most I reckon either don't care or are getting behind the things we've been doing.' He scowled at the flyer he'd ripped from the window of Krista's shop.

Lucy held hers up and looked at it. She didn't need to read it again. Once had been enough. 'The person who wrote this,' she said. 'She's not thinking straight.'

She shifted uncomfortably, letting the impressions from the paper seep into her. 'It's like she's looking at the world though a pair of glasses that aren't the right prescription. Everything is distorted.' Lucy cringed. 'It's awful,' she said. 'There's only the tiniest grip on reality.'

Morghan nodded. 'Throw it away, Lucy,' she said. Then repeated, 'I'm going to go see Winsome.'

'I should go,' Ambrose said.

But Morghan looked at him and shook her head. 'No,' she said. 'Not yet.'

They stared at each other for a long moment, then Ambrose nodded.

'Do you want a lift?' Lucy asked, forgetting that they couldn't hop in the car together. She clapped a hand to her head. 'I forgot, I'm sorry. When is this lockdown going to end?'

'Thank you anyway,' Morghan said. 'I also need to finish dressing first.' She touched her hair, loose down her back, and looked at her feet. 'Winsome will go on at me if I'm not wearing any footwear,' she said, smiling.

'I'd go back with you, if I could,' Stephan said. 'Got a lot going on.' He glanced at Morghan as if he wanted to say something.

'What is it, Stephan?' Morghan asked.

He winced. 'I think Erin needs you,' he said.

Morghan smiled. 'Tell Erin to continue her gardening. She is stronger than she realises.'

'But she's been through so much already.'

'We all go through a great deal, Stephan. How are things with your father?'

Stephan rolled his eyes. 'Awkward,' he said after a brief pause. 'He doesn't like taking directions from his son, that's for sure.' Stephan grinned suddenly. 'He's coping surprisingly well though, considering. There's been a bit of grief, and it's painful all the way, but we're getting there.'

Morghan smiled at him. 'You're doing brilliantly,' she said. 'We're proud of you.'

'But what about Erin?' Stephan asked, then searched around for the right words. 'She hasn't well, you know, had time to develop the same sort of resiliency, you know?'

'No,' Morghan agreed, knowing everyone was following the conversation with interest. 'She's on a bit of a crash course, I know. I'll be seeing her shortly, don't worry. I've not forgotten her, in amongst everything else.' It was difficult to suppress her sigh, but Morghan did it, breathing out and calming herself as she did so.

'Right,' Stephan said. 'Well, I've got a million things to do, so I'll be off.'

'Me too,' Lucy said. 'The renovations for the Green Man are coming along nicely. They're not extensive, but the place has been closed for months now, so needs a good spruce up and a lick of paint.' She grinned, excited by her plans. 'Stephan, we're going to need live music for the grand re-opening.'

Stephan lifted a hand, on his way back to the path between the trees. 'Gather the rest up and I'll be there,' he called.

Lucy nodded. 'Right, then. I can leave this with you?' She held up the piece of paper to Ambrose and Morghan.

Ambrose took it, holding it by a corner as though it was contaminated.

MORGHAN, FULLY DRESSED, HER FEET IN HER STURDY BOOTS, her hair fastened and tidy, stepped into the trees, ducking her head at the memory of them on fire. She reached out and touched a tree trunk, pleased that it was cool and damp under her fingers.

'My friends,' she whispered. 'How hard it was to watch you burn.'

The tree murmured in the light breeze and Morghan continued on.

What a morning it had been, and her devotions interrupted. Usually, she would not allow that for anything, and it irked her now that she was doing so. How could she tell

Erin to lean deeper into her practice to see her through, when she did not do so herself?

Of course, one morning's skipped devotions would not make a difference in the scheme of things, but she slowed her steps and walked deliberately now, breathing in the musk of the forest, as she stepped both in Wilde Grove, and the Wildwood.

In the trees, off in the shadows, she glimpsed the White Stag of the Wildwood, and nodded to him.

Wolf grew more visible at her side, his fur thick and dark, and Morghan looked down at him, remembering how the child Blythe had saved had been able to see the spirit animal. What had happened to the little girl, Morghan wondered?

She suspected she would find out – if not the whole of the story, then at least more of it.

There was a loose knot of people outside the vicarage, all of them clutching the white pieces of copier paper. Morghan rounded the corner and walked straight into them.

For a moment, there was complete silence, and Morghan wished immediately that she hadn't come. Then, she straightened her shoulders – this situation was untenable. They had to all find a way to live together.

'Morghan,' a voice said, and Morghan saw Minnie pushing her way forward through the small throng of people, waving the page. 'Have you seen this rubbish?'

The crowd was only seven or eight people, but each held uneasily onto one of the flyers.

'I have, yes,' Morghan said. 'I came to see how Winsome is; if there's anything I can do to help.'

'Haven't you done enough?' muttered one of the women, her gaze resolutely averted.

'Is that what you really think?' Minnie spluttered before Morghan could even open her mouth. 'I mean – really? Is that what you really think?'

The woman shifted, then shook her head.

'I'm sorry,' Minnie said. 'Could you say that louder, please?'

'Minnie,' Morghan said reprovingly. 'No one needs to be badgered.'

'Someone needs their head taken off,' Minnie retorted, waving the page again. 'And I think we can all agree on who it is, spreading this utter garbage.'

'I for one agree,' another of the women piped up. 'It's like some witch hunt.' She shivered delicately. 'I don't want Winsome hounded from the place. She's been amazing since our Grandad Ken died in Banwell at the beginning of the pandemic. I don't know what we would have done without her – I never felt like he could be at rest until she held that service for him and the others.'

Morghan hid her smile. Emily Bright was right, of course. Ken, and the others, hadn't been at rest until Winsome had welcomed them, blessed them, helped them on their way, held the Requiem Mass for them.

There were murmurs of agreement from the small knot of women.

'She's come and sat with me and mine whenever we've needed her. My mother's been very frightened through all this, and Winsome's been a godsend,' Melody Roper said, nodding her head.

'She helped us access the extra money from the government,' Sharon Johnston said. 'Even though she didn't know much how to go about it.' Sharon glanced over at Morghan for a moment. 'She got that woman from the bookshop to help – Krista. Between them, they got us sorted real quick.'

'And once it's back up and running, I'm looking forward to working in the charity shop again.' Denise Scott glanced sideways at Morghan and shrugged. 'Robinson, bless his soul, was a good man – but he never did so much for us as our Winsome has already.'

'See!' Minnie crowed. 'This bollocks doesn't make any difference, does it?'

Denise frowned. 'I don't know. I don't see as how Winsome should be going to these rituals, and the like.' She glanced again at Morghan. 'No offense.'

'None taken,' Morghan said. 'I think it did help her to understand who we are and what we do, to see us in action, so to speak. Is Winsome here?'

All their eyes turned to look at her.

'No,' Sharon said. 'We knocked but she's not in.' She blinked at Morghan. 'You two are friends?'

'We are,' Morghan agreed.

Sharon's face worked as she thought on that one. Finally, she shrugged. 'I guess that might make sense – you're both, like, what would you call it?'

'Village leaders?' Minnie offered helpfully. 'Spiritual leaders?'

Sharon nodded dubiously. 'I guess so.' She seemed to come to a decision, and drew back her shoulders, standing up straighter. 'I mean, and the village ticks along better now than it's ever done.'

There were nods of agreement from the other women.

'And it's nice that you're both women.' Sharon looked suddenly abashed. 'I never got to say, Morghan, but I was sorry to hear about your wife. Grainne was always so full of life, you know?'

Morghan did know. She drew in a soft breath and nodded. 'Thank you, Sharon,' she said.

'Is Clarice still here?' Denise asked. 'Don't see her around much.'

'She is,' Morghan answered. 'But she does spend a fair amount of time...elsewhere.'

'You know, that celebration we had at Halloween was something,' Melody said almost wistfully. 'You got something planned like that for anything?' She tipped her head dreamily to the side. 'I miss getting together, you know? And the dancing was wonderful – this lockdown's easing soon, perhaps you could organise something like that again?' She blinked. 'The beacons were a brilliant touch.'

It was interesting, Morghan thought, feeling bemused. These women were relating to each other, and her, on a human level, not one of conflicting beliefs. They wanted connection and compassion. They wanted Winsome sitting at their kitchen tables offering a listening ear. They wanted a celebration when the lockdown was over – bonfires and dancing.

They were just ordinary women, who knew deep down, that it was connection that was important.

'I'm sure we can organise something,' Morghan said, smiling. 'Perhaps we can make it a joint effort between us all?'

It was Sharon who answered, pulling another face. She held up the piece of paper. 'What do we do about this, though? I don't want to see our Vicar hounded out of here. Especially as it means practically all the good work she's been doing – we've been doing – will be shut down.'

There was another murmur of agreement.

'I mean,' Sharon continued. 'We've seen it happen with practically every other village our size. Conglomerated, or whatever they call it. Down to one service a month, if they're lucky, held by someone who's always somewhere else when you need them, I'll bet.' She shrugged. 'And if we're not lucky, the church will just get shut down and sold off.' She turned to look at Morghan. 'You'd buy it then, wouldn't you? And give it back to us?'

Morghan's head was spinning. This was the last thing she'd expected to hear. Any of it, for that matter. 'Ah, I'm afraid you've taken me by surprise with that question,' she said. Then frowned and decided she was curious enough to ask a question of her own.

'If that happened, it would not be part of the Church of England. Does that not matter to you?'

The women in the small group were silent for a moment.

'Well,' Sharon answered with a glance around at the others. 'I don't know. Nothing would really change, though, would it? I mean, it's mostly about comfort and community, these days, and we could do things the same way, right?'

'I don't know,' Morghan said, bemused that they were asking her any of this. 'That would be up to whatever committee you formed, I expect, and any regulations from the Church you had to be careful of.'

Denise shook her head. 'It's not going to come to that,' she said. 'That's ridiculous.' She frowned.

'I think we need to speak to the Dean ourselves,' Denise continued. 'On behalf of the village, and the Vicar.' She shook her head. 'Mariah and her lot be damned.'

Denise's cheeks flushed at her own words, but she didn't take them back.

30

'I'm not going back to the cave with you,' Winsome said, thrusting her hands in her pockets and speaking with what she hoped was a firm and resolute tone.

Morghan managed a laugh. 'That's fine,' she said. 'I won't drag you there.'

'What happened then anyway?' Winsome mused. 'Where did I go? Can anyone do that? I mean – is that sort of thing accessible to anyone?'

Morghan tipped her head to the side. They walked as they talked, and she thought that Sharon was right in wishing this lockdown were over. She was used to walking and being outside, but even for her, it was getting ridiculous. Everyone was tired of it, and while the village had been coping well, Morghan could see everyone's frustration rising above the place like a cloud, like something she could almost reach out and touch.

It was part of the tinder that was set to ignite over the business with Winsome if they weren't careful.

'You stepped into the Wildwood, as you have done the times you helped me with the healings and soul retrievals,' she said. 'This time you visited what many call the Underworld, and yes, it is accessible to anyone – to varying degrees. Most will only go there in their dreams, but many are able to change their state of consciousness – go into a trance – and visit there if they try, and continue to practice.' She mused upon it. 'It will be becoming easier too, I think, with the veil shredding, the worlds rubbing up against each other so closely now, but even so, it takes a kind of self-hypnosis, the ability to sink into a trance state.' She sighed. 'I think it is almost more important however, for all of us to realise – and act on the realisation – that the world we walk through each day has a spiritual aspect to it. It is not wholly a material world, and it is alive and responds to us, requires much of us.' She reached out and touched her fingertips to a budding tree. 'Travelling to the Otherworld, meeting the gods there, and whomever else, is well and good, but we would do even better to walk in this world knowing everything has spirit and its own experience of consciousness, and that there are many folds and pockets where the worlds join and open easily to us if we expand our spirits and exercise our awareness.'

Morghan sighed. 'It is hard to explain, and you did not ask for one of my lectures anyway.'

Winsome rubbed her hands together. 'I sort of did, but never mind.' She closed her eyes for a moment and felt the breath of the day upon her cheeks. 'It grows warmer,' she said. 'The seasons are turning.' Opening her eyes, Winsome barked a laugh. 'I'm starting to sound like you.' She paused.

'I can't believe Sharon and Denise said what they did this morning.'

'Which part?' Morghan asked, shaking her head in similar disbelief. 'But I suppose it is a good thing, that they would have you leading them even if it means breaking with the Church?'

Winsome touched her fingers to her forehead. 'They're mad,' she said. 'And I doubt it would be that easy. I don't even know how it would possibly work. I don't even want to know how it would possibly work. It's mad.'

'Would it come to that, do you think?' Morghan asked.

'There's a good possibility,' Winsome said. 'The Dean may choose not to continue services here at all – this parish having a full-time clergy has always been a bit dodgy, and now of course, the Church is haemorrhaging money due to this virus, so they may just shut things down – or do the amalgamation thing, of course.' She waggled her head from side to side. 'I suspect it will be one or the other, and neither good for Wellsford. Or me.' She shook her head. 'I've been so foolish, Morghan – giving Mariah and Julia the ammunition they needed.'

Morghan stopped walking. 'Don't be silly,' she said. 'You've done nothing of the sort. You attended one ritual here, but as neither Mariah nor Julia did, they can only speculate as to what that actually means. And they caught you praying in the small temple? What sin could that possibly be?' She paused, weighing her words. 'Winsome, I feel that Wellsford is the right place for you – that Wilde Grove is the right place for you.'

Winsome's eyes widened in shock. 'Wilde Grove is the right place for me? What are you suggesting? That I leave the Church and join the Grove?' She wondered briefly why she felt such horror over the suggestion – she'd had the same thought herself, once or twice, in the deepest hours of the night when none could overhear.

But Morghan was shaking her head. 'No,' she said. 'That is always an option, but it wasn't what I was suggesting.'

Winsome frowned.

Morghan spread a hand – her golden hand – at the land around them that glowed with the slanted spring light. 'This is a liminal place, Winsome – I think I remember telling you so during one of our very first conversations.'

After a moment's thought, Winsome nodded. It sounded familiar.

'Here,' Morghan continued, 'we straddle the worlds. Everyone can walk this way, but here we have been doing it for millennia and we have worn paths between the worlds, in and out of one and the other.' She sighed. 'You have already changed, Winsome – now you belong not just to the village and the church, but to the Grove as well. You straddle both, and I've a good feeling this is how it is meant to be for you. You are a bridge.'

Winsome turned away, stared out at the trees. 'I don't want to leave Wellsford,' she said. 'I don't know past that fact, but I do not want to leave.' Briefly, she shook her head. 'There is so much I can do here – and you are right, I do move between the Grove and the village.' She fell into thought. 'So much is going on, Morghan. I'm confused by most of it.' She thought again of the flyers she'd discovered plastered on every surface in Wellsford.

'What about all the things Mariah and Julia said on that dreadful piece of paper they pasted everywhere?'

Morghan sighed. It really had been a nasty thing. 'You've only to show your Dean that and he will dismiss everything those two have to say. That was tactically a poor move on their behalf. It's impossible to take them seriously now – saying you're part of a wider, satanic conspiracy? It's that sort of talk that will get Julia out of her position, not you.'

'Yes,' Winsome agreed. 'You're right, and I actually feel more secure about everything now than I did before, precisely because of that. They've overplayed their hand.'

'But?' Morghan asked. 'I can hear a but after that.'

'Well,' Winsome answered. 'But what if I feel like I've strayed too far from what I'm supposed to be as a vicar of the Church of England? What if I've done that? You talk about me being a bridge between the village and the Grove, and I think I understand what you say, but in practical terms, how is that going to affect my calling in the Church?' She shook her head. 'That was a rhetorical question, Morghan – I'm the one needs to think upon the answer.'

They were back at the treeline, and the church and vicarage lay beyond the rock that hid the path. Winsome looked over at Morghan.

'Thank you,' she said. 'For your company and your support.'

Morghan smiled. 'Thank you, Winsome – for your precious friendship.'

MORGHAN WENDED HER WAY ALONG THE THREAD OF TREES, watching the afternoon sun seep down in amongst the woods. Spring and autumn, she thought idly as she walked, were perhaps her favourite seasons. She could lose herself in the light, the way it lay upon the world in long golden shafts, setting the dust to shining as if made of precious metal. Letting go of her conscious thoughts, she walked and draped a hand through the light, watching as it moved and danced with the breeze in the tree's branches. She let herself be part of the light, of the shadow, of the dance of dust, of the scent of the forest, the swaying of the trees, their long, low song, the almost-bursting readiness of their buds.

Erin was in her garden, arms lifted, spread to the sky, and Morghan stopped to watch from the woods for a moment before making her way down to Ash Cottage. The girl's hair was like flame in the light, and Morghan felt the weight of the trees burning again as she'd seen them that morning, the air warping around her with the pressure of the vision. She blinked at the glinting red hair, then tipped her chin down and made her way along the path to the house.

Erin had moved into a swaying, stepping dance – just the way she'd been taught – when Morghan let herself into the walled garden she tried not to still think of as Teresa's. She whispered a blessing to her old friend and looked upon Teresa's shimmering granddaughter.

Erin had talents, Morghan thought, seeing the way she danced, almost but not quite holding the worlds within her. She was close, very close.

All she needed was to hold the dedication and keep up the practice.

And to learn some stillness inside that head of hers.

Morghan stepped forward and into Erin's line of vision. Erin's eyebrows flew up and she stuttered to a halt. Morghan shook her head.

'No,' she said. 'Keep dancing. We will dance together.'

Erin hesitated a moment, then nodded, and moved again to music only she could hear. Morghan stilled herself, wrapped herself in the worlds and let them spin around her. She stepped into the rhythm of Erin's movements and danced with her, feeling the expanse of the worlds, and drawing Erin into them with her.

Erin stopped dancing and looked around in consternation. 'Where are we?' she asked.

Morghan recognised the place at once. 'I did not mean to bring us here,' she said, and lifted a golden hand to her cheek and wiped away a sudden tear.

'Your hand,' Erin said, staring at the way Morghan's hand gleamed. 'It's gold. Actually gold.'

'Here, yes,' Morghan answered.

'You're crying.'

'I don't come here often.'

Erin drew her embarrassed gaze from Morghan and looked around. She didn't know what to say or do. 'I don't understand,' she said at last.

There was a rustling behind her, and she turned, mouth falling open at the sight of a great cat stepping out of the greenery and padding towards them.

'What sort of cat is that?' she whispered hoarsely, backing away. It looked like its mouth would be very big.

'A mountain lion,' Morghan answered, bending down to stroke the animal as it pushed against her legs and nuzzled its head against her belly. 'Her name is Amara.'

Erin licked her lips. 'Amara?'

'She is my wife's.'

'Your wife's?'

Erin swallowed and flushed. She was sounding like a twit repeating everything, but really, a moment ago she'd been in her garden dancing before trying to go back to her new garden and maybe decide what she was supposed to do there.

And now she was here. And Morghan was patting a wild animal. And crying.

'Grainne,' Morghan agreed.

'Her, like, spirit animal?'

'Yes,' Morghan said, feeling Amara's heart beating under her thick fur. 'And no, more than that.'

'More?'

Morghan straightened. 'Once, a great long time ago,' she said, smiling faintly even as another tear tracked down her cheek. 'There was a tribe of shapeshifters.'

Erin listened, confused, trying to understand. She pressed her lips together so as not to repeat what Morghan had said. *Shapeshifters.*

'They took the form of large cats,' Morghan said, her fingers resting on Amara's head while the cat made a rumbling noise deep in her throat.

'Cats?' Erin asked, unable to stop herself. 'Not really, though, right?'

'Yes, I think so,' Morghan answered. 'I think they could, for all intents and purposes, turn into cats. People would see them as such.' She blinked. 'They were all women, and they were much feared and respected by those around them.'

Erin shook her head. 'How do you know this?'

'I remember it.'

'What? Were you there?' Erin asked. 'Were you one of them?'

Morghan allowed herself a smile. 'No,' she said. 'But I loved one of them. I would sneak from my family's home to meet her in the hillside.' The smile widened with the memory. 'She called me *kitten*.'

Erin was fascinated, despite not knowing if she believed a word of it. People who could shape-shift? Really shape-shift?

She supposed it wasn't impossible. As much knowledge had been lost over the centuries as had been gained, she suspected.

'Were you a man or woman?' she asked.

'Does it matter?' Morghan answered.

'Well, no, I guess not,' Erin said, wondering now why she had asked it in the first place.

Morghan looked down at the cat, who gazed up at her with great, golden eyes. 'I have spent most of my lifetimes as a male,' she said. 'But have had plenty of experiences also as a woman. It is the same with all of us – we are one, or the other, depending on what will serve best for each lifetime.' She shrugged. 'And perhaps according to preference, as well, I do not know. It is hard to know much at all from this perspective.'

'What happened?' Erin asked. 'In that lifetime, I mean?'

'That, I also don't know,' Morghan said. 'I've not explored much of it, except some of the intimate details of my association with one of the women – who was later to be Grainne, of course, and hence, why Amara is here.'

Erin struggled to follow that logic. 'I don't understand,' she said.

'Grainne kept some of the cat aspect in others of her lifetimes. She had some ability when I knew her to shift into the cat, and the cat also walked beside her much the same way Wolf walks with me.'

The answer brought another question to Erin's mind. 'Why do I not have Fox with me? I still catch only glimpses of her.'

Morghan gazed around the clearing where they stood. 'She will come when she is ready,' she said. 'Or rather, when you are ready.'

'When will I be ready, though?' Erin asked, then winced at her tone. 'Mary said the other day that I whine too much.'

Morghan laughed. 'It's somewhat true, but so do many.'

'You don't.'

'No, and nor will you if you keep recalling the fact that you ought not to be at the forefront of every thought you have,' Morghan replied.

Erin frowned, opened her mouth to ask for clarification, then closed it again. She would think on that one in private, she decided.

'You haven't told me what this place is,' she said instead.

'It is the place I mentioned recently,' Morghan answered, looking around with a sigh. 'My personal place in the Wildwood, where I might come just to be.'

'But you said you don't come here often,' Erin said. It was impossible, she thought, not to ask a great many questions. Morghan didn't tell her things unless she asked.

'Nor do I, anymore,' Morghan replied. She walked across the soft floor of the forest to the stony shore of the lake that twisted around her small promontory.

'There's an island!' Erin cried, delighted at the sight of the small, rounded hump of land rising from the water. 'Do you know that place?'

Morghan nodded, seizing on a way to make this unexpected jaunt a teaching journey for Erin. The tears were dried on her cheeks now and she breathed deeply of the cold taste of the lake.

'This isn't anything like the loch,' Erin said. 'Much friendlier.'

'You did good work there with Kria,' Morghan said, letting herself be drawn off-track. 'She needed you and you found your way to doing what was necessary.'

Erin shuddered beside her. 'I hope I don't ever have to do anything like that again.'

Morghan turned to look at her and Erin raised her eyebrows.

'What?' she said. 'Have you ever had to do anything like it?'

Blythe came to Morghan's mind. And someone else.

'Come,' she said. 'I'm going to show you something I've shown no one else.'

Erin was immediately impressed. 'What is it?' she asked.

But Morghan held up a hand and shook her head. She turned away from the lake's edge and walked between the thin line of trees that rimmed her private clearing. She crossed the clearing and looked for the track that went onwards deeper into the woods. It was there, faint with disuse.

She did not want to walk this way, or to see what was still there. What she was fairly certain was still there.

But there was meaning to everything, and here she was, Erin in tow. Erin who would likely one day be Lady of the Grove, and who must learn that hard things can be done and done willingly and gracefully.

'Wha?' Erin stepped out of the trees behind Morghan and gaped. 'What's this place?'

Morghan stared up at the house with its weatherboards blackened from flame and soot. Burning was the running theme of the day, she thought.

'Is this the original Hawthorne House, somehow?' Erin asked. 'Stephan said the original had been burnt down.'

Morghan shook her head, not taking her gaze from the house. It stood behind a chain link fence, in which a hole had been cut. She took a breath and slipped through the hole until she stood in the grounds of the house, staring up at it, her back to a large tree that grew perhaps as a guardian, perhaps just as a witness.

'What is it then?' Erin looked at the house, able to see inside the front rooms where the tatters of furniture remained. 'It looks like the pictures you see of houses that were bombed in the Blitz. 'It's so out of place.' Erin shook her head. 'Who set fire to it?'

31

'I DID,' MORGHAN SAID.

Erin swivelled her head to stare at her. 'What? You did?'

'Yes.' Morghan could still smell the fire and the smoke, the dark, burnt taste of it.

'You're crying again.' There was a lump in Erin's throat, and she felt suddenly afraid. 'Should we go?' she asked, hoping Morghan would say yes. The tears down Morghan's cheeks were silent, wet trails.

'Maybe,' Morghan said. 'Or maybe we're here because you need to see this place.'

Erin looked at the burnt-out house again. 'Who lived here?'

'Ah,' Morghan said. 'That's the question to ask.' She shifted her weight on the grass and glanced over to the fence. Amara sat there, silent, gaze locked on her.

Erin waited.

'This is not the real house, of course,' Morghan said

after a moment. 'This is my Otherworld version of it.' She paused.

'And you set it on fire here, or in the Waking?' Erin couldn't stop herself asking the question, although she couldn't imagine Morghan doing arson. In either world, come to that. It seemed so...un-Morghan-like. What had happened there? Whose house was it? The question burned in her mind.

'Here,' Morghan answered. Then repeated the word. 'Here.'

Erin waited.

'You are aware that Ambrose is my brother-in-law?' Morghan asked.

The question surprised Erin. She wondered where this was leading. 'Yes,' she said. 'But I don't think you've really mentioned it.' Or anything else much about her personal life. Her wife.

'Ambrose and Grainne had the same father, although Ambrose was fortunate enough not to spend many years under his father's roof. He lived with his mother and a little later, a step-father.'

Erin shivered. 'This isn't going to be a good story, is it?' she said in a low voice.

Morghan turned and looked at her, a sad smile on her face. 'So many stories aren't though, are they?'

'No,' Erin said quietly, thinking of her own situation. Although perhaps she had been luckier than many. And she was certainly fortunate right now. On the whole.

Despite Wayne Moffat.

Morghan's attention was back on the house. 'This is Grainne's house. The one she lived in as a child.'

Erin's mouth was dry. 'With her father?'

'Who molested her, yes.'

Erin closed her eyes. 'You don't have to tell me anything more,' she said. 'I'd burn the house down too, if someone did that to someone I loved.'

Morghan nodded her head slightly, slowly. 'One of the few times I've let my temper get the better of me,' she agreed. 'This lifetime, anyway.'

Erin wanted to explore that tantalising statement further, but she kept that to herself. 'What else happened?' she asked instead. 'Why is the house here in your, well, personal area of the Wildwood?'

'I don't know why it is still here,' Morghan said, gazing again at the broken building. 'The events of Grainne's early life caused her soul to shatter into pieces. Pieces of herself still stuck in the trauma, unable to get away, caught in the fear and horror and pain.'

The tears tracked steadily down Morghan's cheeks. She sniffed a little and smiled. 'She was the cutest little girl. Big eyes in the sweetest face.'

'I don't understand,' Erin said, frowning. 'Did you know her as a child? You couldn't have, could you?'

Morghan glanced at her, then back at the house. 'I retrieved all the shards of her soul, Erin. She couldn't heal until they were gathered up and brought out of their places of horror.'

Erin put a hand to her mouth. 'That's how you know what she looked like when she was little?'

Morghan inclined her head in agreement. 'There were many shards of her soul, but Grainne herself had gathered up most of them and put them in a place for safe-keeping. There were three she couldn't get to. It was too painful for her to go to them, in memory or spirit.' A pause. 'She'd done well to retrieve the ones she had. My Grainne always did have courage.'

'You did it for her,' Erin whispered.

'Yes,' Morghan agreed. 'Of course. It is part of our work, Erin, when needed, to retrieve parts of the shattered soul.' She glanced at the young woman. 'That is how I met Wayne Moffat.'

Erin hadn't been expecting this. 'What? What do you mean?'

'I was called to the hospice in Banwell to see if I could help him. He suffered greatly, because part of him was stuck by guilt and grief in a scene from the past. Except, as with Grainne, it never is the past for the shard stuck there. It is always and forever the present.'

Erin rocked back on her heels, unable suddenly to string together a coherent sentence. 'Wayne?' she gasped. 'My mother's boyfriend?'

'Yes,' Morghan said.

Erin stared up at the wreck of a house, trying to grasp what Morghan had just told her. She groped around in her mind for comprehension, shaking her head.

'What scene was he stuck in?' she asked, looking at the house, at the remains of a child's room, the bed blankets singed in a heap on the floor. What had happened in this house, she wondered? Then blinked, thinking of the terror of the child that had lived there. 'Was it like this?' she asked, gesturing at the house.

'No,' Morghan said. 'But still he suffered.' She drew

breath, knowing Erin now would need her to tell the story. Was it hers to tell, however?

'Was it to do with my mother?' Erin asked, turning her body so that she faced Morghan. She gripped her hands into fists.

Morghan saw her whitened knuckles and moved her gaze to Erin's face. 'Be calm,' she said.

Erin's eyes widened. 'Calm?'

'Your temper flares too easily. You must learn to be calm, not to hasten to judgement.'

Erin shook her head. 'But it was to do with my mother, wasn't it? That's why you brought him to Wellsford – why I have to work at the care home.' She shook her head more vigorously, her loose hair flying. She was not calm. She was rapidly moving far from calm.

Morghan stepped a pace away and turned back to her contemplation of the house. Why was it still there, she wondered?

Next to the fence, Amara got up and began pacing.

Grainne's father was dead. He had died a year before Grainne and released from the toxic tangle he and Grainne had played out over several lifetimes.

Grainne had done that. She had achieved her aim, had done what she'd come to this life for. She had set them both free from each other, allowing him to die without her anger to keep him tied to her.

But, Morghan thought, looking at the husk of the house, had she herself been able to do the same yet? Had she been able to let go of the hurt he had done to the one she loved so well? Had she been able to let go of the guilt she felt over her part in the saga the three of them had played out over lifetimes?

The house cast a long shadow over her, and she shivered. The light was lowering, dusk drawing down over them.

'I brought Wayne Moffat to Wellsford because he needed a place to die, and no others were available,' Morghan said. 'And I brought him into your care because part of each of you needs it.'

'You're meddling in our lives,' Erin hissed.

'Yes,' Morghan agreed, turning her gaze finally from the house to look at Erin standing furious in front of her. 'I am. I follow the Path, and this, today, is where it has led. All wounds must be healed, Erin.'

The house creaked as a breeze sprang up.

'It's too hard,' Erin said. 'It can't be done.'

Morghan walked over to the fence and stepped back through the hole. Amara rubbed against her legs.

'It is only too hard if you constantly put who you are now at the forefront of it all. If you look for the bigger picture, it can certainly be done.'

32

ERIN STUMBLED BACK INTO THE HOUSE DAZED AND BLIND IN the shadows. The afternoon had grown late and dim while she and Morghan had stood in the Wildwood.

Burdock got up from his bed and stretched, going over to greet her with his tail sweeping from side to side. Erin reached for the light switch and flicked the lights on, then bent down and gave the dog a kiss on the top of his head, between his ears.

'Let me put some more wood on the fires,' she said. And then she would try, she thought, to make sense of everything that didn't make sense. Was that possible?

She wished Stephan could come over, could sit at the table with her, and puzzle it out. Talking on the phone was better than nothing, but it was not even close to being enough. She longed for his presence in the room with her, his sunny grin, and she even wanted him to go off on one of his tangents about plants. Any sort of plants. Tea roses. She didn't care.

But he couldn't come inside. They could only walk together when they had the time and opportunity – and that had been seldom enough recently. Erin set a mug of tea on the table and wished she could talk to him.

'I'm whining,' she said to Burdock. 'But it's hard not to, you know? I miss Stephan.'

Burdock wagged his tail at the familiar name and went to the door, looking back hopefully at Erin. He missed Stephan too. Was Stephan coming over?

'It's this lockdown,' she said. 'I'm going crazy with it. It's so hard and frustrating.' She sank down in her chair and looked glumly at the steaming mug. 'Along with everything else, it's almost unbearable.' She tipped her head back. 'Aargh. It's all right for Morghan. She's...'

Erin drew herself up. It wasn't really *all right* for Morghan, was it? That house. The thought of it made Erin shiver. And going in there to rescue a child from...Erin didn't want to even give it words. How did you do that sort of thing? How did you live with having to see it?

It required more fortitude than she had, obviously.

Erin frowned. That was it, though, wasn't it? She had to develop that fortitude. What was it that Morghan had said? Her rather pointed, parting shot?

It is only too hard if you constantly put yourself at the forefront.

Something like that.

Erin shook her head. 'I'm just like Kria,' she said, the understanding blooming suddenly in her mind. 'Just like Kria – so full of resentment that I can't dig deep and find anything else.' She chewed on her lip. Then snorted, and then, after that, sighed.

'Gardening,' she said.

Burdock quit his hopeful post at the door and came and sat down in front of her, ears alert to listen.

'Gardening,' Erin repeated. 'That's why there's so much focus on it,' she said. 'I need new, what's it called?' She grinned suddenly, although there was little humour in it. 'Topsoil,' she said. 'And I need to prune back all the rubbish weeds and stuff and grow more fortitude.'

DEVELOP YOUR PRACTICE SO THAT IT WOULD BE THERE TO FALL back upon when things got rough. Wasn't that pretty much what Morghan had told her? Erin nodded to herself, head on her pillow, staring up at the ceiling. Because things – to varying degrees for everyone – always did get rough at some time or the other. Look how many difficulties she'd had, and she grew up not wanting for anything. Not materially, at least.

Erin closed her eyes for a moment and glimpsed the dragon from Kria's loch, the dragon that lurked in the blackness behind the door in her dream, and the dragon from the last night's tattered remnant. She needed to know what the dragon meant. She'd been putting it off too long. How could she not have been more curious about it?

But there was so much to do already. Erin sat up and threw back the blankets, getting out of bed determined to make the most of this new day.

In the dream, the dragon had set the house on fire. The house in Morghan's Otherworld place.

Erin snatched up her journal and pen, turned to a blank

page and noted the dream down. Later, she decided, she'd draw it.

Burdock was already scrambling down the stairs, his nails clicking on the wooden boards. A few minutes later, she let him out for his morning meet and greet session with the apple tree, and went to fill his bowl, ready for him. She left the door open, the early morning light reaching in with golden fingers that reminded Erin of Morghan's hand. She stopped and held her own hands up for a moment, imagining them glowing as Morghan's did. What did it mean, she wondered? To have a golden hand. She'd not met the Queen of the Fae. Would she ever?

Everything had been happening so quickly, and yet also so slowly. A creep of impatience inched its way through her, and Erin shrugged it off with effort.

The basics, she reminded herself. Everything had to be built on strong foundations. She was building something long-term here; she needed to do it step by step, with care and intention.

'Listen to me – I'm talking correctly to myself,' she said to Burdock when he dashed in the door, damp and happy. He perked up his ears, but his breakfast bowl called to him.

The garden was sparkling in the first touches of sunlight, even while Erin's breath steamed in the air. She smiled, delighted at the unexpected beauty of it, and on impulse, held out her palm. The shining dew reminded her of the diamonds she'd been given, and she took a breath and conjured them onto her outstretched palm, imagined holding them so that they too glittered in the light of the sun. Her heart lifted and she decided that she would try holding onto the diamonds, keeping them with her during the day, imagining them perhaps in a pocket, so she had something to remind herself of when faced with...well...Wayne Moffat, for instance.

But it wasn't time to think of him yet. It was morning, and Erin needed to begin her day correctly, and not look forward at things that had not yet occurred. She walked up to the well, her diamonds gripped loosely in her palm.

With her other hand, she dipped her finger to the cold water that lapped above the grate placed in the well for safety, then anointed her forehead with the dripping water, closing her eyes.

'Bless me, holy water, with your clarity,' she murmured, knowing that people had uttered such prayers over holy springs for thousands of years. She took her place amongst them with a warm sense of belonging.

Stepping down from the well, she looked around for a moment for a place to put her diamonds, since she couldn't hold them – imagined though they were – for the next part. She had no pockets. Frowning slightly, Erin put them down on the rim of the well, and took a position facing the east, towards the rising sun. Bending her knees, she swept her arms down and up around in a circle, standing up to stretch them to the sky, breathing in the sweet, damp air, the light from the sun, letting it out slowly as she lowered her arms. She moved her arms out to the side, embracing the air, then drew her hands forward towards her chest, breathing in again, breathing the world into her lungs and then exhaling, offering her breath back to the world and spreading her arms in a gesture of generosity.

'Air,' she said, the word a sigh on her lips. 'Breath of life.'

There was a hot breath on her neck and Erin froze for a

moment. But it was not repeated, and she strained to sense what was there, but found nothing. She had imagined it.

She reached upwards again, toward the rising sun, reaching for its fire with her fingertips until they glowed with flame.

'Fire,' she said, and her voice crackled with heat. 'Spark of life.'

The dragon from her dream coughed fire into the air and Erin swallowed, staying still for a long moment until it faded, leaving only streaks of flame behind her eyelids.

On a long, shaky exhale, Erin relaxed her arms, drifting them down through the air as though it was water. Her eyes closed; she floated in the well for a moment, and then for the merest blink of an eye she stood in front of the dark loch again, watching the great beast from under the waves rise, water streaming from its scaled head, wings, flanks.

'Water,' Erin said, her voice wavering. 'Womb of life.'

It was a relief to lift her feet, to feel herself on solid land, the ground rich and fertile under her feet, and she looked as the land spread out, green-humped and curling around with head and tail and wing.

Keep going, Erin told herself, and she licked her lips, stayed with it.

'Earth,' she said, her voice gravel-rough. 'Root of life.'

She reached back to the sky, then swept her arms down to the earth, bending over to almost touch it with her fingers, then drew herself up and brought her hands to her chest, letting herself make the familiar movements, holding her palms to her heart.

'Above,' she said. 'Below. All around.' She took a breath. 'I am part of the wheel.'

And around her the wheel turned, air, fire, water, earth, four dragons rising, spinning.

Erin breathed out through pursed lips, eyes closed, seeing, feeling, holding her fear away from herself so that she could see.

She watched the dragons rise and fade, until only one, its scales red and gold, enveloped in flame, remained burned behind her eyelids, and then it too, shimmered away to nothing.

Erin opened her eyes and stood panting, gazing about her garden with eyes still dazzled from the dragon's flames.

She should go inside and draw them, she thought, while they were still fresh in her vision. Almost, she made to move towards the house, but she stopped herself. She was not done here. She had not done what she'd come out here for, and she had to work this morning. The need to ground herself was imperative.

So, Erin closed her eyes again, letting herself feel the warmth of the sun on her face. She stepped over to the well in her imagination and picked up her diamonds, holding them in her palm up to the morning sun so that they jumped with sparkling light. She closed her fingers around them and concentrated on her breathing and conjuring the garden around her to her mind.

There was the well, the lid still up, the water a dark, cold, deep, and mysterious funnel into the depths of the earth. She looked away from it, her eyes still closed. There was the first circle of beds, the plants that had been cut back for winter now showing their first tentative shoots of green as they woke and felt blindly for the sun.

There was the second ring of beds, where the rosemary,

316

Erin's favourite, stretched its roots and limbs, coming out of its winter dream.

And the third circle of beds, most of them empty, waiting, the soil full of potential, ready to press around new seedlings, to feed and nurture them.

And there was the stone wall that enclosed Ash Cottage's garden. There was the glasshouse and potting shed built into it, and the grapevine that was also shaking off its winter stupor.

There were the apple and pear trees espaliered against the back wall where the sun warmed the stones behind them and the buds of their new blossoming.

There was her garden all about her, and Erin looked around it in her mind, smelling the plants and soil, feeling the breeze, looking upon the plants, breathing it all in. Breathing it all in.

And so, it was only a short step, and she was in another garden, where the layout was the same, but this one was wholly of her own devising. Except, she thought, gazing about it – she may have woven it from sensation and imagination, but she did not bring the level of detail it had to it. That was the magic, she thought. Whether it was in an inner, outer, or other world, it was real. On some level, it was real.

And someone had been doing some work in one of the beds. Erin frowned and walked over to it. Yes, it was tidier than it had been last time, as though she'd come here during a dream, perhaps, and snipped and clipped and cleared some of the wild growth. Just the corner of the bed, not a great deal, but it was tidied all the same.

Suddenly, Erin turned and walked down the path

towards the potting shed, where she knew her grandmother's old tools were stored. Or at least they were in the real garden – the other garden. She ducked under the overgrown branches of an apple tree, then stopped, frowning, and lifted her face to look closer at the tree.

Or rather, the fruit that hung from the tree. There was a proliferation of apples, hanging from branches that waited to burst into bud with new life, and with a glance, Erin saw it was the same with the pear trees. So much fruit, all of it unharvested. She lifted a hand and plucked an apple from the branch and examined it, her lips turning downwards.

The fruit was small, pockmarked, barely good enough to eat. The thought of biting into it made Erin cringe – she easily imagined it sour and hard. Her hand dropped to her side and she gazed at the trees in dismay, then around at the garden.

It was beautiful and wild and completely overgrown – except for that one small corner of the bed. There was so much work that needed to be done. How was she ever to manage it? How would she bring order and discipline to this place?

And wouldn't that destroy the beauty of it? It had to be beautiful. It had to flourish. She frowned over the apple again. It had to bring forth fruit good enough to eat. She sighed. This was going to be a long and hard task and looking about, she didn't even know where to begin.

'Begin where you are,' she said, consciously echoing Morghan's words. She nodded, pushed open the door to the potting shed and looked around in the dimness, then pounced on an old wicker basket, bringing it back out into the early morning sunshine.

The apple dropped into it, and Erin reached for more of the misshapen fruit, letting them fall into the basket. This wasn't the fruit she wanted her trees to bear, she thought as she plucked them from the branches and dropped them into the basket. She'd pick these ones and compost them. That way, they wouldn't go to waste, and the tree would be free of its burden, and could grow more. She could see the new buds forming on the green branches, ready to blossom, ready to grow more fruit.

This harvest, she was determined, would be good enough to eat.

33

'Tell me about my mother,' Erin said, bending down to tie the laces of Wayne's shoes for him. They were ragged, the ends of the laces looking like a rat had chewed upon them, and for the first time too, she noticed the cuffs of his track suit bottoms were frayed, the fabric greasy with age and wear.

'And yourself,' she added, reminding herself that she didn't belong at the forefront of everything, even though that took a great deal of effort. She risked a glance up at his face. It too was frayed and greasy with age, she thought. The man hadn't had an easy life, that much was written large upon his features.

That's what happens, a voice inside her said, when you drink too much and get caught up in drugs. Didn't she know that?

Erin frowned. Yes, she said to herself. She did know that – but what, she made herself wonder – had led him to choosing that life? She remembered the times she'd sought oblivion, looking for it not in substances, but in greyness, in running away. She'd not been strong enough to face everything she'd thought and felt and been, and maybe, just maybe, it had been the same for this man.

Wayne stared down at the head bent over his shoes. For a moment, he didn't want to answer. It was safer to keep himself to himself, and what business of this young chit's anyway? She hadn't been around, so she wouldn't understand. She'd been brought up with a silver spoon in her mouth.

Except here she was, tying his shoelaces.

'She didn't have your red hair,' he said, his voice grudging. He wasn't sure he'd meant to speak at all, but there it was. 'And she was taller than you.'

'Was she pretty?' Erin asked, leaning back, reluctant to get up while he was speaking. But there was a chair beside the bed, and she let herself sit for a moment in that, so that she wasn't standing over him.

'I thought so,' Wayne said. He looked around the room for a moment, wishing he still smoked, but of course, that had stopped when he was in the other care home. He'd thought he was going to die then, hadn't had time to worry about smoking. 'She had a good laugh. Liked to laugh, did Becca.'

Erin closed her eyes for a moment. What did her mother have to laugh about? How could she find life funny when she was giving away her own baby? Maybe the money she was getting for doing it made her happy. She stood up abruptly.

'Breakfast time, I think,' she said. 'Wheelchair or walk?'

Wayne looked at her, startled. 'You look like her when

you're angry,' he said, then touched his eyes with a finger. 'She used to get all squinty like that – just like you.'

'I don't get squinty,' Erin said, widening her eyes automatically. 'And I'm not angry.'

It was a lie. She made herself acknowledge that and took a deep breath. 'Well all right,' she said. 'I am.'

Wayne's watery eyes gazed up at her. 'What for, though?' he asked. 'You weren't there. We made sure of that.'

'For your own gain,' Erin retorted.

But Wayne shook his head. 'Wouldn't you have done the same, though? They were so desperate for a kid they were willing to pay to jump to the front of the line. Leapt at the chance when Becca offered to meet them on the down low.' He sniffed. 'And you gotta understand – we had nothing. Never had anything.'

Erin sat down again, hands gripping each other so that her knuckles were white.

'Becca did – she had her mother, and Ash Cottage, and...' Her voice trailed off. She'd meant to say Wilde Grove.

'Nah,' Wayne answered. 'Her and her mum didn't see eye to eye, you know? Like they'd just been born to do battle, you know?'

Erin couldn't imagine it. 'But...'

Wayne shook his head. 'It was just how it was,' he said. 'She hated this village. Hated that everyone looked at her weird and whispered about her when she was at school down in Banwell. Unmarried mums were frowned upon then, right? And there was her mum being a witch on top of it, and not caring who knew – it made it bad for Becca when she was a girl.' He lifted his bony shoulders in a shrug.

'Everyone's got a story, right? She wanted out, soon as she could.'

Erin sat silently, trying to imagine what it would be like being a little kid at school picked on for stuff you couldn't do anything about. Yes, she decided reluctantly. She could see that.

'Did you ever meet my grandmother?' she asked. 'Becca's mother, I mean?'

Wayne's hands wandered to his pockets before he reminded himself he didn't have any tobacco anymore. He rubbed his fingers and thumbs together, as though rolling a smoke anyway. He wanted a cup of tea. His mouth was parched.

But this was the kid he was talking to. He risked a sideways glance at her then gazed over at the corner of the room. 'Nah,' he said. 'Becca called her on the phone, and that were bad enough. I could hear the yelling from the other side of the flat.'

Erin frowned, licked her lips. 'What about...what about my father? Do you know who he was?'

Wayne's painfully thin shoulders rose in a shrug. 'Never met him. She'd left Wellsford with some lad, but it wasn't him; they'd split early on. I don't reckon Becca really knew who your dad was. She never mentioned him. Just someone she took a roll with one night.'

He paused. 'I need a cup of coffee, love,' he said. 'Mouth's dry especially with all this talking.'

'Right,' Erin said and winced. The story was just as awful as she'd been afraid it would be. Her mother hadn't even known which guy she'd slept with got her pregnant. Erin blew out a breath, trying to stay calm. She swallowed down her disgust, telling herself she had no right to judge. 'Of course,' she said. 'I'm sorry. I'll help you in for your breakfast.'

Wayne was relieved. If he kept talking to the girl like this, she'd end up asking about what happened the night Becca had died. And he didn't want to talk about that. Just the thought of it made him feel shivery and sick. He groped automatically for his pocket again, before remembering for the third time that morning that he didn't smoke anymore.

He wished he smoked.

Hell, he wished he still drank.

Erin took Wayne in for his breakfast, got him a cup of coffee and some fresh scrambled eggs and toast. He was quiet all through it, even though they were alone in the dining room, and Erin had to chasten herself over and over not to keep asking him things, asking him questions that might give her better answers than the ones she'd had so far. He was sick, she reminded herself. Dying, really. She had no right to pester him with her questions.

Still, it was hard, sitting on them, pushing them down, but every time she went to open her mouth to ask something about Becca, she reminded herself sternly that she could not push her needs onto Wayne. Or anyone.

BY THE TIME SHE'D FINISHED HER MORNING SHIFT, HER MOUTH ached from clamping her jaw closed. 'Aargh, Stephan!' she said, a wash of relief coming over her when she saw him standing there waiting for her to finish. 'You are the best sight in the world.'

Stephan grinned at her, hands stuck in his pockets so he

wouldn't reach for her, grab hold of her and pull her to himself so that he could kiss her. And then kiss her again. The lockdown couldn't end soon enough.

'You're an exceptionally fine sight yourself,' he said, letting himself relax into the pleasure of simply seeing her.

She stopped on the footpath a few steps from him and looked at him longingly. 'Pretend I've kissed you hello,' she said.

Stephan shook his head. 'It would get indecent in about five seconds,' he told her.

Erin laughed. 'How are you? I feel like I've hardly seen you.' She wanted to rush into telling him about everything that had been happening, but held her tongue, squaring her shoulders and taking a breath. She wouldn't do that – this was another of her new resolutions. The memory of Morghan telling her sternly to keep calm came back to her, making her cheeks flush.

'Where shall we go, while you tell me about everything you've been doing?' she asked, wishing she could link arms with him and lean against his warm, strong body.

Burdock was already ahead of them on the path, nose down, tail up, sniffing the bushes for recent notices of activity. He glanced around at them, then went back to all the delicious smells.

'Ah,' Stephan said regretfully. 'I can only break for lunch.'

'Is it not done yet?' Erin asked.

'Nope,' Stephan said, thinking of the glasshouse. A marvellous piece of engineering, but he was having an awful time getting it put up. 'It's my dad, see. He's determined to fuss and bother over everything – and I mean every little thing. It's excruciating. He's just enjoying that I had to get him to put it together. Which of course I do – he's the local builder and I'm a gardener. But he acts like it's getting one up on me all the time.'

'It sounds like he's trying to assert his authority over you, Stephan. Because it's your project and you're the one who's really in charge.' Erin let herself relax as she walked beside Stephan, feeling the gentle rub of their energy together. It gave her a bit of a floaty sensation that she liked. Made her feel buoyant, in a good mood.

'It's not like I'm bossing him around,' Stephan said, shaking his black curls and staring at his feet as they walked. He sighed. 'But you don't know my dad. He does not like me.'

'How can a parent not like their kid?' Erin's heart twisted around the thought.

'Happens all the time, Erin,' Stephan said. 'Way too often.' He shrugged, reached for her hand without thinking, then snatched his fingers back as though he'd been scorched.

'My parents – deluded as they are about all manner of things – I'm pretty sure they do actually love me,' Erin mused.

'You should go and see them when things open up again and we can travel,' Stephan said, lifting his face to the sun and feeling its pale heat on his skin.

'I don't have a car, remember?'

Stephan shrugged, shot Erin a smile. 'You can borrow one. That wouldn't be a problem. Morghan hardly uses hers, she'd be fine with it.'

'Huh.' Erin squinted up at the sky, 'Maybe I will. Show

them I haven't grown horns or anything.' She giggled suddenly, and Stephan looked at her and grinned.

'Or antlers,' he said. 'Yet!'

'Oh my goodness,' Erin laughed. 'Maybe you should come though, and show them your bear mask so they know what I have to look forward to.' She shook her head, sobering. 'I miss the rituals and things. Do you think we'll have one for – what's next?'

'Ostara,' Stephan replied. 'It was Imbolc that pretty much got missed.' He sighed, a slight puff of air and watched Burdock lead them down the road that headed to Ash Cottage. 'Maybe we'll be able to hold it. Things are supposed to be relaxing by then, right?'

Erin nodded. 'What are you going to do about your father?' she asked.

Stephan reached up and scratched his beard. 'Well, I'm going to keep on, you know? What else is there to do? I'll be unfailingly nice to him, and try to remember that whatever his problem is, it isn't mine.' He smiled. 'And when the pub's open again, I'll take him for a drink to say thanks for all his help.'

Erin shook her head. 'Stephan, I totally don't deserve such a nice guy as you.'

That made Stephan laugh. 'You wouldn't credit it, Erin, but once upon a time, I used to lie in my bed at night, and think about sticking a knife in the old man's guts. Right to the hilt.' His smile faded. 'Back before I left home – or got kicked out, rather.'

'I'm sorry,' Erin whispered, wishing like anything she could touch Stephan. Hold his hand. Wrap her arms around him.

Stephan shrugged. 'Teresa took me in, and here I am today, so I'd say things worked out pretty well.' His grin was back. 'Now, you haven't said a word about Wayne Moffat today – you've let me ramble on about my problems.'

Erin told him about Morghan having rescued Wayne – or shards of his soul – from some sort of dark place, but she didn't mention Morghan's special place in the Wildwood, or the burnt-out house. That would have seemed wrong, somehow, like she'd been somewhere personal, seen something she hadn't really been meant to see.

'So, I'm trying to be like you,' Erin said.

'Like me?' Stephan's eyebrows rose.

She nodded. 'I'm trying to remember that everyone has a story, and not everything is about me.' She rolled her eyes and laughed at herself. 'It's surprisingly difficult.'

THE RAVEN WAS PERCHED ON HIS FAVOURED KITCHEN CHAIR when Erin stepped into Ash Cottage, Burdock bounding after her. She saw the bird and came to a sudden halt, keys in hand.

'Okay,' she said slowly. 'I'm not even going to bother asking how you got in.' She blinked at the large bird, not entirely convinced it was made of feather and bone. Could spirit animals seem this real, this three dimensional? She cleared her throat.

'We all know you can fly through walls and windows,' she said and skirted around the table into the kitchen. The bird's eyes followed her. 'What do you want today?'

The air changed behind her shoulder, thickened,

stirred, and set the hairs on the back of Erin's neck prickling.

'Macha,' she breathed. 'It's been some time.'

For a moment, she could feel only Macha's presence there in the room while the raven watched her with unblinking eyes. Burdock had gone to sit on his bed, keeping well out of the way.

'The dragons are rising,' Macha said.

Erin gave an involuntary shiver. 'I saw them this morning,' she said. Then shook her head. 'But what do they mean? One came from the loch, but the others?'

'Look to the Lady,' Macha said. 'She faces the fire.'

Erin whirled around, sudden questions filling her mouth, but Macha was gone. Erin gazed around the kitchen, hair flying, but only the raven was there, perched on the chair, staring at her.

'Come back,' Erin said into the air. 'Macha, come back. Tell me what you mean?' She shook her head, wishing she hadn't spun around so suddenly like she had. Maybe the movement had made Macha disappear.

But the air in the kitchen neither thickened nor stirred nor shimmered. Macha had delivered her cryptic message and gone. She'd left her bird behind, but she herself, the one who could talk, was gone.

'You can't talk, can you?' Erin asked the bird, not entirely sure whether her question was a joke.

But the bird simply looked at her, fluffed his feathers, and settled more comfortably on the back of the chair.

Look to the Lady, Macha had said.

The Lady?

Erin crossed the room, on legs that felt more than a little

unsteady, and gave Burdock a shaky smile as she skirted around his bed. 'It's all right, boy,' she said.

He didn't look like he really believed her, and she couldn't fault him for it.

Look to the Lady.

The tiny sunroom off the sitting room was where Erin kept her magical tools, and her altar. She was really just following her grandmother's lead there, but that didn't matter. On the altar was a statue of the Lady of the Ways – not exact, but close enough to how Erin had seen the Goddess, when they'd met. Her fingers went unthinkingly to her pocket and touched the diamonds she'd carried there in her imagination during the day.

'My Lady,' she whispered, bowing her head at the altar.

Was this the Lady?

It didn't feel quite right, and Erin frowned. Why would a goddess be in danger?

Her bag of runes lay on the table and she scooped it up, slid her hand into the velvet bag and swirled the cool stones around, letting them run through her fingers while she calmed and slowed her breathing, focusing her attention on what Macha had said to her.

Look to the Lady. She faces the fire.

The dragons spun for a moment behind her eyes, four of them, one for each element, each direction, each...what?

Erin breathed deeply, drew three stones with her eyes closed, and laid them on the altar. Biting down on her lip, she opened her eyes and gazed at the stones with their enigmatic symbols.

Touched a finger to each.

Kaunan.

Ehwaz.

Jera.

She'd learnt the names, and the meanings too, or a glimmer of understanding of them, and she shook her head. *Kaunan.* Pain. Mortality.

She turned and nipped up the rune book Krista had given her from the shelf, flipping through the pages.

Here is what we must all face – the fragility of life, the agony of being alive. Each unfurling is a risk, each reaching can bring pain. We must live with the knowledge of our body's deaths, that we can be pierced at any moment, and we must find a way to thrive even in the shadow of this knowing.

Erin shook her head. That was grim. Pain, death – was this what Macha spoke of when she talked about facing the fire? A frown made deep furrows in Erin's brow.

She shifted her attention to the next rune, her heart beating too quickly.

Ehwaz. Trust, faith. Companionship. She blew out a breath. Was this what she was supposed to do to help? To look to the Lady?

Connection must be looked for, as we are in this universe always in constellations, never alone. Reach for those you may trust and bring faith to your companionship with each other. We are surrounded by those seen and unseen who wish our growth and we must be that also to each other.

Erin picked up the runestone and held it in her palm until it warmed. Its symbol looked like an M to her, and it represented the horse. There was a feeling of movement about the rune, she thought.

Of questing.

And what was life, she wondered, putting the stone down, if not something of a quest?

Jera. Erin let out a breath. This one was better. Not quite so scary as the first, and she thought its placement was good – the third she pulled, where she liked to think it represented the outcome. Ideally. *Jera* was the rune of the harvest and rewards, which had a positive force to it. Erin turned the pages of the book to find it.

What needs tilled and tended here is the fertile ground of our own soul. And what we may harvest, if we are diligent, is nothing less than our own growth, the ripened, seeking bloom of our spirits who gaze upon the whole of the world around us and know how it is to be rooted in such beauty.

Erin curled her lip at the meaning printed in the book, then closed the pages and set it back upon the shelf.

So, she thought to herself. The drawing was actually pretty clear, in conjunction with what Macha had said. Erin leaned back and looked out through the doorway.

The raven was still there, black and grey feathers rich and glossy in the stream of afternoon light from the kitchen window.

She looked back at the runes. The Lady, she thought, faced fire, and pain. Perhaps death.

Erin shivered, even though she still wore her coat.

She herself needed to offer trust and her companionship, to face with the Lady whatever was necessary.

And if successful, they would harvest their reward.

Erin closed her eyes. This reward would hopefully be on this side of the life and death equation.

The only question now was:

Who was the Lady?

34

'WE NEED TO THINK ABOUT OSTARA, MORGHAN,' AMBROSE said, coming across her finally outside at the well. 'I cannot see us holding it, things being as they are.'

Morghan had been standing lost in thought but looked up as Ambrose strode up to her. She searched his face.

'Are you faring well, Ambrose?' she asked.

He frowned at her. 'What do you mean?'

Morghan smiled and shook her head, drawing herself back to the present. 'Sorry,' she said. 'I was miles away. I meant to ask – how are you?'

'I'm...fine, I suppose,' he said.

Morghan nodded, gazed off into the trees. 'These are difficult times,' she said, then barked a laugh. 'I know I say that every week it seems, but every week there is something new to tax us.'

'We didn't sign up for an easy life,' Ambrose said, even while thinking in the back of his mind that that was exactly what he'd thought he'd be getting when he found his way finally to Wilde Grove. It had felt such a homecoming that he'd never anticipated then the turmoil that he would now be struggling with. He cleared his throat.

Morghan looked at him with raised eyebrows.

Ambrose licked his lips. 'Do you think I ought to go away?' he asked.

Morghan's eyes widened in shock. 'No,' she said. 'Why are you asking that? What have you been thinking?'

He shifted uneasily on his feet, all his usual certainty deserting him. It was alarming, to feel this way.

'Because of Winsome,' he choked out.

Morghan shook her head. 'I don't understand,' she said.

'Well, it would be one less complication for her, wouldn't it? If I weren't here?'

Morghan touched a hand to her forehead. Her fingers were cool against the warm skin of her face.

'Ambrose.' She dropped her hand and went to him, put her hands on his shoulders, then pulled him close into a hug and stood like that for a long silent moment, her arms around him, his body rigid against hers. She held him until his spine loosened and he relaxed against her.

She stepped back, cupped his beloved face in her hands. Smiled at him.

'You may not leave for such a reason, Ambrose,' she said. 'Your destiny lies here in the Grove. This we both know.'

She kept her hands to his cheeks even as he shook his head.

'But I am a pressure she doesn't need right now.'

'Have you spoken to her?' Morghan asked.

Ambrose's gaze skittered away for a moment, then returned. 'No,' he said. 'I've been avoiding her.' He cleared his throat. 'I've not wanted to...complicate things any further for her. Not after...not after the other day.'

'When you called her darling?' Morghan asked, a soft smile on her lips. She dropped her hands, her fingers warmed by his blush.

Ambrose gave a short cough. 'Yes,' he said. 'Then.'

Morghan turned away, looked back to the tree line. 'What is it you always tell me, Ambrose?' she asked.

'In what circumstance?' he asked, knowing he was always fairly liberal with his advice. Never again though, he vowed. Not after this.

Morghan laughed. 'In almost every circumstance,' she said. 'But particularly when things grow difficult, and I would wonder what I am doing.'

'Ha. I don't know,' he said. 'I've quite a few things I say.'

'Yes, and all of them I find are exactly what I need to hear, when I need to hear it,' Morghan told him. She glanced back at him, her face softening again. 'Ambrose, my dearest friend,' she said. 'Things happen as they do. We play the parts we were born to. You and I do not go blindly through our lives – and we do not go alone. You can be sure that running away from this would not be the right thing to do.' She blinked. 'There are times to turn away and there are situations that would be best avoided, but this is not one of them.'

'Perhaps just for a few weeks?' Ambrose asked, hating the pleading in his voice. 'I do not...want to be in the way of whatever must happen.'

Morghan swung around and stared at Ambrose. 'This is what you really think?' she asked. 'This is how you really feel?'

She could barely believe it of him – Ambrose, who had always been so steady, so sensible.

A sudden ember of anger burst to light inside her and she shook her head. 'Answer me,' she demanded, her voice rough. 'This is what you think?'

Ambrose stared at her. 'Don't look at me that way,' he said.

She shook her head. 'Love,' she said, 'can make us soft and foolish – but it should never make a coward of us!'

'Leaving someone free to make an unencumbered choice is not cowardly!'

Ambrose reined himself in, stood panting a moment at his outburst, then shook his head. 'This is affecting you, Morghan,' he said, and waved an arm at the forest. 'She is affecting you.'

Morghan closed her eyes. 'Who do you mean?' she asked.

'The one killed for witchcraft. Blythe Wilde. You've never gone this deeply into another lifetime as you are with this one.' He wiped the back of his hand across his cheeks. It came away damp. 'What is going on?'

'She's going to die,' Morghan spat. 'That's what's going on.' She shook her head and looked away to stare at the trees. 'Today, maybe. Soon, if not.' A glance back at Ambrose. 'Where would you go? Travel is disallowed.'

'Whitewolf has offered me a place to stay for a while. It is not far. I will risk it.'

'Whitewolf,' Morghan repeated, keeping her gaze steady upon his face. 'And you, *Iolair*, Eagle-heart, you would run from the lake of your heart rather than risk the plunge?'

Ambrose paled. Bright spots of colour appeared high on

his cheeks. 'I will not make matters worse for Winsome. She has enough on her plate as it is, without my pushing in there.'

Morghan closed her eyes. Shook her head. 'The Grove crumbles,' she whispered.

'No,' Ambrose said. 'No – I would only be gone a week, perhaps two. At the most. Our Grove is stronger than it's ever been – we're in the best position we've been in since...'

'– Since the Romans razed us to the ground,' Morghan said. 'It's true. And before they came with their daggers and their torches, we were strong and true and keeping the ways of the gods.'

Ambrose was silent.

'What you must realise,' Morghan said, turning her back to him to look out upon the trees, and narrowing her eyes against the memory of flames upon the branches. 'Is that on the verge of breakthrough, something will push back.'

'Something like what?'

Morghan's shoulders were tight. 'A force of disruption. A force that requires you to give more than you thought you had. A force that would trip you up, cause you to turn away, defeated.'

Ambrose shook his head. 'I've not heard you speak like this before.'

Morghan held up her golden hand, seeing it catch the light, and laughed. 'Things have not been like this before, *Iolair*. Or not, at least, this time until now.' She paused, then spoke more softly. 'Things threaten to fall apart.'

'You have the aid of the Fae,' Ambrose reminded her. 'Call upon them.'

Morghan laughed. 'Are you being deliberately dense,

Ambrose? That is not like you. The Fae cannot help when it is us who fall apart, when it is the village divided, the Grove separated.' She dropped her hand, rolled her neck on her shoulders, the muscles sore from holding herself so tensely.

'We have always run this Grove in a reciprocal manner, have we not, Ambrose?' she asked, fatigue seeping into her voice. 'Discussing and agreeing amongst ourselves, is that not true?'

Ambrose did not know where Morghan was going with this. 'It is true,' he said. He looked at the back of her head and waited.

She turned slightly, so that he stood in her peripheral vision. 'You may not leave, Ambrose,' she said, then drew breath and strode away, into the woods, into the past.

Blythe. She waited there, in the dimness of time.

Sometimes, Morghan thought, slipping between the trees and into the Wildwood, following the thread, the pin cushion, back into the past – sometimes, the break that needed setting, the wound that required tending, the energy used by that disruptive force, lay not in the immediate vicinity, but deep in the tidelines of the past.

It was so now, she knew. And if she did not tend to Blythe, the fracture caused many years ago would split them all apart now.

Mariah Reefton drifted into her mind but Morghan shook her head. One thing at a time, she told herself. Follow the Path one step at a time.

35

WINSOME ZIPPED UP HER SKIRT, SMOOTHING THE BLACK WOOL down over her hips and looked in the mirror. Above the dog collar, her face was pale as an uncooked pastie. She tried to scowl at it, but the frown crumpled and wavered and she had to press her fingers to her mouth to keep her lips from trembling.

'Come on, girl,' she whispered into her hand. 'Pull yourself together – what's the worst that can happen?'

Well, let me see, said that annoying voice she'd been trying recently to root out of her head. *You could lose your church and your job, or you could just lose your church, in which case you'd be sent somewhere else and lose, well...*

'Shut up!' Winsome stared at the mirror. Its surface was old, slightly wavery. Made her look even more like the cheese in a Ploughman's lunch. She spun away from it and searched the floor of her bedroom for her shoes.

Actual shoes. Not the wool-lined booties she'd been wearing under her cassock to take services all winter. Proper shoes. Heels small, but heels, nonetheless. She found them collecting dust bunnies under the bed, brushed them off, and shoved them on her feet.

Ready, then.

No more excuses, out the door, in the car. Off to see the Dean, toodle oo.

She locked the vicarage door, handbag over her shoulder, keys in her shaking hand. The car door squealed as she opened it. Hardly been used all winter, the car. No cause to go anywhere beyond Wellsford, and well, couldn't if she'd needed to.

Winsome got the car on the road, stabbed blindly at the radio, listened for a minute as a Christian pop band sang about getting scared sometimes, losing their minds.

Well, Winsome thought, pressing the button and putting a halt to the song. She knew about that. But it wasn't her mind she was afraid of losing – not anymore. Once she'd realised that yes, she really could see spirits, and that there were things she could do about that, she'd felt less and less like her mind was some broken and weird thing she didn't know much about.

Overall, actually, she felt stronger. Better. More...in love with the world.

The drive down out of Wellsford was narrow, the road winding its way out of the hills and Winsome looked out through the windshield at the blue sky, at the early flowers bending their heads over the lane, at the wash of green grass that spread out, the stone walls, the trees, and here and there a house, smoke wafting out of its chimney like it was smoking and dreaming in the sunlight. It was supposed to rain the next day, so Winsome breathed the beauty in like it had calories.

She thought of the story that ancient and wild woman – a goddess, perhaps – had told her when she'd ventured to the Otherworld. The wind, plucking at the girl as she walked, hand over ears.

Winsome didn't want to walk with her hands over her ears. She didn't want to have to block everything out. This beautiful day. This wide spread of the world. The white horse who had shaken his head at her to follow him. Cù, faithful dog made of spirit and message. The smoke in Morghan's cave. The look in Ambrose's eyes when he'd called her darling.

THE DEAN'S OFFICE WAS TUCKED AWAY IN A PLEASANT building in sight of the church, with a garden that spread out in front of it, and which had used to be magnificent, and was now bedraggled and neglected. Winsome's mouth drooped as she walked past it, and she was still looking at it when the door opened and almost hit her in the face.

'Julia!' Winsome said. 'What are you doing here?'

Julia licked her lips and smiled, displaying a row of small, neat white teeth behind her lipstick.

Bugger, Winsome thought. She'd forgotten to put her lippy on.

'Why Winsome,' Julia said, her voice as sweet as saccharine. 'I've been having a most illuminating time with the Dean.'

Winsome squinted at her, looking for the woman's

colours. They swirled about her – her usually slightly putrid green – and through it threaded broken capillaries of red.

'You've been illuminating him on things?' Winsome asked. 'Rather more than I suspect you know, I would say.'

'Winsome,' Julia said, unable finally, to help herself. 'I really don't like you.'

'It shows, Julia,' Winsome answered. 'It shows.' She blinked, stood back out of the doorway. 'But I'll let you go on your way. I suspect you've had a rather difficult hour.'

Julia frowned, moved the folders she was carrying from against her breast to under an arm. Then put them back and hugged them against herself. 'I don't know what you mean, Winsome,' she said. 'I'm sure I don't. You never make much sense; do you know that?' Her lips made a little moue of distaste. 'Always being so cryptic. Always acting like you know more than you possibly could. Like you see more.'

Winsome just nodded. 'I think you ought to get home, Julia, and get your feet up for a while. I don't think your blood pressure is doing good things.'

Julia turned up a lip and shook her head. 'I'll be glad when you're gone, Winsome Clark. More glad than you could ever know.' Her face smoothed out to an expression of triumph. 'And whatever the Dean thinks,' she let slip, 'he has to take some things seriously.'

'I'm sure Dean Morton will take all evidence in front of him seriously, Julia,' Winsome said, still musing upon the threads in her Churchwarden's colours. 'Now, off you go.'

It was mean, Winsome thought, to dismiss Julia like that. Julia Thorpe was, after all, a grown woman.

Bethany looked up from her computer as Winsome let

herself into the room. She took off her glasses and put them down on the desk.

'Hello Bethany,' Winsome said, trying to resist the urge to shuffle her feet as though on the way to the head teacher's office for a dressing down. Still, came the thought, that's pretty much exactly what was happening there that day.

'Winsome,' Bethany said. She nodded her head, which had very tidy blonde hair in a neat chignon. 'How are you?'

Winsome grimaced. 'Not looking forward to this, Bethany, I can tell you.'

Bethany shook her head. 'Tell me it's not all true, for goodness sakes?'

'It's not all true,' Winsome said promptly. She was fairly certain she could get away with saying that – if Julia had brought that disgusting flyer in, then definitely it was not all true.

'I'm relieved to hear it.' Bethany nodded towards the door. 'The Dean is waiting for you.'

Winsome swung around and looked at the door to Dean Morton's office. The last time she'd been in there her mood had been effervescent. She'd just been appointed to the Wellsford Parish and excitement had fizzed in her veins like she'd had nothing but Berrocca to drink. Which had actually been the case, she remembered, having been too nervous to eat proper food.

This morning, however, she'd forced herself to sit down at the table and eat breakfast. Or at least, push the food around her plate and take a bite from each of the two pieces of toast, as though that meant she'd eaten them.

'Go on in,' Bethany said suddenly. 'After your Churchwarden, I've a feeling you'll come across almost completely sane.'

Winsome glanced over at Bethany who had put her reading glasses back on and was looking at Winsome over the top of them.

'It was bad?'

'The woman screeched,' Bethany said. 'At the Dean.' She blinked and her mouth tightened in distaste. 'She screeched.'

'Hmm.' Winsome blew out a breath, pushed her shoulders back with an effort, and opened the door.

'Good morning, Dean,' she said, closing the door behind her, determined there would be no screeching from her for Bethany to hear. No raised voices at all. Simple, reasoned conversation, that was the ticket.

'Is it?' David Morton asked, with a sigh. 'I seem to have lost my taste for today after speaking to your Churchwarden.'

'Julia Thorpe,' Winsome said. 'I met her on the way in.'

Dean Morton looked down at the piece of paper the Thorpe woman had given him. His lip curled in distaste and he pinched it between finger and thumb of one hand and held it up.

'Have you had the pleasure of seeing this?' he asked.

Winsome recognised it straight away. 'I have,' she said. 'Although I assure you it was no pleasure. I woke up the other morning to find them plastered all over Wellsford.'

'Yes,' David Morton said on a sigh. 'She said she'd done that – in order to spread the truth, apparently. Sit down, Winsome, please.'

Winsome stepped around the chair in front of the

Dean's desk and perched upon the edge of it. A shadow of movement caught Winsome's eye, and she glanced over to the side of the room where Cù had stretched himself on the floor, looking at her with an open, panting mouth that she would have sworn looked like a grin.

If she'd looked properly at him, that was. But now, she told herself, was not the time to acknowledge the spirit dog.

Although, what was it that Morghan had said about having a dog for a spirit animal?

Winsome shook herself. This wasn't the conversation she needed going on in her head right now. She was here, in the Church, capital C. Speaking to the Dean, capital D, about her Future, capital F.

If she had a future, that was, of course. The F might stand for something else entirely.

She guessed she was about to find out.

David Morton stared at the piece of paper, grimacing. 'What do you make of this, Winsome?' he asked.

Winsome shifted on her chair. 'Well,' she said. 'Shall I try to be diplomatic, or just blunt?'

'Let's go for blunt, shall we say?' David answered. 'You know Julia better than I.'

'I had not realised Julia's issues, and those of her aunt, went so deep or wide.' She looked at the flyer. 'Or far.'

'They're preposterous,' David broke in. He stabbed a finger at the paper. 'This offends me. It's offensive.' He shook his head. 'And the woman had the temerity to stand in front of me and pass it to me like it would mean something.' He let out a long breath.

'I'm going to insist she steps down as Churchwarden, Winsome – you know I have to,' David said. 'This awful thing says that the pagans in Wellsford are taking over the village and sacrificing animals and all sorts of other nonsense. That they're putting poison in the food they're giving everyone.' His gaze met Winsome's.

'They're not sacrificing animals, and they're not putting poison in the food. I'm sitting here as healthy, living proof of that.'

'Satanic rituals?'

Winsome shook her head. 'They don't even believe in Satan, David.'

'But they do hold rituals, don't they?' David leaned back in his chair and looked levelly at Winsome. 'The accusation that you attended one. Is it true?'

It was such a direct question. There was no squirming out from under it. Not, Winsome had decided, that she wanted to.

'Yes,' she said. 'I took part in their Yule – winter solstice – ritual.'

Dean Morton's eyes widened. 'Took part in it? I assumed you were simply present.' He sat straight. 'As a sort of onlooker, so to speak.'

'It was beautiful,' Winsome said faintly, then cleared her throat. 'It was beautiful, and I danced with them for part of it.'

'Danced?' David's eyes strayed to the flyer where, in bold capitals, it claimed that the pagan rituals were dances with the devil.

'Yes.' Winsome shifted uneasily. 'It was in the woods, at the stone circle at dawn. It was snowing.'

'Stone circle?' David's voice was thin. 'At dawn?'

'Yes. They were, erm, dancing the sun back up and the

seasons to turn, I suppose is the easiest way to put it.'
Winsome locked her fingers together, the knuckles
whitening.

'And you danced with them?'

'Yes.'

'Danced the sun back up and the seasons to turn?' David
shook his head. 'How did this come to pass – did they invite
you? Did they invite your parishioners? Was this to be a
shared...celebration?'

'No.' Winsome glanced away from David Morton's face,
which was slowly turning the colour of a ripe plum. Cù
looked at her and thumped his tail against the floor.

It made no sound.

'I wasn't invited, either.' She swallowed, tried a smile. 'I
erm, followed some of the Grove members when they
walked up to it. I was up early, you see, couldn't sleep, for
erm, various reasons. So, when I saw some of the younger
members, who live in the village, walking through the
churchyard, I just sort of...followed them.'

Did that sound as completely lame as she thought it
did? She glanced over at Cù and was rewarded with what
was most definitely, a hairy, doggy grin, white teeth
shining.

But the Dean had a hand up in the air, as though stopping traffic. 'Wait,' he said. 'Wait a minute here.' He
squinted at Winsome. 'Did you just say they walked through
the churchyard?'

Winsome nodded. 'There's a path, behind a rock on the
edge of the old graveyard, almost behind the vicarage, actually, that leads into the woods, and eventually onto Wilde
land.' She paused, put together another smile. 'It's a lovely

347

walk. I've taken it often lately. There are all sorts of tracks through the woods. Very relaxing.'

David Morton shook his head. 'So – forget this whole ridiculous flyer for a minute, or forever, actually – let me get this straight?' He sucked in twin lungsful of air. 'The preferred method to getting to the Wilde Grove rituals is to walk through the churchyard. And you yourself went uninvited to one of these rituals?'

Winsome swallowed. Nodded.

'Why did they not send you away?'

This question was the rub, thought Winsome. She could either stick herself right in it or try to skirt around the outside of things and maybe, maybe, get away with it.

'I've been working closely with Morghan Wilde,' she said, sticking herself right in it.

David narrowed his eyes. 'I see,' he said, not seeing at all. 'In what capacity, Winsome?'

'Erm, we've consulted together on a number of village concerns.'

David nodded.

'We've come to know each other rather well, over the last few months,' Winsome said. 'She is a remarkable woman.'

'She's a lesbian, isn't she?'

Winsome's eyebrows shot up. 'I believe she was married to a woman at one stage, yes,' she said. 'Her wife died tragically,' she said pointedly.

'So, you've just been consulting each other on village concerns?'

His tone confused Winsome, and she didn't like it. She

decided to ignore its ambiguity and simply answer the question.

Except there was no simple answer to the question. Not if she was determined to be honest.

'Look,' she said. 'What are you thinking? About...everything?'

'I'm trying to determine what is going on with you, Winsome. You were entrusted with the Wellsford parish – by myself – and here we are with a great mess on our hands. I want to know the parameters of it.'

'Of what?' Winsome was still confused.

'Of the mess,' David said. 'Now, walk me through exactly what has been going on in Wellsford, between you and these pagans, if you please.'

Winsome squeezed her hands together in her lap even tighter. Here it was, the moment of reckoning. Did she lie and gloss over things? Or did she take three deep, even breaths, and go where the truth took her?

Did it matter?

It did, she decided.

'All right,' Winsome said, taking the first of her three breaths and holding it for a moment. 'Well, here's how it's been, I suppose. The first time I met Morghan Wilde was in church. She attended a service there and I introduced myself afterward.'

Winsome took a perverse pleasure in watching David Morton's eyes grow round.

'She was in the church? At a service?' he asked.

'Yes. And I invited her over to the vicarage for a cup of tea afterward, once I learned who she was.'

Now, he was blinking like a blind owl at her. If this had been any less serious, she might have giggled.

'And?' he asked.

'And I liked her. She is intelligent, calm, and knowledgeable.'

Now, David's eyes slitted. 'Knowledgeable about what?'

'All sorts of things, I'm sure.' Winsome shifted slightly. Took the second of her deep breaths. 'The village, it's history.'

'Why was she attending a service?'

Winsome didn't alter her expression. 'I'm afraid you'd have to ask her that,' she said.

'I'm asking you.'

'I do not break the confidences of my parishioners.'

David shook his head. 'She's no parishioner, Winsome,' he said.

'My friends, then, Dean,' Winsome answered.

David frowned over the answer and glanced at the flyer. Maybe he ought to take it more seriously after all. He tapped a finger on it. 'What's this about you praying in some pagan temple?'

'There's a very old stone summerhouse in the woods not far from the vicarage. It's a lovely spot, and yes, I've been known to stop there on a walk and pray.' Winsome blinked. 'I'm a vicar. We do tend to pray quite a lot.'

David shook his head. 'That tone is inappropriate, Winsome,' he said. 'You do yourself no favours.' His finger hovered over the flyer again. 'And this – getting drunk in the church. That is absurd to the point of I don't know what. Why is it there? It has a date and time. What is that about?'

36

W<small>INSOME SIGHED.</small> 'J<small>ULIA MET ME THAT MORNING AS</small> I <small>WAS</small> coming out of the church after a particularly...intense...time of prayer. She mistook my disorientation for being drunk.'

'That's quite some...disorientation.'

'It was quite some prayer.'

David stared at her. 'Winsome,' he said. 'You don't seem to understand the gravity of this situation. In fact, you seem to be being deliberately provocative.'

Winsome stared at him. 'I don't know what you want, Dean,' she said at last.

'I want you to explain this!' he exploded. 'Rationally, calmly, giving me the reasons I need not to move you on from your position in Wellsford. Can you do that?'

Winsome looked down at her side, where Cù had come to sit. She could see him there in her mind as well as if with her eyes. It had been the same with Reverend Robinson and the others.

'Well?' David demanded. 'Can you?'

Winsome shook her head. 'I don't know,' she said. Then looked straight at the Dean. 'But here's what I can tell you – I've done a lot of good since I took up my position. These have been extremely trying times, and yet I've still managed to institute several excellent community projects, and our congregation has actually grown.' She took the last of her three breaths and let it slowly out. 'I am entrusted with the spiritual needs of Wellsford parish, and I have been meeting those, tending to them, and deepening them where I can.'

'You've also been consorting with a group of radical pagans and attending – and participating – in their rituals. Which is well outside the scope of a small village vicar.'

'Perhaps it is a sign of the times, Dean,' Winsome said. 'Perhaps it is time that we stopped proclaiming that it's our way or the highway, and actually acknowledge that there is beauty and worth in many other religions. That there is more than one way of knowing the world.'

David stared at her. He was silent for several moments, then shook his head. 'Yes,' he conceded. 'But when we talk about interfaith dialogue, we're generally not talking about a bunch of pagans dancing around an old circle of stones.'

'What is the difference?' Winsome asked.

David shook his head. 'And besides, Winsome. I'm afraid that when you joined in with their ritual on their grounds and on their terms, you were not defending Christ, or living His word. And I cannot ignore that. You are, first and foremost, a spokesperson for Christ and His Church.'

'It was...unorthodox of me,' Winsome admitted. 'I'm not even sure why I went. Only, it seemed so apt – to sing the sun up after the longest night.' She shook her head. 'What a beautiful idea that is. It really makes you aware of where you are, the world you live in, and how alive and wonderful it can be.'

'We have our traditions, Winsome. The birth of the Lord Himself celebrated at that time of the year.'

'Yes, that's true,' Winsome said. 'And it's a lovely little myth, the birth of Christ. The star of Bethlehem, three wise men, and the virgin birth of course. It's all very nice, really, and I can't help that think if we actually viewed it as the mythology it really is, then we'd be better off. We could really explore the symbolism, the deeper mystery of it, and concentrate of experiencing the truth of the story, and the world. We could look to our souls and see how deep they really are.'

Winsome stopped talking, pressed her lips shut in consternation at what she'd just said.

Cù grinned up at her.

David, however, was silent for so long, Winsome began to wonder whether she ought to just get up and leave.

He cleared his throat. 'That was quite the speech, Winsome.' He closed his eyes and rubbed his hands over his face. 'I can't help but blame myself,' he said eventually, peering through his fingers at her before dropping his hands.

'Blame yourself?'

'Your first parish. You were already of a romantic, Celtic bent. I thought it would allow you to navigate the sensitivities of Wellsford, but now I realise I was wrong. It has made you an easy target.'

'Target?' Winsome repeated stupidly.

'You've been seduced by them, Winsome. Dancing in the dawn, calling the sun to rise, or whatever. I'd say you're besotted.'

He got up from behind his desk and walked to the door. 'I'll be in touch, Winsome,' he said.

'I don't understand,' Winsome said, getting awkwardly to her feet.

'I need to think about things,' David said. 'If the issue were just you – I would move you on, or better yet, back where you came and where you can't do any harm...'

Winsome interrupted him. 'Harm?' she asked, disbelieving what her ears were telling her. 'You think I'm doing harm?'

'I think you're muddying some very dangerous waters, Winsome.'

Winsome shook her head and fumbled for her handbag. 'I think you're forgetting the number one reason for our existence, Dean,' she said, drawing out a sheaf of letters. 'I wasn't going to show you these – it's embarrassing, really, but I think it might be a good idea to remember the human side of what we do.' She looked at David who still stood by the door, one hand on the knob, about to open it and usher her out, probably jobless.

'What I do,' she said, speaking around the lump in her throat. 'The hours listening to the needs of the people in the parish. The people – the souls it's actually all about. Tending to the flock.'

She held out the small bundle of letters.

David looked at her for a moment, then down at the

papers she held out to him. Whatever these were, he doubted they could change his mind. The whole thing was an appalling mess. He should have got another man like Robinson for the job. A bit of a plodder. Smart, but no real imagination.

Only, no one else had applied for the position, stuck out in a tiny village with only one road in and out.

He took the letters reluctantly. Most of them were written on cheap paper in a variety of pen colours and legibility.

'How many do usually attend services, Winsome?' he asked.

She licked her lips. 'Around thirty, Dean,' she said, then blinked. 'Which is more than did when I came to Wellsford.'

'Thirty,' David repeated on a sigh. 'Once, everyone in the village would have.' He blinked. 'Including the local witch.'

'She still does, on occasion,' Winsome answered. Okay, it had only been the once, but still.

David grunted, flicking through the letters. 'They do seem to love you, Winsome,' he said.

'I didn't ask them to write these for you, Dean,' Winsome hastened to say. 'I wasn't even going to bring them out and give them to you.'

'What's this one about?' He held up one written on pink paper and waved it like a small flag.

Winsome didn't need to read it to know who it was from. Emily Bright. Her grandad had been one of the ones who had died in Banwell at the beginning. Winsome shivered. That seemed so long ago now. So long since she'd come to

Wellsford and seen Robinson and the others waiting for her. Dead, but still waiting.

'It says you held a service for her father and the others? What others?' He puzzled over the letter. 'A what? A Requiem mass?' David looked over at Winsome. 'Surely she means a memorial service? They had already been buried at that stage, had they not?'

Winsome cleared her throat. She should have kept the letters in her bag. 'Erm, yes, this was some months after they'd passed on.'

'So she has it wrong then – she's talking about a memorial service, correct?'

'No.' Winsome shook her head. 'She's correct. I held a requiem mass for the small group of souls who had passed on at the care home in Banwell.'

'Why on earth would you hold a full mass for them?'

Winsome looked down at her feet, saw Cù at her side staring at the Dean, and raised her head. 'I was concerned that the souls of the departed might not...well...have actually departed, according to the manner of their deaths – frightened and alone as they had been.'

David stared at Winsome for a long minute. 'This just keeps getting worse,' he said. 'Let me see if I understand you correctly – you were concerned that what? These people might be what? Ghosts?'

The question made Winsome grimace. She really should have kept the letters. She'd meant to leave Emily's at home, at least. 'Yes,' she said. 'They'd died in great difficulty. I thought it would ease them at the same time it eased their families.'

'This is extraordinary.' David closed his eyes for a

moment, then sighed and folded the letter in his hand. 'I'll be in touch, Winsome,' he said. 'But I think we can safely say that the days of St. Bridget's in Wellsford have effectively come to an end.'

'What?' Winsome squeaked.

'There's not the money, anyway,' David said. 'This pandemic has had a terrible effect on the Church coffers, and St. Bridget's should have been closed years ago.' He straightened where he stood and made up his mind. Wellsford had always been a bit of a problem, a bit of a grey area in the scheme of things, but it was obvious it couldn't go on.

'What about me?' Winsome asked. 'What do I do?'

'You could see if there is a place still available in the community you were part of before, I suppose,' David said.

'I don't want to go back there.'

'Well, I think you'd fall under pastoral reorganisation then,' David said. 'Redundant, effectively, with one year's stipend, and accommodation for that time.'

Winsome stared at him. 'Redundant?' she echoed.

'Unless you'd like to be removed through a capability procedure?' David shook his head. 'I think we can forego that, don't you? A waste of our resources.'

'What about – what about another parish?'

'No,' David said on a sigh. 'I don't think so.' He opened the door a crack. 'Take the year's stipend, Winsome, and move on. Away from Wellsford, if you've any sense.'

Winsome walked out of the office on legs she couldn't feel. She drifted in a daze past Bethany's desk, not seeing Bethany's sympathetic look. Somehow, Winsome's feet took her all the way outside and stood her next to her car.

Cù sat in the back seat, waiting for her.

'I've lost my job,' Winsome whispered, just to hear the words out loud. They didn't sound real, not coming from her mouth. She loved it in Wellsford. She loved the people she served, all the things they'd grown together, despite hardly being allowed outside their doors the last months. She even loved taking services – okay, really not the preaching so much, but the prayers in the church, looking over the bent heads, and lifting their voices in praise. She loved that. She even liked the new website, was getting quite good at navigating behind the scenes on it, putting together her little blog posts, all of that. Even making the video hadn't been too awful. Not when it was part of something so worthwhile.

When she was part of something worthwhile.

Winsome discovered the car keys in her hand and opened the door, slid in behind the wheel.

'I don't know why I'm so stunned,' she said out loud. 'I knew this was a possibility, after all.'

She had. She'd known. But now it wasn't just a possibility, it was a fact. And where did that leave her?

Side-lined. Pastoral reorganisation. No job – and what else could she do?

'I'm forty, for crying out loud,' she said. 'All my job skills are rusty, and there are no jobs anyway.'

She blinked at the blue sky outside the car. Looked over at the building she'd just come out of. The blinds on the first floor twitched and Winsome jolted as if shocked and rammed the keys into the ignition. That was the Dean's office, she was sure of it.

She couldn't bear the thought of him looking out his window and seeing her sitting shell-shocked in her car as though she'd been such a fool not to anticipate this would happen.

Of course she'd known it could happen.

She'd just not known how it would feel.

And it felt terrible.

37

Erin walked down the path towards the well at the centre of her garden. It was foggy this new-born morning, as though the day was reluctant to unveil itself and commit to either sunshine or cloud. Her footsteps were muffled, and the mist pressed against her exposed hands and cheeks with a delicate, damp touch.

She was trying to put aside the gnawing seed of worry she'd been carrying around since Macha had appeared and told her to look to the Lady, and instead see the garden with a type of double vision. One garden was damp, smelling of mist and soil and another, inside her mind, was a maze of plants with early morning sunlight slanted across them.

It was an odd sensation, to be almost in two places at once, and yet it was also...interesting, she decided. Almost freeing. It was like an extension of the exercise she'd been doing pretty much since coming to the Grove, that sort of slow spreading of consciousness beyond the bounds of her body until she could see far in every direction.

Erin stopped in front of the well and tried that exercise now, hoping it would calm her, stop the vaguely itchy feeling she had that something was wrong.

But she knew something was wrong, or was about to be wrong, or something along those lines. Macha wouldn't have appeared to her and said something, if not.

If only though she'd been slightly less cryptic.

Raising her hands and breathing deeply, Erin began, calming and centring herself, then she lowered her arms as she exhaled, as if she were going to start spinning and dancing. She didn't though, instead she repeated the stretch and the breath, and on each longer exhale relaxed her body and her mind so that her awareness spread and expanded as she let go.

She relaxed into the mist, damp ribbons winding around her as she felt the familiar shape and size of her garden and cleared everything else from her mind.

And she relaxed into the new garden as well – the one that existed only in her imagination. Or somewhere.

It surprised her so much that she almost pulled back, almost reeled herself in. But she caught herself in time and let herself go again, and reach. She reached for the edge of the second garden, feeling its sunshine on herself.

Then Erin got curious and lifted herself upwards, like she'd done many times to peer over her garden walls at the trees that grew almost down to the plot of land on which Ash Cottage looked.

It was still there, just like that, the trees dripping fog from their branches, wreathed in the mist that glittered here and there where it thinned enough for the sun to shine through upon it.

And the second garden was there as well – her space she was making for herself in the Otherworld, and she looked down on it as though she were a bird and saw the garden with the well in the middle, and the radiating beds full to bursting with their plants and flowers. She breathed in, and there was the garden wall, and beyond it...

Beyond it was the Wildwood. Not the woods she was used to, but their ancient counterparts, the woods that straddled the line between here and there, the forest that was part history, part myth.

Something moved within it, and the white stag of the Wildwood stepped out from under the branches and lifted its tined head to look at Erin, as though she truly had taken on the shape of a bird and rode the lazy air currents above the gardens and between the worlds.

Erin collapsed back into herself with a whoosh of surprise and stood in her garden again, surrounded by the mist, eyes blinking. She shook her head.

So much was possible, she thought.

So much more than she'd ever believed. More than anyone had ever told her.

She raised her hands and cupped her palms in front of her and looked into the bowl they made. One day, she thought – one day she'd make fire, pluck the spark from inside her as Kria had done, and make fire.

It was possible. Magic such as that had been done in the past. She lifted her eyes and gazed out at the mist-ridden sky. All the elements had been manipulated; she knew. She'd been reading Ambrose's history books, the story of the slaughter of the Druids at Anglesey, where the Druids had cast imprecations and incantations to the sky and brought down clouds and storms.

It hadn't been enough, against iron and war, but it had been done.

And one day, Erin decided, she would make fire in the palms of her hands. Just as Kria had done. There was so much magic that was possible.

And she would walk between the worlds also. She closed her eyes and spun her garden in her mind again, vowing to keep tending it, walking there as well as here, coming back to it over and over, and when she was ready, stepping through the gate and into the Wildwood.

Erin sighed, drew herself back to the garden her grand-mother had planted, and walked over to the well, tugging up the heavy lid.

'I am blessed,' she whispered. 'To walk, and see, and spin. I am a spoke on the great wheel of the world, and I am blessed.'

She reached into her pockets and touched her diamonds with her fingers and her mind. Later, she decided, she would make a pouch to hang around her neck, and she would put her diamonds in there, so that she could always remember the treasure of her soul.

For a moment, she bowed her head, a sense of wellbeing flooding through her as though it filled her bloodstream.

When she closed the lid on the well and headed back to the house, she felt calm, despite the returning niggle of concern about Macha's message.

· · ·

'WHAT'S HAPPENED TO WAYNE MOFFAT?' ERIN ASKED, POKING her head around the door of Mary's tiny office.

Mary looked up at her. 'What do you mean?' she said, frowning.

'He's not able to get out of bed this morning,' Erin said. 'Usually he's up and waiting, dressed and everything – or mostly dressed. This morning I go in there and he's barely visible under the blankets.' She nipped at her bottom lip. 'I've only been off a day.'

'He's feeling under the weather, I'm afraid, Erin,' Mary told her. 'I don't know if he is nearing the end, or not, however.'

'But we'd barely talked – he'd barely told me anything!'

So that's what the problem was – and Mary thought she could sympathise. It was hard, Erin's position. 'It's not his responsibility to, Erin,' she said gently. 'His only responsibility at this stage of things is to live and die as well as possible.' Mary nodded. 'Spend your shift by his bedside. He'll be glad of the company, although he's not been strong enough to talk much. It will matter though – not being alone.'

'Me?' Erin asked.

'Winsome sat with him yesterday afternoon, and she will be along later to look in on him, but for now, I think it would do both of you some good.'

Erin nodded. 'All right,' she said. 'I can do that.' She withdrew her head.

Mary looked at the empty doorway. The girl had looked as though she was having to convince herself that she could indeed do that, but Mary sighed and turned back to her paperwork. This was why Erin was there, after all. To be with Wayne Moffat as he took his last exit.

Erin crept into Wayne Moffat's room to find Burdock already there. Burdock sat beside the bed, his head on the mattress, big brown eyes luminous in the dim light.

'Hey boy,' she whispered. 'How's it going?' She patted Burdock and sat down on the chair next to the bed.

'That your dog?' Wayne asked. His voice was paper thin and seemed to come from a long way away. He groped a hand from the bedcovers and Burdock licked the fingers.

'Yes,' Erin said. 'I inherited him along with the cottage.'

'Always liked dogs. Had one once, but he got out when I was...under the weather, and hit by a car, he was.' Wayne shifted his gaze to the ceiling. 'Never got another after that. Weren't no good for looking after anyone. Not even a dog.'

Erin winced at Wayne's tone. Filled with self-loathing. 'I'm sure that's happened lots of times,' she said.

'Doesn't make it any better.' His gaze drifted towards Erin. 'Don't look like Becca, you don't. I thought you would, but it's only really in your expression sometimes.'

'Did you love Becca?' Erin asked, her voice soft.

Wayne didn't answer for a long time. 'We had some good times,' he said at last.

'You must have missed her after...afterward.'

Wayne closed his eyes. Flicked them open again. The door, the stairs. Still right there. Not as bad as it used to be – he'd used to dream of that night all the time. The way Becca had run off through the house, yelling and screaming at him.

'I chased her,' he said, before he knew he was going to say it. 'That night – I chased her. We were arguing. We argued a lot. Great screaming matches. Becca was a volatile woman, you know.' He subsided into silence.

Erin stared at him, her hand on the blanket clenching a handful of wool. 'That night?' she asked, her voice barely more than a whisper.

'Yeah.' Wayne's voice was leaf-light. 'I chased after her. She turned around and shoved me and I shoved her back.' He screwed his eyes shut. 'God help me, I pushed her back. And the door...it wasn't latched, you know? She just crashed right through it.'

Erin lifted her hands and placed them carefully on the sides of her head. 'The door to the basement?' she asked and now it was her own voice that sounded far away.

'I called an ambulance,' Wayne said, watching it playing over inside his head, the way he'd stood on the top of the stairs staring down into the darkness, waiting for her to move, get up, say something at least.

But she hadn't said anything. Just laid there, and he'd turned and run skidding through the house for the phone. Pressed the buttons for the ambulance with a finger that couldn't quite hit them square on.

Then the lights outside from the ambulance, and the paramedics, coming in with their stretcher, picking her up off the cold dirt floor and bringing her past him, and he'd thought she was dead then, her face still, white, like she was already a ghost.

'She wasn't dead,' he said, his voice scratchy now. Hoarse, like the words had thorns on them. 'Died later, in the hospital, when they were operating on her.' He turned his head and looked at the far wall. 'Didn't help none though that she didn't die at the bottom of them stairs. She might as well have. I killed her as soon as I pushed her back.' He swallowed and his adam's apple bounced in his scrawny neck. 'Should never have pushed her. Was just mad as hell, and she was screaming at me.'

Erin got up stiffly from her seat. 'I need some fresh air,' she said.

Wayne looked at her. 'I'm sorry,' he said. 'I'm real sorry. I didn't mean to do it.'

Erin sat back down again. 'Did the police come?' she asked, thinking of Bernie.

'Yeah. Asked some questions, took some notes. Looked at me like I was scum, but nothing ever came of it. Why would it? Just a couple junkies ruining each other's lives, that was as far as they thought.'

Erin got up again, turned to leave, her mind blank with shock. A hand snaked out and grasped her arm. She turned to look at Wayne, just sticks and stones in the bed.

'But she wasn't a junkie then, you gotta know,' he said. He licked his lips with a tongue that was barely wet. 'Let me tell you the rest, girl. I'm not feeling my best today, and I know there will be more days like this for me – but let me tell you the rest.'

Erin looked at him and after a moment, she nodded. Reaching over to the bedside table, she picked up the glass of water and helped him drink.

'Thank you,' he whispered. 'I know I don't deserve that – don't deserve anything from you, I know that.'

Erin sat in silence beside the bed, waiting.

'She'd stopped most of the drugs you see – during the pregnancy. Knew it wouldn't be good for the baby, and even though she wasn't going to keep the mite – you – she didn't want to do it any harm, either.' Wayne sniffed. 'I had a habit though, and I always thought the plan was we'd use the money your hoity toity parents gave us to play a bit, you see?'

Erin saw, but wasn't sure she wanted to.

'And that's how it went down, after you were born and tucked up sweet in your new mansion. Becca and me – we went back to our ways.' He blinked. 'Fora while, at least. Made a nice dent in the money. And then, Becca, she saw something.' Wayne lapsed into silence, his memories swirling inside his skull.

Erin waited, frowning. What had Becca seen? She shook her head. The whole story – it was sad – sordid, left her with an awful taste in her mouth. She closed her eyes, and there was her mother, the mother she'd never met, screaming at a younger version of this husk of a man, and then a push, a shove, and a door that wasn't latched.

And then blackness. A blow to the head – Charlie, she'd said Becca hit her head on the stairs, never regained consciousness. Died after the ambulance had come for her, taken her to hospital. Erin snapped her eyes open. Shook the vision away.

'What – what did she see?' she asked, her voice rusty sounding, as though she hadn't used it for a long time.

In the bed, Wayne swallowed. Shook his head minutely. 'I never understood it,' he said. 'And I'm ashamed of what I did.'

'What did she see?' Now Erin's question was hissed. She wasn't interested in the old man's shame. She shared his contempt for himself.

'Was one day when we were going out to, you know...'

Wayne cleared his throat. 'Visit our dealer,' he said. 'About to get into the car, we were, and suddenly Becca stops still, staring into the air over the roof of the car.' His voice faded out again, then started up, reluctantly, and Erin had to lean close to hear what he said.

'She didn't tell me what she saw right then,' Wayne continued on a sigh. 'Only turned around, went back inside, and when I followed her, demanding to know what she was on about – we needed to go out, didn't she know? She looked at me and said she wasn't going to do it no more.'

Wayne blinked, a squinting of his eyes.

'Do what no more?' Erin asked.

'The drugs, you know,' Wayne replied. 'The drinking. I thought she was crazy, of course, but she shakes her head and says to me that she saw two orbs over the top of the car, and knew they were there to tell her something.'

'Orbs?' Erin's eyes rounded. 'What do you mean, orbs?'

Wayne moved his shoulders in the bed, shrugging. He closed his eyes. 'Dunno,' he said. 'She just called them orbs. Two of them. One small and bright, one large and dark.' He paused again, and the seconds ticked by as he made himself look at the memory.

'She told me she knew they were a message. She could choose, she said. Keep drinking, doing the drugs, and the black one, it would get bigger, and that would be her life – something big and dark and useless. Or she could choose the smaller, the one that glowed like diamonds, she said. She could concentrate on that one because it was beautiful and her life could be too, maybe, if she just kept her mind on that one.'

Wayne let out a breath, spent. There, he thought. He'd

done it. He'd told the whole sorry story. He looked at Erin. She'd hate him now, he knew.

But at least she knew. Becca had been going to turn her life around.

'I reckon it was because of you,' he said. 'Having a baby changed her, even if she didn't keep it. It was going to be good for her.' His voice trailed away again. There was nothing left to say. He'd told her all of it.

Erin tipped her head back, stared at the ceiling for a moment trying to gather her thoughts together but they were skipping all over the place. 'Was that...was that the night she died?' she asked.

Okay, Wayne thought. So maybe he wasn't quite done, then. 'Yeah,' he said. 'We argued, you see. And we'd been drinking. Me more than her, though I know that's no excuse.' He looked over at the girl. 'I know I've no right to ask you to forgive me for what I did, or anything,' he said. 'But I am sorry. I wish I hadn't done what I did. I never intended...'

He stopped talking because he'd been about to say he hadn't intended to hurt Becca. Which wasn't true, was it? He'd wanted to hurt her. Wanted to reach out and shove her into the wall. She'd scared him. He knew the moment she told him she was quitting it all, getting straight and sober, that it spelled the end for him. He'd never manage it, not him.

'You never intended to kill her?' Erin asked hoarsely.

'No,' Wayne whispered. 'I never intended for her to die.' He turned his face to the wall, and suddenly all he felt was tired and empty.

'Erin?' It was Mary, standing in the doorway. 'Come away now,' she said. 'Mr Moffat needs to rest.'

Erin, one hand on Burdock, gazed over at Mary with glassy eyes. After a moment, she nodded, and got up on legs that were unsteady. She walked over to Mary, Burdock trailing after her, and Mary put a hand on her shoulder, and led her from the room, steering her to the kitchen, where she sat her down at the table.

'She all right?' Alan asked, there to make lunch for everyone.

'She just needs a minute,' Mary said. 'And a cup of hot, sweet tea.'

Alan looked at Erin, then nodded. 'Coming up.'

He slid a mug in front of Erin a minute later and Erin put her hands automatically around it. She looked over at Mary's face, which was creased with concern.

'How much did you hear?' she asked.

Mary smiled sympathetically. 'Enough,' she said.

'He killed her,' Erin said, shaking her head. 'Because she was going straight.'

Alan glanced over at the pair of them sitting at the table and decided it was high time he took a break. In a different part of the house. Maybe outside.

Burdock pressed his chin down on Erin's lap, and looked up at her with worried brown eyes.

'He didn't know she would fall through the doorway and down the steps,' Mary said.

'Why didn't the police do something about it?' Erin asked. She sipped at the tea, relieved to feel as though she was coming back to herself. Another thought struck her, and she held up a hand. 'Wait,' she said.

Was this what Morghan had been talking about – was it this scene that she'd said Wayne Moffat was stuck in? Erin shivered, imagining part of herself being forever imprisoned in the dark basement where Becca had laid, her head damaged because of an argument and a fall.

'What is it?' Mary said.

Erin chewed on her lip for a moment. 'I just remembered something Morghan told me – she said that part of Wayne was stuck in a scene from his past, held there by grief and guilt.'

'That sounds likely, don't you think?' Mary asked. 'It would be hard to live with knowing you played any sort of part in something like this. Especially if you were just a silly, ignorant young man.'

38

Erin stumbled out into the day like she was coming out of a dark room. She stood on the footpath for a moment, staring up at the sky, shaking her head. Burdock looked at her for a moment, then sat down and scratched himself before going over to her and pressing his warm side against her legs. She petted him absently.

'It's okay, Burdock,' she said. 'It's okay. I'm okay. I'm going to be okay.'

Her voice with its whispered words made him feel better. He twisted around and licked her hand, then with a last look at her, wandered off to explore the bushes. Sometimes other dogs left interesting messages in these bushes.

'Erin?'

Erin swung around, saw Krista coming towards her, and found she still knew how to smile.

'Erin!' Krista laughed. 'We must stop meeting like this!' She shook her head. 'I can't wait until we can all be out and about again.'

'Me neither,' Erin said. 'I've missed coming over and seeing you.'

Krista nodded. Then narrowed her eyes a little. 'Erin,' she said. 'Are you all right?'

'Well,' Erin said, giving an odd little laugh. 'I don't know, actually. I just found out that one of the old guys in the care home killed my mother.' She blinked. 'My birth mother, of course.'

Krista's eyes widened in shock. 'What?'

Erin shook her head. 'Remember we were talking last time we met about how weird it kind of was that my mother had gone to the loo at night without turning the light on first? Well, this guy was her boyfriend way back when. And the night she died, they'd been arguing, and she pushed him, and he shoved her, and she fell against the basement door, which wasn't closed properly, and she went crashing through, hit her head, and well, died a few hours later.'

Krista put a hand to her mouth. 'Wow,' she breathed. 'I mean, wow.' She shook her head. 'How do you feel about that?'

'I've honestly no idea,' Erin said. She looked up at the sky, grey and cloudy, although the mist had cleared. 'I mean, I knew there was something fishy about the whole business, right? But to hear it from the horse's mouth, so to speak.' She shook her head. 'I'm just really gobsmacked.'

'Is there anything I can do?' Krista asked. 'I mean, I'm supposed to be going for a walk with Minnie, but she'll understand if I reschedule.'

'Minnie,' Erin said. 'How is she?'

'Oh, you'd barely recognise her,' Krista said. 'She's doing

amazingly. Totally headstrong and opinionated, but I think that's just her personality. She's great, really.'

'She's, like, over what happened?'

Krista nodded. 'She is. It's amazing, isn't it – how much we can go through? We come out the other end a bit battered and worse for the wear for a while, but still. Living and learning, all part of it, really.' Krista looked ruefully for a moment down at her leg, the one that was now no longer made of flesh and blood. 'I think she'll eventually have quite a feel for spirit work, having had the experiences she did.' She nodded. 'Yeah, I can see her going in that direction one day.'

Krista looked over at Erin. 'Oh, I'm sorry,' she said. 'I didn't mean to go on – I know you've had a shock. Honestly, let's walk a while together. I can let Minnie know.'

'No,' Erin said. 'It's all right.' She nodded. 'I'm all right - I mean, it's been a shock, and I don't know how I'm ever going to look Wayne Moffat in the eye again, but I think I'm all right. I just need to keep busy a while, you know? And I also promised Stephan I'd do the grocery run again.'

STEPHAN CAME OVER AS SOON AS HE SAW ERIN HOVERING ON the edge of the gardens. He knelt and ruffled Burdock's fur. 'Man,' he said. 'I sure have been missing you two.'

'We miss you too,' Erin said, unable to help smiling at him, at the way his blue eyes danced in his face at the sight of her. She touched her hand to her heart.

Stephan saw the gesture and nodded. He touched his chest too, then held out his hand and let himself relax for a moment, so that all he was doing was reaching for Erin.

She held out her fingers, and although they didn't touch, both could feel the sweep and swirl of energy between them, the tingling of their fingers, the way the energy shivered its way up their arms and set the hairs on the backs of their necks tingling.

This was it, Erin thought. This was what she needed. Stephan. The glorious way they fit together even when they couldn't touch each other. It made her smile.

'You look suddenly...radiant,' Stephan said. 'That's the word, right?'

'It's the one matches how I feel, thanks to you,' Erin said. She relaxed and closed her eyes for a moment, soaking up the sensation of him.

'How's your day been?' Stephan asked.

Erin shook her head. 'The story of my morning can wait until later,' she said.

'Have you figured out what Macha meant, by telling you to look to the Lady?' Stephan asked.

'Oh.' Erin looked down at her feet. 'You know – I'd completely forgotten about it.' She shook her head. 'But she hasn't sent her raven back to harass me, so maybe it's not about anyone specific? What do you think?'

'I don't know,' Stephan said, coming around to her side to lean against the low stone wall that separated the garden from the property next to it. 'I mean – every leader of the Grove has been called Lady, right? So, considering how, you know, flexible time is, it could be anyone.' He eyed Erin. 'It could even be you, right?'

'Me?' Erin looked at him in surprise. 'I hadn't even thought about that.'

'But it could be. I mean – you've had a lot of things going on, right?'

Erin nodded. 'And I've been seeing dragons.' It was possible, she supposed. 'I guess we'll just have to keep thinking on it,' she said, then decided to change the subject. 'How are you getting on here?'

'Done, thank goodness,' Stephan said. 'Well, practically done. Dad and his crew can go, at least, which is a bit of a relief, I have to say. We're getting on better, but it's been a long journey.'

Erin beamed at him. 'You've done brilliantly,' she said.

'Thanks. I'm really pleased with it all, actually,' Stephan said, gazing out over the long strip of land where the big glasshouse now took pride of place. 'It's been a lot of planning and a lot of organisation, and I guess that's just the start of it, really.' He gave Erin a sidelong glance.

'What?' she said. 'What are you thinking?'

Stephan winced. 'I've been doing quite a bit of puzzling things out, you know?'

Erin did know. She'd been doing a lot herself. 'There's been almost nothing but time for thinking,' she said. 'What with normal life being pretty much at a standstill.'

Stephan scratched his head. 'Yeah.' He swept a hand at the garden and the glasshouses in front of him. 'This has taken up all my time for the last few weeks, which has been great and all, and I'm really thrilled with everything we've achieved and the massive plans we have.'

Erin sensed there was more to it. 'But?' she asked.

'But.' Stephan whistled for Burdock and patted him when he came trotting over. 'But I'm thinking there are some other things I want to do – and maybe I can, since like,

I'm not the only one on this community garden project now.'

'What sort of other things?' Erin asked. She leaned against the wall as well, wishing she could tuck herself under Stephan's arm while he talked. She couldn't though, so she patted Burdock as well.

'Like, you know the training that Bear Fellow's had me doing?' Stephan blinked his dark-lashed eyes at Erin.

She nodded.

'So, I'm thinking I'd like to take that further – here in this world too, you know? Morghan and Ambrose are talking about bringing a doctor into the town if they can find anyone who might be interested, and I'm wondering if there wouldn't be room in whatever centre or house or whatever for, like, an herbalist. A proper, qualified one, you know?'

'You, you mean?'

Stephan nodded, his cheeks pinking. 'Yeah. I'm thinking it would be like, bringing knowledge from one world to another – and isn't that what we're supposed to do, really?'

Erin nodded, then grinned at him. 'I think it's a brilliant idea,' she said.

Stephan was delighted. 'You do?'

'Of course! And it's the natural progression from what you're already doing.' Erin stood up and faced him, Burdock in between them. 'Stephan,' she said. 'It's wonderful. I think you should totally go for it.' She shook her head. 'In fact, I think you were probably born for it.'

'Wow, all right then, yeah,' Stephan said. 'You can help me look for courses to do. There are way too many of them. I don't know how you're supposed to pick one.'

Erin nodded. 'I'd love to do that with you.' She tucked her hands protectively under her arms. 'God, Stephan. It's really hard to stay away from you.'

Suddenly, the air was shimmering between them again. Stephan shook his head and marvelled over it. Shifted just like that, it did, their energy. 'I think,' he said carefully. 'When I'm actually able to hold you, I might just, like, explode.'

'I'm thinking it's going to be dangerous,' Erin said, and laughed. 'I gotta go away from you now,' she said. 'Before, you know.'

Stephan knew. Before they said bugger it all and just threw themselves at each other. This was the weirdest kind of dating he'd ever known. Not being allowed near each other. It meant they'd done a lot of talking though, on the phone at night. And a lot of, well, reaching for each other. With their spirits.

Which was pretty cool, really. More than that. Fantastically awesome.

But still.

'Yeah,' he said, nodding.

'I'm going to do the grocery run,' Erin said.

'Walk you home afterwards?'

'Yes please,' Erin said.

THIS TIME, ERIN DIDN'T EVEN THINK ABOUT NOT MOVING THE boxes around in the rear of the van herself. She heaved and shoved them into place so that Burdock could hop nimbly into the back. He promptly stuck his head between the front seats, and she patted his rump and slid the side door closed, careful to miss the long tail that whipped from side to side.

Burdock loved his car rides. If he wasn't squeezed into a pretzel. The van was perfect. Standing room. Good view. He was ready to rock and roll.

Erin swung into the driver's seat and slammed the door shut. The list was on the seat next to her, just like last time, and she picked it up, scanning the deliveries she needed to make. She reckoned, by the time she and Burdock had deposited every box on its doorstep and made small talk for five or ten minutes at each address, the sun would be heading well over to the west.

'Still,' she said to Burdock who stuck his cold nose on her neck when he heard her speaking to him. 'Still, it's better than thinking about the fact that Wayne Moffat killed my mother.' She paused, putting the van in drive. 'Accidentally,' she added. 'Sort of.'

Why had the police never done anything about it? How had they bought the story that it was an accident?

'It was an accident,' Erin told Burdock, who simply thumped his tail and waited for them to get on the road.

'I mean, he didn't mean her to die, right?'

Burdock licked her neck again. He was impatient to get moving. He loved this new job. The old one was okay, but sometimes the people at the other place got worn out and then they laid down and their bodies died. He saw their spirits leave, but the bodies smelled funny afterwards. Sort of empty. It made him happy-sad.

'He didn't know the door wasn't closed properly, right?'

Burdock thumped his tail. They were on the road. Soon, they'd be stopping, and he'd get out to supervise the box of yums being put on the step. Then he'd get pats and good boys. Which was how it should be. He was a good dog.

'But still,' Erin said on a sigh. 'He shoved her. I mean, that's wrong, whichever way you look at it.' But stuff like that happened, didn't it? People yelled and pushed and shoved, and sometimes they died afterwards.

'Doesn't make it right,' she said. 'Doesn't make it okay.'

Erin glanced over at the list, checking the first address again. Her gaze caught on one of the names.

'Huh. Mariah Reefton.' Erin took the corner and slowed for her first stop. It didn't take long to get anywhere in Wellsford. There just weren't that many streets.

She was surprised to see Mariah's name on the list though – after that flyer the woman had pasted up everywhere. Erin shook her head. The flyer that accused the Grove of delivering poisoned food to everyone in Wellsford.

And here she was getting some of that food.

'Guess it's just not poisoned then, is it?' she asked out loud. 'The only thing that's poisoned, Mariah, is your mind.'

Hers and a lot of other people's, Erin thought. She'd caught up with the news and a whole lot of current affairs stuff the other night and come away from it feeling like she'd been wading in sewerage. The things people were believing just blew her mind. The conspiracies, the weirdness.

'It's like we've gone back to the Dark Ages, Burdock,' she said and pulled on the park brake. 'Or maybe we never left it. Who the hell knows?'

She didn't come to any conclusion on that one as she made the deliveries, stopping to talk to everyone who came out onto their doorstep to say hello. But she did leave Mariah Reefton's box until last.

This was one person Erin didn't want to stop and pass the time of day with, however, so she pulled the van up down the street a little way and hushed Burdock when she drew open the van door.

'No,' she told him. 'I want you to stay here for this one.'

He quirked his ears and looked quizzically at her.

'She doesn't like dogs,' Erin said, and gave Burdock a smooch on the top of his head. 'I know – I don't understand it either.'

Erin hefted the box and shook her head over the contents. There was the soup mix in a pretty, handmade fabric bag, just like in every other box. Winsome had organised a group of people in the village to make them just for this purpose, but Erin was quite sure Mariah hadn't been in that group.

Mind you, not all that many had, but they all got the cheerful bags. Just because Mariah was so awful didn't mean...didn't mean what? Erin frowned and slowed her steps as she made her way up the path towards the door.

Didn't mean she wasn't going to be treated with the same courtesy as everyone else. It would be petty, Erin knew, to swap out the pretty bag for a plain paper one. And, as she sighed, the Grove didn't do petty. They did grace and consideration.

The front door was open, and Erin slowed even further. She wanted to sidle up to the step, put the box down, and run. She'd almost decided she wouldn't even thump on the door to let Mariah know she was there, but simply dump the box and run, when she heard raised voices.

Erin froze.

'You can't tell me to calm down!' someone screeched. 'I've had my job longer than that bitch Winsome has – I was supposed to keep it.'

Erin flattened herself against the wall and debated creeping back to the van and forgetting about the whole thing. Julia Thorpe – because of course who else was saying those things – she had a car. She could collect the damned box of groceries.

'I can tell you to calm down when you're being a pain in my rear end,' an older, angry voice said.

Mariah.

'But we've got to do something!'

Julia again.

'We will, you've just got to stop screaming long enough for me to think about what.'

Erin squeezed her eyes shut but decided she wasn't going anywhere just for a minute. Maybe she needed to overhear this conversation.

'We'll get back on who really is the problem in this town,' Mariah said.

Who was that? Erin wondered. Her heart sank. She thought she had a rather good idea who Mariah Reefton thought that was.

'It's that nasty woman Morghan Wilde we ought to be getting even with,' Mariah said. 'Lady of the Grove as she calls herself. I'll show her what happens to Ladies of the Grove. We've done it before, we can do it again.'

Erin's fingers hanging onto the box were suddenly numb. Lady of the Grove, Mariah had said.

Erin had forgotten – how had she forgotten?

Look to the Lady.

Morghan.

'What do you mean?' Julia asked. 'What are you talking about Morghan for? It's Winsome Clark who has done me out of everything I ever wanted.'

'No. It's Morghan behind it all,' Mariah said. 'We got one of them once, you know. My mother told me all about it, and her mother told her, and her mother before that, all the way back.'

Her voice floated out of the open door, gloating.

'We got one of those filthy ladies once you know. Had her hanged for witchcraft as she deserved. Always frolicking with the Fae, she was, just like this one now. Except this one is even more brazen about it – and she's taking over the whole village, that's what she's doing, and we've got to stop her. Today. Tonight. The other one, she ought to have burned – hanging was too good for her. Burning's what you do to witches. Smoke them out. Burn them. We burnt the house down – but she was gone by that time. This time, she won't be.'

Erin pressed against the wall, eyes wide with shock.

Inside the house, there was silence following this pronouncement. Then it was Julia's voice. Harsh as though she was already breathing smoke.

'When?' Another pause. 'No one can know it was us.'

Mariah cackled. 'No one will, Julia, no one will.' She clapped her hands. 'Oh, the lovely symmetry of it.'

Down on the street, in the van, Burdock suddenly started barking and Erin flattened herself further against the wall. Shush, she told him in her mind, but he carried on barking.

'Why's that so loud?' Mariah asked. 'Did you leave the door open, you silly cow?'

There were footsteps in the house and Erin closed her eyes, prayed in a tiny whisper. 'Please, Lady, don't let her come outside.'

Burdock kept barking.

'Please don't let her come outside.'

The steps stopped, the door slammed, and Erin sagged against the wall.

39

Winsome had been going on autopilot. Up in the morning, bathroom, shower, get dressed.

Hold the dog collar in her hands, staring at it, blinking her eyes, blinking away the tears that threatened.

Don't cry. Keep the numbness a while longer. The white noise between the ears.

Was she supposed to wear it now, she'd wondered? Or was she already out of a job? When did that start – not being part of the Church anymore?

Now, or later? When proper notice came?

Later, she'd decided. Let them tell her officially. Black print on white page. There like a brand, services no longer needed.

But she'd left the collar off – experimentally. She kept touching her neck, the skin there bare, oddly vulnerable. She didn't even wear the thing every day so why was she missing it so badly now?

It was...what day was it? Two or three days after she'd lost her job?

More than a job. Her calling. How had God called her to this, then let her go?

She bent over her desk and checked her diary. It was already late afternoon. She wasn't quite sure where the day had gone. She'd been to the church, knelt before the altar, the steps hard against her knees, and prayed.

Tried to pray. The words looping in her mind. Round and round until she didn't know what she was saying, what she was trying to say.

And then, into the woods, along to the temple, staring at the stone it was built from, touching the Green Man's face with her fingers, thinking of the story the wild goddess had told her. The wind that caught the soul.

Always the soul was caught.

Now, she was back in the house, the vicarage – would she be able to stay here, when the church was barred to her?

Did she want to stay on?

Winsome's head roared with questions she had no answers to.

There was nothing in her diary. Yesterday, she'd been in to sit with Wayne Moffat, who was fading, as though now he'd reached a place of safety it was all right to let go.

She should go to see him again. Sit at his bedside, holding space for him. She still had that – the soul midwifery course she'd been doing. Rocketing through it, really, thanks to the on-the-job training she'd had with Morghan.

She didn't want to give that up, she realised. She was only getting started with it.

Winsome sighed. That was the problem, wasn't it? She was only getting started with a great many things, and now she had to get stopped with most of them.

'Don't think about it yet,' she told herself, standing in her study, hand upon her diary, her notes for next week's sermon spread over the desk. Should she still give the sermon? She couldn't remember what it had been going to be about.

And what about the website? No church, no website.

No Winsome.

She wandered from the room, Cù trailing behind her, head down, tail low. Back into the kitchen. She'd been doing this restless perambulation of the house every time she came inside. Study, kitchen, front room, upstairs, downstairs, study, kitchen.

There was someone outside, standing in the trees. Winsome opened the door, stepped out into the fresh breeze that smelled as it always did of soil and tree and history. But she wasn't paying any attention to that. She was looking at the figure in the shadows of the trees.

There was something odd about it.

Winsome pressed her fingertips against her lips. That was what was wrong, she thought.

The person wasn't solid.

She hadn't seen a spirit since Robinson.

Cù looked up at her. Apart from the dog, of course.

'Who is it?' She whispered.

Cù looked intently at the apparition between the trees.

A woman, Winsome answered herself, and stepped across the lawn to see more closely. A woman in a long dress, and she held something in her arms.

Not something. Someone. A child. Pressed to her breast. Winsome saw the small white face of the child. Only young, she thought. Barely two years old.

The woman turned and stared at her, as though she'd felt the weight of Winsome's gaze. Her eyes were dark shadows and Winsome gasped at the fear she saw there. She held up a hand.

'Let me help,' Winsome said. 'Tell me what's wrong.'

But when the woman opened her mouth as though to speak, Winsome was too far away; she couldn't hear anything. She walked further across the lawn, stepping between the gravestones, shivering slightly as a cold wind brushed up against her.

The woman stared at her again, then looked behind her at something in the trees, something that made her flinch over the child, hunching protectively, shying away from whatever it was she could see.

Winsome couldn't see anything. Nothing but the woman, shimmering slightly in her dark red gown, the baby clutched to her chest. The baby had light brown curls escaping a white cap. The woman's hair was tucked up under a coif too, but it was her mouth that Winsome watched. It opened and closed, crying out words she couldn't hear.

And then, the woman and child were gone and Winsome stood amongst the old graves staring into the trees at nothing. She shook her head.

Who had that been? What had she been doing? Winsome hugged herself.

The woman had been frightened of something. Or desperate.

Desperate about something. Keeping the baby safe, perhaps.

Winsome didn't know.

She didn't know the history of this place – because surely this was something to do with Wellsford's history? The woman hadn't come from modern times.

Winsome shook her head. She'd been from hundreds of years ago. Her clothes had said that loud and clear.

Ambrose would know.

The thought startled Winsome and she hugged herself, looking at the empty woods. Empty of ghosts, at any rate.

She hadn't seen Ambrose since he'd made himself scarce the day she'd been to see Morghan at Hawthorn house.

The wind pushed her hair into her eyes, and she turned, made for the vicarage and her jacket.

MRS. PALMER OPENED THE DOOR AND HER SHOULDERS SAGGED with relief at the sight of Winsome.

'Mrs. Clark,' she said. 'I'm so glad you're here!'

Winsome looked around, bewildered at the welcome. 'Is everything all right?' she asked.

Mrs. Palmer's head shook rapidly from side to side. 'No,' she replied. 'It decidedly is not.' She reached for Winsome's arm and all but dragged her into the house.

'What's happening?'

'It's all in uproar,' Mrs. Palmer said. 'First young Erin and Stephan came careening up the drive in that old van and were out the doors before the engine had barely stopped. Something about overhearing Mariah Reefton plotting terrible things.'

Winsome's cheeks paled at the mention of Mariah Reefton. 'What's she going to do?'

But Mrs. Palmer shook her head. 'That's not the least of it. There's Morghan.'

'Morghan?' Winsome looked around the hallway, but if there was bustle and urgency in the house, it wasn't here by the door. The house sat on top of them, silent.

'And we can't find Clarice to bring her back.' Mrs. Palmer shook her head. 'Though that's no surprise. That girl's never here anymore except to eat and sleep.'

'Mrs. Palmer,' Winsome said, shedding her jacket and hanging it up, taking a deep breath. 'What's going on?'

Elise Palmer stopped, pressed a hand to her aproned chest and blew out a big lungful of air.

'You'd best talk to Ambrose,' she said, then frowned. 'But didn't he call you? Isn't that why you're here?'

Winsome shook her head, remembering why she was there. 'No,' she said. 'He didn't call me.' Her heart thumped against her ribs. 'Where is he?'

'Everyone's upstairs, in Morghan's room.' Mrs. Palmer gestured at the stairs. 'I'll put the kettle on,' she said, and hurried away.

Winsome looked after her then walked to the bottom of the stairs and gazed up them. She paused for a moment to calm her breathing and her heart thumping behind her ribs. She didn't know what was going on, she told herself, but she'd find out.

And perhaps she would be able to help. The thought of

something wrong with Morghan was alarming, almost frightening.

Morghan's bedroom door was ajar, and the sound of voices wafted from it. Winsome, swallowing down her nervousness, pushed the door open and stepped into the room.

'Can't you try something else?'

It was Ambrose's voice.

'I don't know anything else!'

Erin.

'This isn't working, and we need to do something about Mariah.'

That was Stephan.

The silence that followed this seemed to Winsome to be her cue. 'Hello?' she said, looking quickly around the room.

'Winsome!' Ambrose strode over to her and grabbed her shoulders as though for a moment he was going to kiss her. Abruptly, he stood back and dropped his hands. 'Sorry,' he said. 'I'm just very pleased to see you.'

She stared up at him, at his green eyes, warm with sudden relief. He'd touched her, she thought inside her head. None of them were distancing. Something must truly be wrong.

'What's happening?' she asked.

Immediately, Ambrose ran a hand through his hair, shaking his head.

Erin ducked around beside him. 'We can't get Morghan back,' she said, face pale except for two bright spots high on her cheeks. 'I've been trying, but I don't know what I'm doing.' She waved a hand in front of her face. 'And I think

I'm about to start hyperventilating.' She blew out a puff of air through pursed lips.

Winsome stepped over to her, touched her arm. 'It's all right,' she said. 'I feel like this all the time.' She glanced at Ambrose, then looked back at Erin. 'Bend over a little,' she said. 'Hands on knees, nice long slow breaths, in through the nose, out through the mouth, that's the way.

Erin did as she was told, glad for Winsome's steadying hand on her arm, her nice, clear instructions. She took a deep breath, let it out slowly. Nodded.

'Thanks,' she gasped, and took another breath, doing the same. 'This is helping.'

Winsome shook her head. 'Will someone tell me what is going on, please?' Morghan was lying on her bed, eyes closed, and for a moment, Winsome thought she must be dead, she was so still.

'Is Morghan...breathing?' she asked.

Ambrose nodded. 'Yes, but who knows how long she's been like this – it's not good to stay in this state too long,' he said. 'Her pulse is steady, but it's slow. Because she's just not here!' His fingers dragged through his hair again. 'I can't lose her too, Winsome. You have to bring her back.'

Questions crowded around inside Winsome, jostling for space. She patted Erin, who was bent over her knees, breathing more slowly.

'Bring her back from where?' she asked, keeping her voice mild and slow, as though she were in the kitchen of one of her oldest parishioners, keeping them calm, finding out what was going on in their lives. 'And there's some urgency?' She looked over at Morghan again, who had Stephan on his knees beside the bed, holding her hand.

KATHERINE GENET

It was Stephan who answered. 'I don't think it's so good physically for her body to slow down like this,' he said. 'And Erin overheard Mariah talking,' he added.

'She said she was going to burn the house down,' Erin said, straightening. 'Her and Julia – I heard them talking when I went to deliver their groceries.' Her mouth grimaced. 'Not talking – plotting. They've lost their minds, Winsome,' she added.

Mariah and Julia. Winsome gaped at Erin, took in the worried faces of the others. 'Burn the house down? How long ago did you hear this?' she asked.

Erin shook her head. 'I don't know – I couldn't believe it at first. Not long ago, I guess. I went and got Stephan and we came straight here, told Ambrose.'

Winsome looked down at the carpet, unable to fathom the news. 'Have you called the fire brigade, in case, you know?' She directed the question at Ambrose, and he nodded.

'I have, but they say they can't come all the way out here on just a threat from some old woman.'

'What? What does it take then?' Winsome asked.

Ambrose winced. 'An actual fire, I'm assuming.'

Winsome rolled her eyes. 'The police then? Can't they go and have a chat to Mariah? Check she's not stockpiling petrol or whatever?'

Ambrose shook his head. 'They weren't inclined to take it seriously, I'm afraid.'

'Why ever not!'

He winced. 'They think that a four-hundred-year grudge is a little unlikely.'

Winsome closed her eyes for a moment. 'I think I'm

missing something,' she said, and walked past Erin and Ambrose over to Morghan's bed.

'Mariah,' Erin said, 'Says that they burned down the house once – the house that used to be here, Ambrose says, and they need to do it again, because witches ought to be burnt.'

'Oh God,' Winsome said. 'She has lost her mind.'

Stephan got up so Winsome could take her place. Winsome perched on the side of the bed, looking down at Morghan.

'Yes,' Erin agreed. 'But what's set her off? I mean, I know there were the flyers, but it's a big leap between nasty letters and burning someone's house down.'

'Things are stirred,' Ambrose said. 'Blythe Wilde – hanged for witchcraft as Mariah says – her life is near the surface of the river.' He cleared his throat. 'Time,' he said. 'It flows, but it's wide and deep.'

Morghan's hand was cool to the touch, but they were right – she was still breathing, her chest rising and falling - slowly. Winsome looked over at Ambrose.

'Morghan told me about her,' she said. 'The Lady of the Grove hanged as a witch.' She swallowed. 'By Mariah's ancestors, isn't that correct? Or her ancestors were the ones who made the accusations, at least.'

'That's correct,' Ambrose said.

'And Julia lost her position as Churchwarden the other day,' Winsome mused. She didn't say she herself had lost her position as vicar as well. Instead, she was recalling something that Morghan had said to her. Something about belonging to the village and Grove, straddling them, bridging them. She blinked, bent over Morghan's outstretched hand, working out the puzzle.

She was the bridge between them all, Winsome thought. It was true. She walked amongst the villagers, sat on their sofas, and listened to their problems. And she also walked in the woods, travelled to the Wildwood to meet ancient goddesses who wove stories out of the wind.

Winsome turned to look at Ambrose. 'Where is she?' she asked.

'Morghan?' Erin said.

Winsome nodded.

Ambrose cleared his throat. 'Back to her past,' he said. 'Reliving the last days of Blythe Wilde's life four hundred years ago.'

Erin shook her head, clutching her hands together. 'Why doesn't she come back?' she asked. 'We need to get out of the house, in case, well, you know. In case Mariah and Julia weren't just talking mad.'

'Can't we just pick her up and move her?' Stephan asked. 'We could carry her out of here, couldn't we?'

Ambrose shook his head. 'No,' he said. 'We move her when she's this deep, we run the risk of jolting her back, and she might not come back in one piece, or even if she does, it will make her sick. Really ill.' He rubbed at his face. 'You need to go in there and bring her back,' he said, looking at Winsome.

She gazed at him for a long moment. 'What makes you think I can?' she asked softly. 'Why can you not?'

Ambrose blanched. 'I have many skills, but this isn't one of them. I can travel, but I have no hope of being able to find her.' He tapped a finger against his temple and scowled. 'I'm too much up here,' he said. 'Always analysing.' He gave a tight shrug. 'And...'

'And it should be me, anyway,' Winsome agreed. 'Because I belong to both worlds, but particularly the village.' She nodded. 'Balance. Harmony. Morghan talked about the need for things to be brought back into balance.' She looked over at Erin. 'It should be you as well.'

'Me?'

Winsome nodded. 'Of course. This is your work, as Lady in training. And you are of the Grove. Between us, we are in balance.'

'But I've barely begun. I mean, Morghan and I travelled together only a few days ago, but still...'

'I could try too,' Stephan said.

But Winsome shook her head. 'No, the two of us is right, I think.' She looked down at Morghan, astonished that she was even contemplating doing this. How, for crying out loud?

'You and Ambrose need to keep a look out for Mariah,' Winsome said on a long, low sigh. 'Let us do what we need to.'

'You want us to leave the room?' Ambrose asked.

'I think it would be best,' Winsome agreed. She looked over at him, met his eyes.

'I can't concentrate so well when you're near.'

40

'WHAT DO WE DO?' ERIN ASKED AS SOON AS SHE AND Winsome were alone with Morghan. 'I'm serious – how are we supposed to do this?'

Winsome looked down at Morghan, still lying as though completely comatose on the bed and shook her head. 'I've only travelled once without Morghan,' she said.

'I've never done it without her at all,' Erin answered. 'Not this sort of travelling. Back into the past – to a specific place and everything.'

'Well, now's when we figure it out.' Winsome gazed across the bed at Erin, lifting her eyebrows and waiting for agreement.

'I suppose so,' Erin said. 'But she is in a past life, right? Rather than the Otherworld?'

Winsome hadn't had time to think any of this through. She frowned over the question, then shook her head. 'I can't see that it makes any difference. If we seek her, I think we should feel confident that we will find her.' She glanced down at Cù, who stood looking up at her. 'After all, we're not alone in this, are we?'

Erin looked around the room for a moment. 'What do you mean?' she asked. 'It's just us, here.' She shook her head. 'You shouldn't have sent Ambrose and Stephan away. They both know how to walk the worlds; they could come with us.'

'No,' Winsome said. 'We need them to make sure we'll be safe, physically. And we can't all go tromping around not knowing what we're doing.'

Erin nodded. 'So,' she said. 'How do we start?' She looked at Morghan on the bed. 'She's been teaching me to hold the worlds inside me,' she said. 'To be here and there at the same time.'

'That sounds good,' Winsome said.

'Yeah,' Erin agreed. 'She's made me make the garden at Ash Cottage like, a fixed point. My own personal place in the Wildwood.' Erin narrowed her eyes. She'd just thought of something.

'What is it?' Winsome asked.

'Well, last time I was with Morghan, she took me to her own personal place, right?' Erin shrugged. 'I just wondered if we could go there, somehow, and find her?'

Winsome considered it. 'You have a garden in the Wildwood?' she asked.

Erin nodded.

'Let's go there,' Winsome said. 'Is there a gate to take us outside the garden and into the Otherworld?'

'Yes,' Erin replied. 'But how will we know where to go from there?'

Winsome smiled down at Cù who gave her one of his

toothy grins. 'We will trust in our helper spirits to guide us.' She looked over at Erin. 'What else can we do?' She shook her head, unable to believe she was here, contemplating this. Like it was real. Like it was possible.

But it was real, and she looked down at Morghan, and hoped to God it was also possible.

'You have a helper spirit?' Erin asked.

'I do, of course – don't we all?' Winsome said. 'Mine is a dog who looks a great deal like your Burdock.'

'Burdock?' He was down in the kitchen with Mrs. Palmer.

'Yes. Who is yours?'

Erin shook her head. 'A fox, I think, but I've only caught a few glimpses of her.'

'Right. Then you'll have to call her to you, I think,' Winsome said. 'And let's do this, shall we?' She put her hand gently to Morghan's wrist. 'Her pulse is very slow.'

Erin nodded, body electric with nervousness. 'Where should we, um, sit or whatever?'

Winsome frowned, thought about it. 'I think we should lie down next to Morghan and take one of her hands in our own. It's a big bed so there's room, and then we are, well, sort of connected to her.'

Erin caught on. 'It might make it easier for us to find her,' she agreed.

They lay on their sides, looking at each other's pale faces across Morghan's. Erin reached for Winsome's hand with her free one.

'I think we should hold hands too,' she said. 'After all, you have to come to my garden with me.'

Winsome nodded. She'd followed Morghan places

before; she could do this. Erin's fingers were cold in hers. 'Let's do this,' she said.

Erin closed her eyes, felt the pillow under her head, its cool cotton, its softness. She made herself breathe slowly, evenly, relaxing her neck, easing the tight tension in the muscles there. It was the same with her shoulders. The one that pressed into the blankets and mattress of Morghan's bed. On an exhale, she let the tension seep out of it, and moved on down her arm, doing the same, until it felt almost as though there were no bones in her arm, and all was relaxed, her fingers holding loosely to Morghan's. She relaxed her chest too, so that it no longer ached, but her ribs moved slowly, steadily with her breaths. In. And out. In. And out.

In. And out.

Her hips. The leg she lay on. Relaxing further and further each time she breathed slowly out. Her ankle. Toes. Then the toes of her other foot. Her ankle. Knee. Hip. Back to the chest. The arm that reached across Morghan, lying gently on her. Her hand, fingers in Winsome's.

Shoulders. All the tension eased away, deeply relaxed. Her neck. Face. Eyes closed but still looking. Gently looking.

Seeking the garden.

The scent of water from the well. Strong, cold, ancient water from deep within the earth, travelling its dark, secret byways.

The carvings on the outside of the well. The four directions. Erin pictured herself there, drawing herself down into her relaxed state and then through somehow into her garden, gathering it around herself until she stood there.

East. 'Air,' she murmured. 'Breath of life.'

She reached upwards, made the familiar movements. Arms out wide to the side, embracing the world with her hands, drawing its breath into her lungs, then exhaling slowly, offering it with a gesture back to the world.

Winsome watched her, standing in the garden that was Ash cottage's, and yet not. Erin's hair was loose, its colour a dark and wild red. Winsome blinked, thinking for a moment that she saw spiralling tattoos on Erin's cheeks. She lifted her hands to her own face.

Erin turned. Reached again for the sky. For the sun.

'South,' she said. 'Fire. Spark of life.' She felt flames lick at her fingers and drew her arms down, turning a third time.

For a moment, she floated in the dark silk of the well, feeling water all around. 'Water,' she whispered. 'Womb of life.'

Now the ground was solid under her feet again, and Erin turned toward the north.

Winsome echoed her movement. Lifting herself onto her toes, rocking back onto her heels. Feeling the great spread of the earth below her.

'Earth,' Erin said, spreading her arms as though they were the branches of a great tree. She dug her toes deep into the ground. 'Root of life.'

They reached for the sky again, both of them, and a moment after Erin drew her hands back down to her chest, to her heart, Winsome did so also.

'Above,' Erin said. 'Below. All around. We are part of the wheel.'

And they were. Winsome closed her eyes and felt the spin of the world around her.

Great Creator, Winsome whispered inside her mind, full of awe and tears. Thank you for this.

Thank you.

It was all there. This beautiful, wild, unruly garden, and beyond it, something else, something more. World upon world upon world, hidden and visible.

Erin, eyes closed, arms outstretched again, felt her garden around her, and now it was only one garden, one walled garden and outside the walls? She glanced over at them, then at Winsome, uncertain suddenly, about taking the next step. What if she became lost? If she couldn't find her way back here?

If she couldn't find Morghan?

Winsome had a dog standing beside her and Erin frowned at it. First, she thought it was Burdock, but Burdock was darker than the wolfhound standing beside Winsome.

Winsome saw Erin looking, and reached out a hand, touched it to the back of the dog. 'This is Cù,' she said softly. 'He walks at my side all the time, now.'

Erin shook her head, then looked around for her fox, wondering where she was, why she was not with her.

But she was there, Erin realised. Sitting by the gate in the wall, the one that would lead to the Grove, if this was Ash Cottage's garden. But it wasn't that garden. This one was in a different world and the sight of the gate made Erin shiver.

'Fox sits beside the gate,' she said to Winsome, who turned to look.

'She is waiting to lead you,' Winsome said.

It was true. Erin felt the truth of it vibrate in her bones.

'Will she know where to take us?' she asked.

Winsome looked at the small red fox, sitting front feet turned neatly together, the plume of her tail tucked against them. 'I believe so,' she said.

Erin nodded, stepped down the path towards where her Fox waited. Her heart lifted and sang a moment – here was Fox, not darting away between the trees, a red shadow in the corner of an eye, someone barely seen, Fox fleet of foot and never sticking around.

Here was Fox, sitting waiting for Erin, as though it was time now, as though Erin had come finally to the place where she was ready.

Was she ready? Erin was unsure, and she pressed a hand to her heart. It beat there, behind her clothes, behind her ribs, steadily, as if it didn't know to be cautious, afraid. As if this spirit body she walked in, that worked and felt just as her own, trod paths natural to it. As though it were born to walk like this.

Erin put her hand to the gate, Fox standing up now, nose to the wood, and she pushed it open. She remembered lifting herself to look over it the last time she'd come to her garden to do her exercises.

And it was the same.

The Wildwood spread around them.

'This looks like the Grove,' Erin said, turning to glance at Winsome, a frown on her face. 'I thought, when we first stepped through the gate that it was different, but...' she trailed off and looked again.

It was different.

And yet, it was so awfully familiar.

It was Winsome who guessed first, pressing herself

closer to Erin as they walked after the fox and up a path into the trees.

'I think we've stepped into Morghan's past,' she whispered. 'Which is also Wellsford's past. The Grove's.'

Erin didn't answer except to nod.

'I didn't think it would be so easy,' Winsome murmured, half to herself. Her hand strayed again to Cù's solid, warm back, and he turned his head to look at her, eyes lively.

'I guess we had enough intention,' Erin replied, ducking under the branches of the nearest tree. It was in leaf, and the air was warmer. 'It's not the same season, see?' she said in wonder.

It wasn't, Winsome realised. 'Do you think anyone will be able to see us?' she hissed suddenly.

Erin turned to look at her, eyes wide. 'Surely not?' she said.

Cù chuffed as though laughing and Winsome glared down at him. 'Aren't spirit animals supposed to be able to speak?' she asked, not knowing where she'd heard that.

She swore he raised his eyebrows at that, but he said nothing, turning away instead to look intently at Fox, who led them deeper into the woods.

They followed in silence.

'This is the path that leads to Hawthorn House,' Erin said after a while. 'I recognise it.' She pointed. 'Over that way is the stone circle.' She paused. 'And I felt us cross over into warded land.'

Winsome nodded. 'I did, too,' she said.

'Someone has set protection spells around the land, just like Morghan and Ambrose do.' Erin found herself quickening her pace, impatient now to find Morghan, and to see.

Whatever there was to see.

Winsome thought of Ambrose. Back in the real world. Or, since this felt so very real, the waking world. Or whatever. The world in which Mariah Reefton's mind had finally snapped.

She wouldn't burn the house down again, would she?

Winsome decided she wouldn't like to test it. She was glad Ambrose and Stephan were there, looking out for Mariah.

And Julia. She couldn't forget Julia, who would be furious that she was no longer Churchwarden. Winsome shook her head. What had Julia thought would happen?

Of course, Winsome reminded herself, Julia wasn't thinking properly. Somewhere along the way she'd veered off into her own private, conspiratorial, warped little world.

It really was important to keep an eye on what went on inside your head, Winsome thought.

Erin's hand landed suddenly on Winsome's arm.

'There's something happening up there,' Erin hissed.

Winsome peered through the trees. 'What?' she whispered.

Erin's shoulders were tight. She shook her head.

'Can you see Morghan?' Winsome asked. Morghan must be around here somewhere. Briefly, she wrangled with the urge to scream out Morghan's name. She clamped a hand over her mouth and Cù turned his head to look at her, a frown on his shaggy face.

Erin's hand tightened around Winsome's arm, fingers digging in. 'Around this way, quickly,' she said, and dived off the path dragging Winsome with her.

They skirted through the trees, ducking under branches

that threatened to tangle in their hair, and now Winsome could hear the commotion too.

And then she could see them.

A woman, on the back of a small red horse, bags bundled on the saddle in front of her, fair hair tucked under a cap.

Tendrils were escaping the cap and Winsome stopped walking, amazed at the details of what she could see. The rough stuff the woman's dress was made of. The tension in the long, smooth neck. The woman was barely more than a girl, she thought.

And she was twisted around in her seat, the horse half in and half out of the woods – they were at the treeline, and when Winsome looked out, she could see a house in the near distance.

'It doesn't look like Hawthorn House,' Erin whispered, crouching down behind a shrubby bush, pulling Winsome with her.

'The original was burned down, remember?' Winsome said. 'By Mariah's ancestors.'

'What's going on, do you think?'

'Blythe Wilde is about to be taken away as a witch.'

Winsome spun about on her feet so quickly she almost tumbled.

'Morghan,' she said.

'You needn't hide,' Morghan said. 'They won't see you – or Blythe might, if she were being quiet, but that is unlikely at this stage.'

Winsome and Erin drew themselves up and stared at Morghan, but Morghan nodded her head towards the drama playing out on the edge of the woods.

'Watch,' she said. 'You can tell me why you're here later.'

But Erin shook her head. 'No,' she hissed. 'You have to come back with us – you're in danger.'

Winsome wanted to add to what Erin had just said, but she'd glanced at the young woman on horseback and been captured.

There was another woman, on a black horse, behind the first. Blythe Wilde, Winsome decided, thinking she'd know her anywhere even though they'd never, of course, met.

It was something about the way the woman held herself, Winsome thought. There was something about her, something inside her, some indefinable thing. A sort of strength.

Winsome shook her head.

A sort of strength and a sort of knowing.

Finally she realised what it was.

It was whatever Morghan had. The same weight to her presence.

41

Tomas had wanted her to leave, to flee and run. She'd known this by the set of his mouth, the way his back turned stiffly from her when they got back to the house.

'I cannot,' she'd told him, though he'd not said it to her. 'You know that I cannot. I am tied to this land.'

At that, he'd spun around in their room and faced her, furious. 'Tied to this land?' He shook his head. 'It is only land, Blythe. Stone and dirt and tree.'

'It is more than that, Tomas, as well you know. And I'll not leave.' She swallowed. 'I'll not leave you either, or Leah or Cecily, or the child.'

He wouldn't listen to her. 'They'll drag you from here, Blythe. You won't have any choice.'

'They'll not believe the stories of Agnes and Pauline and the others, Tomas,' she said. 'The magistrate, if it comes to that, won't take their tales as true.'

Tomas gaped at her then slowly swung his head from

side to side. 'Listen to yourself, Blythe.' He stepped forward until his face was in hers. 'They hang witches in this land, Blythe Wilde. Tie a rope around their necks and let them swing until they are suffocated, or their necks broken – and these are women who cannot do half of what you can. Half of what you are known to be able to do.' He dropped suddenly to the bed and put his head in his hands. 'I told you not to go see the child, Blythe. We all told you that, did we not?'

'I could not leave a child to suffer!'

'Aye, perhaps,' Tomas said, rubbing his tired skin with his hands. 'But now we'll all suffer, and you most of all.'

'The villagers will not dare,' Blythe said, grasping at the idea. 'They will not have the courage to lay formal complaint.'

But Tomas just looked at her. Shook his head again. 'Leah will help you pack your things, Blythe, and her own. You must travel light. I shall set two of the horses to readiness.'

Blythe stared at him. 'I cannot leave,' she said.

'You can, and you must, or this will all be for nothing.' He swept a hand at the window. 'Your knowledge is what is precious. This land will abide, but you, my Lady, are but flesh and blood and easily crushed.'

Blythe hung her head and looked at the floorboards. They were worn to a low sheen with use. With the steps of her own feet. She looked around the room, out the window. She was everywhere she looked. In the walls, in the trees, in the stones.

'I will return,' she said, her voice low, stubborn.

Tomas enfolded her in his arms, and she felt him shaking against her. 'You will, my love. When it is safe.' He stepped back and held her at arm's length, to look in her face. 'I would have you go for my own sake too, Blythe. I've no wish to watch you swing from a gibbet.'

She nodded, defeated by the energy that swirled around him, and herself. It was love and loss and fear and love and strength. She let it wash over her. Breathed it in as though it was air for her lungs.

'I will pack my things,' she said. Then lifted her eyes to him. 'You will keep the child? She can see the spirits. If I do not return, she will learn the ways naturally, I think.' She blinked. 'Or enough of them, with your teaching and Cecily's.'

Tomas sighed. 'I will keep the child as if she is my own if it is possible.'

Blythe nodded and turned away before the dampness in her eyes could overflow. She went to her cupboards, calculating quickly what to take with her.

Now that it was decided, and Tomas seeing to the horses, Blythe flew about the room, snatching clothes from her chests and flinging them on the bed, trying to think ahead, to where she ought to go, even while part of her reached for the trees outside the house. Her precious trees, her beloved Grove.

'Lady,' Leah said, coming into the room and scooping up an armful of clothes. 'These will have to do. We must make haste.'

Blythe stopped in the middle of the room. 'You think they will come?'

Leah thought about the looks on the faces of those she had known all her life. 'They will,' she said. 'I am assured of it. They will be away for the bailiff even as we speak.' She paused in stuffing the clothes into a bag. 'You have money?' she asked.

Blythe nodded. 'You are coming?'

'I am, Lady.'

Tomas strode back into the room, took in the disarray, and looked at Blythe. 'You are ready? I have the horses waiting.'

Blythe shook her head. 'I've clothes packed but I need my jewellery and – some other items.'

'You cannot take anything that gives you away, Blythe,' Tomas answered.

'There are things I need!'

They stared at each other. Tomas folded his arms, although anxiety made him quiver slightly. 'What are they?'

'They won't catch me,' Blythe said. 'I am only going because you tell me I must. I need only a few items. My talismans, ritual items.' She drew breath, brushed past Tomas to the cupboard she kept in the room and looked in the open door again.

'We cannot keep any of it,' Tomas rasped. 'If they search the house – and surely they will – these things are damning.'

Blythe didn't hear him. She touched the fan she'd stitched carefully together from feathers. Duck, her spirit bird, who swam deep in the water of emotion.

She picked it up. Felt her fingers among the other objects. A smooth wand of wood, the grain silky under her touch. She drew it out of the cupboard. And the bag of stones, nuts, and bones she used for divination. Turning her back carefully to Tomas, she tucked the bag down the front of her dress where it could not be seen.

'I must take these,' she said. 'The rest you may hide in the woods. Wrap them carefully and place them in Grandmother Oak. She will keep them safe until I return.

She could not believe she was going.

The child, she thought. She ought to stay and be with the child. The girl would need her as she grew.

Leah touched her on the arm. 'We have tarried overlong,' she said. 'We must be away now or not at all.'

Blythe wanted to tell them not at all, but she could not bring herself to meet Tomas's eyes with her own. Instead, she nodded, and walked across the room, brushing against him for a moment and pressing a hand briefly to his chest, closing her eyes and sending a pulse of love into him. He grabbed her hand for a moment, held it, then let her go.

Outside, the sun was improbably high in the sky and Leah hurried ahead of her, carrying their bags, making for the tiny stables where the horses would be waiting. They only had two horses, and Blythe half-turned to ask Tomas what he would do without one, but Leah's hurrying drew her forward.

Tomas would only tell her to not mind it, to make haste.

My Lady, Blythe thought, walking down the path through air that was like syrup, hazy and thick. This could not be your wish, surely?

Better she should stay. They would not come for her. She had helped them too often, the people of Wellsford.

Helped with illness and birth pains. She healed people; she did not harm them.

She healed and kept alive the ancient ways. It was how it was meant to be. How it had been for centuries, and now suddenly she must walk away from it all? From all she held dear?

'Lady,' Leah hissed, turning. 'You must hurry.'

'I want to bid the child goodbye,' Blythe said in return.

But Tomas was behind her, in the doorway to the house as though he knew that she would bolt back to it, inside to the kitchen where Cecily held the child.

The child who had taken its place in her heart already. Next to the hole from the one she had lost.

The horse smelt of dust and hay and moved nervously under her hands as though sensing her unease. She pressed her forehead to his neck for a moment and made herself still.

'Hush,' she said. ''Tis all well.'

On his back, she watched as though from a great distance as Leah mounted the other horse and settled their bags in front of her. Smaller, her horse was, and red to Blythe's black.

'Where do we go?' Blythe asked, gazing around the small farmyard like she'd never seen it before.

And she never had, not under these circumstances.

Not to leave it. For who knew how long.

Perhaps forever.

'Lady,' she whispered. 'Don't let it be forever.'

Leah was talking, urging her horse forward, reaching over to snatch the reins from Blythe's numb fingers, leading the horse under Blythe behind her.

'We cannot go by the village,' Leah said. 'Nor can we go down to Banwell. We must go through the woods and around.'

'It would be faster on foot,' Blythe said, for some of the paths were narrow, the branches hanging low over them.

But Leah shook her head, and they were already moving. 'No,' she said. 'We shall need them when we reach open ground. Tomas says to make for the market town of Barrowby.'

'But that is miles away!' Blythe exclaimed.

'Aye,' Leah said grimly, biting down on her own fear and dismay. 'The better to find accommodation and blend in as two women on our own, strangers.' She clicked her teeth to the horse, upon whom she sat precariously, and the beast moved hesitantly into the woods, more used to pulling a cart than picking her way through the trees.

Blythe turned in her saddle, thinking to take a last look at the house she'd called home for as long as she could remember. She'd been born under that roof, brought up amongst these trees, and now, could not believe she was leaving.

'Leah,' she called urgently. 'You must give me the reins.'

Leah twisted around, confusion on her face. 'Why?' She brought her own horse to a stop.

Blythe shook her head. ''Tis too late,' she said. 'They've come.' She could see them, by the house, the magistrate's men, burly and self-important, and Tomas, standing cross-armed in front of them. She knew he was deliberately not looking across the yard at where she was about to disappear into the woods.

Their voices raised, and the men turned their heads, scanning for a view of her.

'Lady,' Leah called, her voice low and tight with tension. 'We must move.'

But Blythe shook her head. They were too late. She'd taken too long.

A shout. They'd seen her. Tomas lunged for the man, but he pushed him away.

Blythe slid from her horse.

'They cannot see you, Leah,' she said. 'You must go, and quickly, lest they drag you along with me. I'll not have that.' She flicked a glance at Leah's stricken face. 'Go quickly, and return when I am gone, and they will not know.'

She grasped her horse and turned him, leading him towards the man who came towards her. He took the horse roughly from her hands.

'You were thinking to run off?' he asked.

'I was going for a ride,' Blythe said, staring up at him, refusing to look behind her to check that Leah was away.

The man's face twisted. 'You were thinking to run from justice,' he said.

'I was going for a ride in the woods,' Blythe replied. She turned as though casually and gestured at the path between the trees.

There was no sign of Leah. She closed her eyes, whispered her gratitude.

Thank you, my Lady. If this is to be, I would face it alone.

The man grabbed at her with his other hand, and turned, dragging her along beside him, her horse on the other side. He smelt of sweat and grime and Blythe turned her face away from his nearness.

He shook her. 'You know why we're here, witch?' he asked, then laughed.

'I've got her,' he called, although why he did, Blythe did not know. Surely it was obvious?

'She was trying to escape.'

'I was going for a ride,' Blythe said. 'On the back of my own horse, through the woods on my own land.'

He shook her and her teeth bit down on her tongue, the taste of coppery blood flooding her mouth. She swallowed it.

'Your husband's land, you mean.' It was said with a sneer. 'Does he know your crimes?'

Blythe's eyes widened, and she ducked her head as though contrite. 'I have done no crimes,' she said. 'My husband works the fields and provides for us as a good husband does.' She would not look at Tomas.

She was shaken again, like a rag dolly, and then marched over to the others.

'Aye,' the man said, letting go of her and shoving her towards the cart. 'Well, we'll soon be seeing about that much, that we will.'

'I will be back in a day,' she said.

Blythe climbed onto the cart without looking more than a moment at the house where Tomas stood outside in the yard, a broad-shouldered, glowering presence, his fair hair glinting in the sun so that the faint redness in it set it to flame. She turned her face away and stared at the trees, at the sky, and pressed her palms against her knees.

The cart rumbled down the track from the house and through the village, where everyone came out of their doors and followed, jeering and shouting at her. She caught sight of Agnes Reefton and watched her for the space of a heartbeat, seeing the fury and the hate in her eyes.

Then Blythe turned her face away and stared at the hills, the trees, switching off her mind, not allowing a single straggling thought into it.

Her jaw ached with tension.

42

Blythe stood before the Justice of the Peace as the afternoon sun peered suspiciously in through one of the windows. Her stomach gurgled. There had been no food given her and she had not broken her fast before they had fetched her.

Nonetheless, she stood straight, shoulders back, her face schooled to calmness.

'You are accused of witchcraft, Mistress Blythe Wilde,' Robin Collington said.

Blythe looked at him, made no answer.

The Justice stared at her for a moment. Looked over her dress, her demeanour. 'You are not the usual sort brought before me on this charge.'

Blythe did not reply.

'Cat got your tongue, eh?' Robin Collington sniffed. Looked over her again. She was a comely woman. Perhaps, when he had this one's naked body searched for witch's teats, he would stand in the back of the room and watch.

'We shall begin simply, then, shall we?' he asked. 'You live in Hawthorn House, outside the village of Wellsford – is that not correct?'

'It is,' Blythe replied, her tongue sticking to the roof of her mouth. They'd not given her more than a cup of water either.

'Ah, so you can talk.' Robin sniffed, settling back in his chair. There had not been many accusations of witchcraft in this area, and he had to admit to a little thrill at the thought of the questioning ahead.

Although this one looked immovable. What other options were at his disposal? He would decide as things progressed.

'I'm inclined to take the charges against you seriously,' he said, lifting his head to look down his nose at her. 'The way you stand before me and the manner in which you are dressed tell me you are neither a simple nor a poor woman.'

Blythe merely blinked. She wanted to draw the trees of the Grove around her so that she could stand amongst them while she also stood in this room that smelt of masculine sweat and contempt. But she made no move to straddle both places, for that would put an aura of the glamour upon her, and she did not wish even an inkling of it to be seen.

'Ah,' Robin said. 'A tough nut to crack, are you?' He smiled. 'We shall see, of course. Now, you are charged with consorting with spirits, sending forth such spirits to cause the death of a child, weakening the health of cattle with your curses, and not least, causing some sort of mischief with a changeling child.' He wrinkled his nose. 'Would you care to elaborate upon this mischief?'

Blythe did not care to elaborate at all.

The silence stretched out between them.

'Tell me how you caused the death of the child, then?' He consulted his notes. 'The child's mother being one Agnes Reefton.'

Blythe licked her lips. 'I did not cause the death of the child.'

'The mother is mistaken?'

She inclined her head. 'The mother is mistaken.'

'But would not a mother know what is done to her own child?'

Blythe did not answer.

'How old was the child?' He leaned forward. 'And I warn you – I expect answers to my questions, and I will have them. Things will go much easier for you – and your family – if you answer my interrogations.'

Blythe flicked her gaze to the doorway, rattled by the threat, but it was blocked by one of the bailiffs. The only other person in the room, besides the Justice and herself, was a clerk, bent over paper, pen waiting to note her replies.

'How old was the child whose mother was Agnes Reefton?'

'Three months,' Blythe replied reluctantly.

'And you saw this child with your own eyes?'

Blythe closed the eyes in question. 'I did, yes,' she said.

'I'm sorry – could you speak up please, for the benefit of my clerk?'

She cleared her throat. 'I did, yes. I saw the child with my own eyes. He was sickly since birth.'

'What were you doing when you visited Agnes Reefton and her baby?' Robin paused, let the silence stretch out just a little. 'Was it a social call?'

Blythe opened her eyes and stared at the Justice. 'No,' she said. 'Agnes came to me for help.'

Robin's eyebrows rose and he smiled slightly. 'What sort of help did she think you could offer her?'

Here, it was necessary to step carefully.

'Have you your own children, Mistress Wilde? Perhaps she sought your expertise based upon experience?'

Blythe stared at him. He knew, she thought, that she had no children of her own. But it was a trap she could not see how to avoid. She shifted minutely on her feet and looked about at the long room with only wide hearth – unlit – and the Justice's chair, and a long desk. The floor was bare boards, and she thought she could feel the chill seeping up from under them.

'I did not at that point,' she said.

'I see. So it was more of a social visit, then?' Robin Collington narrowed his eyes slightly and looked at her through his lashes. 'You'll understand me saying, I'm sure, that you do not look quite the same social position as Agnes Reefton.'

'We live in the same Village,' Blythe said. 'There are no strangers in Wellsford, and it is common for me to visit the women.'

'It is? For what purpose?'

'For the purpose of neighbourliness and companionship.'

The Justice gazed a moment at the ceiling. 'And yet, Mistress Wilde, when Agnes herself, and several of the women of Wellsford were here making their complaints against you, not even one claimed you as friend, or companion.' He blinked slowly. 'What do you say to that?'

She could not tell the man that things had soured between herself and the others of Wellsford. That would lead places she could not afford to go.

And they hadn't even gotten to the meat of the claims yet.

'May I have a drink of water, please?' she said. 'My throat is dry.'

There was a pause. 'Perhaps,' Robin said. 'After you've answered my question.'

Blythe looked down at the floor. 'I am good with herbs,' she said. 'For when one is ailing. I can offer a tonic for fever, perhaps.'

'I see,' Robin said, shifting in his chair so that it creaked under his weight. 'And did you look to do this for the Reefton baby?'

'I did,' Blythe said.

'And what was its ailment?'

'The child had been born early, I believe.' Blythe wiped her hands in the folds of her dress so that the man would not see her nervousness. 'So 'twas always a sickly, crying child.'

'Carry on,' Robin said, beginning to really enjoy himself. She was talking. He had got her talking, and they had the entire afternoon.

'It was not that which caused the ailment I saw when I visited to offer any assistance I might be able to, however,' Blythe said.

'It was not?'

'No,' Blythe said on a sigh. 'The boy had fallen from his cradle.' Or been shaken. She'd suspected the latter.

'The mother told you this?'

'When I questioned the nature of his injuries, yes,' Blythe said.

'So you were unable to offer any of your...tonics.'

'No,' Blythe said. 'They would have done little good.' She had made one up for the child's pain but was not about to say so.

'And the baby died?'

'Yes.'

'And you had nothing to do with the death?'

'No.'

The justice abruptly changed tack. 'You are accused of consorting with spirits. Is this true?'

Blythe swallowed. The black wolf was by her side now as always.

'I require an answer, Mistress Wilde.'

Blythe stayed silent.

'Very well,' Robin said. 'We shall return to that question. Tell me instead about the changeling child.'

'There is no such thing as changelings,' Blythe said.

'The parents say differently. The mother in particular, said that she gave you the child so that you could take it back to the fairies and retrieve her own.' Robin smiled at Blythe, a baring of teeth. 'Did you take the child?'

'Yes. She forced it upon me.'

'Believing that you have access to the fairies and could swap the child for her own?'

Blythe didn't answer.

'Mistress Wilde, I am discerning a pattern in your replies here – when you are able to say no to my question, you do so without hesitation.' He looked at her. 'Answer my question.'

Blythe cleared her throat. 'What was the question?'

'Did the mother believe you had access to the fairies and could fetch her real child for her?'

'May I have some water, please?'

'No. Answer the question.'

Blythe looked down at her feet, at the spirit wolf pressed close to her side. 'Yes,' she said. 'She believed so.'

'Why?'

'I beg your pardon?'

'Why did this woman think you could do such a thing?'

'I don't know,' Blythe said.

'I don't believe you.'

'I do not know another's mind,' Blythe said, pressing her lips together.

'You know the words issued from their mouth. What was this woman's argument for you to do as she wished? Surely there was some discussion?'

'Superstition,' Blythe replied. 'There is no such thing as a changeling. The child is an imbecile, that is all.'

Her heart broke for baby Olive.

'Ah, you present yourself as a woman who does not believe rural superstition.' Robin Collington tapped his fingers on the arms of his chair. 'Unfortunately for you, I believe you are dissembling. And you have not answered the question yet again, Mistress Wilde. Why does this woman think you have access to the realms of spirits and fairies?' He paused, then asked more. 'Why do they accuse you of witchcraft? Of whispering charms to hurt and harm.'

Blythe pressed her lips together. 'I do not know,' she said. 'And I do not whisper charms, only blessings.'

'Blessings? On whose authority? Are you a priest now, with the direct ear of God?'

'I have not hurt anybody,' Blythe said. 'And I will not answer any more questions. I am no witch.'

'I believe you are,' Robin said mildly. 'My bailiff brings me report that your family has been whispered about in such terms for generations. And that only two Sunday's since, you did make a dreadful racket in the church, coughing and vomiting while the Lord's prayers were being heard. And have not crossed the threshold of the Lord's house since.'

Blythe's heart sank further. It was that the vision she'd had that day had surprised her so that she'd sucked in a great lungful of smoky air and then choked on it – after she'd thrown up the invisible black tar that had gouted from her when the woman, shimmering as a spirit, had touched her. A misfortune, that had been. The spirit had disappeared as quickly as she'd appeared. Blythe looked around now, as something tickled inside her mind. A presence, watching, with her.

The same spirit?

No. That could not be.

'Take her away,' the Justice of the Peace cried, gesturing for his bailiff. 'Prepare her for her examination.'

'Examination?' Blythe said, startled back to the room.

Robin Collington leaned forward. 'Yes. For you required to be searched for witch's marks and teats – for all know a witch must feed her spirits for them to do her bidding.'

Blythe opened her mouth again, to say what, she did not know, but the bailiff grabbed her by the arm and marched her from the room.

43

Morghan drew back, through the walls, taking the other two with her, until they stood outside on a street, Winsome and Erin blinking in the sudden sunlight.

'We do not want to see the next few days,' Morghan said.

Erin looked at her. 'What happens?' she asked, not wanting to know, but still needing to.

Morghan stared down the street, watching the few people going about their day, only avoiding the pocket of shadow in which she stood with Winsome and Erin.

'She is interrogated, examined, walked until she confesses.'

There was a moment's silence. 'She confesses?' whispered Erin.

'What is walking?' Winsome asked.

Morghan took a breath. 'Walking is where a suspected witch was kept awake for days on end and made to walk the length of the room over and over without respite.' She blinked. 'It was believed that if this were done, eventually her spirits would return to her, and be able to be seen, thus confirming that she was indeed a witch.'

The others stared at her, appalled.

'Of course, the accused would be going crazy by that time, and would confess just to bring it to an end.' Morghan shifted slightly, chilled inside. 'You heard the questioning also. There is no way for Blythe to avoid incriminating herself, whether they go on to walk her or not. Which they do.'

Winsome reached out and touched Morghan lightly on the arm. 'Morghan,' she said. 'We must get back to Hawthorn House and our proper time.'

But Morghan shook her head. 'I cannot leave yet.'

'But you've just said what is to happen – what is there we can do?' Erin asked. 'And you've been here a long time – your body isn't in great shape. Your heart is beating too slowly.'

Morghan turned and looked at her. 'It will hold out a little longer, I'm sure,' she said.

'How can you be certain? It's dangerous.' Erin asked.

'I have not much more to do here,' Morghan said.

'What do you have to do?' Winsome asked.

'Yeah,' Erin said. 'We've seen what is happening – what else is there?'

'Just one more thing,' Morghan said, resolute, her mouth firm around the words.

'I must help her die.'

For a moment, there was an appalled silence.

'I don't understand,' Erin said. 'She's already going to die

428

– she doesn't need help doing it – she needs help stopping it!'

'I can't stop it,' Morghan said, and she looked over at Winsome. 'Do you understand?' she asked.

Winsome gazed at the ground for a moment, then lifted her head and met Morghan's eyes. 'I think so,' she said. 'You need to make sure she doesn't get stuck there.'

Morghan nodded and smiled sadly. 'Because she has been.'

Erin looked wildly from one to the other. 'I don't know what you're talking about,' she said. 'I do know that we need to go home. Even if Morghan's okay, there's still Mariah's threat to burn the house down.'

Morghan held up a hand. 'It's all right,' Erin, and I've come this far, I can't turn back now.' She shook her head. 'I can't.'

'But you might die!' Erin said. 'Your body might die.'

'That's a risk I'm prepared to take,' Morghan said, her head tipped to the side, the sun from a day hundreds of years in the past shining on her silver hair.

'What about us, then?' Erin asked, wildly changing tack, feeling her blood freeze in her veins at the idea of having to take Morghan's place as Lady of the Grove. She wasn't ready. Not even nearly. She was years away from being ready for that. 'We're there in that room with you – what if the building is on fire around us? We might die from that.'

For a moment she thought she saw a shadow of worry in Morghan's eyes and wanted to grab her by the arm and draw her away. Wish themselves home, or however they would do it.

But Morghan shook her head. 'I will make sure that doesn't happen,' she said.

'How?' Winsome asked, surprised.

'Like this,' Morghan said, and took their hands.

The worlds wrapped and folded around them, and they stood in the circle of stones, Erin and Winsome looking about themselves, blinking in astonishment.

'How?' Erin asked.

'When?' Winsome asked.

'We are in spirit,' Morghan said in answer to Erin. 'And still on the same timeline,' she said to Winsome. 'It is easier and quicker this way.'

Winsome nodded at the same time Erin shook her head.

'What are we here for?' Erin asked.

But Morghan didn't reply. She was still instead, questing behind the veil, looking for someone. She smiled when she found him.

'Maxen,' she said.

The faerie man stepped from the woods and strode up to stop in front of the group. He bowed slightly. 'We are well met, my Lady,' he said.

'You recognise me?' Morghan asked.

'I recognise your hand, and so I recognise that which you are,' he said. 'If we have had the pleasure of meeting previously, I do not recall it.'

'We have not,' Morghan said. 'But we are friends many years from now.'

Maxen nodded in understanding. 'How may I serve the Lady of the Golden Hand?'

Morghan drew breath. 'I am here to help the Lady of the Grove.'

'They will hang her,' Maxen said, regret passing over his features.

'Yes, and I will be there with her – but there is danger facing me in my own time.' She smiled slightly. 'The time in which I know you well.'

'We are friends?' he asked, a single brow raised.

'You play at all our gatherings,' Morghan said.

Winsome and Erin stood silently, watching, and listening, astonished.

Maxen's face broke into a wide smile and he bowed again. 'We are friends indeed, then,' he said. When he stood straight again, he nodded, his face solemn again. 'I shall rally help for you, my Lady,' he said, then lowered his chin to indicate Morghan's hand. 'I know our Queen's work when I see it,' he said. 'We are in alliance.'

Morghan bowed her head. 'My thanks,' she said.

'Give the Lady Blythe our good greetings,' Maxen said, turning for the woods again. 'Bless her and speed her on her way for she is a friend also of ours.'

ERIN PRESSED A HAND OVER HER MOUTH TO STIFLE HER HOWL of horror. She turned and looked wide-eyed at Morghan and Winsome.

Winsome shook her head, but there were tears in her eyes and she put a hand on Erin's shoulder, for Erin's support, and her own. Here again was the woman she'd seen in the woods, her spirit standing between the trees.

But Blythe was much changed. Her clothes were filthy, the skirt stained from the dirt and muck of her prison cell, and she had lost weight. Her cheekbones were sharp under the skin of her face as she stared out from the back of the cart that took her to the gallows set up in the small square, and her wrists looked tiny and too delicate for the thick hempen rope around them.

Erin stared at her. It was Blythe's eyes that hurt Erin the most, she decided. Under the dirty cap, that had once perhaps been white, and from which escaped tangles of wild hair, Blythe's eyes burned as she stared out at the gathered crowd. Perhaps it was fever that made them look as they did, or perhaps it was fear and fury and failure.

Winsome looked down at the ground as Blythe was dragged stumbling onto her feet, then made herself watch as Blythe was wrenched by the shoulder into position, and her head threaded roughly into the noose.

'I want to be sick,' she whispered, her voice hoarse. 'This is disgusting.' There were tears in her eyes. 'The things people do to each other – I can't stand it.' She wiped her cheek with her sleeve and looked over at Erin's staring, pale face, her other hand still on Erin's shoulder.

Erin shook her head. 'This can't be real,' she said. 'I can't stand here and watch this.' She turned, knees weak and trembling, to Morghan while a man stood on the back of the cart and began his proclamation of Blythe's sins against God. 'Why do we have to watch this?' she asked, dropping her hand to her heart to press against her ribs where it hurt so badly that she wanted to bend over and tuck herself into a ball.

'You do not have to watch this,' Morghan said, staring straight ahead at Blythe, whose eyes scanned the crowd restlessly as she tried to squirm out of the gaoler's grasp.

The other man finished his litany of Blythe's crimes and

turned to her where she stood, the noose grazing the skin of her neck.

'Do you wish to repeat your confessions for all to hear, Blythe Wilde?' he asked.

Blythe turned her head slightly to look at him, her expression stilling, eyes turning to flint.

Morghan put a hand lightly on Erin's arm. 'I must go to her now. You both may turn away, if you would rather.'

'What?' Erin asked, startled. 'What do you mean – go to her? What can you do? There's nothing you can do – they're going to hang her!' She bit down on her lip, stifling the panic that had crept into her voice.

'Morghan,' Winsome said. 'What are you going to do?'

Morghan smiled at them, a slow, sad curve of her lips. 'My job,' she said. 'My duty, my calling, my necessity. And it is also my honour and privilege. Blythe needs me. If she must do this alone again, she will be stuck here forever.'

She took a couple steps towards where Blythe stood, the rope around her neck, and the man in front of them turned and looked at her, startled, then blinked and cried out, shrinking away.

'A spirit!' he shrieked, voice high and shrill, face paling. 'I saw a spirit!'

'What's going on?' Erin hissed.

Morghan shook her head. 'I must hurry,' she said. 'I am becoming more clearly here.'

'What?' Erin glanced wildly at Winsome, then stared back at Morghan. 'What do you mean?'

Morghan was looking at Blythe, who had looked in their direction at the man's cry. They gazed at each other.

'My body weakens,' Morghan said. 'And so my spirit

strengthens.' She drew her eyes from Blythe's gaze and nodded at Erin and Winsome. 'I need to go now.' She stepped away from them, around the man who had glimpsed her briefly and was gibbering to his companion of the spirit he'd seen.

Erin made to go after her, but Winsome pulled her back. 'Let her do what she needs to,' she said.

'But you heard her!' Erin said. 'We need to go home, not whatever she's going to do here!'

But Winsome was watching Morghan climb up onto the cart and take Blythe in her arms. 'She will not come,' she said softly to Erin. 'She will do what needs to be done.' Winsome blinked back more tears. 'We cannot stop her, so watch her instead, Erin. See what it really means to be human and spirit entwined.'

Erin shook her head, but lifted her frantic eyes to watch, trying to understand what was happening.

'Hush, my love,' Morghan said, taking Blythe in her arms. 'All will soon be well.'

Blythe looked wildly at her, and her spirit spoke to her.

'I have lost all,' she said, the words full of fury and pain. 'I have sacrificed everything because I could not keep my own emotions in check. The Grove for the sake of what? My vanity in my healing skills? The need for a child to fill the hole inside me?'

Morghan shook her head. 'Nothing is lost,' she said. 'Leah makes a fine Lady of the Grove after you, and Olive a skilled priestess. Nothing is lost, except you, and now I have found you.'

Blythe shook her head, dirty hair flying. 'I cannot do this again,' she said. 'I have died here on these gallows a hundred thousand times. I cannot rest.' Her eyes looked at Morghan, deep wells of pain. 'There is no rest for me.'

'Yes,' Morghan said to her. 'There is now. I will do it for you, and then I will take you from here, and you will rest, and you will heal.'

Erin clutched suddenly at Winsome. 'What's she doing?' She shook her head. 'Oh Goddess, what's she doing?'

Winsome's blood ran cold inside her, fingers going numb, legs wooden. Even though she'd guessed.

'Why?' Erin asked. 'Why is she doing that? How?' She jammed her fingers against her mouth, spoke around them. 'How can she bring herself to do that?'

Winsome's voice trembled in her throat. 'I don't know,' she said. 'I don't know how she is brave and strong enough to do this.'

Blythe slipped from her body, collapsed to the dirty planks of the cart.

Morghan took her place, looked out over the crowd of people come to watch Blythe die.

Erin tugged away from Winsome's arms and flitted through the crowd, nothing more than a cool breeze to those there.

'Erin?' Winsome hissed. 'What are you doing?' She followed automatically.

But Erin was already trying to lift Blythe from the cart at Morghan's feet, feeling Morghan's eyes on her but unable to raise her gaze to meet them.

This she could do though. 'Help me lift her,' she said to Winsome.

Together, they carried Blythe's spirit to the back of the

crowd, kept her tucked between them, flimsy and barely there, then looked at each other.

'We should watch,' Winsome said. She didn't want to, though.

Erin nodded, pale and shaking, and they turned back to the gallows.

44

'THIS IS RIDICULOUS,' STEPHAN SAID, RUBBING HIS HANDS compulsively on his jeans. 'Like, the police or someone should be here, right?'

Ambrose shook his head. 'Nothing's happened, except someone overheard talking.'

'Making a threat, you mean. Isn't that supposed to mean something?' Stephan asked, stalking over to the window again and peering out.

'The threat wasn't made to us directly, I'm sorry Stephan. Mariah and Julia could have been just letting off steam.' Ambrose looked towards the door, and the stairs, wanting to go and check on Morghan.

Stephan snorted. 'Well that's all good, then. Let's hope that's just what it was,' he said bitterly. He shook his head again. 'Right, Ambrose, I can't just stop here doing nothing, or waiting, or whatever it is we're doing. I'm going down to the village, going to keep an eye on the pair of them from there.' He cleared his throat. 'There are a million directions they could come here, and we'd never see them. Not now the sun is going down.'

He turned to look at Ambrose. 'You won't let anything happen to Erin – and the others, will you?'

'No,' Ambrose said, surprised his voice was so steady and clear. As if nothing was wrong. How did it manage to sound like that, when his heart was beating dread with every moment? 'It's a good idea,' he said. 'To go down there and check on them.'

Stephan nodded. Reached behind and patted his back pocket for his phone. 'I'll call you if I see anything, you know, untoward.' His breath hitched. 'And you'll call me?' He was already heading for the door, tension making it impossible for him to stay still. 'I'll go through the Grove. I'll be quieter and quicker that way.'

'I'll call you,' Ambrose said. As soon as Stephan was gone, he was going to check on Morghan and Winsome, and Erin, of course.

It had been too long. Morghan had been gone too long. She needed to come back. He waited for the sound of the front door.

Then went bounding up the stairs, taking them two at a time.

All three women were in the same position, and Ambrose stared at Winsome in the dim light for a long moment, seeing her honey-coloured hair over smooth skin, and her hands tucked around Morghan's and Erin's. He took a deep breath, his heart in his throat.

But Winsome was all right. He could see the steady rise and fall of her chest, and there was colour in her face.

It was the same with Erin. She breathed strongly, as

though simply asleep, twitching every now and then as though dreaming.

Morghan, however, was even more pale. And still. Ambrose stood over the bed, holding his own breath as he watched for Morghan's. It was there. Shallow, barely perceptible. He checked his watch. As far as he knew, she'd been in this state for hours. How many, he wasn't sure.

But too many.

He drew out his phone from his pocket and tapped a nail quietly against the screen.

Now, he thought. Checked the time on his phone. By the time they got here, he thought, Morghan would be back, surely?

She had to be.

He bowed his head for a moment. Moved his lips in a prayer.

Please, bring her home quickly.

Ambrose backed quietly out of the room and pulled the door almost closed behind him. The front door opened and slammed shut downstairs, and he stopped, his finger over the buttons on his phone, and frowned.

Footsteps ran lightly up the stairs.

'Clarice!' he said.

'Where is she?' Clarice asked, dishevelled, her hair tangled, a twig dark against the whiteness of it. 'Maxen told me what's happening. How long has she been gone?'

She shouldered past Ambrose before he could answer and into the bedroom, stopping at the end of the bed and staring appalled at the three women lying there.

'Where are they?' she asked. 'Where did they go?' She

held up a hand, shaking her head. 'Maxen said something about the Lady Blythe. Who is she?'

'The one hanged for witchcraft,' Ambrose said.

'And that's where Morghan is?' Clarice demanded. 'And these two?'

'Gone to fetch her back.'

'So why isn't she back?'

'I do not know.' Ambrose answered.

'But they've found her, yeah?' Clarice stared at her step-mother. 'She's barely breathing.'

'I hope they've found her,' Ambrose said. 'Come away, Clarice. I don't think yelling will help.'

She turned and stared at him. 'What are you doing to help, then?' she asked.

He shook his head and left the room, tapping the call button. He listened a moment when the call went through.

'Ambulance, please,' he said, and this time his voice wasn't quite so steady at all.

THERE WAS A LIGHT ON IN MARIAH REEFTON'S FRONT window and Stephan pushed himself back against the wall of the empty vicarage, watching it for a moment, waiting for the outline of a person to flicker behind the window as they walked by.

But the curtains were drawn, and they were thick, blocking out everything but the light that seeped through a gap at the side. Stephan clenched his fist and pressed his knuckles against the cold stone behind him.

He'd have to get closer.

Stephan ran across the road, keeping his head ducked

down. Probably, he thought, he should just have sauntered across as though out for a walk, heading home like he knew nothing, like nothing was going on, but he couldn't make himself do it.

He reached the shadows of Mariah's garden with a stifled sigh of relief. Then shuffled over to the lit window and leaned over the garden to press his eye to the glass.

The room was empty, and Stephan pushed away from the wall, his mouth set in determination as he rounded the house to see if he could find the kitchen window.

Or any window that would let him see what was going on.

He was sure something was. The words Erin had repeated to him rang in his mind. *We burnt the house down, but she was gone by that time. This time, she won't be.*

They couldn't burn the house down, not with Morghan in it.

Not with Erin in it.

Or Winsome.

He couldn't let it happen.

His boots scraped against the concrete driveway beside the house and Stephan winced. It was almost full dark now, and he squinted towards the ramshackle shed at the end of the drive. Mariah didn't have a car – he knew that. But did Julia? They were living in the house together. Surely Julia had a car?

The driveway was empty.

He looked towards the house instead, saw a light behind the glass door, crept closer.

The hallway was empty. He went over to the kitchen window, leaned closer to look in.

Here, there was no light on and no one about. Stephan stood back and his brow creased in thought. The hair on his chin scraped across his hand when he rubbed it.

He looked up at the first floor, but it was dark. The only light was in the front room.

Stephan spun around and looked down the driveway again. Looked closer at the garage. The door was closed.

He inched down into the deeper shadows towards the garage, the hair on his neck standing on end.

There were no windows. The only way to see if Mariah and Julia had taken a car wherever they'd gone – to Hawthorn House – was to open the door and see. Stephan winced at the idea. Then reached out and grasped the handle, twisted it, and pulled the folding door partway open.

Open far enough to see that there was a small car parked in there.

There was also a smell that made his eyes water.

Stephan tugged his phone out and flicked on the torch light, slipped in through the half open doorway and aimed the light at the side of the car as he walked around it.

The petrol tank lid was on the ground. He wrinkled his nose at the sharp stench of petrol, closed his eyes for a moment, then opened them, took a shallow breath, and opened the camera app on his phone, snapping a couple quick shots of the petrol cap and the short length of garden hose that lay on the dirty floor beside the car.

He backed out of the garage quickly, snapped the door shut and shook his head, heart racing. What now, he asked himself, holding his phone and staring at it, thinking. A moment later his call was put through.

'Yeah, look,' he said. 'I just went to check on a woman who made a threat earlier today to set a house on fire – and she's not here, and her car's been emptied of petrol.' Stephan turned and stared back at the garage. 'Yeah, there's the tank lid on the ground next to a hose. The garage reeks of fumes.' He gnawed on his lip, then gave the address of Hawthorn House.

'What?' he asked. 'An ambulance was called out to the same address?' He shook his head. 'Shit.'

Disconnecting the call, he stuck the phone back in his pocket and jogged across the road and back into the trees, making for Hawthorn House again.

If Mariah and Julia weren't driving, though – where were they? How come he hadn't come across them on his way down?

'Don't be silly,' Mariah hissed. 'Of course we're still going through with this. That young man went right past us.' She shook her head. The silly fool had been going so fast that he'd made plenty noise enough to give them warning he was coming. They'd ducked off the path and behind the trees, and a moment later he'd come and gone, and they were back on their way.

Or they would be if Julia would stop her whining.

'You've no backbone, that's your problem,' Mariah said, hefting the milk bottles full of petrol in her wire carrier. They were heavy, and her arm ached. Her legs ached too, from climbing steadily up the hill, but she'd be damned if she was going to let her old bones stop her.

How many times had her mother talked of doing something like this? Sat in her chair in the corner of the sitting room with her wool and her needles like a great black spider knitting its poisonous web.

'What are you mumbling about?' Julia asked, pushing away a twiggy branch that had reached out of nowhere to scratch her on the face. She shook her head, looking down at the milk bottles full of petrol she carried.

She couldn't believe she was doing this.

Was she insane?

A glance over at her aunt and she shook her head. Mariah was the insane one. Not her. Julia licked her lips.

She was mad. Furious even, and she wished all sorts of nastiness on Winsome Clark for making her lose her job – but it was Winsome she was mad with, not Morghan Wilde. And all that stuff about the conspiracy, that she'd come up with?

She'd been deluded. Temporarily. The stress had gotten to her.

'I didn't say anything,' Mariah said. 'Hurry up your miserable feet, will you? We'll never get there at this rate, with you lagging behind like you're in preschool.'

Julia stopped walking altogether and set the milk carrier at her feet, holding it between her legs so that it wouldn't tip and spill. Although maybe, she thought, that would be a good thing.

Except, no.

'What are you doing now, for crying out loud?' Mariah hissed. 'We've got to get this done.'

Julia shook her head. Tried to speak, cleared her throat, and tried again.

'I'm not doing it,' she said.

Mariah turned around and stared at her in disbelief. 'What?' she squawked.

'No,' Julia said. 'I've gone along with you so far, but this is too far.'

Mariah narrowed her eyes. Julia's face was little more than a pale oval in the creeping dark, her eyes black sockets.

'You're a fool,' Mariah said, spitting. 'You always were, you and your no-good mother. Getting herself knocked up while working at that fancy job she had.' Mariah licked her lips. 'Coming home with her tail between her legs. I should never have let you into my house just like my mother never let yours back through the door.'

Julia stood there in the middle of the woods with four milk bottles filled with petrol she'd siphoned from the tank of her little car. Her mouth still tasted of the foul liquid, and she had a sudden, terrifying feeling that she'd never get rid of the taste, that it would always be there on her tongue until the day she died.

The tree tangled in her hair again, and she jerked her head, smacking it away. Around her, the night shivered and grew darker. She shook her head.

'You're ugly,' she said.

'Ugly!' Mariah cackled. 'It's an ugly world, my dear,' she said. 'We are simply fighting fire with fire, doing the work the Good Shepherd is too meek to do.'

'You're ugly, and you're crazy,' Julia said. 'I've gone along with you, but I'm done now. This is too much. This is too far.' She shook her head, and the branch caught at her again, snagged on her hair. She tugged away from it, almost lost her balance, almost overturned the petrol bombs. Her hand landed on the tree's trunk, solid and rough. She steadied herself.

'I'm going back,' she said, and a breeze whispered through the woods, catching at her words with a soft sigh.

Mariah peered at her niece, standing like a stick in the woods, cloaked in darkness. She shook her head and turned away, hefting her bottles with their rag wicks. 'I shouldn't have expected anything else from you,' she said, and flung her free hand out. 'Go on, then, be a coward. Run for safety.'

Julia stared at the bent figure of her aunt scuttling off through the trees like a great black beetle. She opened her mouth and yelled before she could stop herself.

'You're the witch!' she cried.

Mariah laughed, and the wind picked that up too, caught it and rolled it around the Grove like high-pitched thunder.

Julia watched her move off into the darkness, and she shivered, tugging her jacket closer around herself. Then there was a movement, off to the side, and something bright was over there. She gasped and backed up against the tree, knocking the bottles at her feet so that they rattled. She snatched them up, cradled them carefully in her arms, mouth open, eyes wide.

More shapes between the trees, glowing painfully bright, moving towards Mariah.

'Aunt,' she tried to call, but her voice was just a croak, and she couldn't make her throat work to try again.

Julia watched instead, her body white and rigid with terror as the shapes coalesced in the darkness, their light growing dimmer as they took form.

'Oh my God,' Julia groaned. 'Oh my God.'

The worst thing was their beauty.

Julia slid down the tree, the bottles clanking against each other in her arms, the sharp stench of petrol making her light-headed.

That was it, she thought. That was what was happening. It was only an illusion. The men and women in the woods, the beautiful, luminous men and women with their sharp, elven faces and their glowing eyes, they weren't real. She'd just breathed in the fumes of the petrol. That was what had happened. She was seeing things.

One of them walked past her, and Julia cowered back against the tree, would have burrowed whimpering and deep into the mulch, had she been able to. But she sat frozen, only her eyes moving, as the creature looked down at her with a face more beautiful and unearthly than anything Julia had ever seen before. Its lips twitched in a smile, and Julia felt hot tears upon her face.

The figure moved on, moon-bright in the darkness of the forest, and Julia closed her eyes for a moment, her cheeks wet and warm. She shook her head.

No, she told herself. They weren't the Fae. They weren't real.

She was high, she decided. High from the petrol.

That was all.

Scrambling to her feet, Julia turned tail and skidded down the path, holding the milk carrier out to the side with one hand, flailing for balance with the other.

She would get back to her car. Pour the petrol in the bottles back into its tank – she had the right sort of funnel somewhere – and then she'd drive home. Stay there, door locked, curtains drawn. She wouldn't look back.

And she didn't look back. Didn't think about her aunt. Didn't think about anything except getting home.

MARIAH TURNED AND STARED AT THE FIGURE APPROACHING her through the woods.

'No,' she said, shaking her head. 'Not you.'

The faerie man bowed his head. 'Do you recognise me, Mariah?' He smiled and gestured at the sky, where behind the tree limbs the moon floated high and narrow in the sky, a crisp curve between the clouds. 'We danced together under this moon once before.'

'We didn't,' Mariah said, backing away. She shook her head so forcefully her teeth clacked together.

'Ah, but we did,' the faerie said. 'And 'twas a glorious night full of music, do you not remember?' He pretended to pout. 'I remember it well,' he said. 'You were young and lithesome in my arms, and your smile lit up my night.'

Mariah put down the milk carrier full of bottles she'd so carefully filled with petrol and plugged with rags made from an old summer dressing gown. She shook her head again.

'I don't remember,' she said.

But she did. Her body remembered even while she tried to deny the memory. It quivered under her clothes, the wrinkled skin feeling suddenly taut and sensitive.

'No,' she said.

He held out a hand to her, head cocked to one side. 'I hear the music again, Mariah my dear,' he said. 'Don't you hear it?'

The worst thing was that she did. A whistling and lilting

piping that threaded through the air, silver and perfect, stirring her blood in a way it had never been since...

Since she was young, sneaking from her mother's house to come watch the Grove dance.

She shook her head again, trying to deny it even while her nerves prickled with longing. She half lifted her hand to reach for the faerie man's then snatched it back again.

'Come now,' he tempted her. 'Do you not want to dance again with me under this fair sky, on this beautiful night, amongst the trees and the stones?'

Mariah looked wildly around and sure enough, there were the stones of the circle. She'd come the wrong way, taken the wrong path, come too far.

She choked out a sob.

Other figures danced around the stones, their skin soft and smooth, glowing softly as though they each held the silver of the moon inside them, and Mariah shook her head again, crying openly now.

'I'm not young anymore,' she said, a last attempt.

The faerie man smiled at her and held out his hand again. 'Ah, Mariah my love, but you are. Look.'

She sniffed back tears but looked anyway, unable to stop herself. When she held up her hands to her face, they were long-fingered and lovely, the skin smooth and unblemished upon them.

The music soared and dipped on the wind.

'No,' she said, and touched her face. 'No, it can't be.'

Her long ago lover smiled at her. 'Yes,' he said simply.

'I want to go back,' she said. 'Take me back to my world.'

'I can't do that,' the faerie man said, and for a moment he sounded genuinely regretful. 'You will do too much damage there.' He stepped closer. 'Here though, we can dance.'

Mariah shook her head.

'We can dance and feast and celebrate the sacred union.'

A couple flitted by them, feet light as the wind, eyes bright like stars.

Mariah sobbed again, then took his hand and he smiled at her, leading her to the dance.

45

THE CROWD HUSHED SUDDENLY AS ERIN AND WINSOME watched Morghan on the back of the cart, the noose around her neck.

They understood why everyone was silent, transfixed by the figure under the gallows.

'Tis spirits,' the man in front of them said, his voice harsh against the quiet of the crowd. 'Tis the work of spirits, I tell you.'

Morghan stood on legs now steady, her face relaxing into calmness.

'How can she be so calm?' Erin asked. 'How can she do this?'

Winsome shook her head. She was crying. 'I don't know,' she answered.

But Morghan looked out over the crowd, as the man on the cart repeated his question.

'Do you wish to share your confessions?' he asked, his voice rough and loud.

Erin winced against the question and shifted slightly to hold Blythe's spirit more securely between herself and Winsome.

'I do not,' Morghan said, and her voice was calm, and clear as a bell. 'For they were gained from me through the callousness of human actions, not from the grace of God.'

The crowd shifted as though one animal, consternation and shock whispering through it.

'Do you wish to pray then, for your immortal soul?' the priest on the cart asked.

Winsome shook her head silently.

Morghan smiled slightly, her eyes searching out over the crowd, coming to rest upon Winsome's own gaze.

'I do,' she said.

The crowd shuffled on its feet.

Morghan looked at Winsome, her gaze steady, her eyes clear.

When she spoke, Winsome's eyes filled with fresh tears.

'Our Father,' Morghan said, gaze still fixed on Winsome. 'Who art in heaven.'

'Our Mother,' whispered Winsome. 'Whose body is the land.'

Morghan spoke. 'Hallowed be thy name.'

'Blessed be thy flesh,' Winsome said.

Morghan smiled at her. 'Thy kingdom come, thy will be done, on earth as it is in heaven.'

'As above, so it is below,' Winsome said. 'As it is without, so also it is within.'

'Give us this day our daily bread,' Morghan said, and she looked at the knot of three women at the back of the crowd, there in spirit, there in witness and connection.

'And forgive us our trespasses as we forgive those who trespass against us,' she said.

A breeze sprang up and sighed through the crowd, ruffling their hair and clothes before wrapping itself around Morghan, bringing with it the scent of her beloved trees.

Winsome lifted her voice. 'Your bounty is also our own,' she said. 'We are in service to your needs.'

'And lead us not into temptation,' Morghan said, taking a breath of the wind. 'But deliver us from evil.'

Winsome lifted her wet face to the breeze. 'For compassion lives in our hearts,' she said, 'and kindness moves our hands.'

Morghan closed her eyes. 'For thine is the kingdom, the power, and the glory, forever and ever.'

She waited for the last line, looking at the forest behind her eyes.

Winsome answered her. 'So it is,' she said.

'So it has always been,' she continued. 'And so shall it remain, world beyond time, world without end.'

The cart moved, and Morghan slipped from it to dangle at the end of the rope until Blythe's body was suffocated.

46

AMBROSE SHOOK HIS HEAD. 'YOU CAN'T GO IN THERE YET,' HE said to the two paramedics standing outside Morghan's bedroom door.

They gaped at him.

'Why did you call us then, mate?' one of the men asked, his Australian twang harsh in the silent house. 'You said you had an emergency.'

'A woman who had been unconscious for an amount of time,' the other added. His name tag said he was called Matt.

Ambrose shook his head.

'You don't then?' the first, Nick, asked.

'No,' Ambrose said. 'I mean, I do.' He took a deep breath, glancing over their shoulders into Clarice's strained face. 'It's...it's just not that simple.'

Nick reached for the door handle. 'Let's just take a look, eh?'

Ambrose shook his head, but let the man open the door and they all pushed into the room.

'What's this about, then?' Nick asked, looking at the three figures on the bed, perplexed. 'What's happened?'

'Is it an overdose?' Matt asked, carrying his bag around one side of the bed and reaching for Erin's wrist. 'This one's pulse is strong enough,' he said, frowning.

'It's not her I'm worried about,' Ambrose said, running fretting fingers through his hair. 'It's Morghan – she's in the middle.' His voice faltered.

Matt reached for Morghan's hand, disengaging it gently from Erin's. He pressed his fingertips lightly to the vein that beat in her wrist, his face intent as he counted the beats. He shook his head. 'Hers is faint, man,' he said, then reached over to move her head, lifting her eyelids.

'Don't,' Ambrose said. 'You'll bring her back too soon.'

Nick raised his eyebrows. 'Right,' he told Ambrose. 'Why don't you tell us what exactly is going on here?'

It took long, painful minutes for Blythe's body to stop jerking and swinging and Winsome counted each one of them with the hollow thudding of her heart. She kept shaking her head, and when she looked over at Erin, they met each other's gaze over Blythe's head with reddened eyes.

When at last, though, the rope hung more still, creaking slowly with the weight of Blythe's body, they held their breaths, and waited, hearts thumping louder, for Morghan to slip free.

Erin shifted her arms around Blythe, who slumped

against her, barely sensible to what was happening, and touched Winsome with urgent fingers. 'Where is she?' she asked.

Winsome couldn't take her eyes from the woman hanging from the gallows. She paid no heed to the crowd as it stirred restlessly on its hundred feet, murmuring in its low voice, unsettled for no reason it could discern. She looked at Blythe spinning slowly and shook her head.

'I don't know,' she said, and she pushed through the crowd, a cold draft, and stood at Blythe's feet. 'Morghan,' she called. 'Morghan, please, come back to us. It isn't your time, don't get caught.' She licked her lips, clasped her hands together and thought she would never be able to erase the image of Blythe's purple and bloated face from her mind.

She stumbled backwards as the body moved suddenly, and Morghan slipped her spirit from its flesh and stood in front of her. Winsome flung her arms around her and hugged her tightly.

'That was terrible,' she said. 'That was awful – don't ever do that again,' she bawled through her tears.

Morghan lifted her arms and held Winsome for a moment, feeling the grief shaking through her. 'It's all right,' she said. 'It's all right now.' She stepped back and held Winsome at arm's length. 'We must do the rest,' she said. 'And get back before it is too late.'

Too late? Winsome stared wide-eyed at her, then nodded hastily. 'What do we do now?' she asked.

Morghan took her hand and led the way through the shifting crowd back to Erin and Blythe. She put her hands on both and glanced at Winsome.

'Put your hand on my shoulder,' she said, her face luminous in the sunlight. 'I can smell the trees.'

Winsome did as she was asked, and they were in the forest.

'It's your place,' Erin said, the tears still wet on her cheeks.

'Yes,' Morghan said briskly. 'Now come – we must make Blythe comfortable here and then get back.' She thought of Hawthorn House, of Ambrose, Clarice.

Winsome looked around as she followed the others. It was dim, evening here in this place, wherever this place was. Lake water lapped at a stony shore, and everywhere was the scent of pine trees and water and soil. She quickened her steps.

Blythe was no longer sensible of anything, and Erin and Morghan laid her down gently in the nest of blankets waiting in the clearing.

'I don't have time to tend to her now,' Morghan said. 'But she will be safe here and can sleep. She will heal as she sleeps.'

'This is what we did for Wayne,' Winsome said, her voice rough with sudden exhaustion.

'For Wayne?' Erin asked, lifting her head from the pale figure on the forest floor. 'Wayne Moffat?'

Winsome nodded. 'We didn't bring him here, though.'

'No,' Morghan said. 'This is...my place.'

Erin gazed at them both. 'You did this for Wayne?' she asked. Hadn't Morghan said as much when she was last here with her? Erin shook her head slightly. She hadn't known it meant anything like this.

Like what Morghan had done for Blythe.

It probably hadn't been like that, though, she thought. But similar. Maybe it had been similar. She was dazed.

'Now,' Morghan said, reaching for their hands. 'We go. Ambrose will be beside himself.'

ERIN GROANED, SQUEEZED HER EYES TIGHT THEN BLINKED them open, saw a strange man leaning over her and yelped, leaping up to sit scrunched, disoriented, against the headboard.

'What's going on?' she squawked, the room spinning around her. She looked over at Morghan and Winsome, and Winsome stirred, blinked, sat up in the dim room.

'Oh thank the Goddess,' Ambrose said, pushing Nick away and grabbing Winsome. 'You're back.'

'Who are these guys?' Erin asked, staring with wide eyes at the two strangers.

'Paramedics,' Ambrose said, and he got Winsome on her feet, led her to one of the chairs. 'They're here for Morghan.' He turned back to Erin.

'Are you all right?' Matt asked, still not knowing really what was happening here. But two of the women at least had burst back to life.

Erin nodded. 'Yeah,' she said. 'I'm fine.'

Ambrose reached for her, and she grasped his hand, scooting from the bed and over to where Winsome stared back at Morghan, still pale and unmoving on the bed.

'Did she come back with you?' Ambrose asked.

Winsome nodded. 'Yes, I think so.'

'Okay,' he said. 'That's good.'

Nick looked at him. 'We can get to work now?' he asked.

'Yes,' Ambrose said. 'Help her, please.'

But Nick was already inserting an IV for fluids, to stabilise her blood pressure. Ambrose turned back to Winsome. Looked at her.

She looked back at him. 'Ambrose,' she whispered, then pulled herself up and tottered over to him, wrapping her arms around his neck, and leaning against him while the room spun.

THE FIRE ENGINE'S SIREN WAILED AS IT DROVE THROUGH Wellsford's main street. Julia froze on the path to her house, car keys in her hand. She glanced back at her little VW Rabbit, grimacing, then scurried to her front door, ducking her head as lights went on all over the village and curtains were drawn, faces peering out into the darkness.

'Damn you,' she muttered. 'Damn and bother you.' Had Mariah gone through with it? It was crazy – the whole thing was crazy. Mariah had lost her mind.

And so too had she, almost. Julia pushed her front door open and all but collapsed into the hallway. She slammed the door shut and leaned against it, heart pounding, feeling sick. Pushing herself to her feet, she stumbled through the dark house to the kitchen and twisted the tap, grabbing a glass.

The water didn't take away the taste of petrol.

47

WINSOME POPPED HER HEAD AROUND THE DOOR. 'HOW ARE you feeling?' she asked, slipping into Morghan's room.

Morghan shook her head and gave a short laugh. 'A bit like I've been run over by a bus, to be honest.' She glanced out the window. 'I want to go outside, but Ambrose won't let me. He's been hovering over me all day.'

'That's probably because you almost died a few nights ago,' Clarice said acerbically from where she stood leaning against the wall looking out the window.

Morghan didn't answer, simply looked thoughtfully over at Winsome. 'So,' she said. 'In the middle of this, you went to see the Dean. What did he have to say?'

Winsome glanced over at Clarice, who heaved herself onto her feet and came over to bend over Morghan's chair and kiss her on the cheek. 'Be good, Mother,' she said. 'Do as Ambrose tells you.' She gave Winsome a quick smile and left the room.

'I didn't know she called you mother,' Winsome said, looking after Clarice as she closed the door.

'She doesn't, usually,' Morghan answered, and there was a small smile on her pale face. 'I think I gave her a bit of a fright.'

Winsome transferred her gaze to Morghan, narrowing her eyes at her. 'You gave us all one,' she said. 'That was skating too near to the edge.'

Morghan tipped her head back and closed her eyes. 'Obviously, it wasn't supposed to take so much from me,' she said. 'But as I'm still here and whole, it was worth it.' She looked over at Winsome. 'And you did brilliantly,' she said. 'You and Erin. I'm proud of the both of you.'

Winsome laughed. 'Your crash course in walking between the worlds worked out, I guess,' she said.

'Yes,' Morghan agreed. 'Helped along by the fact that you're both naturally talented at it, have probably spent lifetimes doing it.' She sighed, rubbed a hand to her neck.

'And Blythe?' Winsome asked.

'She sleeps and heals,' Morghan said. 'Thank you again for your help. It was easier to have you with me.'

Winsome nodded, thinking about the night two days before. About watching Blythe's body spinning on the end of the rope, Morghan's eyes looking out from it as she went through the agonies of the slow, drawn-out suffocation. She shuddered. It had taken a long time for Blythe's heart to finally stop.

She shook her head. 'How did you do that?' she asked. 'Take her place?' Winsome looked down at her hands. 'I don't know if I could have done that.'

Morghan turned her head and looked out the window. 'I

didn't want to,' she confessed. 'I was frightened of the pain it would involve.'

'You didn't look frightened!' Winsome stared at her.

But Morghan just smiled sadly and shook her head. 'What's that saying about courage? That it's being terrified and doing it anyway?' She looked down at her golden hand, glowing softly in the overcast light. 'It's Ostara today,' she said. 'The day of coming into balance again begins and the energy changes to that of the dragon, of renewed and vigorous energy.'

Winsome sat back. 'That seems apt, somehow, doesn't it?'

'Yes,' Morghan agreed. 'We will need all that extra energy to pick up the pieces and forge the path ahead.'

'I thought everything was going so well,' Winsome said. 'Especially as we've all been in lockdown.' She shrugged. 'Hardly any cases of the virus in the village, and the new initiatives both of us have been working on.' She smiled wistfully. 'It was all coming along nicely.'

Morghan leaned over and touched Winsome's hand gently. 'The Dean,' she said. 'What did he say?'

'Oh,' Winsome said, and looked down at her hands. 'I've lost my position,' she said. 'But I suppose we knew that would happen.'

Morghan was silent for a moment, letting Winsome's words sink in. 'You will be going to a new parish?' she asked.

Winsome shook her head. 'No.' She tried to smile. 'Not that either, I'm afraid, for me. I'm being put out to pasture – they're going to put it down as parish reorganisation – redundancy, effectively. I'll get housing and salary for another year, but I'm not going to be a vicar anymore.' She shrugged tight shoulders.

'I'm sorry,' Morghan whispered. 'I'm deeply sorry to hear that.'

Another shrug, this one slightly looser. 'Well, it's not surprising, really. The surprising thing is that Wellsford wasn't made part of a parish conglomeration years ago. It's very unusual that it wasn't.'

'Is that what will happen now?' Morghan asked.

Winsome shook her head. 'No. They're closing St. Bridget's down completely. Probably sell the building or lease it out – if there's any interest in it.' She sighed. 'Morghan – how am I going to tell my congregation this? How am I going to tell them I let them down so badly that their church is being closed?'

'They already knew it could happen,' Morghan said. 'As soon as those flyers went out.' She stretched gingerly in her seat then tried to relax again, feeling restless. 'Remember when I went down to see you at the vicarage when you weren't there and one of your parish ladies asked me if I would buy the church if it were shut – so that you could simply carry on?'

Winsome wrapped her arms around her middle and hugged herself. 'I still can't believe they asked that.'

Morghan laughed. 'I know,' she said. 'I had much the same response.' Her face turned serious. 'It just goes to show, however, that it's what you and these families have been doing together on a personal and village level that matters to them.' She nodded. 'That's something to think about, if you're going to stay on here, in Wellsford.' Morghan paused. 'Are you?'

'I...I don't know,' Winsome answered.

'Well, there's plenty of time to think about it,' Morghan said. 'To consider the options.'

'You would buy the church?' Winsome asked, still flabbergasted that this conversation was going on.

'I don't know,' Morghan mused. 'I think it would be better if it were a village asset, don't you?'

Winsome shook her head. 'I've no idea,' she said. 'Just thinking about it makes me light-headed.'

'Ah,' Morghan said, pushing aside the blanket Clarice had insisted she have over her knees. 'Light-headedness we can do something about.' She stood up, testing out the steadiness of her legs before moving over to the door. 'Shall we?' she asked.

'Shall we what?' Winsome said.

'Go outside,' Morghan replied. 'Ambrose has been a bear about not letting me, but with you at my side I think he will be unable to say no.'

A long slow flush crawled up Winsome's cheeks. 'What has he said to you?'

Morghan shook her head. 'Nothing,' she said. 'Nothing about the two of you, if that's what you're asking. He wouldn't.'

Winsome looked down at the floor. 'If I'm no longer vicar,' she said, then trailed off.

'Yes,' Morghan agreed. 'There's usually a silver lining to things, as they say. But for now, let's go outside. I've a need to walk amongst the trees and give thanks.'

Winsome gave Morghan a flat look. 'Are you up to it? They did have to pump you full of fluids and things the other night.'

'I am up to it,' Morghan replied. 'And it is also what I need.'

The reply made Winsome nod. 'All right, then,' she said. 'But only if you wear boots. It's still cold out there.'

Morghan looked across at Winsome and a sudden grin appeared on her pale face. 'You're never going to let me live that down, are you?'

'No,' Winsome said, getting to her feet and walking with Morghan to the door. 'No, I am not.'

AMBROSE APPEARED AT THE BOTTOM OF THE STAIRS AS THEY came down. 'Where are you going?' he asked.

'Outside,' Morghan replied. She smiled impishly. 'And you can't stop me this time, for I've found myself a companion.'

Ambrose narrowed his eyes and looked at Winsome. A smile quirked his lips. 'A co-conspirator, more likely,' he said.

Morghan thought of something and interrupted. 'Has Mariah been found?' she asked.

Ambrose shook his head. 'The only sign of Mariah was her pair of shoes at the stone circle.' He paused. 'And, most oddly, a carrier of milk bottles, the bottles filled with soil.' He raised his eyebrows. 'I don't think we'll be seeing the woman again.'

'No,' Morghan agreed. 'The Fae have taken her, it is sure.' She leaned against the bannister. 'What do the police say?'

'They are scratching their heads. The whole of the woods have been searched – myself and Stephan and Erin and the others were out there helping, but...' He shrugged. 'There are only her shoes.' He sighed.

Winsome cleared her throat. 'What about Julia?' she asked. 'What is she saying about it?'

'Nothing. Says Stephan has the wrong end of the stick – that the smell of petrol in the garage was only because she had to fuss around trying to fill her car from a can. And that she and Mariah went for a walk around the neighbourhood, then Julia went home and hasn't seen or heard from Mariah since.'

They were all silent for a moment, then Morghan sighed. 'Are they still searching?'

'Yes,' Ambrose said. 'They've moved around the hills, and over on the far farms looking for her.'

Morghan nodded. 'Then I am going outside,' she said, and walked to the door, where her boots were placed nicely under the coat stand. She tucked her feet into them, one hand on the wall to balance herself.

Ambrose looked after her a moment, then turned to gaze at Winsome. She stared back, chewing on her lip. He cleared his throat.

'Perhaps we could ah, go for a walk together later?' he asked. 'Or I could cook you a meal when the lockdown is scaled down in a couple of weeks?'

Winsome couldn't find her voice. She nodded, drew a breath. 'A meal would be nice,' she managed. 'In a couple weeks.'

Ambrose nodded, paused, then reached out gingerly and touched a fleeting finger to the back of Winsome's hand where it rested on the bannister. 'Thank you,' he said, and turned, disappearing back into the sitting room.

Winsome drifted across to the door where Morghan was waiting. The back of her hand tingled. She swallowed, smiled vaguely in Morghan's direction.

'Come,' Morghan said kindly. 'Grounding for both of us, I think.'

Outside, on the grass, Morghan stumbled a little, and Winsome threaded their arms together. 'I think we've established a new support pod,' she said.

'Thank you,' Morghan replied.

They walked in silence towards the trees then stepped into the dimness of the woods. Morghan stopped and closed her eyes, breathing in the greenness. 'The trees are budding,' she said.

Winsome looked around, seeing everywhere now the knobbly bursts of leaf buds on the trees. 'Yes,' she said. 'Soon the woods will be green again.'

Morghan reached out to touch the sturdy trunk nearest her. 'Their sap is rising,' she said. 'After the long drift of winter, they're waking.' She turned to Winsome. 'Which is also what we must do,' she said.

'Help me to the circle.'

Winsome nodded, and they walked together, listening to the birds chatter and squabble and build their nests.

'It's so peaceful here,' Winsome murmured.

'A balm to the soul,' Morghan agreed.

Winsome stopped walking and looked around, then stared at Morghan. 'How do you do that?' she asked, realising they were no longer on the path but on the shore of Morghan's lake, the waves lapping gently at the stones on the shore.

Morghan gave a wan smile. 'Practice,' she said. 'Only that.'

Winsome shook her head and looked around. 'The world is so big,' she whispered. 'And once you know that – nothing is ever the same again.'

'It's not just the world, Winsome,' Morghan said, turning and picking her way through the fringe of trees to her clearing. 'It is us. We are big. Bigger than most of us imagine.' She stopped and spread a hand at the forest and lake around her. 'I must go inside myself to find the way here. We really do need to learn to plumb the depths of our own souls, and not to be afraid to do so.'

Blythe was still in her soft nest, curled up on herself, hands tucked under her chin. Winsome kneeled down beside her.

'Has she woken up yet at all?' she asked.

'No,' Morghan replied. 'And she won't. When she is rested, she will re-join our soul family, from whom she has been separated for too long – and that is the reason we did what we did.' Morghan brushed back a strand of hair from the sleeping woman's cheek.

'It was that important?' Winsome asked. 'To take the risk you did?' She studied Morghan's face, still pale from the strain her body had been put under.

But Morghan nodded. 'That important. Our connection is all-important, Winsome. Our soul suffers when one of us is lost to it. And it is strengthened – we are strengthened, each aspect – when we are returned.'

Winsome touched the springy moss and grass under her and frowned. 'But not all of us have your strength and ability, Morghan,' she said at last. 'What do we do?'

The question made Morghan smile. 'Practice,' she said, the smile broadening on her lips.

Winsome looked up at her, shook her head, and laughed too. 'Touché,' she said. Then, 'that easy, huh?'

'Yes. That easy,' Morghan agreed. 'Lifetimes of practice. Once you wake up, you must not go back to sleep.' She looked down at Blythe and sighed.

'She didn't go back to sleep,' Winsome demurred.

'Oh, no, she didn't. She was simply caught in her own fear and fury and grief and guilt.'

Winsome thought about that for a moment. 'I saw her,' she said, remembering.

Morghan looked across at her. 'Saw her?'

A nod. 'Yes. It's why I went looking for you. I saw her... spirit, ghost, whathaveyou. In the forest.'

'Ah.' Morghan's grey eyes glowed in the speckled light. 'This place – Wellsford – is good for you, Winsome. It is where you belong.'

Winsome didn't know what to say to that. She felt the truth of it though, in her heart, deep under her skin. 'I don't want to leave,' she said, and there was a lump in her throat. 'Tomorrow is Sunday, and I have to tell everyone that St. Bridget's is closing.'

'Only in its current form, if that is the way you wish it,' Morghan said, getting to her feet and holding out a hand. 'Let us return.'

Winsome scrambled upright, touched her fingers to Morghan's, and a moment later they had returned to the path through the trees, Hawthorn House at their backs.

'That is very disorienting,' Winsome said, shaking her head briefly. She glanced over at Morghan. 'Erm, are you all right?' she asked. 'You look a bit done in. We should go back to the house.'

But Morghan shook her head and released Winsome's hand. 'I will be fine in a moment, and we've yet to do what we came out here for.'

Winsome's eyes widened. 'We haven't?' she asked. 'What did we come out here to do, then?'

'Grounding,' Morghan answered. 'And gratitude.'

'Ah,' Winsome said, not really understanding. It sounded good though. She could do with feeling grounded. And gratitude, well, wasn't that always a good thing?

Morghan reached the stone circle with gladness in her heart and walked over to the tallest of the stones, planting her hands upon it and bending her head toward it, closing her eyes.

'Spirit of stone,' she said. 'I am grateful for your presence, your slow, solid song.' She let the strength and age of the stone seep into her, hearing its ancient song wend its way through her, quiet and sacred.

'My blessings upon you for your gift,' she said after a minute, pressing her forehead briefly to the stone before standing back and walking over to Grandmother Oak.

Winsome watched, reached out a hand to touch the stone that stood at her back. It was cool and rough under her palm. And solid. She swallowed, let herself relax, her spirit unfurl, and she breathed into touching the stone.

And realised it was alive. That it too had some form of consciousness.

That it sang.

For a moment, she hummed with it.

'Grandmother Oak,' Morghan said. 'I would have roots

such as yours.' She imagined them, digging deep into the soil, seeking the secret networks of trees, reaching for each other, in sustenance and song.

'I would have branches such as yours,' she said, and felt herself taller, strong, nourished by the light of the sun. She pressed her palms against Grandmother Oak's tough bark, her eyes closing.

'I would seek some of your strength, Grandmother,' she whispered now. And felt the slow run of sap under her hands, and the welling green energy that built up between them, spilt over from Grandmother to her, until she was filled, invigorated, sustained.

'I am blessed by your gift, Grandmother,' she said. 'My heart is full.'

'Your colour is better,' Winsome said in surprise when Morghan turned around.

'Yes. Grandmother is generous with her energy when she is asked and honoured.' Morghan raised an eyebrow. 'Would you like to try?'

'Erm,' Winsome replied, not knowing what to say. But she had touched the stone, had she not? Felt its slow song?

Why not the Oak too?

She nodded, took a breath. 'This is a whole new world, my friend,' she said.

But Morghan shook her head, smiled.

'No,' she corrected Winsome.

'This is the Ancient Path.'

PRAYER OF THE WILDWOOD

Spirits of Air, I greet and honour you.
Breath of my life,
Hold this space with me.
Spirits of Fire, I greet and honour you.
Spark of my life,
Hold this space with me.
Spirits of Water, I greet and
    honour you.
Womb of my life,
Hold this space with me.
Spirits of Earth, I greet and
    honour you.
Root of my life,
Hold this space with me.
As above, so below.
As outwards, so inwards.
We are the wheel.

ABOUT THE AUTHOR

Katherine has been walking the Pagan path for thirty years, with her first book published in her home country of New Zealand while in her twenties, on the subject of dreams. She spent several years writing and teaching about dreamwork and working as a psychic before turning to novel-writing, studying creative writing at university while raising her children and facing chronic illness.

Since then, she has published more than twenty long and short novels. She writes under various pen names in more than one genre.

Now, with the Wilde Grove series, she is writing close to her heart about what she loves best. She is a Spiritworker and polytheistic Pagan.

Katherine lives in the South Island of New Zealand with her wife Valerie. She is a mother and grandmother.

Printed in Great Britain
by Amazon

44152437R00273